rhythm

∞

jennifer willis

Second release: Copyright © 2011, 2012 by Jennifer S. Willis

All rights reserved. No part of this book may be reproduced in any manner whatsoever without the express written permission of the author, except in the case of brief quotations embodied in critical articles or reviews.

Published by Jennifer Willis
Portland, Oregon
Jennifer-Willis.com
Author photo by Rachel Hadiashar.

This ebook is licensed for your personal enjoyment only. This ebook may not be resold or given away. If you did not purchase this ebook, or it was not purchased for you, please visit your online retailer to purchase your own copy. If you would like to share this ebook with others, please purchase an additional copy for each person you share it with. Thank you for respecting and supporting the hard work of this author.

First release: Copyright © 2001 by Jennifer S. Willis

GREAT BALLS OF FIRE, by Otis Blackwell and Jack Hammer
(c) 1957 (Renewed) Unichappell Music Inc., Mijac Music, Chappell & Co. and Mystical Light Music
Unichappell Music Inc. administers all rights o/b/o itself and Mystical Light Music
All Rights Reserved   Used By Permission
WARNER BROS. PUBLICATIONS U.S. INC., Miami, FL 33014

Cover artwork designed by Jennifer S. Willis and Al Marschall

Library of Congress Control Number: 2001117326

For Peter,

We are our own lights in the darkness, illuminating the way home, map already in hand.

Two friends, two bodies with one soul inspired.
—Homer

In the depth of my soul there is a wordless song.
—Kahlil Gibran

Preface to the 2011 Edition

It's been ten years since RHYTHM was first released, originally via a 500-book print run through a printer in West Virginia, and subsequently through a print-on-demand set-up with Booklocker.

I've made no revisions to the original text of RHYTHM. I was tempted to revisit my "drivel" vs. "dribble" angst from the first publication — I deliberately had Robin using the latter in place of the former, then worried that readers would think I was an idiot for not knowing the difference. But I figured I made the right call back in 2001, so left it alone.

It's a bit curious to go back over the text and gauge how far technology has come in the past ten years. In 1999, Robin was excited about Mary K's colorful iMac, and she praised his work in multimedia CDs. Cell phones didn't play a major role in this story as they would in VALHALLA (2011), and the internet in RHYTHM is still sputtering along — with no Netflix, Wi-Fi or even iTunes. There's nary an MP3 player in sight. Kindle didn't exist, and no one had heard of an iPad.

At the conclusion of RHYTHM, September 11, 2001, is still just another day with no significance, two-and-a-half years in the future. There are no full-body scans or tightened security measures at airports. There is no "Ground Zero" in New York City. The U.S. is not fighting wars in Afghanistan or Iraq. George Harrison, Ray Charles and Michael Jackson are still living.

My writing style has also changed significantly since I wrote RHYTHM. This is not at all the book I would write today, but people still seem to like it so maybe I wasn't a complete hack back then. Ten years ago, there was a much more intellectual bent to my work, with less emphasis on action or humor. Mostly what I see, though, as I look back now from the perspective of slightly more experience is the anxiety that permeated my words then. In 2001, I worried that I didn't have a right to tell any story — much less a groovy tale of "visionary fiction" — or to think of myself as writing professionally. I was more than a little ambivalent about self-publishing, and I internalized the negativity of that stigma. As much of a champion worrier as I am today, I was even better at it then.

Ten years on, I make my living with words. I'm very much a professional writer — journalist, essayist, author — and though there remains a prejudice against self-publishers, this is lessening by degrees with each indie author taking the ebook and POD world by storm. I hadn't foreseen a re-release of RHYTHM even 12 months ago, but readers and friends nudged me in this direction. We'll see what additional leaps and bounds occur in literary technology in the next ten years, and whether that will urge a 20th anniversary edition.

Jennifer Willis
Portland, Oregon, 2011

Chapter One

20 May 1999
New York City
9:25 a.m.

In the twenty-eighth floor men's room, Robin Michaels stood at the sink and took a long, hard look at himself. His reflection revealed his age, and as he considered his thinning hair and sinking cheeks, he was again amazed that time had moved so swiftly.

His hands dripping wet, he glanced out the window to his left, looking down on the busy Fifth Avenue traffic below. New York was such an exciting city, so raw—a far cry even from London. It didn't take much to lure him here, and the synchronicity of Amnesty International's human rights conference and Mary Katherine's interview request provided ample justification for this visit.

Robin's life didn't always offer opportunities for quiet introspection, so he found some satisfaction in moments like this one, alone in a corporate restroom. The familiar reflection of his deep-green eyes had a humbling effect these days, and he laughed as he thought again on the angle Mary K's editor had proposed: "The Next Incarnation of Robin Michaels: Rock Star to Renaissance Man." What a joke.

"Who am I?" he whispered to the mirror. No answer. Some final piece remained to be integrated, having eluding him for years. Robin's focus softened, his reflection beginning to blur. He wasn't unhappy. He did not feel incomplete. But there was something missing; he wasn't grounded. A gentle glow brightened within the glass. Robin rested his hands on the sink basin for balance as the luminosity of his reflection grew. He could almost hear that voice...

The door from the hallway swung open. Robin shook the water drops from his fingertips and reached for a paper towel. The mirror caught the double-take of the man in the three-piece suit headed for a nearby stall. Robin had been recognized. He said a silent prayer that the fan in question wouldn't start humming some old, tortured tune as an indication of his appreciation for the musician's work. He had had enough of such encounters in the nearly thirty years since he and his mates had recorded their first song.

Robin checked his watch. It was almost 9:30 a.m. Glitter time. He looked one last time into the mirror to practice the smile he would give the photographer. The next incarnation indeed.

As he balled up the damp towel and walked toward the trash bin, he heard foot-tapping from the stalls, accompanied by a strained voice quietly singing, "Walk me down to that ocean, feel the sand shift under my feet..."

Robin shook his head and sighed. The well-dressed fan had been listening to his music for some time. "Not many people remember that one. Cheers," Robin said politely as he reached for the door.

* * * *

Sharing a wall was the ladies' room. Angela Harris leaned her hands on the rim of the sink and took a deep breath. She turned her head to the right to look down at the passersby on the sidewalk below, so many people rushing about while the automotive traffic progressed in spurts. She had tried to open the window for a breath of fresh air, but these climate controlled buildings did not allow such luxuries. It was just as well, as she doubted the air quality on the other side of the glass.

Angela turned again to the mirror above the sink. She had hoped for a quiet moment of introspection but was overwhelmed by the day's prospects.

If the finer details of her business plan found favor with the investors this morning, she and her partner would soon launch what promised to be a truly revolutionary company. Thrilled by the fantastic possibilities, Angela was still battling nervous nausea.

Here she was in the big city. Even though the crowded, fast-paced world outside the window was foreign to her, there was a certain excitement in being in New York. She had made it to the big leagues. Too bad she wouldn't have any time to explore once her meeting had concluded.

She regarded her reflection squarely and was satisfied with what she saw. Her eyes were alive and sparkling—always a good sign. The light in her gaze was a reliable indicator of her attunement, the flow of her creativity, and her command over the day. This morning, her green eyes glistened. This day would be hers.

It was nearly 9:30 a.m. She adjusted her tailored jacket for the forty-second time and made sure she didn't have any food in her teeth, even though her nerves hadn't allowed her any breakfast.

Then Angela stood still. She listened to the dripping faucet several basins down. She thought she heard singing coming from the air vent. With a sudden tingling in the middle of her back, her thoughts flashed on her twin... Angela shook it off. She was leaving her old world for a new one of her own design. She knew in her heart she was on the right track, at last.

Thirty years old, she thought to herself. Time to get on with your life.

Angela flashed herself a quick, confident smile in the mirror, then walked past the sinks and stalls and opened the door.

Chapter Two

It was all a marvelous game.

It was too long ago to measure when the pact had first been made, the simple agreement with Self that steadily influenced and guided all decisions, actions, and states of being. This eternal exercise in Self-knowing was renewed in various forms, various shapes and sizes. Splitting apart to come back together again in conscious understanding was nothing new.

It happened all the time.

There was the delightful illusion of risk, though there had only ever been one possible outcome, encompassing all choices and paths. Individuating from the Whole and the Universe it had created, the Soul repeatedly broke apart to envision and experience Self, one aspect connecting with another. The Soul toyed with circumstances of birth, choosing where, when, and how. The polarities of male and female were one more interesting twist.

The Soul had its own frequency, its own rhythm. This was one of the Old Ones, choosing its path at the Beginning, mapping out its playful course over what would be called eons. The Soul loved learning and had gained great wisdom, embodying teacher and slave, warrior and mystic, ruler and peasant. A wandering missionary, the Soul delighted in the dramas it played out with itself, feeling and breathing the lesson.

The Soul laughed and sang and dashed itself against the rocks. It felt the pain, tasted the blood, and rejoiced in the learning. It turned the One Consciousness back on itself in an endless hall of mirrors. So very many reflections, each with a personality, an individual knowing, a name.

For this round of the dance, the Soul divided itself across a wide ocean and a generation of years. There would be only two this time, a single pair of incarnated twins to walk the earth, dancing around each other inside the world they would create. Similar backgrounds, the same blessings and challenges, different pathways, one core personality.

Twin stars. To experience the physical world from these two perspectives, to play with twice as many pieces on the game board, to stack the deck. The Soul boogied to its own dual rhythm.

Chapter 3

October 1968
St. Anthony's College
Lewes, East Sussex, England

Having just turned sixteen, Robin was again away from home, at St. Anthony's preparatory boarding school for boys, but this time for his first year in sixth form.

Robin was miserable at St. Anthony's.

The mornings found the boys rising near dawn to file into the shower room where they waited their turn for a few minutes of hot water and soap. After donning their traditional grey jackets, the students stepped out into the heavy morning air, their leather shoes collecting dew from the crisp grass along the short walk to the dining hall where every breakfast featured the same, dull mush as had no doubt been served the days and years before.

In this afternoon's intramural football match, Robin stood apart from the other players on the field—poised, his cleats digging confidently into the soft ground, a faint glistening of perspiration on his brow. Knees bent, Robin was ready for action. He felt powerful, a jungle panther awaiting its prey, crouched low, muscles taut. He was ready for anything, floodgates of adrenaline threatening. Robin envisioned himself on the fields of Agincourt, moments before the bloody battle, trying on the raw, fatalistic courage required to step so readily into close combat. He clenched his fists and deepened his stance, imagining the cold cunning of the broadsword in his hands.

Something wet hit him in the ear. George had thrown a divot of grass and mud. Shaking off the dirt, Robin turned to find his friend laughing at him.

"St. Anthony's finest! Get your mind on the ball, old man!" Without hesitation, George tore up the field to wrest control of the ball from the opposing team, unintentionally inflicting a bloody nose in the process.

Engaged in this modern battle, Robin cheered and ran up the field to provide passing assistance at the goal, scored by George.

George was one of the larger boys in Robin's class, growing into his man's body sooner than others. He was a hero, enthusiastic for what interested him and pleasantly disregarding the rest. Outgoing and handsome, he had already had a string of girlfriends.

His day-dreaming friend, Robin, was still short and thin, uncomfortable in his own skin.

Under George's leadership, their team had won the match. Boisterous from the excitement of the game, the boys from both sides packed themselves into the small locker room, the air alive with sweat, banging lockers, and raucous laughter. Robin carved out what space he could to quickly stow his gear while the others ran in and out of the showers, soaking the floors and littering the benches with damp clothes and muddy cleats.

Robin changed clothes, saving the shower for later. George did the same on the opposite row of lockers. The two squeezed between the sweaty bodies and stepped out into the fresh air, still sweet with the humidity of the waning summer. The sun was setting. They only had a hour or so before the evening meal. They broke into an easy jog across campus to the music room, which they were happy to find deserted.

The boys stood together just inside the heavy double doors, surveying the possibilities. There were two pianos—one baby grand and one upright—standing marimbas, large black cases containing the new hand bells, boxes of recorders, triangles, maracas, and tambourines on the shelves, along with a half-dozen acoustic guitars leaning against the back wall. The cymbals and drums were safely locked away in the music director's office, following an unauthorized exploit the previous year involving Robin's older cousin, Gareth, and other members of The Chippers, a popular band on campus.

The Chippers would likely practice shortly after supper, and these walls would echo with better structured chords and vocal harmonies than George and Robin could muster; but for now, the room was theirs.

George smiled sideways at Robin. "A bit of rock and roll, then?" he said mischievously before dashing to the bench of the baby grand. Robin sauntered over to the upright piano, though George had always encouraged him to experiment with percussion. Backs to each other, the boys sat before the black and white keys. Robin turned his head to call out, "Feeling a bit like Jerry Lee this evening..."

George laughed and struck a familiar chord before counting out an empty measure. His fingers flew across the keys, missing a few notes here and there, but still playing a great deal better than Robin, whose enthusiasm for dramatics easily overshadowed his limited musical abilities.

"You shake my nerves and you rattle my brain!" Robin howled, drowning out his friend's less animated voice. "Your kind of lovin' would drive a man insane!" Robin made up the bits he didn't know, trying to effect an American southern accent.

With George carrying the music, Robin attempted some of the singer's trademark acrobatics, pretending to play the piano with the heel of his right foot. He sprinted across the room and pulled a bright blue maraca from one of the boxes, shaking it for all it was worth and using it as a microphone. "Goodness! Gracious! Great balls of fire!"

He was dancing now, gyrating around the piano that vibrated under George's control. Robin wished he might play half as well as his friend, but for the time being he expressed himself through spontaneous percussion and strange dance movements. Two maracas now in his hands, he jumped from side to side behind George. "Ooh! Kiss me, baby! Ooh! Feels good!"

A stray glance toward the doors unexpectedly revealed the three figures of The Chippers, watching. Intimidated, Robin nevertheless strutted over to the older boys and half-sang, half-shouted the lyrics to them. "I want to love you like a lover should." Two years older and more than six feet tall, Gareth towered over his cousin, whom he observed with obvious amusement. Robin twisted his body this way and that in his exuberant, haphazard rhythms, while at the piano, George neared the song's final climax.

"Goodness! Gracious! Great balls of fire!" Robin bellowed from the center of the room, his hands thrown down to his sides and his feet a bit too far apart. George banged out the last notes and sprang to his feet, jumping up and down at the piano. "Woo! Woo!"

The Chippers offered a bemused round of applause. Robin exaggerated a bow before them and smiled nervously. The older boys filed into the room to choose their instruments, save for Joe, who had the luxury of his own bass guitar, though he hadn't yet been allowed to bring his amplifier to St. Anthony's. Ken chuckled as he passed Robin on his way to select an acoustic guitar. George stepped around from behind the piano, "Do you want to sit in with us, then?"

"Actually, we have the room reserved," responded Gareth, rummaging through the boxes on the shelves. "Sorry."

"It's just as well," George replied, tucking his wrinkled shirt tail into his trousers. "We need to shower anyway." George jogged toward the door as Robin approached his cousin to hand over the maracas. "Could I stay?"

"You want to stay and watch?" Gareth looked to his bandmates. Joe and Ken simply shrugged their shoulders. He turned back to Robin and smiled. "Why not? George?"

With one foot already out the door, George stopped to consider the unusual offer. "No, I've got some studying to do. Thanks, though." He waved and ran off into the darkening night.

Robin gave a quick, startled laugh and announced, "He's a bit shy."

Joe, with his impossible red hair drifting into his eyes, shot back, "And you're not?"

Gareth clapped his hand on Robin's thin shoulder, handed him a small tambourine, and guided him toward a row of chairs. "Why don't you help me keep time, eh?"

Gareth and Robin sat down close to Ken and Joe, who were tuning up. Gareth reached for Joe's bass guitar case and balanced it across two chairs. He retrieved a pair of worn drumsticks from his back pocket and beat out a quick pattern on the plastic case in front of him. "In another few weeks, I'll have my own kit," he winked at Robin, then turned his attention to the band. "What's on the programme?"

"Well, as I recall, *Saw Her Standing There* is pretty pathetic." Joe launched into a chaotic bass line, warming up his long fingers. The muscles in his face tensed as he concentrated. "We'll need it for our set next month."

"We've got a bigger problem than that, you well know." Ken leaned his guitar against a chair and crouched down next to it. Ken had a reputation for being difficult. Though it was never his conscious intention to incite tempers, he felt obligated to point out problems, and to frequently beat them into the ground.

"I'll say again that someone has to replace David, more permanently. You know I can't keep singing and playing at the same time." He ran his fingers through his short, blonde hair. He was attractive enough, but he lacked the stamina to be the band's front man. And he simply didn't want it. Every Chippers rehearsal since their lead's departure had begun with this same discussion. "I'm not that versatile. It's just one awful sound added to another."

Joe sighed heavily. Gareth deliberately studied his wooden drum sticks and the positioning of his makeshift instrument. Ken clasped his hands together and sank lower into his crouch, leaning his weight against a chair, producing a loud squeak as it slid slowly across the floor.

"I could do it." Robin couldn't believe his own ears, and judging by the raised eyebrows around the room, the others were having much the same reaction. He looked immediately at his shoes, already needing a polish. The Chippers were not a professional band, but they were a popular group on the public school circuit. Robin was too young, and he was woefully inexperienced. Robin raised his head and was surprised to see the older boys actually considering his suggestion. "If you can't find anyone else," he added.

"This one won't finish his studies and leave us high and dry, like David. He won't be ready to sit for the Oxford exam 'til next year." Joe rested his fingers on his bass strings and stared at Robin, sizing him up. The boy fidgeted under his gaze. Joe liked Robin and his quirky awkwardness, but it was easily apparent that he lacked confidence.

Ken was less receptive. "Look at him. He's got a stick of a body. He's too young. David had a presence, he was a good front man." Robin tapped his feet together, frustrated and partially relieved. Seeing Robin's downcast eyes, Ken tried to soften his words. "No hard feelings, Robin, but you don't cut a striking figure. What about that George? He's a big, good-looking fellow."

"He can't sing to save his life." Joe stepped across the room toward Robin, balancing his bass with his strides. "Robin may not have the cleanest voice, but it's not half bad. And he's got some personality to him. You saw him with the bloody maracas."

Robin glanced up to Joe and gave him a polite smile, then turned to his cousin. Gareth always looked wiser than his eighteen years, and while Robin generally preferred to be left alone, his cousin's presence on campus was often a comfort. Gareth read the tentative eagerness in Robin's face. Turning to

Ken, Gareth cocked his head to one side. "What do you say? We could use him in rehearsal at least, to free us up to focus on the instruments."

"But I want to play," Robin interjected. "I know I'm not the best musician, but I'm getting better." Robin pointed to the baby grand. "You don't have anyone on piano."

Ken laughed derisively, but was quickly silenced by a cold glance from Joe.

"A piano is an impossibility for staged set-ups. Besides transporting the thing, it has to be retuned every time you move it. And we're not stylish enough to have something more sophisticated." Gareth tapped the tambourine Robin held. "You can give me a hand on supplemental percussion. But we need your voice. Let that be your instrument."

* * * *

A great excitement coursed through Robin, swirling in his toes and tickling his scalp. He was on top of the world.

The rehearsal had not begun especially well, with Robin too nervous and too enthusiastic to effect an easy performance, though his singing had helped the others concentrate on their instruments. Once he had gotten used to Ken's rolling eyes and occasional grimaces when his voice broke, Robin had relaxed enough to enjoy himself.

"We rehearse Tuesdays and Thursdays, with occasional Saturdays and Sundays," Gareth explained as they made their way across the grassy quadrangle toward St. Anthony's main administrative building. "Tonight wasn't part of the usual routine, but we figured we needed the practice."

Robin didn't respond. He was lost in his own surge of energy, bobbing his head and taking strides much larger than his normal gait. He smiled at the terrific collection of butterflies in his stomach as he thought of himself on stage with The Chippers only five weeks away.

Easily pacing him, Gareth observed Robin for a few metres, then laughed. "You've caught the bug, eh? Don't let it go to your head. This practice was easy, and short. Some nights nothing goes right and we all flat out want to kill each other."

"Good," Robin said too loudly, enjoying the sound of his voice as it echoed back from the walls of the stone and brick buildings. "I look forward to that."

His companion shook his sandy curls. "Your enthusiasm will wane, believe me." Gareth pulled open the heavy wooden door to the administrative building and held it for Robin. "But you can tell that girlfriend you'll be breaking schoolgirl hearts all over the district with those green eyes of yours, once you're up on stage."

Robin lowered his head and flashed his cousin a truly devilish grin. Gareth liked seeing him in such good spirits. "Go on, see if you've received something from Marianne. I'll save a seat at dinner."

Gareth turned up the grand hallway toward the dining room while Robin skipped down the steps to the cellar, where he hoped a letter waited in his mailbox. It had been a month since he had last seen Marianne, whose family had taken up residence down the road from his home during the summer. His friends envied Robin his American girlfriend, assuming her to be free from the Victorian bonds which had such a tight grip on the rest of them. But he had only kissed her a handful of times, and this friendly correspondence between boarding schools would be their only contact until the holidays.

He didn't bother turning on the light in the mailroom. He reached his mailbox in the corner and found a letter waiting. Following St. Anthony's strict honour code, there were no combination locks or even hinged doors on the student mailboxes; their very presence would be an insult to the institution.

Stepping into the dim light of the hallway, Robin recognized Marianne's flowery handwriting on the envelope. He happily tucked the letter into his jacket and flew up the stairs, his empty stomach rumbling.

* * * *

It was nearly 10 p.m. before Robin found some time to himself. He was lucky to share a double room with George this year, and there were only six boys altogether in their suite, with a lavatory to themselves, though they still shared the showers with the rest of the boys on the hall.

Robin stepped gingerly over the books strewn in a haphazard trail from his bed to his desk. Although the reading lamp on Robin's desk had been left on, George had already retired. Perhaps it was the afternoon football match, but it was always possible, even probable, that George had been coaxed into several rounds of wrestling in the hallways after dinner.

Robin tossed Marianne's letter onto the bed and hung his jacket on the back of his chair. The rest of his clothes he folded and stored at the bottom of his closet before pulling on his linen pyjamas. Getting into bed, Robin made himself comfortable. He opened the envelope carefully and laid one hand on his thigh, considering a masturbatory fantasy as he began reading.

Robin liked the chattiness of Marianne's letters, telling him about her studies, her new friends, and her continued adjustments to English culture and boarding school. Her descriptions of her school uniform and her athletic activities sent a warm thrill through his body. He slid his fingers under the crisp fabric of his pyjamas and over his own skin. He thought of her long, blonde hair that always smelled of strawberries and the freckles highlighting her cheeks. He thought of holding her hand as they walked along the beach after a dinner party at his grandparents' house. He read on about the colours of the leaves outside her window and thought of seeing her again in another six weeks.

There was a quick knock at the door. Robin glanced over to see if George had been disturbed, though he lay still. Before Robin could respond, the door slowly creaked open. Robin dove under the bedcovers and feigned sleep. He heard someone slip quietly into the room and step toward his bed. Robin kept his eyes closed and tried to slow his breathing.

"Robin," a voice whispered. "Robbie?"

It was Timothy. Robin unconsciously pulled the bed clothes closer around him. He pretended to stir in his sleep.

Timothy bent down over him. Robin felt the familiar fingers touch his hair. He tried not to flinch. "I haven't much seen you this term," Timothy whispered. "I hear you have a girlfriend."

Robin gripped Marianne's letter under the blankets and prayed George would wake and throw Timothy out. He faked snoring.

"Alright." Timothy stood up straight and finally turned toward the door. Robin listened to his bare footsteps retreating across the floor. "You know where to find me, Robbie."

Robin cracked open one eye as far as he dared without being found out. He saw Timothy's back as he faced the door, disappointment visible in his shoulders. He made some incomprehensible gesture with one hand and then turned back to face the bed. Robin shut his eyes tight. It was a long, anxious moment before Robin heard the door close behind Timothy.

Robin sat up in bed. He filled his lungs, then slowly let the air escape through his nostrils. He looked down at Marianne's letter still in his hands, then glanced back to the closed door. Damn St. Anthony's and its blasted honour code. There were times when a simple door lock was absolutely necessary.

He reached over to his desk, dropped the letter on the wooden surface and switched off the lamp.

Chapter 4

November 1968
McLean, Virginia, USA

The soul had been watching, studying the partnership between Mark and Marie Harris. Watching and waiting. These prospective parents would provide a suitable environment for the necessary work. Their baby would have an appropriate launch platform into the world. The soul made a decision; the couple announced that they were pregnant.

Preparations were underway on many levels. The soul was more heavily concentrated in these incarnations, choosing only two avatars. Much of its more earthly energy was already contained in one form; now a higher vibration would manifest. The limbs and organs took shape in Marie's womb, all according to plan. The soul laughed when it felt the delicate fingers and toes, trying them on for size. The soul danced, hearing the mother's heartbeat, smiling at the muffled sound of her voice, "The baby just kicked!" That time was gone quickly, and the soul fused itself into this new form. Angela.

Accepting the heavy imprisonment of flesh, the child was born, thrust out into a cold world. It seemed an eternity that the squeezing pressure and pain assaulted her. She could feel the sympathetic strain in her mother's body. Agonizingly slow.

There were hands on her. She was held aloft by her ankles, exacerbating the painful throbbing in her head. Her diaphragm contracted, then expanded, and she took her first breath. The frigid air shocked her fragile system, and she cried, her body erupting in searing spasms.

She heard her own small cries as her physical senses took hold. She remembered this trauma, but was still unprepared. There was another sound, a human voice, the doctor speaking to her mother. Everything was alright; she was healthy. She wiggled her fingers and sent little electrical pulses down to her toes. She kicked her legs. She had forgotten the inherent ache and sluggishness of the physical body. She continued to cry.

They were poking at her, cleaning out her mouth and nostrils, wiping the fluids out of her eyes, and drying her skin. She heard the sweet music of her mother's voice, the joy in her laughter, so far away. She wanted to touch her, to be reassured by her heartbeat and the rise and fall of her breath. This sudden separation was frightening. She saw formless shadows pass over her closed eyelids.

Finally, she felt warmth. Someone had wrapped her in a soft blanket and had covered her bare head. They were taking her away, farther from her mother. Her body was so tired, her tiny muscles exhausted. Her cries became quiet whimpers. She wanted to open her eyes and see, but something blinded her, stabbing at her new eyes and sending painful shards ricocheting through her brain. Then she remembered: light.

She was completely helpless, bound by this blanket, though thankful for warmth after the icy coldness of the delivery room. Everything happened so fast in this world. She would adjust to this new perspective soon enough. She struggled against sleep, for sleep meant forgetting. She wanted to remember, to stay firmly on her chosen path. But there lay ahead many years of meandering, so much growth. She took a deep breath into her tiny lungs, already growing used to the pain, and she drifted off to sleep.

It was perfect. Everything. A gentle relaxation spread across Angela's newborn features as she rested.

Chapter 5

April 1970
London

While the small audience dispersed, Robin stepped down off the stage and made his way through a dark, narrow hallway to the oversized closet of a dressing room, where George and the other boys in the band were already enjoying the complimentary drinks that came as partial payment for their performances at the Bidder's Suite. With only a pair of chairs and a few crates as furniture, The Wombles made themselves comfortable and talked excitedly about their most recent set.

Stepping over his lounging bandmates, Robin ducked into the corner to retrieve a towel from his rucksack on the floor. He mopped his dripping brow and pulled out a spare jumper, as his shirt was soaked through with sweat.

Robin had lingered on the stage after the set, as was his habit, interacting with audience members. While George, Matthew, Ian, and Terry packed up the instruments, Robin sat on a wooden stool at the edge of the raised platform that served as a stage, with friends, acquaintances, and a few total strangers gathered in front of him. They bantered back and forth, each taking a turn at telling part of a story they were creating together in the dingy, upstairs parlour of the pub. Improvisational Myth Making, Robin called the process, and he used these spontaneous tales in his own compositions, though he never found the confidence to share these with his band, much less an audience.

Terry thrust a beer toward him, but Robin shook his head and took off his damp shirt. Wrinkling his nose, the seventeen-year-old leaned back against the cool, cinderblock wall and observed the other boys' enthusiasm—save for George, who remained quiet like himself.

Robin was glad Ken had made it to tonight's gig. The two had encountered disagreements and massive creative differences with The Chippers. They couldn't even agree on simple stage lighting, much less the songs for any given set. The Chippers had disbanded after the graduation of all members but Robin—with still a year to go—though the stubborn contest of wills would have split the group eventually.

The sudden change in this strained relationship had everything to do with Alice, Ken's sister.

Robin ran the towel across the back of his neck, smiling as he thought of his golden-haired, raven-eyed sweetheart who both excited and intimidated. A year older than himself, Alice had latched on to his own passion, quietly considering the possibilities. She believed in him.

This night would be their first truly alone together. For not quite a year, they had only seen each other on occasional weekends when Alice made the journey by train to see him. Even then, Alice had to be sandwiched between Robin's rehearsals, his growing performance engagements, and his rigidly enforced "studio time"—Robin's hours in seclusion fitting together the ideas and phrases constantly swimming through his head.

Terry and Ian laughed at a joke Matthew was telling about elephants in ladies' undergarments. Robin crouched down on the floor. A furtive glance to George confirmed their plan.

Tonight's performance was Robin's last with The Wombles. Their meager but loyal following and even the few pounds they occasionally brought in were not enough to counteract his impatience with the same, tired playlist and lack of originality. George had already thundered at him several hours before the show when Robin announced his intentions. George tried to convince him that The Wombles offered good performance experience while The Chippers were re-forming, but Robin held firm.

He just couldn't bring himself to tell the other boys.

Standing up, Robin pulled the dry jumper over his head and felt the cotton knit sticking to his moist skin. He worried about not showering before meeting Alice, but then decided the sweat would enhance his masculinity. He thrust his damp shirt into the bottom of his bag and took a quick look around before making his escape. George caught his glance. Robin just shrugged and headed toward the door.

"Goodnight, lads," Robin announced cheerfully. The others returned his salutation, and Ian gave him a quick pat on the shoulder. Robin felt his resolve waver as he reached for the dented metal doorknob, but in the next second he found himself again in the dark hallway and heard the door close shut behind him. George would break the news. The Wombles were through.

A handful of people still lingered in the club, kids barely older than Robin. He was amazed at the small size of the room, holding only a handful of tables. He felt the walls expand exponentially whenever he took the microphone into his hands, due to stage fright, the love of being the center of attention, or perhaps a combination of the two.

Alice hadn't moved from her seat in the back corner, where she sat quietly during these shows. She never came forward to participate in Robin's fantasy roundtables, preferring to admire the proceedings from her obscure vantage point. As he approached her, nearly lost in the shadows, Robin was in awe of her loveliness.

Alice was no great beauty, though Robin saw deeper. She was intensely endearing, holding out to him some mysterious promise. Her pink lips curved into a smile as she reached for his hand. Robin's pulsed quickened as her slender fingers curled around his, and he hurried with her down the stairs and into the London night.

* * * *

Within the space of a few minutes, Robin had turned into a blabbering idiot.

He knew he was jabbering on excessively about insignificant details of his day and plans for the summer, but sitting on the subway car holding Alice's hand as they made their way to her flat, the meaningless stream of words issuing from his tired lips was the only thing that kept his mind from exploding.

Alice smiled and nodded politely, complimenting him occasionally with a quiet giggle. She was caught up in the nervous tension in her hands and shoulders and wasn't paying much attention to what he was saying anyway. Her mind flitted from one vision to the next, focusing first on the image of Robin electrified by the stage lights, balanced precariously on the edge of the platform, hovering over his audience as the room filled with the strange sound of his howling; then flashing ahead to the possibilities of the next few hours. Her toes curled inside her shoes, and she bit her lip when she felt his knee press against hers.

They didn't speak of the fact that it was late at night and the underground would be shutting down shortly, that Robin would be stranded at Alice's apartment. Nor did they discuss Alice's roommate conveniently visiting family in Brentwood. There was no mention of Robin's excited afternoon visit to the chemist in search of prophylactics.

Reaching the top of the stairs at Alice's tube stop, Robin fell silent. It had rained while they were in transit, and the humid night air mingled with the traces of sweat on Robin's brow and the back of his neck. The wet street hissed as a stray automobile drove past. Robin was distracted by a humming street lamp a few buildings down.

Alice fumbled for the keys in her coat pocket as they mounted the cement stairs to her apartment building. Robin scarcely noticed, distracted by the lonely sounds of the wet road late at night. Alice pushed open the door just as Robin softly touched the back of her neck with only his fingertips, his slight caress a gentle breeze playing with her hair.

They entered the apartment without a sound. They took off their jackets and slipped out of their shoes in the darkness. Alice took his hands into hers and led him carefully through the hallway to her bedroom.

Robin would not be her first lover, but she was most certainly his. Alice was touched by his inexperience, neither timid nor self-conscious. She watched his eyes, illuminated by a street lamp outside her window, as first his gaze and then his hands moved over her, discovering every ounce of her sensuality. She had imagined a more natural performance, a carefully choreographed and instinctive pairing, but a sincere innocence seeped deep into their pores as they fumbled around the bed in the dark, learning how to love each other.

* * * *

Robin's departure from The Wombles proved less than popular. Reluctantly, George broke the news as gently as he could. He understood his friend's fear of confrontation and ambiguous insecurity, even if Robin himself couldn't see it.

Matthew accepted the news the best, his shocked excitement revealing a desire to front the band himself. Long frustrated with Robin's eclectic leadership, Matthew crouched low on the floor and ran his fingers through his hair, scheming. At last, with Robin the prima donna out of the way, he would have his chance.

Ian, on the other hand, was immediately despondent, giving into his quiet brooding about which Robin had vented endlessly in private to George. Terry exploded, angrily cursing this abandonment, convinced Robin thought himself too good to associate with simple school boys now that he was to be a university man.

George had always been the peacemaker, attempting diplomatic solutions to even the most trivial conflicts within the band. In the midst of this tumultuous news, he wanted to stay with these three in the small dressing room to help reach some resolution. But as Matthew frantically paced the floor, masterminding his rise to power, while Ian silently drummed his fingers on his corduroy trousers and Terry ranted aloud about artistic subservience and entitlement, George felt a murky resignation take hold, and he slipped quietly out of the room.

George had returned alone to his parents' home, where he and Robin were staying the weekend. His parents had already retired for the night, and it was no surprise that Robin was nowhere in sight. George smiled when he thought of Robin with Alice. He had watched them as the band was setting up for the show, Alice hovering on the outskirts as usual. Robin had gently touched her cheek, engaging her in an intimate, soulful gaze that wasn't quite a smile. In that moment, George understood the depth of Robin's feelings for his lady. He was truly in love.

* * * *

The telephone woke George the next morning. He was alone in the house, his parents out on Saturday morning errands and Robin having never returned. His eyes heavy with only a few hours' sleep, George stumbled into the hallway and lifted the receiver.

"Hullo," he grumbled into the phone. His voice was hoarse from the smoky Bidder's Suite, and he could taste the tar at the back of his throat as if he had been smoking those cigarettes himself. There was a chaotic racket at the other end of the phone. Assuming it was Robin phoning, he began to laugh but quickly coughed up bits of blackened mucus instead.

"... you sure picked your timing. I bloody knew you were a gutless leech, just using our talents to fake your way through," Terry's voice came into focus. George squinted against the early morning tirade and scratched his head.

"Terry, you're over-reacting..."

"I'll tell you who's bloody over-reacting! Your impossibly inflated opinion of yourself and your so-called musical stylings. It was an embarrassment playing with you. Can't even hold a simple note without inventing some wild excuse of a tortured animal sound to mask your own ineptitude." Terry had probably not slept and had quite possibly had several pints too many. George imagined he was prompting himself with written notes.

"Terry, you've got to calm down. Listen now, this is George."

Terry sputtered a few unintelligible syllables before shouting as loud as he could. "Then you put that slimy maggot on the phone right now!"

George held the receiver far from his ear and raised a hand to his brow to stave off the pounding headache he felt threatening. Even with the telephone at arm's length, he could hear Terry shouting and cursing, raving like a lunatic. It was too early in the morning for this. George gently returned the receiver to his ear.

"Terry, Terry, listen to me. Robin isn't here. You've had a long night and need some sleep. You'll just have to take this up with him some other time. I'm going back to bed now, Terry." Out of patience, George rang off while his former bandmate was mid-invective.

* * * *

Alice awoke to the vague clattering of pots and pans.

She stretched her long, slender body and blinked her eyes lazily in the golden light creeping in through the window. Warm in bed, listening to the birds outside, she drifted out of slumber into consciousness. Alice took a long, deep breath and smiled at her tingling muscles, luxuriously musing on the previous hours with Robin, tangled together in love and in sleep. Her heart beat faster as she remembered cradling his head as he slept.

She turned to regard her lover in the morning light, but her bed was empty. Propping herself up on her elbows, she recalled the earlier noise in the kitchen. How long ago had that been? There was a rhythmic tapping coming from down the hallway.

Then she smelled the burning.

She found him sitting at the small breakfast table that separated the tiny kitchen from the cramped sitting room. Robin had an army of wadded up paper balls on the table and many more scattered about the floor. Tapping his feet, he kept time with the music in his head and banged out a series of rhythms on the table top with a pencil and his fingers, pausing only to scribble in Alice's notebook.

He was completely oblivious to the smoke rising behind him in the kitchen.

Alice rushed past him, quickly grabbing a towel to keep from burning her fingers as she lifted the smoking saucepan from the stove and dropped it into the sink. Robin appeared vaguely aware of some activity behind him. Alice turned off the stove and flooded the charred pot, trying to make out what Robin had attempted to cook.

She wanted to yell at him, but checked this angry impulse. After their first night together, she had awakened alone. He had chosen music instead of her in the early morning hours. And then he had tried to burn down the building. But she rationalized that he had been inspired to write a song for her, music so deeply felt it could not be contained for a single moment, and that he had intended to bring her breakfast in bed.

Alice turned off the faucet and stepped up behind Robin, leaning down to wrap her arms around him. She kissed his ear. "Good morning," she mumbled into his neck.

He clasped a gentle hand around her wrist, frowning as he jotted down one last bit of nonsense before turning to smile at her. "Sorry about that," he said cheerfully, nodding toward the smoking saucepan in the sink. "I was hungry, and then forgot about it..."

"Didn't you at least notice the smoke?" Alice ran her fingers through his red-brown hair, suppressing a sigh in her throat. He was simply adorable in the morning.

"Oh, umm, yeah... I was just..." Robin motioned weakly to the mountain of papers on the table. He knew this was not the most auspicious start to the morning, though he was thrilled with the energy pouring through him onto these scattered bits of paper. He felt guilty for the sneaking irritation at her interruption but quickly forgot everything outside of her eyes the moment she smiled at him.

"No permanent damage." Alice laughed and kissed his nose, brushing a few stray wisps of unruly hair from his emerald eyes. Delighting in the boyish smile that played across his lips, she felt a vague tugging within. She turned her head and shook it off.

"What's all this scribbling about, then?" Alice settled into his lap as Robin collected the papers into a more organized stack and glanced through his messy notes.

"Is this a song about last night?" Alice surprised herself with a coquettish giggle.

Her question didn't even register. Robin had not yet made the transition from his musical muse back into the real world. "It's about Pepsi Cola."

She began to laugh, but he was completely serious. His description of the creative thoughts behind the stylings and story was quite detailed.

"So then this chap in the pub orders some cola, takes a few sips, and then makes his way to the toilet. But when he opens the door, he's actually opened a door into another world, another realm. I'm working out what happens to him there... He will step inside. And then what happens to him when he comes back."

"Pepsi Cola," Alice said more to herself than to Robin.

"Yeah. They used to make the stuff with cocaine, before they knew what it was."

"Coca-Cola," Alice commented as she rose from his lap and stepped into the kitchen.

"Yeah, okay, so people were drinking this stuff and not knowing what they were putting in their bodies, and to be sure they were tripping right and left, but they didn't know it, so this bloke steps through the doorway into this kind of drug experience—"

"I don't think they put that much in there." She washed out the saucepan and took stock of what was available in the apartment for breakfast. Going out would be easier.

"Okay, but it's the whole idea of the thing. These huge companies introduce all these great new products without really knowing what they're putting out there, things we won't know about for years, after damage may already have been done. Like maybe some of these miracle drugs, the food we're eating... We put so much trust into the companies making these things, products, not stopping to consider how we're guinea pigs."

Out comes the activist, Alice thought as she dried the saucepan and stored it below the counter. She knew Robin as a surprisingly romantic fellow and was disappointed not to see that now. That's alright, she told herself. Robin had within him the workings of a great and important man. Minor and occasional frustrations, like this one, would no doubt be a part of their life together.

He was tapping again, striking the table with a pencil in one hand and a ball-point pen in the other, his foot counting out on the floor as he read through his notes. Feeling her eyes on him, Robin smiled. "I always start from percussion first, and then move forward from rhythm. Gareth taught me that."

Robin stopped his drumming and laid his hands flat on the table, disengaging from *The Cola Trip*. He turned in his chair to regard Alice, standing in the kitchen and staring at him. God, she was beautiful, wearing nothing but his shirt and a pair of socks. Her early morning hair hung in tangles around her pale face, her dark eyes piercing through this golden halo, as if she were the captive of another realm. He wondered if she had similar thoughts when she gazed on him. She looked lost, waiting for his direction.

"Right. Breakfast." Not until he stood did he realize he was clad only in his underwear. He looked down, then blushed as he laughed, lifting his eyes to smile at Alice from beneath his brow—that mischievous, penetrating look that so thrilled and disarmed her. He playfully strode toward her, and Alice took a few unconscious steps backward, her breath quickening. But instead of taking her forcefully into his arms, as she expected, he gently reached for her hand and raised her fingers to his lips.

"But first," he said smoothly, "I'm going to brush out your hair."

Chapter 6

April 1970
McLean, Virginia

It was spring when Angela's Daddy came home.

She had never seen him before. He had been deep in the jungles of Vietnam when she was born. A picture of his new daughter had arrived several weeks later, and Mark Harris carried her photo with him at all times. The jungle planted the seeds of superstition in the hearts of even the most practical men. His buddies had their rosaries, St. Christopher's medals, and lucky coins; Mark had his picture of Angela, his baby angel.

He had written Marie asking for a taped recording, to hear his daughter's tiny voice, though he would have settled for the quiet sound of her breathing as she slept. There was no such peace for him. He closed his eyes at night, but sleep would not come.

At last the recording arrived from home, but Mark never heard it. Within six weeks of Angela's birth, Mark was a prisoner of war.

Marie had moved in with her parents just after her husband boarded the military transport taking him away from her. She was only a child herself, soon to be a mother. In Mark's place, Marie's mother held her hand through morning sickness, restless nights, and two false labors. In his stead, Grandmum welcomed Angela into the world.

The news of Mark's capture had been devastating. Unwilling to burden others, and terrified of her own rage and fear, Marie put on a strong face and retreated inside herself. Marie hated living with her parents, though she needed them desperately. What if she were a war widow? Marie lay awake at night, wondering at her own breaking point. She couldn't sleep for nightmares of what they must be doing to Mark, if he was even still alive. She shut her eyes tight against the screaming inside her head.

Her daughter's tears flowed freely, enough healing water to cleanse them both. Angela didn't need words to understand. She felt it every time Marie reached for her. She heard it in her mother's heartbeat when she held her close. And she tasted it whenever she was pressed against her mother's breast.

She was a quiet baby. She needed all her strength to defend against this psychic invasion from without. The slightest touch sent a confusing mixture of fear, rage, pity, and hope coursing through her. She struggled against every embrace. At each feeding she consumed Marie's dark desperation, and the milk turned in her stomach. Unable to process so much heavy energy, Angela began to vomit uncontrollably.

Several frantic visits to the pediatrician and the emergency room produced the same diagnosis: Angela must be allergic to her mother's milk. One formula after another was prescribed as the doctor tried to find nourishment her system would accept. But each feeding meant more contact with the same adults. She tried to show them how their energy was making them all sick, but they just kept taking her back to that cold doctor's office.

Now she was close to eighteen months old, living with her mother and grandparents who doted on her, delighting in her mental strength and creative interaction with her environment. Her tiny fingers reached out to grab hold of the whole world.

There had been some excitement several days before—a man in uniform at the door and a flurry of telephone calls. Noticing the incredible roller coaster of emotions in her mother, Angela kept playing with her brightly colored, plastic blocks.

Marie gave Angela an extra bath and put a yellow ribbon in her red-brown hair. They both wore brand new dresses from the department store. Angela even had new shoes, and they hurt her feet.

Angela watched Marie curl her own long, dark hair and put on her makeup. She sat quietly on the bed, fingering the lace hem of her dress as she studied her mother's movements. Marie darkened her lashes and streaked sparkling powder across her cheeks. She drew color on her lips. Catching Angela's eye in the mirror, Marie winked at her daughter's reflection, and they laughed together.

Angela, Marie, Grandmum, and Granddad all hurried to the car. Angela liked getting in the car. She especially liked going places with her grandfather, even if only to pick up eggs or laundry detergent. Today everyone was dressed up, so fancy. She worried they might be going to church. She didn't like church, so dim and dull, where she had to sit still and pay attention to a man she couldn't see saying things she didn't understand.

She didn't recognize the landmarks outside the car window as they drove along. Angela ignored the bubbling banter of Marie and Grandmum. She patted her mother's thigh and got up on her knees on the back seat, pressing her hands and face against the glass window to blink her big, green eyes at the world passing by.

It was always a long trip when they took her someplace new. Angela pressed her lips against the cool glass, and she giggled when it began to rain. She traced the drops of water with her finger as they meandered down the other side of the window.

"Here we go, sweetheart. We're almost there now." Marie pulled her daughter into her lap. Looking ahead, Angela observed block-like islands of buildings swimming in concrete. This was a very noisy place. While Granddad parked the car, Angela frowned at the roaring she heard outside.

Granddad opened the car door and pulled Angela into his arms. She squealed when he tossed her in the air. As soon as she had her feet back on the ground, another loud roar boomed overhead, and she covered her ears with her hands to block it out. Her mother took hold of her elbow and pulled her along. Angela shuffled her feet along the pavement in the shiny shoes that pinched her toes.

The family entered a massive building that smelled funny—stuffy and electric. The floor vibrated gently, helping to relieve Angela's cramped feet.

They walked very quickly within a stream of human traffic. Angela studied the bags people carried. Some were big and strong, in dark colors, and she imagined they must be very heavy, with people hunched over and dragging their feet to carry them. Other bags were small, brightly colored, slung over shoulders or held in loose fists. Angela saw that her mother and Grandmum only carried their purses.

Granddad mumbled something about being late. Angela was hoisted into the air, settling into her grandfather's chest as he carried her. She watched her mother rush forward, swimming ahead into the river of people. The roaring noise was growing louder. They veered right and walked down a long, carpeted ramp with posters of exotic places on one wall and glass on the other. Angela watched another current of people on the other side of the glass heading back into the main building. Pairs and groups clung happily to each other, arm-in-arm, some with heavy coats, some wearing sunhats. They were laughing together and carrying on animated conversations.

Grandmum and Granddad walked faster to catch up with Marie, passing through an open doorway into the bright sunlight outside. Angela blinked her eyes against the sun glinting off of the wet pavement. The rain had stopped, but there was a new smell that attacked her nose and burned the back of her throat. Her eyes welled up as she coughed to get these fumes out of her system, but she only managed to breathe more of it in.

"What do you think of that, missy? See that big plane?" Granddad was pointing to a long, sideways building up on wheels, its shiny exterior curved outward with funny little windows and people looking out from inside. "That's an airplane," Granddad said. Angela stretched one arm over her head and yawned. Granddad laughed.

She sensed the expectation. Something important was about to happen. Angela studied Granddad's profile, touching his jaw with her small hand. She saw how Grandmum's bony fingers clutched the handle of her purse, then released their grip for a moment, only to tense again.

Angela searched her mother's face, peering into her thoughts and feelings. She followed Marie's gaze to a long ramp extending down from the airplane. Bags and suitcases were being unloaded, but Marie was watching several large boxes come down out of the plane. There were people all around these boxes, people with sad faces and somber gaits. They stood together in small groups, clutching each other as if they would fall down. The boxes were covered with colors and stripes just like the special sheet Granddad hung on the pole each morning in the front yard.

Angela reached for her mother, with her hands and her heart. Making the insistent noises that brought nearly instant gratification, she was quickly transferred from Granddad's grasp to her mother's embrace. She felt Marie's anticipation, grief, excitement, and guilt. She looked at the other clusters of people. Marie was a powerful mixture of conflicting emotions, and Angela shut her eyes tight to block out this psychic flood.

"MARIE!"

Angela heard her mother's breath catch in her throat, felt the explosion in her veins.

"MARIE! I'm home!"

She opened her eyes to find her mother sobbing with delight. "MARK!"

Marie's grip on Angela tightened as she ran forward, nearly stumbling on the tarmac. Angela saw a man in strange clothing rushing down a metal staircase pushed up against the plane. Other people on the stairs happily gave way as he squeezed past them.

"Angela!" the man shouted. "Angela, my baby!"

He jumped the last few feet from the stairway to the tarmac and ran toward them, dropping his bag to the ground. A thrill of excitement tingled inside Angela at his approach. In a flash, he had both her mother and herself in a strong embrace.

This man and Marie were laughing and crying simultaneously, kissing each other, kissing their baby. "This is your father, Angela sweetie. This is your Daddy."

Angela looked into the man's face, watching the happy, proud tears streaming down over his young cheeks. He was touching her hair, smiling as the salt water trickled over his lips and into his mouth. She reached out to touch the water drops on his face. He sobbed as her fingers made contact with his skin.

Chapter 7

June 1971
Arlington, Virginia

A year since his return from the jungle, Mark Harris still had not come home.

Following the joyful reunion with his wife and meeting his daughter for the first time, Mark couldn't relax into a quiet life at home. He was still in prison camp. The family tiptoed around him, waiting for the war to melt away. They missed the Mark they had known and loved before.

Mark had not rested since his return. He was home, a free man, but there was an agitation that would not let go. He needed action. After a few days living with his in-laws, Mark was anxious to establish his own home, no matter how meager.

His first impulse was to flee from everything he had known, to carve out an entirely new existence. He couldn't stand the gulf between who he had been before Vietnam, and the man the war had made him into.

But both his parents and Marie's convinced him to settle closer to home, promising babysitting and other support. Two weeks after her father returned, Arlington became Angela Harris' hometown.

Angela hadn't cried when she left her grandparents' home, though she had seen Marie's apprehension as they walked down the driveway for the last time. Angela was fascinated by this new man called Daddy who played and talked with her, who made her mother smile, and who attracted so many dark souls.

But that was a year ago.

Marie busied herself in the role of wife and mother, thankful to have her immediate family intact. But she slowly acknowledged that her husband had become a complete stranger to her. Only Angela seemed to have a real connection with him, and Marie was jealous of their bedtime conversations.

When they ran out of storybooks, Mark confided in his daughter as he would a confessional priest. Angela liked it when adults spoke to her in their own language. She and Daddy shared a special secret, talking like this with no one else but God and spirits listening.

Everyone imagined the terrible atrocities Mark must have seen and committed in the jungle. No one spoke of what must have befallen him in that POW camp. Nobody wanted to dredge up potential trauma. Marie spoke with her friends and parents. Her parents spoke with Mark's parents. Mark's parents asked Marie how he was doing.

But no one ever asked Mark about it.

Life went on as though there were no war on the other side of the globe, as if he had never been gone. He was numb and exhausted when he returned, anxious to forget. But Mark knew the time would come to release the rage, grief, and pain. When he turned to his wife and his family, they looked away and politely changed the subject.

And so he turned to his small daughter. She was a patient and forgiving confidante. He felt some small salvation when he looked into her eyes and saw love there.

He never imagined there might be a connection between his late night confessions and his daughter's horrific nightmares.

Grandmum called them night terrors. Approaching her third birthday, Angela was a body possessed when these evil dreams took hold. She threw herself on the floor and clawed her way out of the grasp of any who tried to comfort her. She screamed and tore at her own hair. The sobs that wracked her small body shattered her mother's heart.

And then, as suddenly as it started, the terror would wane. Angela's blood-curdling cries became quiet whimpers, and she faded into deep sleep, not waking until morning.

Mark slept through these traumas, night after night—Marie could not rouse him. Such a light sleeper otherwise, he seemed nearly comatose whenever Angela's nightmares struck.

Angela had no memory of these dreams. Marie's haggard and weary visage greeted her daughter in the morning, and Angela worried that her mother looked so tired. But Mark sprung out of bed with renewed reserves, unlike his normal grayness.

Angela was taken to a child psychologist, but she was silent when asked to describe her dreams. He put a piece of paper in front of her and gave her a pencil. She carefully sketched a crude vampire and a Frankenstein monster, like she saw sometimes on television. She couldn't remember any dreams about either of these creatures, but she didn't want to disappoint the doctor.

The diagnosis was that Angela was afraid of the dark. Exercises were applied to calm her fears and to ease her into peaceful sleep. The doctor would sit her down in a room by herself, gradually turning down the lights as he asked her to close her eyes and relax. He talked to her through a speaker from the observation booth. He asked her to imagine a tingling sensation in her toes, spreading across her feet, into her ankles, and up her legs into the rest of her body. And then he read her a story, carefully monitoring her, assuming she was getting used to being in the dark alone.

And she did sleep. At least, her body slept. Now she could keep her mind awake and see for herself these nightmares they kept saying she was having.

* * * *

Mark tucked his daughter into bed and read her a Curious George story. Then they sat together. It was unusual for Angela not to request a second story, and on this night she was particularly quiet.

"Is everything alright, sweetheart?" Mark brushed a few wisps of hair out of her eyes. Angela nodded obediently and then frowned as she looked up into her father's eyes.

"Are you afraid of the dark?" He took one of her hands into his and marveled at her fragile fingers.

"Are you?" She was asking him a serious question. Mark laughed as an unexpected shiver ran up his spine.

"I'm worried about you, Angel. You keep having bad dreams."

Angela nodded again, her dark hair falling back down into her face. "Worry 'bout you, too." She reached up to touch his rough chin, then kissed him on the nose. Angela lay back and closed her eyes. Her breathing was already deepening as Mark turned off the bedside lamp, checking her nightlight before he left the room.

* * * *

She awoke inside her dream. In her weeks and months of practice, she had yet to encounter one of these terrible dreams.

Tonight, her dream was heavier, almost dull. She was dreaming about her bedroom, sitting and waiting. She heard a voice from her parents' room across the hallway and decided to investigate. Making her way across the floor, she turned to look at her bed. She saw her own body there, asleep. She watched the rise and fall of her breath and felt nothing. There was a thin, silver cord running from that dark shape in the bed to where she stood. This was no dream. She accepted this and passed through the door.

Her parents couldn't see her. In their bedroom, Angela saw her mother turn off the radio on the bedside table. Marie had been trying to talk to her father, though he was already drifting off to sleep. She watched her mother brushing her teeth, but then became distracted by movement around her father.

Those souls were leaving him alone now that he was asleep. He closed off his mind to them when he lost consciousness, and Angela knew that must be difficult. She was used to these energies hovering around him, hitchhikers who had come home with her father from the war. Sometimes she could see one or two of them distinctly, but mostly they all blended together, barely aware of one another, focused on the living energy of Mark Harris.

They formed a dark cloud around him, seeping from his energy field as they were forced out. It was a storm cloud encircling her father, complete with thunder claps and lightning strikes. These lost souls played tug of war with each other and collectively struggled with Mark. He slept soundly with all of his concentration focused on recharging his own batteries, though it was still not enough to completely rid himself of these unwelcome guests. Tonight, they fought a losing battle with him, even if their displacement would only be temporary.

The dark, turbulent mass collected itself above her father's sleeping body. Angela heard a low, grumbling howl within the cloud, as it moved slowly toward her. More fascinated than frightened, she stepped aside as the energy mass continued through the bedroom door.

She followed into the hallway and saw the darkness enter her own bedroom. The dark cloud engulfed her small, sleeping body, assaulting with the same frustrated panic. Homeless and afraid, these souls were trying to enter her form as a temporary host.

Standing outside of her body, watching the attack, she saw the night terror begin. Her body clawed and kicked. She heard herself moan. Her mother would rise shortly to make futile attempts to hug, kiss, and shake the bad dreams away. It was no nightmare after all.

Chapter 8

June 1971
London

As with Robin's other traditional endeavours, his university studies had proved a disappointing failure.

His first semester had been an experiment in torture. Robin had honestly tried to put everything but his studies on hold... everything but Alice. But even she felt cut off from him, and he admitted to her that this forced diligence had everything to do with his fear that he would never amount to anything, and he had better have something more reliable to fall back on than mediocre drumming skills.

While he had the aptitude for the mathematics and science required to pursue his chemical engineering degree, he had no patience for theories not immediately applicable to real life. And there was always a pressing creative quest demanding his prompt attention. He managed to complete his course work, producing an average if uninspired showing.

It was during winter holiday that he sat down with his parents by the family fireplace to tell them he wanted to drop out of school. No demands, just a simple request.

Mrs. Michaels was not surprised, having seen Robin's commitment to higher education eating away at him. It was a bad fit. Robin's character and spirit demanded something different.

Robin struck a compromise with his father. He had completed a half-year of schooling and had posted passing marks. He would take some time away, perhaps a year or two, with the understanding that he could—that he would—return when his other prospects failed. His parents would lend financial support for the first six months. Then he would be on his own.

To save on expenses, Robin moved in with Gareth in his London flat, a small but livable space within walking distance of Alice's apartment. While Gareth rose early each morning to accommodate his job and classes, Robin spent the long weeks of February and March lounging lazily in bed, amusing himself with vaguely lucid dreaming as he drifted in and out of consciousness, exploring the partnership of his meandering imagination with the sounds of the city outside the window.

No particular schedule ordered his days. He liked this new spontaneity. All manner of schemes swam through his mind of how this departure from the traditional educational system would set his creative spirits on fire. He was free to compose endless rivers of revolutionary and soulful music that would somehow translate into an ample income.

Instead, Robin ate a great deal of junk food and watched an immense amount of daytime television.

As winter gave way to spring, he rose late in the day, munched on leftover pastries in front of the telly and considered doing laundry, which he always left for the weekend, when he would have Alice's assistance. Occasionally, Robin wandered outside the building, came back indoors to scribble nonsense on random scraps of paper, then lay down for several hours. He was generally awakened again when his cousin returned at the end of the day. He was not terribly productive.

This particular June evening, Gareth came home from work as an apprentice engineer at Triumph, found the flat a bit more of a disaster than the previous evening, and heard Robin snoring away in the spare bedroom. Stepping carefully across the floor, he made his way over scattered clothing and damnable bits of paper littered about. Storing his briefcase and overcoat in his own bedroom, Gareth returned to the front room to begin once again the process of bringing some kind of order to his flat.

Switching on the evening news, Gareth sat on the couch and sighed as he looked about the place, wondering how to break Robin out of this comfortable rut.

Gareth leaned back into the tattered cushions and closed his eyes, thankful for the quiet babbling of the television.

"A girl called for you. Priscilla."

Gareth opened his eyes to find Robin sitting on the arm of the couch. His hair had not been combed out after this latest nap. His clothes were wrinkled, and he wasn't wearing shoes. Gareth realized he must have dozed off himself. He yawned loudly, stretching his long arms. "What's that? Who called?"

"Priscilla," Robin answered, his own yawn mimicking Gareth's. "Said something about cooking dinner. I couldn't really follow. I was sleeping when she called."

Gareth jumped to his feet, eyes wide. "What time is it?!"

Robin blinked at his cousin's alarm. "I don't know. Half-past six?"

"Oh!"

Robin frowned as Gareth sprung into action like a man possessed, trying to straighten the mess into more orderly stacks and piles of clutter so at least some of the floor was visible. On his knees picking up Robin's precious paper scraps, Gareth looked up to his cousin. "Are you going to help me with this or not? Priscilla will be here in no time, and this is your mess we've got to get in order."

Robin dutifully got down on the floor to collect the notes for his latest mastermind creation, still trying to shake off the heavy sleep and the strange dream. He had seen a little girl, warm brown hair, sparkling green eyes—just like his. She had been standing in the center of a dark room, in vivid colour, while shadowy shapes and other nefarious forms full of sadness swam around her. Robin had instinctively feared for her safety, but this tiny creature had raised her eyes to meet his, and an intense, blinding radiance had shot forth from her to engulf him, nearly knocking him off his feet. The flash of her eyes found him sitting bolt upright on the bed, his mind clawing its way back to consciousness.

It was not unpleasant, this energy from the dream child, though he was still reeling. On the living room floor, Robin rested back on his heels and looked at his own hasty handwriting scrawled across these paper strips. All of these crazy ideas had made so much sense in the previous hours and weeks. In this incredible moment of clarity, they appeared instead only so many mad ramblings destined for the wastebasket.

Gareth was washing up the breakfast dishes. "You're welcome to stay for dinner with us if you'd like."

Robin looked up at Gareth, wiping down the sparse counterspace to make the kitchen more presentable. He watched in a haze, so disconnected from his cousin's frantic energy. He felt instantly intuitive, able to read his surroundings in a way he never could before. He placed his hands on his thighs and raised his dull body to standing.

"That's alright. I don't know how impressed your date would be with me hanging around all evening. I'll, umm, head out."

It only took a few minutes to comb out his unruly hair and brush his teeth. He found a clean pair of socks under the bed, though he had to hunt for a matching pair of shoes. After slipping his feet into the brown leather, he sat on the edge of the bed in silence. He could still see her eyes, her image burned into his retinas. His heart was beating too quickly. His mind was not racing, but he felt overwhelmed all the same.

The quick knock on the apartment door was followed promptly by voices in the living area. Robin pulled on a light jacket as he listened to the nervous glee in his cousin's tones. He grabbed his keys from the bedside table and stepped out into the hallway.

"Robin, this is Priscilla. We met in the book shop a few weeks back. This is my cousin, Robin." Robin brushed his hair from his eyes and shook the young lady's hand. She was comfortably attractive, with a warm and reassuring smile. Robin liked her instantly and was pleased with Gareth's good fortune.

"I'm on my way out, actually. It was nice meeting you." Robin reached into his pocket to confirm that his keys were still there.

"Are you sure you won't stay? We'll have plenty for three." Priscilla had friendly eyes, too.

"No, you go ahead. I've got a project I need to sort through tonight."

Gareth was puzzled as he watched Robin exit the apartment. There was something about his cousin this evening that hadn't been present earlier that morning.

Priscilla stood next to him at the sink to wash vegetables for dinner. Gareth laughed under his breath, certain that after a few moments of meandering, Robin would head straight for Alice's flat.

* * * *

Robin had been wandering round and round the same small park for nearly two hours, crisscrossing back and forth along the pavement, skirting the perimeter of the grass, watching the colours deepen and fade with the day's dying light.

It was the image of the girl. Especially her eyes, the energy of her. She was a small but able master of the forces swirling about her, yet she was just a tiny child. He couldn't get her out of his mind, still fearing for her safety amongst those dark spirits.

It was more than a dream. It was inspiration, his muse sending a visual message, a fast flash of material to use in his creations. He had no idea what to do with this. It wasn't relevant to his current efforts about electricity, nor did it speak to the now abandoned *Cola Trip*. If he just kept walking, kept his body in motion, somehow these pieces would jostle around enough to come together and congeal, integrating the new theme of the little girl.

But his stomach protested. He departed the quadrangle and crossed the road, dodging traffic. He found himself carrying a cheap bottle of wine, a box of crackers, and a small wheel of cheese. He must have stopped at the store. He didn't like it when his mind checked out like this, though it was not uncommon when he was preoccupied. He was growing tired. Would sleep again bring the image of the little girl? Maybe getting pissed would allow some rest without dreams.

He felt every step along the pavement. Just as he became more present in his body, he looked up to find himself standing at the door to Alice's flat.

She took the groceries from Robin's tired arms as he walked across the threshold. Used to Robin's odd moods, which she attributed to creative genius, Alice had never seen him so dazed. She deposited the cheese, crackers, and the bottle of wine on the modest dining table and then joined Robin on the couch.

Shoulders slumped, he had such a far-away look in his eyes. Alice wanted to cheer him up, to break him out of whatever cloud he was in, but she remained quiet. She studied his profile as he gazed ahead. They sat in silence, with only occasional traffic noise from the street below. The light from the kitchen played across his eyes, nose, and mouth, the shadows deepening his features and making him appear more sullen.

Alice sat cross-legged on the couch, facing Robin. They sat this way for long, powerful moments, until finally she rose. Stepping over him, Alice reached for the wine and opened the bottle. She retrieved two glasses from the counter by the sink. Covering the short space to the couch, she knelt on the floor by Robin's feet and poured the wine. She felt his light touch on the top of her head and smiled. Looking up to offer him the glass, Alice was shaken by his deep, shadowy stare. A gentle softness played across his face, and as he took his next breath, she could see his body relax.

"Do you want to get married?"

Chapter 9

1 January 1972
Arlington, Virginia

It was New Year's Day, and the Harrises were hosting a party in their new home.

Mark was in graduate school at George Mason University, pursuing a master's degree in education in the evenings. During the day, he worked as a salesman at Thomas Brothers office furniture retailers.

Even with his paltry income, the real estate market was tepid enough to allow the family to purchase their first home in a quiet suburb, and with a second child on the way, the Harrises had packed up their small apartment the previous November and moved into an 1,800-square-foot house.

Settling in was rocky. Mark was almost always gone, busy with work and classes, leaving his wife to manage the household. Marie was constantly moving furniture between rooms and up and down the stairs. Mental deliberations about wall colors and paper patterns kept her awake at night. She was still getting used to the idea of putting a nail in the wall wherever she wanted without having to check with anyone first.

The Harrises inherited antiques from both families, mixed pieces that had been placed in storage long ago by relatives who had run out of room in their own homes. Mark and Marie did not complain; they would fill their home with fine furniture, even if it required an eclectic style of decorating.

Mark did what he could for Marie in executing her plans for this party. He didn't want her to strain herself with the baby coming. Though Mark was also proud of their new home, his enthusiasm for the New Year's event paled next to Marie's manic levels, and he started to retreat into his studies for solitude, though he was still on winter break.

In the midst of this activity, Angela kept mostly to herself, enjoying the Christmas holiday and playing with her new dolls, creating stories in her head for them to act out.

But at the party, she watched the adults instead. They were more interesting.

Angela had been put to bed shortly after the guests began to arrive. But she couldn't sleep with all of the carrying-on downstairs. So many animated conversations. She lay awake listening to the laughter, the clinking of dishes and silverware at the buffet, and the footsteps on the hardwood floors from one room to the next. Marie was a popular hostess, and Angela could hear her mother's voice distinctly among the others.

Angela found her slippers next to the bed and padded out into the hallway. She ran her fingers along the spokes of the banister as she approached the stairs. She stepped down carefully onto the landing, walked to the top of the main staircase, and sat down. In her pale pink nightgown and Big Bird slippers, Angela watched the adults circulating below.

She knew some of these people, old friends and family members gathering in their new house. She had met some of the neighbors. But there were many new faces and voices. Her father's co-workers from the store, her mother's friends from the Women's Club, students and professors from George Mason. There were no children.

She watched her mother pass through the hallway from the kitchen to the living room, playfully balancing on her swollen belly a fresh tray of the biscuits Angela liked. Marie had told her there was a baby coming, a little brother or sister. Angela was uneasy about this prospect, but she liked seeing her mother so happy.

Angela also watched the "other people" making their rounds. They were attracted to the party, so many vibrant people concentrated in these downstairs rooms.

The usual entourage surrounded her father, a dark barrier against the world. Her parents couldn't see them. Angela thought they were very sad. Sometimes she tried to talk to them, especially when her father took naps on weekends. She asked why they were here, why they were so sad and angry. Maybe they couldn't hear her.

At least they had stopped bothering her. Her night terrors no longer disturbed her sleep. But she was more keenly aware of them, since they had touched her. She had been afraid of them, fearful they would attack her, that they were hurting her father.

And there was a new group in this house. Several roamed about, oblivious to Angela and her parents, performing the same tasks over and over, tracing the same paths across the floor. She couldn't always see them very well—sometimes not at all—but they offered a strange comfort, like when Angela had already seen the episode of Sesame Street on television and knew what was going to happen next.

There were guests at this party with a shadowy figure or two in tow. An older neighbor wore a strained smile as she walked to the threshold of the living room with a spectral teenager trailing, pleading all the while. Angela was the only one who could hear her murky, desperate voice repeating, "I'm sorry! I'm so sorry!"

"It's alright," she whispered from the top of the stairs.

She also saw a man had brought his dog, always at his master's side. Angela wanted to go downstairs to pet the dog, but she could tell by his translucence that he would not want to play with her. The man picked up a few crackers from a small serving table, and the dog sat back on his hind legs, raised his front paws in the air, and barked. Angela giggled, but he received no treat from his master, who could not see him.

Though fascinated by the roaming crowd—both the living and the ethereal—she was growing sleepy, and the features of her face contorted as she yawned.

Then she noticed man she had not seen before in the hallway. He stood by the radiator close to the front door, also observing the party guests. He was older than Daddy, but not as old as Granddad, and his red-brown hair was turning salt-and-pepper gray. Angela watched him instead.

Out of the way of the hallway traffic, he engaged no one. He had no beverage and held no plate of food. Standing partly in the shadows, he radiated his own gentle light. His arms hung comfortably at his side, and he was smiling.

As a boisterous threesome passed through the hallway, this man looked up at Angela sitting atop the staircase, and his friendly smile broadened. She had been discovered at last. She grinned back down at him.

Sharing this smiling secret, he crossed the hallway, easily weaving between the guests, though no one noticed him. Angela was eager for some company. He climbed the staircase quickly and took a seat at her side.

"Good evening, little one," he said in a melodic voice. "Aren't you up past your bedtime?" Angela smiled up at him, mirroring his own expression, and giggled. "I like to watch people, too," he confided.

"Nobody sees me up here, so I can see the party." Angela pulled her knees close to her chest and wrapped her arms around her ankles. Her companion nodded.

"Do you like parties?" he asked her.

"Sometimes," she responded. "I don't like when they talk like I'm a baby. When they don't know I'm looking, I can hear what they really say."

"Grown-up conversations aren't so different from what children say. Adults and kids often say pretty much the same things. Just different words."

Angela looked up at him. "I like grown-up words."

He laughed quietly. "What do you see when you watch people from up here?"

She peered down into the hallway, studying a dark-haired woman in a sparkly red sweater and high-heels who was laughing too loudly. Angela caught a flashing glimpse of a dim, muddy-colored shadow whispering in the woman's ear. Angela frowned.

"There are a lot of strangers." She was quiet for a few moments, blinking her eyes at what transpired below. "Some people have invisible friends."

The man followed her gaze. "Yes, I see what you mean."

She turned to him, her eyes wide with surprise. "You see them, too?" He smiled at the hope in her voice; she wanted so badly not to be the only one.

"They're not really invisible," he began. "They just live in a different place than we do. On a different plane, you might say."

Her eyes were trained on him as he spoke.

"People who are still living their lives, like your parents and the people at this party, people you meet all over, are paying so close attention to what's going on right in front of them, that they have difficulty seeing anything else. They don't usually see these other people, the ones who have given up their bodies."

Looking into her small face, he was touched by her rapt attention. He knew this might be too much for her to absorb, but she was hungry for this wisdom. She waited for him to continue. "You know you have a soul, that isn't the same as your body?"

Angela looked at her feet. She pulled one foot out of the slipper and wiggled her toes. Marie had painted Angela's toenails pink at Christmas, and not all of the polish had flaked off yet. "Sometimes when my body goes to sleep I get up and go places."

"Right. People use their bodies as a kind of vehicle, like when your Mom drives the car to the grocery store. The car helps her get there, and your body helps you do the things you need to do in your life."

She picked at the remnants of pink polish on her big toe.

"And then when the body dies, when you don't need it anymore, the soul—who you really are—just leaves it behind, like when you change out of your dirty clothes at the end of the day."

Angela nodded. He could see the gears turning behind her sharp green eyes. He wondered how long it would take her to figure out who he was.

"So the invisible friends, as you call them, are just people who have left their bodies. Only they hadn't finished all of their business yet. Without a body, they can't finish, even though they still want to. So they keep trying, but people don't see or hear them anymore."

She was beginning to frown. He had to be careful not to upset her or plant any seeds of fear. She sensed that he was done with his explanation. Her foot was cold now, and she slid it back inside her slipper. She turned to him and cocked her head to one side.

"Are you my Daddy's friend?"

"I'm your friend right now."

"What's your name?"

He extended his hand to shake hers. "You can call me Michael."

"My name is Angela." She felt a delicate warmth as her fingers touched his palm. "Thank you for talking to me, Michael."

He laughed at her sudden sophistication. "I think it's time for Miss Angela to go back to bed."

She smiled sleepily. Placing a hand on his knee, she raised herself from her seat on the top step and ambled off to her bedroom.

Chapter 10

March 1972
London

The days were getting longer, but not long enough. Nightfall only made the draft in the apartment worse. Robin and Alice had been married three months, and they were practically starving.

Alice's parents had been wary of the relationship from the outset and regarded their unpromising new son-in-law with cool suspicion. But Alice was as stubborn as her young husband, and her parents' disapproval was no small factor in her strong devotion to Robin.

The couple had been living with Gareth since the wedding, a small but formal affair with which Robin had been spectacularly uncomfortable. With Priscilla maintaining a constant presence in the flat, the four young adults spent their days and nights trying to get out of each other's way. At least they would never run out of body heat, Gareth joked.

Alice worked as a clerk in an actuarial firm as she continued her studies. Robin was embarrassed to be supported by his wife at the tender age of nineteen, but it was their only source of real income and helped off-set the financial drain of Robin's artistic aspirations.

The new band, Imbolc, was in the studio, working on a hopeful debut album. Three earlier singles had sold well amongst friends and fans. Danceable *Ten Tea Biscuits*, whimsical and upbeat *My Michelangelo*, and just plain quirky *Tarantula* were standards of their frequent gigs, though the money was hardly enough for equipment repairs. Covering popular hits and performing random improvisational pieces simply wasn't enough. They had to find out if they could sustain a full-bodied work.

Priscilla was the inspiration behind this album. With different visions dancing through their heads, the lads couldn't agree on sandwiches for lunch, much less a concept for an album. Priscilla had also named the fledgling group. Launching her own Wiccan studies, she first suggested to Robin naming the band after the festival of lights and fertility, the sabbat of purification after the long confinement of winter. Robin sat with this for a few hours as it took root. By morning, he had made the decision for the entire group.

IN THE BEGINNING, Imbolc's debut album, would follow traditional pagan mythology through the seasons of the year. Drawing upon youthful and artistic ideals of the way the universe should work, they would build a body of rhythm and melody to deliver veiled philosophies to the world in a pretty vinyl package. The five young men were exhilarated in their work, giddily riding a wave of anticipation that they were creating a breakthrough in music and awareness.

Cecil Thornton had heard the boys in one of the smaller London clubs and was sufficiently impressed by the creeping strains of *Tarantula* to approach them about representation. His brother-in-law owned the start-up Caterpillar label, and he was anxious to see the record company succeed. It was Cecil who arranged the recording studio, the equipment, and the personnel to make it happen. While the band scrounged to make rent each month, prepaid studio time awaited them.

Locksmith Studio was no state-of-the-art facility. The old warehouse had once housed the padlocks, combination locks, and other security products of the defunct Coppermine Company. Locksmith now offered basic production space to advertising and public relations agencies, and to the occasional musical group.

Imbolc already knew the process, having recorded *Ten Tea Biscuits* in Joe's parents' garage, though they had been working with borrowed equipment and the singles had been pressed by a favour-owing friend of George's father. The cost had barely been recouped through various gigs and modest record sales to audience members.

Imbolc was learning that an entire album does not come together overnight. Earlier songs had appeared spontaneously, one at a time, with no true pressure bearing down. They had at least agreed on a theme before heading into the studio. But they hadn't thought about what they were getting themselves into with a concept album.

"Alright, let's get to work." Robin launched himself from the tattered sofa shoved against the wall in their studio space. Their instruments had been waiting for some time, and although there had been a few false starts of varying promise, Imbolc had failed to accomplish much of anything thus far.

Gareth dug his fingers into his hair and propped his elbows on his knees. "I'd like to have a more solid plan mapped out, instead of just popping around haphazardly."

"But we've got a plan." Robin pointed to the sheet of paper that had been posted on the wall twenty-four hours earlier.

"We've got a piece of paper," countered Joe. The former Chippers' bassist sat on the floor, drawing random geometrical patterns on the soles of his shoes.

Robin jogged over to the wall. "We've got a whole list right here." He lifted the paper with two fingers to get a better look at it. "*Lady Evening, Bonfire, Green Man, Yule Log, Mistress of Winter, Queen's Consort,* and *The Reaper.* Which shall we try first?"

"Those are just title ideas. They're not real songs." Danny, the group's newest member, also sat on the floor, resting against the couch with a notebook balanced on his knees. He held a pen between his fingers, poised to capture any flash of inspiration, as soon as one should strike.

A fixture at band meetings Priscilla busied herself collecting the remnants of their lunch from the grocery up the street. She tousled Gareth's hair as she passed him, kissing him quickly on the forehead.

"They're not real songs... until we make them real songs." Robin was smiling, scheming, sparking his own fire. His own enthusiasm would ultimately be enough to go around for everyone. "It's obvious we're not accomplishing anything just sitting about waiting to be magically gifted with the Right Idea. Let's just pick one and give it a go."

Gareth rose and stepped up beside Robin to examine the possibilities that had seemed such good ideas the day before. He ran his finger slowly over each title. They were so abstract, just words with no grounding in rhythm or lyrics.

"Tell me more about the Green Man...?" Gareth inquired of the room.

Robin smiled. "The Green Man, yes."

Sitting on the arm of the couch, Priscilla thumbed through her journal. Robin stepped away from the wall and stood in front of the worn coffee table to address the group.

"Alright, we all have some familiarity with the folkloric Jack O' the Green, the Green Man, whatever you want to call him. Right? So we take this jolly fellow... Alright, he has a lifespan, spring to autumn when he's a man. I don't want to do anything around his being a child, do you? He is the God of Light! He brings the harvest, the sunshine, that sort of thing. Let's think about... What's he like? Umm, there's this bloke, covered in ivy and leaves and such, sort of, in the forest, like he's dancing or skipping his way... He's a good natured God. So what's he doing? What's his personality? If he were to show up here today for an interview, what do you think he'd say?"

Robin was riding his own train of thought, expecting no answers to his questions. He paced in front of the coffee table, gesticulating broadly with expressive hands as he thought out loud. The other fellows watched and listened. Danny took notes.

"Okay, there's an invocation of the God," Priscilla offered. "This is how the priest or priestess would call upon him."

She looked up to find Robin staring at her, his brow knitted in deep thought, eyes squinted and lips pursed, his right hand clasping his chin. If she hadn't known him better, she would have taken this frown personally. After a moment of silence, he waved a finger in her direction and turned to pace around the table again.

"Yes... Yes, alright. Good." He had his hands in his hair now. "We can use that. How about a conversation? Between the people and the God, the people of the village. We talked about a community of more or less simple people, living off the land. So they call to him... Mmm. No." He shoved his hands into his trouser pockets, took a few more steps, then stopped suddenly, the mental workings clearly visible in his face.

"Yes!" He unconsciously centered his weight, pushing his shoulders back and inclining his head upward. He looked as though he were about to launch heavenward.

"Not a conversation with the peasants, but a dialog between the God and the Earth itself!"

A few heads nodded cautiously in curious agreement. Priscilla smiled.

"Sure, okay." Joe was still drawing on his shoes. Though they had played together with The Chippers, he was only now becoming accustomed to Robin's impulses. After this demonstration, Joe was sure to be asked to conjure a bass line that was more "earthy" or "dripping with foliage."

* * * *

Gareth and Joe had split off to work out the Green Man's rhythm, the foundation for melody and other accompaniment. Danny and George sat in on these sessions, absorbing the potential for their own pieces and offering criticism, solicited or not.

Robin was just as likely to listen in as he was to be romping around the nearest green quadrangle, embodying the Green Man himself. Alice was finding bits of grass and leaves in her husband's clothing, from all of his jumping and rolling about on the lawn.

Gareth and Joe had been playing for hours on end, allowing Danny and George to build their parts on top of the bass and drums, experimenting with melody and mood, Robin came bursting in with a paper shopping bag and a wild expression on his face.

"Lads, I've got it!"

He wore a green turtleneck shirt and rust-coloured trousers, his hair more unruly than usual. Dirt was streaked across his face, and his shoes were caked in mud.

Mildly annoyed, Joe rested his fingers on his bass strings. "You've got what?"

Robin's self-congratulatory grin spread across his face as he dropped his bag on the floor. Placing his hands confidently on his hips, he threw his head back to look about at the other musicians, dumbfounded by his entrance. They were surprised he didn't start cackling.

"Ah, and how is it coming, then?" he asked instead.

Gareth got up from his kit, gently taking his crash cymbal between two fingers as he stepped out from behind the drums. "Still making progress," he offered. "Rhythm is in place, melody is getting close. Same as always." Gareth looked down at Robin's bag, which had pieces of straw peeking over the top. "And what bit of inspiration have you brought us this afternoon?"

Gareth knew he wanted this attention, and Robin raised his eyebrows appreciatively before he reached down into his bag. First retrieving the dried straw, which he stuffed into his trouser pockets, Robin next pulled out two winding vines of garden ivy, supplemented by grass and tangled clusters of leaves and berries. Robin proceeded to loop the vines around his neck and then wrapped them about his arms and torso, letting the loose ends hang off of his hips and wrists.

"What are you supposed to be," George interjected, "the creature from the black lagoon?"

"Just wait." Robin reached down again, this time producing a green wreath which he wedged down over his impossible hair. With the complementary colours of his clothing and the cosmetic effect of the dirt and mud, his transformation was complete. Robin extended his arms to his sides so the others could admire his costume. "Well, I've found him!"

"Oh, bloody hell," Joe muttered.

Gareth bit his tongue to stifle his laughter. Danny put down his guitar and crossed his arms over his chest, studying Robin's garb and frowning. "You look like some mad gardener."

Delighted, Robin pointed at Danny and laughed. "Yes! I am the Green Man!" He launched into a spontaneous jig about the studio. "I am the God of Living Things! The Bringer of the Harvest!" As he sashayed and skipped, his wraith-like form executing less than graceful manoeuvres, the others stepped back, instinctively protecting their instruments.

Robin made a final, spinning leap into the centre of the room, his slight limbs flung about with enthusiastic abandon. Out of breath, Robin recovered his balance, the wreath now falling down into his eyes. He laughed. "This is it! I've become the Green Man; now I can embody him in song."

George stepped behind the piano and sorted through his notes. "I am going to attribute this to malnutrition."

Robin skipped over to his old friend and hung an ivy-draped arm around his shoulder. "Perhaps. Perhaps this is why artists must first starve before achieving greatness. It loosens the creative juices."

"It's loosened your connection to reality," Joe muttered under his breath.

George looked into Robin's excited, mud-smudged face and sighed.

"But there's more." He leapt from George's side back across the room to retrieve one more item from the paper bag: a flute. Ignoring the deep scratches in the metallic surface, he took the instrument carefully into his fingers and raised it to his lips. Regarding Robin's ivy-covered figure, his raised elbows pointed sharply outward, Danny speculated that he looked more like a stunted tree covered with Spanish Moss.

Robin took a deep breath, closed his eyes, and released the air from his lungs. What emerged from the flute was a strained series of tortured squeaks. Joe covered his ears and shouted to the others, "That's worse than the costume! They'll throw us out of here with that racket."

The young Green Man lowered his instrument and smiled sheepishly. "Well, it needs some work. But you get the idea. The flute is sacred to the God. It's a means of calling him forth. So, we need a flute."

George didn't bother to look up as he jotted down a few notes. "At least Pan could play his flute. As a mythological archetype, you leave a great deal to be desired."

Robin smiled at this good-natured barb.

The amusement past and his patience worn thin, Joe was ready to work. "Alright, then. George, could you play that last bit again? I liked it with the bass hits, but I want to hear what you're doing."

Though Robin had lost the group's attention, he retained his enthusiasm. He raised the flute for closer inspection, toying with the levers as he watched them pop in and out of place.

Gareth crossed the room and stood close to his cousin. "You've put on quite a display."

Robin beamed up at him. While he had gained in stature, he was still a good bit shorter than Gareth. "It feels right to me. I know it seems a little off..."

Gareth laughed and put his arm around him. Robin did indeed appear a spirit of the woods. "It's no matter. We need this kind of thing. But where did you get the flute?"

* * * *

Alice was furious.

Robin had nearly wiped out their modest savings for the whimsical purchase of a worn musical instrument from a second-hand shop. While they had not been saving for anything in particular, Alice had cut every conceivable corner to build some small buffer, should even harder times befall them.

Gareth had quietly excused himself from the table when the bickering began. While Robin and Alice maintained a tense silence, he left his dinner plate in the sink, anxious to depart the flat. Alice kept her hands close to her face, hiding her expression. Robin's focus was split between his wife's fragile composure and his cousin's hurried efforts to vacate. Gareth grabbed his coat from the narrow closet, shoved his keys into his pocket, and dashed out. He could hear the apartment explode as he closed the door behind him.

"What were you thinking?!" Alice threw her hands down on the table in exasperation. She was torn by so many emotions it was difficult to choose which would express itself first. Her breathing was deep and deliberate, her stare boring holes in the dinner plates as she tried to make sense of her husband's latest frivolity.

"We need this for the album. To be a success, we need to put everything we've got into our efforts." Robin was reasonable and calm, further aggravating Alice. "We're all making sacrifices." He honestly didn't understand how she could be so upset.

"Sacrifice!" she cursed angrily. "Robin, you just have no idea, do you?"

He rested his fingertips on the rim of the table. "Well, obviously I don't." He heard the bitter edge in his own voice.

Alice took a deep breath through her nostrils, then held the air in her lungs. She kept her eyes down. She wasn't ready to look at him.

"But we've talked about this." She tried to bring her voice down to his level of control, straining to contain her emotion. "If we're going to have any kind of real start we needed that nest egg, small as it was. That money was for an emergency..."

"This was an emergency," Robin interrupted. "The Green Man couldn't have lived otherwise."

"There is no Green Man! It's just a song!" She managed not to scream, "stupid song." "And for what? A worn out piece of junk, scratches and dents all through it."

He pulled his chin to his chest, feeling the tightness there. "It was the only one I could find. The only one I could afford." She had wounded him.

She clasped her hands in her lap. "I know how much this means to you..."

Robin leaned forward, trying to engage her from across the table. "How much it means to us, you and me. To all of us. We've got to do this, Alice. It's more than just a song, more than just an album."

"I know that." Her voice was very small as the tears flooded her eyes, blinding her momentarily. "I want you to be successful. I do. But we need to be thinking of what we're building for us. We'd been putting that money aside, so we could get our own flat, or in case something happened. In case..."

"In case it doesn't work out?" Robin practically had his chin on the table now, trying to catch Alice's eyes underneath her long, blonde hair. His voice was soft, consoling. "It's going to work out, Alice. This is going to happen. It has to."

She looked up to find Robin's emerald eyes swimming with reassurance, bringing her heart into her throat. She managed to smile as she coughed. Robin reached across to touch her hair.

"I know it's difficult right now. I know this is hard on you. I've not exactly been a great provider." The golden strands of her hair slipped from his fingers, and he leaned far back, balancing his weight on the back legs of the chair. "We're doing what we have to do. If this is the way it has to be, then so be it."

Alice blew her nose into her napkin.

"I know I should have told you about this first. I should have asked you."

She dismissed him with a wave of her hand. "Ask, don't ask. You would have done it anyway."

The front legs of Robin's chair hit the floor with a thud as he leaned forward. "I know I'm hell to live with."

Her voice dropped in pitch, flat and expressionless. "You seem to know a lot of things right now. I wish you'd known them earlier."

Robin sighed loudly and pressed his palms into the table as he stood. He turned his back to Alice and took a few steps toward the living area, crossing his arms over his chest. He dropped his head and looked at his feet.

Alice watched him, seeing in his spine and shoulder blades everything she knew he couldn't say. She shook her head and almost laughed. "You don't even play the flute, Robin."

She saw the weight lift. He turned toward her, wryly smiling sideways. "Not yet."

* * * *

After Alice had fallen asleep, Robin quietly rose from the bed, pulled on a track suit and jacket, and left the apartment, flute in hand. Gareth had not returned, no doubt taking refuge at Priscilla's.

Climbing the narrow staircase to the roof, he wrapped a scarf around his neck and ears against the cold as he opened the door to the outside. March in London. It was dark and chilly, and wet. He was still trying to get used to the smell of the city, and it didn't sit well with him.

He walked out to the edge of the roof and looked down into the empty street many floors below. The wet pavement reflected the street lamps. It was too warm for a layer of ice on the roadways, but it was cold enough to give him a headache. He heard the rattle of trash bins as neighbourhood cats scrounged for a midnight snack.

Robin's hands hung at his sides as he let go a long, lingering breath. "Ah," his body reverberated, the sound seeping into his toes as it escaped his lips and dissipated on the crisp air. He closed his eyes, feeling his body sway gently as he began to lose his orientation. He was desperately happy. Even with the struggle, the gnawing hunger, and the uncertainty in the faces and voices of his friends and family, he felt as though he were standing on the threshold, ready to cross over.

How could Alice possibly doubt this album would be a success? It wasn't that she was questioning his talent or vision, but by stashing away funds, wasn't she admitting a lack of faith and fear that failure was nearly upon them?

Robin opened his eyes and inhaled sharply, feeling the cold, damp sting inside his nostrils. He loved his wife. He was also convinced he knew nothing about how to handle himself inside this relationship. So, he would do his absolute best in his work to prove to her, and to everyone else, that this was all simply meant to be. He had to make music. There was no other life for him in this world.

Looking around, he found a dry patch of cement beneath his feet and sat down on the roof of the apartment building. The flute was ice in his bare hands. He raised the metal instrument to his mouth, feeling the shocking chill against his moist lips. He blew the air out of his lungs gently, clasping the flute with a delicate confidence. The sound they made together was infinitely more satisfying as Robin stumbled through his scales. In the middle of the March night, sitting alone in the dark, he searched for his own music.

*   *   *   *

It wasn't unusual for Robin to disappear when possessed of an idea needing to come through him, so no one worried when he didn't appear at the studio for a few days. Gareth saw continued evidence of his existence back at the flat, although even Alice didn't know where he went at such odd hours, returning only for an occasional nap.

Robin was on the roof. Surveying his environs, he couldn't understand why he would have picked such an in-organic setting to craft his "song of the god," surrounded by the city and its noise, smells, and late winter dinge. Normally, such an atmosphere would only have depressed him, but somehow he was inspired.

Flute at his side, he considered Priscilla's texts and reflected on his own fantasies about the earth deity he endeavoured to bring to life. He alternated attempts at lyrics with practice sessions on the flute. He had no idea how to play the thing, not sure if he were even holding it properly, but its simple presence connected him to his protagonist—the Green Man.

He sauntered into the studio, where the other lads had already begun work on *Lady Evening*, not wasting time waiting for Robin and his lyrics. While the rest of the band jammed on a new groove, Robin set his collection of papers and his flute on the floor and removed his jacket. His posture was strikingly serious, his earlier enthusiasm replaced by a quiet determination. His bandmates took notice.

Sensing their lead singer required an audience, the four wound down their playing and crossed the confined studio space to sit down on the couch and the floor. Robin kept his eyes on his notes, looking up once the group had settled.

"I've got something I'd like you to hear," he said quietly.

"Well, here's your captive audience," George responded cheerfully. "Let's have it."

Robin cleared his throat nervously. "Could you play back what you've already laid down? I want to see how this fits."

Danny got up from the floor and headed toward the sound board.

"So this is the song of the Green Man, his calling to the Earth." Robin felt the weight of the flute in his hands as well as everyone's eyes on it. He laid the instrument down on the coffee table in front of him. "I still need to work out the flute bit some more." He cleared his throat again.

The playback started with a loud blast, then cut back dramatically as Danny toyed with the controls. "Sorry about that," he called out. Finding the proper levels, he started the music up again. Danny shoved his hands into his trouser pockets and looked over at Imbolc's front man as the heavy bass and percussion lines of the earth god filled the room.

Robin self-consciously tapped his foot in time, keeping his eyes trained on his own handwriting. With each measure, he tried to root himself in the Green Man's pulsing rhythm. He dared not look at the others.

"I am the glowing God of Nature, pouring over Earth warmth and light," he began, more speaking than singing. He thought he heard Joe snickering. Robin searched for the playful melody he had sung to himself, alone on the rooftop.

"I call forth the glory of creation, awaken from the long winter's night." The notes weren't quite right, but he was getting closer. His voice was gaining confidence.

"My springtime sun laughs, the Earth's joyfulness will grow," Robin sang, aligning with the leaves and branches of the green god's song. "Life returns, rest and rewards, from the seeds of peace I sow."

As the guitar and keyboard blended into a deep, chanting cadence, Robin opened his eyes, looked only at Gareth, and said, "I've not worked out the entire chorus that goes here. Something about life being infused with blood and spirit." The melody climbed out of the percussion's rhythmic mantra. "Here we go again." Robin took a breath and continued singing:

Call me Sun of all Worlds, darkness flees as the days grow long
I am the great beastmaster, the stag running free and strong
Hear my merry voice echoing through forest, across glen
With eagles I soar, carry my song, filling the hearts of men

"So there's another chorus here." Robin took a deep breath, diverted his eyes quickly to George, and saw him smiling, impressed. The heart-beat music continued:

To you I bring the harvest, yielding fruits, gourds, and grains
To feed my beloved creatures, I call the healing rains
Reap my soul, feast on my body for strength with retreating light
Faith I come again, with the sun, blessing the Earth with my might

The melody dipped down again. "Alright, another chorus." Robin chanced a glance to Joe, sitting on the floor. He was looking away, nodding his head appreciatively with the grounded beat. He was hearing Robin's words. The singer launched into his last verse:

I am the spirit of the bountiful harvest, as such worship me
I am the great gold sun, rises and sets, my glory for all to see
I die, unconquered, in this cycle that has come to be
The power of my regeneration is your right and destiny.

"I thought there might be some improvisational, you know, statements or something from the Green Man." The experimentally earthy music played on, punctuating his words. "And interspersed throughout, we could have voices of the Earth calling back, sort of answering him..." The song was fading out. Danny cut it off.

Joe kept nodding, still thinking over what he had just heard. "Not bad." He looked up at Robin. "It's not what I expected." He got up from the floor.

Sitting on the couch, George smiled up at Robin. "Didn't know you were a poet, did you? Some of the words are a bit contrived, we might change a few things, make syllables fit better. But it works."

Robin still stood in front of the coffee table, clutching his papers. His face flushed red in relief, his ordeal over. He picked up his flute and found Gareth at his side. His cousin gazed down on him, pleased.

"You've done well. Now let's get to work."

Uncomfortable giving creative feedback as the newest member, Danny simply walked past Robin, not even making eye contact. Taking his signal from Joe, already playing the new bass line, Danny retrieved his guitar and was ready to move on.

"Okay," Joe called out, looking directly at Robin. "Let's see what we can make of this next one then."

Chapter 11

13 November 1972
London

IN THE BEGINNING, Imbolc's first album, had not fared as well as expected.

None of the songs could be released as singles to the radio stations, though the band played through the entire album in concert, and audiences responded enthusiastically in venues around the country. Ticket sales were not bad, thanks to Robin's increasingly outrageous antics on stage—a sharp contrast to his shy embarrassment during his first gigs with The Chippers.

He spent three times longer backstage than his bandmates, streaking wild colours across his face and donning homemade costumes to embody his characters. He and Alice routinely combed through second-hand stores and family attics, searching for pieces that might come together in these incredible outfits.

The Green Man was an easy favourite. Robin delighted in throwing live flowers and rubber earthworms into the crowd as he pranced and tumbled across the stage. *The Reaper* was also popular, a dark and horrifying character for whom Robin designed specific lighting effects, even convincing several stage managers to experiment with pyrotechnics before fire codes shut them down. Hidden beneath a black executioner's cloak, he would glide ominously across the front of the stage on rollerskates. Two electric red lights attached to eyeglass frames punctuated Death's dark gaze as he wielded his scythe, made mostly of wire and foil.

Following his lead, the other members of the band embraced some new tricks of their own. Joe and Gareth used lighting effects to emphasize rhythm, punching up particular moments and creeping through others. Danny wrapped himself in electric Christmas tree lights to be illuminated during guitar solos, though he later attached the lights to his instrument only after tripping himself up a few times. Shying away from elaborate effects, George was happy to let the others have the attention.

While Robin was in costume, the others gradually adopted a simple uniform to further offset their front man. Fans started appearing at concerts in the same dark green trousers and black turtleneck shirts the band was wearing.

Concert sales of the album were brisk, but IN THE BEGINNING was not doing well overall. Depressed by the commercial defeat, Gareth and George skulked around despite Cecil's assurances that the recording was destined to be a cult classic. Fans reveled in the earthy ties to pagan mythology and revealing observations on life and death.

Robin was unconcerned with album sales, even after pouring so much of himself into the recording. People were noticing who and what Imbolc was, and gigs were more frequent and in better locations. There were mentions of the band in MELODY MAKER and thrilling moments of being recognized on the street. With advances against album sales, they could better care for their instruments and upgrade their diets. But with proceeds not meeting expectations, there was growing pressure to figure out what to do next.

Imbolc now shared a communal home closer to the recording studio. It was a tight squeeze for seven adults—Gareth and Priscilla had married in June—sharing four bedrooms and a single bathroom. Only Joe had his own room, having drawn straws with George and Danny.

But the house had a substantial cellar—ample rehearsal space for the band. Robin had worn out his welcome practicing his flute on the roof—once the neighbours opened their windows to the spring air, they started complaining about the racket.

Alice spent little time in the house. Finished with school, she took a full-time position with a financial consulting group. She enjoyed the creative atmosphere of her new home but wasn't overly fond of the cramped quarters. What time Alice did have alone with her husband was usually spent talking in bed before going to sleep, although she made a date with Robin at least twice a month to get out of the house together. Their usual destination was a small park ten blocks away, where they enjoyed picnics in nicer weather. The distance brought on by Alice's work schedule and his Imbolc commitments frustrated Robin, though he was mollified by his growing enthusiasm for the studio.

In October, Cecil agreed it was time for Imbolc to record again, though he saw the group having difficulty coming to consensus on what to tackle next. They generally sat around in the basement, occasionally working out a new rhythm, but mostly pissing away their time drinking and griping.

Cecil was afraid they would run out of steam, and that Gareth's wariness and George's brooding would infect the lot. But he was a tenacious manager. He brought the boys into the studio, set out a hearty lunch of soup and sandwiches, and proposed a compilation of singles from their beginnings as a group. Cecil estimated the album could be released by mid-November, for the holiday buying season.

The three previous singles—*My Michelangelo*, *Ten Tea Biscuits*, and *Tarantula*—would be included without re-recording. Several standards from club dates over their year-long history would also be on this new release. Familiar with Imbolc's repertoire, Cecil selected the remaining songs for the album: *Somnambuman*, *Eggs and Toast*, *What's Your Fancy? Bartholemew*, *The Sausage Man*, *Promise Me Little*, and *Layers of Love*. All were Imbolc originals and would be recorded with a minimum of rearranging.

This idea was not an instant hit with the band, who were not especially anxious to climb out of their rut. With some effort, Robin convinced the others that this would at least give them something to do and might relieve their financial obligations to the label.

Cecil had been right on the mark with the production timeline. Imbolc spent an average of one studio day for each song recorded, passing the morning working out any kinks, then recording and mixing tracks in the afternoon. They were finished in time for dinner at home. The challenge was the non-stop exposure to each other, in the studio and at the house. After finishing the first four songs in rapid succession, the boys began taking off a day or two between sessions, to spend some time apart.

The recording was still completed ahead of schedule. There was a minor delay for a debate about artwork, but Alice dug up a watercolour painting she had made as a child. It was endearingly whimsical—a scene of two children jumping rope on a rainbow asteroid while a purple spotted cat and pink dog looked on. The decision to feature this as their new album cover was unanimous.

Claiming the uninspired title of CALLOW CONVICTION, the new Imbolc album was released on Monday, November 13, 1972.

At 9 a.m. on the thirteenth, Robin was camped out at the front door of HMV Records on Oxford Street. He had dreamed of crowds of people waiting with him, all anxious for the first available copies of the new Imbolc album. But he stood vigil alone. Still, he smiled to himself and imagined the years to come, when his music would be featured on radio programmes across the country—across the globe?—when he would tell magazine reporters the anecdotal story of how he alone awaited the open doors of HMV.

Robin's toes complained of the cold through his thinning socks. The twenty-year-old paced back and forth before the store's display windows, his hands shoved deep into his pockets. He hunched up his shoulders and laughed when he saw the man approach the main door from inside, coming to open the store for the day's business. Watching his frozen breath dissipate on the brisk morning air, Robin ran a hand quickly through his hair, felt in his pocket for the money to buy the record, and stepped casually into the store, offering a wry smile to the clerk as he passed.

He walked directly to Imbolc's meager cubby, where he found seven copies of IN THE BEGINNING lending company to only twenty copies of the new album.

What a travesty, Robin thought to himself. He pretended to study the front and back covers of CALLOW CONVICTION, making a great show of quiet appreciation for the artwork and the album's content, though the only other people about were a handful of clerks. Robin challenged himself to make this new album a single-day sell-out.

A sparse string of customers trickled into the store. Instinctively, he held CALLOW CONVICTION at chest level, displayed prominently as he nonchalantly strolled the aisles with a serene smile. He didn't stop to look at any other albums, just scanned the titles on either side as he lovingly clutched his Imbolc prize.

He passed the other customers, looking them in the eye and smiling as he circled round, still holding up his copy of the new album. Most simply thought he was high on one drug or another and tried to ignore him.

Within the hour, three copies of CALLOW CONVICTION had been sold. Robin congratulated himself on his quiet cunning, though he could not prove his ambulatory strategy had anything to do with the sales.

Robin had been at HMV for several hours and was arousing the staff's suspicion, when he noticed Ken Campbell enter the store. Though they were now family, the former bandmates saw each rarely. Ken was at Oxford studying classical mythology, and Robin generally avoided family gatherings as best he could. Robin smiled as he watched Ken searching through the aisles, finally stopping in front of the Imbolc recordings.

As Ken picked up the newest album, he was surprised to find Robin at his side.

"Shall I autograph that one for you, sonny?" Robin cracked.

Ken smiled at his brother-in-law. "Alice rang me and told me this was the day. I figured I'd drop in and see what you blokes have been up to."

Robin retrieved a copy of the band's first album. "Don't forget this one as well."

"Yes, I have that one. Strange stuff this is." Ken took the debut album from Robin and studied it a moment. "You could say I've a scholar's appreciation for the ties to earth-based religions you incorporated." Ken returned the record to the display and tucked CALLOW CONVICTION under his arm, noticing the copy Robin was carrying. "What are you doing here, anyway?"

Robin again lifted his record to attract the attention of any passersby. "Oh, you know, just watching and waiting. I thought it would be exciting to witness one of our albums go on sale. But it's actually rather dull. I'm glad you stopped in."

Ken rested a hand on Robin's shoulder, smiling. "It's a good thing I happened to be in the area this morning, to liven things up a bit."

Ken looked around. The store had filled considerably since he came in. "There's a better crowd in here now," he said quietly to Robin, then stepped back from him.

"I know you!" Ken exclaimed loudly. A few heads turned, and Robin regarded him strangely. "You're Robin Michaels, the singer for Imbolc!"

More shoppers stopped and looked over. Robin saw what was happening and smiled, his face turning slightly pink.

"Would you autograph your new album for me?" Ken shouted excitedly, pulling a pen from his coat pocket.

Infused with excitement and moderate embarrassment, Robin accepted Ken's pen and signed his name across Alice's watercolour.

"I was sure they would be sold out of your new album, CALLOW CONVICTION." Ken turned his head as he spoke, watching the reactions of other customers, now making their way over to Robin. "Your first album—IN THE BEGINNING—is so great! I very much enjoyed the mythological basis and the pagan overtones which permeate the music and lyrics and lend an exciting earthy-quality to the entire recording."

Robin shot Ken a look from beneath his brow. "Tone it down a bit, eh?" he whispered.

"Sorry," Ken mumbled back.

"Here you are," Robin said with exaggerated volume as he returned the pen and album to Ken. "It's always grand to meet a fan. Cheers."

Ken noticed the line forming behind Robin, with anxious customers jostling each other to snatch up remaining copies of both CALLOW CONVICTION and IN THE BEGINNING. He could feel several other people at his own back.

"Thank you, Robin Michaels! I can't believe it's Robin Michaels, singer for Imbolc, right here in this store!" Reaching out to shake Robin's hand, Ken whispered to his brother-in-law, "I can't very well have my sister starving, now can I?"

Robin returned his smile. "Cheers, Ken."

He handed his pen back to Robin. "You might need this."

Ken headed for the store register. The small, enthusiastic crowd parted to let him pass, then swarmed around Robin. The mostly teenaged shoppers emptied the shelves of Imbolc recordings and pressed Robin for autographs. Some customers had no idea who he was and had never heard of Imbolc, though they wouldn't pass up the opportunity to have a signed copy of a new album. It was not yet 2 p.m., and Robin had his sell-out.

* * * *

At a public phone on the street, Robin scrounged for a few coins in his pocket and rang Cecil Thornton. He was surprised to find his manager expecting his call.

"You may want to press a few more copies of both albums," Robin began giddily.

"Yes, I heard about your adventure at HMV this morning." Although Cecil's voice was stern, he still laughed. "Just what did you think you were doing?"

"It was Ken's idea, actually. Brilliant. I'm surprised I didn't think of it myself." Robin was talking too fast. "The people in the store were getting angry with the clerks, because they didn't have any more copies of the albums. But they were so wonderful to me. It was a thrilling experience."

"We've already gotten the call from the store about reordering. I understand small gatherings have amassed at a few other stores, hoping other members of the band might surface. Didn't hurt album sales one bit."

"I knew this would happen!" Robin exclaimed, his excitement barely contained by the phone box.

"It was a good first day. We'll see how we fare going forward." Cecil's friendly voice turned sober. "Robin, you had better come to my office, this afternoon if you can. There's something you and I need to discuss in confidence."

* * * *

Robin headed to Cecil's office straight-away, though empty-handed — he had at last, reluctantly, given over his copy of CALLOW CONVICTION to a genuine fan in the record store. Robin had been to Cecil's management office only once, when the band signed their contract. All other meetings had been at the studio or in their respective homes.

The young musician waited nervously in his manager's office, alone, studying the walls. There were several Monet prints, though Robin was more interested in the press clippings—some framed, others simply tacked up—concerning Caterpillar Records. Academic and business accomplishments were displayed prominently. There was also an Imbolc collection, sparse in comparison: a few mentions in local journals, a favourable article in a neighbourhood newspaper, and the like.

When Cecil at last entered the room, he found Robin seated uncomfortably in one of the upholstered chairs opposite the uninspired, industrial desk. "Sorry to keep you waiting." Cecil handed Robin a lukewarm Coca-Cola. Robin took an obligatory sip as Cecil seated himself behind the desk.

"I won't bore you with pleasantries, Robin. There is serious business to discuss."

Robin shifted uneasily. After his exhilaration at the record store, he feared this roller coaster might plunge to some dark depth. On the way to Cecil's office, he had convinced himself the band was in even greater financial trouble than he had imagined.

"I received a call last week from Alec French at Oracle Records. They've been watching your band, despite less than stimulating album sales. Mr. French himself attended one of the Southgate concerts over the summer. Are you familiar with his label?"

Robin's eyebrows shot up. "Of course. The Fantastic Freds, Tracey Shreds, Ted Jennings, The Wannamakers. It's a good label." Robin paused. "But Caterpillar is a good label, too..."

Cecil waved off further comments. "Yes, it's a very good label. Oracle launched the careers of The Observers, Satchel Waters, Whack Pack, Black Currant, and Danny Gregory, to name a few." Cecil placed his hands squarely on the desk and looked Robin in the eye. "Now Alec French is interested in you."

Robin took a moment to let the news sink in, then slowly got up and paced about the chair. "This is progress for the band, obviously. I knew we would be noticed." He was thinking out loud as the gears turned.

"No, Robin," Cecil stopped him. "Not the band. Alec French is interested in you alone. Robin Michaels."

Robin stopped pacing and rested his hands on the back of the chair.

"You can see why I didn't call the rest of the band into this meeting." Cecil got up from behind the desk and walked around to sit on the front corner, facing Robin. "After your scheming this morning, I got another call from Oracle, requesting a meeting this week. A sell-out record gets attention. Mr. French heard about the incident at HMV. Quite simply, he wants you to quit the band and launch a solo effort on his label."

Robin brought his hands to his hips and frowned. He kicked at the feet of the chair. "What did you tell them?"

"Naturally, I replied that I would have to speak with you on the matter. As your manager, it is my job to represent your interests, whether they lie with Imbolc... or elsewhere."

Robin was honestly stunned. He stared at Cecil for a moment, then dropped his gaze to the beige carpet. He recommenced his pacing, his hands still squarely on his hips. "I don't know about this, Cecil. I'm just part of a band — one bloke out of five. Five friends."

"No one is pressuring you to do anything, Robin. The offer is on the table. We can pursue it if you want to. I understand you may not feel ready for a solo push, but I think you have it in you. If not now, then some other time." Cecil returned to his seat behind the desk. "Or I can ring Mr. French and tell him, 'Thank you for your consideration, but my client must decline at this time.' The choice is entirely yours."

Robin sat down in the chair and buried his hands in his hair. "I wasn't expecting this," he looked up at the ceiling and sighed.

"Listen, Robin, you boys pushed hard on this last album, and you need to take a break. I'll tell Oracle you're on hiatus until the beginning of the year, and you can take some time to think about this."

Robin crossed his arms over his chest and looked blankly at Cecil.

"In the meantime," Cecil continued, "this conversation does not leave this office, as far as I'm concerned. If you want to discuss this with anyone—your wife, your bandmates—I leave that to your discretion. I'd say the best thing for you at the moment is to not think about this much. HMV, Clements, Hooper, and Rhythm Jungle have just sold out of Imbolc's new album on the first day of release! Take Alice out to dinner. Host a celebration party at the house with the other lads. Don't worry about this business for a time."

Chapter 12

20 May 1999
New York City
9:30 a.m.

Angela slowly exhaled as the door to the ladies' room closed behind her. She relaxed her hands, wiggling her fingers to let go of her anxiety.

She was right on time, neither late nor early. Punctuality was her trademark. She would be in the right place at the right time today.

Balancing her weight evenly between her feet, she looked down the hallway to the conference room where they were expecting her.

Coming up with the ideas was never the problem. It was unusual for Angela to sleep through the night without a brainstorming session waking her in the wee hours. She would never run out of potential projects. The challenge was choosing which ones to tackle. Now she was learning to build a solid business plan and then, in meetings such as this one this morning, to sell the right people on the finished package. Not always confident in her ability to share her vision, Angela was relieved to have her partner, a true businessman, with her.

Taking her first step down the hallway, she heard another door close behind her.

"Hello, Mary Katherine. How are you, my dear?" The voice stopped Angela dead in her tracks. An excited surge ran up her spine as her eyes widened.

Was that his voice?

She felt as though she had been kicked in the stomach. It took an eternity to turn around and look. There was a lump in her throat, choking her. Angela saw a man and woman walking in the opposite direction, away from her.

Could that be..?

Narrowing her eyes, she studied the man's gait, his clothing, his thinning hair. Her heart pounding, the only sound she heard was the throbbing in her ears. He was walking away from her. What should she do?

It couldn't be him, she decided at last. He was too short, his stride too small, and he was too thick around the middle. Angela shook her head and laughed quietly.

"I thought we had let that go," she chastised herself under her breath, again turning down the hallway. She was at least thankful for this momentary distraction, something to take her mind off of her nerves.

Jeff appeared from a contiguous corridor. "Angela," he boomed in his smiling voice. "You're just in time, per usual." With a gentlemanly gesture, her business partner escorted her into the conference room.

* * * *

Mary Katherine had been waiting outside the men's room for him. Robin had a habit of getting distracted or lost in interesting buildings, and she wanted to make sure not a moment of her friend's time would be wasted, though he frequently protested that he rather enjoyed his adventures down unexplored passageways.

Robin had never been to Mary K's new office in New York, and as she gave him a quick tour, he thought back on their first meeting, years ago, and smiled.

"You're looking well for a man your age, Rob," she jibed.

"Oh, please. I'm finally feeling comfortable in my own skin, and you come at me with that." He winked at her.

"Down this hallway is where we have our copy editors and layout artists, and my office is a few doors further down this way. You know, I saw an autographed copy of CALLOW CONVICTION up for auction on eBay. I bid on it myself, but last I saw, it was up to $15,000!"

Robin laughed incredulously. "Did I ever tell you that story, about autographing those albums in the store the day they were first out?"

"About a dozen times," Mary K responded.

They were about to turn down another hallway, identical to all the others in this building, when Robin heard a strong voice behind him: "Angela!" He turned and saw a flash of warm, brown hair atop a slight frame. So familiar... Robin couldn't place her. He frowned for a lingering second as the young woman disappeared through a doorway at the far end of the corridor. Robin continued on after Mary K and chalked it up to the usual, vague déjà-vu.

Chapter 13

December 1972
London

So here it was Christmas, the end of a lean but productive year as Robin and Alice celebrated their first wedding anniversary.

Pursuing a career in finance, she had naturally taken over the couple's accounts. Robin had no interest in such matters—money only frustrated him. Alice had control. All he knew was that resources were tight and that for his occasional expenditures—such as the surprise purchase of his flute—Robin had to answer to his wife.

But Alice was keeping a secret from her husband.

On her wedding day, Mr. Campbell had taken his daughter aside and silently handed her an envelope. Returning from a modest honeymoon in Paris (thanks to the generosity of Robin's parents), Alice Campbell Michaels promptly took that envelope to the bank and established her own savings account.

Alice's wages were scarcely enough to buy food each week, much less cover rent.

She had lunch monthly at her family home, after which Mr. Campbell routinely walked his daughter outside and handed her another envelope. Alice never mentioned this arrangement to her husband.

So it was with great excitement that Alice privately discussed with Robin the possibility with Oracle Records. Alec French had sent Cecil detailed terms of the agreement he hoped to strike with the young singer. The contract guaranteed particular sums with the completion of each of three albums, with a percentage of sales on top of that.

Alice was thrilled. This would ease their financial burden and might allow them to break free from her parents, while offering her husband the creative freedom she felt he needed. She disliked his vision being tempered by the consensus of Imbolc. She was strongly in favour of the Oracle contract and managed to work this discussion into nearly every conversation.

In the wee hours of Christmas morning, Robin sat on the edge of the bed in the Campbells' guest bedroom. As his wife slept, he watched a few, brave flakes of snow float past the window, gracefully dancing their way to the ground. He had barely slept all weekend, mulling over the good news from Cecil: due to popular demand, a third pressing of IN THE BEGINNING and CALLOW CONVICTION had been ordered, and the single *Layers of Love* was getting more radio air time. Caterpillar was anxious for a third album, and the boys had been discussing ideas from Friday onward. Robin had escaped Saturday evening with Alice to her parents' home for the holiday weekend, but he still had Alice privately pressing for the Oracle deal.

Robin was determined not to think about anything. He just stared out the window, his naked shoulders and feet oblivious to the chill in the bedroom. His breath held steady in a relaxing rhythm. When had he last had a few peaceful moments alone? Robin smiled at this Christmas present he had somehow managed to give himself.

Alice stirred in her sleep. Robin turned to study her face, so soft and calm. He loved to watch her sleep. He imagined that with her brow unfurrowed, he could see who she really was, without the worries that plagued her. Alice's breath was slow and deep, unlike her excited gasps when they argued or made love.

Robin wanted to do right by his wife. She had accepted a secondary role in his life, though he saw her efforts to shift his priorities. Alice had struggled just as much as he had—possibly more, because all she could do was wait.

Wait for Robin to be a success. Wait for Robin to be a failure. Wait for Robin to grow up. Wait for Robin to find some real direction in his life.

He touched her cheek. He felt so indebted to her for all she had endured for his sake, for the sake of his career. Perhaps he should accept the Oracle contract, to leave Imbolc and try a solo career. In his heart, he felt he wasn't ready, but this agreement offered financial security. His intuition told him to stay with the band to complete whatever cycle he was on with them. But he was a husband now. He wondered when he might finally step up and accept that responsibility, to put the welfare of his family first.

Alice shifted again in her sleep, and a book fell to the floor. Robin leaned across her body to retrieve the copy of Malory's MORTE D'ARTHUR she had been reading before she went to sleep. He picked up the book and placed it on the bedside table.

Catching sight of her face just then, Robin suddenly saw Queen Gwynevere in his wife's frame, her eyelids closed in peaceful slumber, dreaming of Launcelot while Arthur despaired over his failing kingdom. Robin held his breath, hearing the echoes of ancient voices playing out their bittersweet tale. He slid off the bed and crouched down on the cold floor, peering at Alice for long, luxurious moments. He watched the entire story unfold on the sheets before him as she slept.

CAMELOT would be his next album, a new concept collection. And he would record it with Imbolc.

* * * *

Robin announced his decision to his wife when she awoke several hours later. He had already gone to work, scribbling fragments of verses on a pad of paper from the study. He had appropriated Alice's book, nearly wearing out the binding as he searched for references. He spent long moments reading, caught up in the legends.

She didn't respond when he told her he would turn down the Oracle offer. He intended to ground himself with Imbolc, he explained, and might consider an independent effort after he had worked through his rough edges. Everything would work out, he promised.

Naturally, she was disappointed. No, she was frightened. They needed security, now more than ever, despite Imbolc's recent gains. But she saw how happy Robin was to be inspired again so suddenly, enthusiastically launching himself into this new creation. This passion and its frustrated joy were vital to him.

She offered her husband a smile and nodded. Then she pulled on a bathrobe and a pair of thick socks and went downstairs to the kitchen. She and Robin were the first awake in the house. She started the coffee brewing and collected breakfast ingredients on the kitchen table. Tomatoes, eggs, bread, cheese, beans, sausages. Pulling her mother's iron skillet from the cupboard, Alice said a silent prayer.

Please, let everything work out. For all of us.

She rested the skillet on the stove top and burst into tears. Lowering herself to the floor, she felt the whole world weighing down upon her thin shoulders. There was nothing she could do to change any of it. Why couldn't she be as carefree as Robin? Why couldn't she simply let go and let everything work itself out? Alice was just not that person.

And then without warning, the tears were gone. She was sitting on the floor in her parents' kitchen on Christmas morning. Soon the rest of the house would be wandering in. She could hear her mother stirring upstairs. Alice picked herself up and dried her wet cheeks on a dish towel. At the end of an anxious exhale, Alice marched out of the kitchen, back up the stairs, and into the guest bedroom to talk with her husband.

He hadn't moved, still hunched over the writing desk and taking notes as he ploughed through her book. She closed the door.

"Robin, I want to give you your Christmas present before anyone else's, before everyone wakes up."

She sat down on the bed and watched his back as he disengaged from his work. He put down the pencil deliberately and released the creative energy streaming through him. Robin turned to her and smiled. "Are you sure?"

Alice's eyes again filled with tears. She hated feeling so raw, but she smiled. "Yes. Come sit with me."

Smiling curiously, Robin rose from his chair and sat down beside her. "Right. Here I am."

Alice took her husband's hands in hers. The tears streamed down her flushed cheeks as she looked into his eyes. "Robin, we're going to have a baby."

Robin was stunned into silence, his face threatening to explode into joy. Alice's heart leapt seeing the light dancing in his eyes. But then his sparkle faded, and he frowned, looking down at his hands. Alice reached out to her husband, placing a worried, clutching hand on his shoulder.

"Robin? What's wrong?"

"Well…" Robin's face brightened as he enjoyed a quick chuckle at his own expense. "All I got you was some jewelry."

Chapter 14

1 January 1973
Arlington, Virginia

Angela was tired. At four years old, she felt uncomfortable and alone.

She sat at the top of the stairs, again watching her parents' annual New Year's party. She had to be extra quiet, so none of the adults would see her. She was also wary of waking Anthony, her nine-month-old brother.

She was happy to have her friend Michael beside her on the steps. Though she had looked for him during the year at dinner parties, she had only seen him occasionally, late at night, when everyone else was asleep. They sat together and watched the adults pass through the hallway below.

Angela was used to the shadows around her father, and she understood that no one else saw them. No one but Michael. She had learned not to ask about the hazy images she saw at the periphery of the sunlit world.

This was a difficult evening for her father, and she flinched whenever he came into view. Her mother also looked concerned, mentally tracking the amount of alcohol he was consuming. It was not the drinking Angela noticed, but the violent gang of smoky shapes constantly on the attack, scratching and clawing, growling in discontent.

Mark stood in the hallway, engaged in a strained conversation with a co-worker from the office furniture store. With a beer in one hand, he unconsciously warded off the metaphysical blows with the other. He touched his brow, the top of his head, his solar plexus, his left shoulder.

Assuming these were the aches and pains of aging, Mark ignored the telling twinges in key areas of his body. It was particularly bad tonight. The exaggerated effects of a New Year's Eve hangover, he told himself.

"They don't listen," Angela said to her companion. "They won't go away."

"They can't listen just now," Michael said bluntly. "Won't listen."

She rubbed her hands over her shoulders and crossed her arms. The dark struggle below sent a disturbing chill along her spine.

"Is Daddy sick?" She faced Michael, her green eyes full of confusion and fear.

Michael sighed and gazed down into the hallway again to examine the situation. He clasped his hands in front of him. "He himself isn't sick, no. But these others, they are making him sick. He can't get better until they leave him alone."

Angela looked down again at her father, who had disengaged from his tedious conversation and was going to retrieve another beer. Mark raised a tight hand to his temple, fighting a bad headache.

"Did Daddy do something bad? Is that why they are here? Is that why they hurt him?" Angela's eyes were again trained on Michael. He was the only one she could talk to. Her father seemed to have some understanding when she approached him, but there was a cloudiness about him. He was disconnected, caught up in the struggle. Like the other adults, he too turned her away.

"There's no easy answer to those questions, Angel." Michael rubbed his eyes and thought for a moment. "Do you know where your Daddy was when you were born?"

"He was far away. In the jungle." Angela was pleased with herself for knowing the answer.

"That's right. Your Daddy was in a place called Vietnam. He was in a war there."

Angela's eyes grew wide. Her parents hadn't told her specifically about the war, or she hadn't understood. Mark's earlier confessions had just been bedtime stories to her.

"Did he get hurt there?" she asked in a small voice.

"No, not really. He was captured by some enemy soldiers and put into a prison camp. But your Daddy is okay. He came home, in one piece."

Angela frowned. "But the others, they're not okay, are they?"

"No," Michael replied. She knew where he was headed. She needed only slight prompting to get there herself. "A lot of people died in the war while your Daddy was there. People from all different places. Some just lost pieces of their bodies, but others lost everything, like these others you see with your Dad tonight."

"They aren't very happy." She pulled at her short fingers, trying to imagine what losing them would be like.

"No, they aren't happy one bit." Michael turned to face Angela. He had to adjust to this physicality every time he took it on. "They had their bodies taken away from them before they were ready. There was a lot of confusion surrounding them when they died."

"So they're confused? Why are they confused?" Angela was playing with the pink and yellow ribbons on her nightgown.

"They lost their lives in a war zone. I don't want to frighten you by trying to describe that." He peered into her small face.

"I'm not scared," she responded, still toying with her clothing. "You can tell me."

"No, I don't want any more nightmares for you, young lady." Michael smiled as she shrugged her shoulders and waited for him to continue. "They were very afraid right before they died. And then suddenly they were free of their physical forms. And they were even more frightened, because they didn't know what was happening."

"Okay." Angela folded her hands loosely in her lap and looked up at Michael.

"So they looked around, looking for their buddies, the people who had been their friends, because they were afraid and wanted help. Sometimes they looked for their enemies instead, because they were very angry about what had happened."

"They thought it was their fault?" Angela asked. "They think it's my Daddy's fault?"

"Some of them." Michael saw Mark cross through the hallway in the company of one of his professors. The black, swirling cloud followed every step of the way.

Angela saw this, too. Her lip trembled. "Did my Daddy kill them?"

She was visibly upset, but Michael couldn't lie to her. "Some of them."

Angela's mouth opened, her face flushed. Her eyes brimmed with tears as her lips formed words that had no sound.

Michael placed a hand on top of her head as she looked down at her knees. He gathered her into his lap and rocked her slowly.

"I'm sorry, Angel. I didn't mean to make you cry," Michael said softly, stroking her hair.

Angela sniffed and wiped her nose across the back of her hand, then smeared the tears away from her eyes. "It's okay." She got up from Michael's lap and sat down beside him again. "I know my Daddy isn't a bad man."

"That's right," he reassured her. "He's not a bad man."

In silence, Angela leaned forward and rested her entire torso on her knees as she peered down into the hallway. Her mother was laughing at a joke a neighbor was telling. Mark passed through again and touched his wife on the shoulder. Marie watched him as he entered the dining room and started a new conversation. Angela sat back up.

"Some of them are mad at Daddy, and some are just scared."

"That's right. They don't know how to move on, to let go," Michael searched for the words to help her understand. "They are supposed to go to a different place, but all they can see is your Daddy. He is alive, and they cling to him because they are still angry and afraid. They are trying to hold onto the lives they had, so they hold onto your Dad."

"They pay more attention to Daddy than to God," Angela offered.

Michael was impressed. "Yes, something like that."

Angela pulled at her fingers again, and her feet were fidgeting. "I ask them questions. 'Why won't you leave Daddy alone? What do you want?' But they don't listen."

"They can't answer questions like that, Angel. But you can talk to them. You can see them. You can help them."

* * * *

Angela stood beside her brother's cradle, watching him through the wooden rails as he slept. There was so much inside her head, so many thoughts and new ideas swirling around. Whenever she felt like this, she came into this tiny room to watch Anthony sleep.

He is just a little baby, she thought. He's closer to God than I am. He was just there. I wish I could go there, too.

Angela touched his cradle, giving it a small push. Gently rocking him back and forth, Angela shut out the noise of the party downstairs. She thought about her conversation with Michael. She thought about her Daddy. She didn't understand how he could have killed anybody. Daddies don't do that.

She wished the baby would wake up, so she could ask him questions. Maybe he could help her understand. She listened to him breathing and saw how his tiny fingers grasped the warm blanket. His eyelids fluttered, and she knew he was dreaming.

"I wish you didn't sleep all the time," she whispered to Anthony.

Chapter 15

March 1973

London

The London skies were dark, the thick blanket of clouds dropping a low ceiling over the city. Winter always felt claustrophobic to Robin, when the air itself turned grey. The threat of depression loomed, just behind him, over his left shoulder.

He made his way along the pavement toward the recording studio where Imbolc had already completed half of their new album. He preferred to walk alone, the rhythm of his footsteps a back beat for his busy mind. The band was working quickly, and remarkably well, with unprecedented concentration and direction.

Robin rounded the corner and was nearly upon the warehouse, his mind swimming with the day's agenda. He kept his head down, focusing on the pressing details of his work, lest he look up and panic that the granite sky itself might be falling on him.

Robin always rushed to the studio, convincing himself that his absence was delaying the album. More often than not, he was the first to arrive, and he would have a few moments of solitude in the comforting company of the band's instruments.

Once inside the main building, Robin unlocked the door to Imbolc's rented studio space and stepped into the dark room. Not bothering to turn on the lights, he glanced around at the instruments, partially illuminated by the light from the hallway. A quiet thrill crept up his spine and raced out through his fingertips. He was making music in this room! Ideas born in the depths of imagination bubbled to the surface through the unlikely medium of these young musicians, taking shape through sound, donning the glowing raiment of full-bodied song, self-duplicating on these funny vinyl discs so all the world might hear... It was magic, spirit itself, all happening in this small, unassuming space.

Robin enjoyed blowing his own mind like this, tasting the exciting alchemy that infused the process. It was easy to become mired down in the minutiae, playing the politics of whose instrument would solo where, worrying that one song wasn't quite long enough or that another might drag on unnecessarily.

Robin stepped across the floor to the darkest corner of the room. He laid his coat on the corduroy sofa and sat down. The space was quiet, even with the door to the hallway standing open. He relaxed into the comfort of the couch, resting his hands gently on his knees as he closed his eyes and drifted. He knew how much he needed these moments alone, though he sometimes felt guilty for taking time out, especially now that Alice was expecting and Imbolc had another major project in the works. But these moments, for him, held open the gates for his greatest inspiration and his worst fears to enter.

"Sitting around in the dark again, Rob?" Joe entered the studio and snapped on the lights. Momentarily blinded by this intrusion, Robin held up a hand to shade his eyes as he watched Danny follow Joe into the room.

"Just enjoying the quiet," Robin responded absently.

Joe dropped his coat on the floor and reached for his bass guitar. "Sometimes I worry about you, you know that?" he said to Robin with a good-natured wink.

George and Gareth appeared soon after, and the day's work began. They had completed four tracks and were closing in on a fifth. CAMELOT would consist of ten songs, though only eight had been mapped out. Robin had volunteered responsibility for the final two, though the vision of how they were supposed to fit together had thus far eluded him.

Gareth settled in behind his drum kit as Danny and Joe tuned up. George sat down at his keyboard and cracked his knuckles, one by one. Gareth frowned in painful distaste. "Must you really do that every bloody time?"

George chuckled and managed another loud "POP!" for Gareth's benefit.

"Cecil stopped me in the hallway, as I was coming in," George announced to the group. "He wanted me to convey his congratulations on *Morbidity*. Seems he was listening to the tapes again over the weekend. Said he really likes the dark, mournful strains of that one."

"Yeah, well, when you're writing music in winter, dark and mournful is about all you're going to get," Danny commented, adjusting the volume on his electric six-string.

"I think his words were… yes, 'deliciously deep and ominous.' That's what he said," George continued with a wry smile.

"It's just as well he likes that one, seeing as it's done." Joe relaxed his shoulders and ran his fingers though the shock of red hair on his head. "Don't misunderstand. It's a good song, and I'm proud of it. But I was going to chew through my own scalp if we had to play through that one again."

George and Danny laughed in agreement.

Joe checked his connections. "Ready," he announced to the room.

"Right, let's dream of that queen once more, shall we?" Gareth eyed Robin, still immersed in thought on the far side of the room. "Robin? You care to join us, love?"

"Hmm?" Robin looked up to find the amused expressions of his four bandmates waiting for him. "Ah, right. Sorry." He picked himself up off of the couch, retrieved his pencil from the floor, and took his place behind the microphone.

A gentle blend of keyboard and guitar started off *Dream of a Queen*, the tender sound evoking a sunlit, grassy meadow from Robin's imagination. They had worked out most of the layers, though Gareth was still pondering some supplemental percussion which hadn't yet made itself quite clear.

Robin had quickly completed the lyrics for this bittersweet, cynical song of Queen Gwynevere, frustrating his mates with the deliberate misuse of vocabulary. For the first time he had let sound take precedence over meaning, though he was still dancing his way through a careful mingling of the two. He admitted privately to Alice his pleasure in thumbing his nose at his privileged education through willful misplacement of words.

After the fanciful and light opening measures, the mood of the music turned somber as Joe dropped the bass line down, and Danny and George introduced a subtle layer of minor chords. A few more vaguely ominous bars, and Robin delivered an opening narrative, which changed significantly with each run.

"Across the horizon at dawn, sped the intuitive vision of the great wizard," the singer spoke in calm, mellow tones. "His king's heart had been captured by a lady, a maiden of unsurpassed loveliness, and the Druid's mission was to the seal the marriage."

Joe listened, nodding in agreement with this incarnation of Robin's introduction.

Robin softened his voice, allowing it to become another soothing element of the music as the song took on a tragically hypnotic tone. "But a fortuitous love match was not meant to be, spoke the Fates, whispering into the wise magician's attuned ear. This queen-to-be had another destiny, and it would mean the downfall of the kingdom."

The music swept upward, toward a false crescendo, pulling back into a simpler scheme of synthesizer and bass that heralded the main lyrics.

"Fair, gentle maid, born of noble blood," Robin sang tentatively, his voice hardly more than a whisper. "Alabaster skin and hair of sunspun gold. Destined a legend, so innocently begun. Blue eyes of the sea, her beauty is foretold."

He wasn't comfortable with the cadence or melody, which featured unusual transitions. But he loved the music itself—so interesting and delightfully evocative.

"Beloved of many, beholden to two," he continued, his voice more grounded and full. "Gwynevere, the queen, mistress, pawn. Her folly a kingdom's ransom. Fabled child, spritely spectre here and yon."

Despite the queen's treason, Robin could not help picturing his own lovely Alice as the tangled, legendary Gwynevere. He embraced the building chorus, "Is her devotion so easily won? Boldness and courage—"

One of Danny's guitar strings popped, sending a high-pitched "ping" across the amplifier. "Sorry about that," he grimaced. He unplugged and went hunting for a replacement in his guitar case. Gareth got up from behind his drums and followed Joe down the hall in search of hot coffee.

"Robin, come work with me," George waved him over. Robin stepped up next to his friend and scratched his head, looking again at the lyrics written in his notebook.

"I can still hear you straining," George confided. "You don't have to work that hard, once you really have the feel for it. You want to start up again at the chorus?"

Robin cleared his throat. "Please."

"I'll give you a couple of bars. Two-three-four." George launched into the music, playing supporting chords while emphasizing the melody for Robin to follow.

"Is her devotion so easily won? Boldness and courage have their own measure," Robin sang quietly, more self-conscious now without the full band backing him. "Loyalty is a more lasting pledge. A queen's hand, a king's treasure."

George stopped abruptly. "You see, you're fighting it there. Naturally, you expect the melody is going to go up on 'lasting pledge,' but it doesn't."

"Right, I'm anticipating something that isn't going to happen," Robin frowned.

George smiled. "Just think of yourself as being on a raft, floating on the current of the music. You don't have any paddles, any way of steering or controlling where you're going. You're totally at the mercy of the melody."

"Yeah, okay," Robin acquiesced.

"And if you try to fight it, your raft will fall apart, and you'll drown."

"Great." This was Robin's least favourite part of the process. He didn't often need vocal coaching, but every once in awhile he simply couldn't make it happen, no matter how simple the song. Late at night, as Alice slept, he had practiced, singing quietly to his wife's swelling abdomen, serenading his child. In those moments, it came easily. But now, he was beating his head against a brick wall.

"Again, from the chorus," George prompted.

* * * *

"Loyalty is a more lasting pledge," Robin sang. "A queen's hand, a king's treasure. A queen's heart, a knight's pleasure."

The recording engineer listened and smiled, making an adjustment on the sound board as Imbolc played. Robin turned to the engineer and nodded as he sang:

Her heart bleeds like a comet
Shooting bright across the sky
Her heart, her soul for her people
Crowned by judgement's eye

Is her devotion so easily won?
Boldness and courage have their own measure

Loyalty is a more lasting pledge
A queen's hand, a king's treasure
A queen's heart, a knight's pleasure.

Lady, what is this treachery?
What binds you thus to your fate?
The wizard behooves your caution
Against becoming evil's unwitting bait

She weeps silent, secret tears in grace
Crossed swords are her cross to bear
Refuse to open her eyes to her own truth
Catching kings and fools into love's snare

Is her devotion so easily won?
Boldness and courage have their own measure
Loyalty is a more lasting pledge
A queen's hand, a king's treasure
A queen's heart, a knight's pleasure.

Robin stepped away from the microphone and sipped some water as his bandmates played out the song on the other side of the glass. Smiling at the mesmerizing and almost ethereal rhythm, he watched their intense concentration, especially visible in Gareth.

This was the final recording of *Dream of a Queen*. Five songs down, five more to go, and CAMELOT would be ready for release.

* * * *

Alice stirred in her sleep. Robin's bedside lamp was on, and she heard his voice, half-speaking, half-singing. She opened drowsy eyes to find her husband on his knees beside her, hunched over a notebook as he addressed her navel.

She reached out to touch his head, burying her fingers in his thick hair. Gently stroking his scalp, she let the soft hair slide between her fingers. Robin lifted his face to kiss her wrist.

"What are you doing?" Alice asked, her eyes closed.

"I'm writing a song for the baby." Robin jotted down a few more words on the tattered pages of his notebook.

"Hmm," Alice murmured happily as her fingers dropped sleepily to his shoulder.

Robin took her hand and lightly pressed her knuckles against his cheek before resting her hand down on the bed. "Go back to sleep, sweetheart." He reached up to kiss her on the forehead as she turned her head and drifted off.

He looked again at his notes and tapped out a simple rhythm with his pencil.

* * * *

It was just before five in the morning. Robin had been up all night. He looked once more at the torn-out pages of notebook paper in his hands, then knocked on George and Danny's door. He grimaced at the sound, hoping he wasn't waking the whole house.

After a few moments, he knocked again. There was a thud and some crashing about on the other side of the door.

In his underwear, Danny cracked open the door and squinted. "Rob?"

"Yeah, I'm sorry to wake you. Listen, can you get George for me?"

"You want George?" Danny scratched his head and leaned against the door.

"Yeah, could you rouse him, please?"

Danny stepped back into the bedroom to wake his roommate. Standing in the hallway, Robin could hear some confused syllables from inside the room, followed by George's appearance at the door. Pulling his robe over his pyjamas, he closed the bedroom door behind him.

"Is everything alright, Robin? It's five in the morning."

"I'm sorry to wake you." Robin fumbled with the pages in his hands. Through his fatigue, there was still a small spark left after the night's vigil. "Umm... I've been up, I've been working. That song I told you about. It's done."

George ran his hands through his matted hair. "It's done? I didn't know you had even started it."

"Well, it's mostly done. See?" Robin handed the pages to George. "The words are all there. I've made notations about melody and rhythm. I'm hearing... I'm not sure what I'm hearing. We'll have to play with the arrangement."

George read, following the words across the paper with his fingers as he listened to Robin and nodded. "You know some of this doesn't rhyme in here."

"Uh, yeah. I know about that," Robin stood next to George to see where he was pointing. "I wanted it that way. I kind of like it."

"Mmm." George kept reading.

"Anyway, I was getting ready to go to sleep. I'm going to be down for awhile, and I didn't want this to wait." Robin rested his hands on his hips. His hair was disheveled, his shirt untucked and partially unbuttoned, his socks falling down. "Could you help me?"

"Yeah, sure. I'll, uh, I'll fix some coffee and take a look, see what I can do with this." George placed a hand on his friend's shoulder. "You go on to bed now."

Robin managed a weary smile. "Thanks." He made his way back down the hallway toward his own room, where Alice still slept.

George glanced down at Robin's pages, then quietly called after him. "Robin."

Robin stopped in front of his bedroom door and turned to look at George.

"This is good work. Thank you." George waved to him on his way down to the kitchen.

Robin looked at the floor and smiled. He opened the door as slowly as he could, trying not to make any sound that might disturb Alice.

Chapter 16

April 1973

Arlington, Virginia

Angela was now in school. Marie had felt overwhelmed looking after two small children on her own every day—and some nights, given her husband's class schedule. At her urging, Mark reluctantly enrolled his four-year-old at the local Montessori school. Angela began going half-days at the start of the year.

She was suddenly surrounded by other children when she was more accustomed to interacting with adults. Coming in at the middle of the term, Angela was the new kid, not knowing the other children as well as they knew each other. But she made a few friends easily and was content within a cluster of playmates who appreciated her imaginative games.

But she also wanted to stay home. In her familiar surroundings, the comfort of home leant her confidence. And she was keenly interested in her younger brother, who made things at the house much more interesting.

Marie was concerned about Angela requiring a long nap after school almost every day, but she assumed it was the stimulation of new friends, games, and lessons. She never guessed what her four-year-old was up to.

Months earlier, Granddad had surprised the family with a cat for his granddaughter. Angela and the green-eyed feline took to each other at once. She loved to touch his dark gray fur and to hear him purring when he curled up beside her. She called him Jasper. When questioned by her grandmother, Angela replied simply, "That's what he said his name is." Jasper slept with

Angela at night, sat in a chair next to her while she ate breakfast, and waited patiently by the door for her to come home from school.

Shortly after her last New Year's conversation with Michael, Angela began to wake in the middle of the night, and she could not fall easily back to sleep, despite Jasper's comforting purr. She tossed and turned in her small bed, wide awake.

She began to get up out of bed when she awoke. She roamed the house in silence, her slippered feet padding along the dark hallways while Jasper followed. Sometimes she went downstairs and turned on the television, but she couldn't find Ernie and Bert.

Other nights, she stood in her parents' bedroom, just inside the doorway, watching. The same dark cloud festered and grumbled around her father. He had built up his defenses, erecting great psychic barriers. The shadows kept hovering, waiting to find a chink in his armor and slip inside.

And while they waited for Mark, Angela waited for them.

They were attracted to her father's light. Michael had explained this to her. She thought it was sad and imagined they must be very lonely with no one to talk to.

"I want you to come downstairs with me," she would whisper to them. But every night it was the same. There was no response.

Then they began to gradually disengage from her father when she made these requests. She had gotten their attention. The cloud moved slightly away from Mark, separating further each night to regard this tiny child standing in the doorway, only to race back to their host. All the while, Jasper circled Angela's feet.

It was late at night, and again, Angela was awake. She lay on her back, staring up at the ceiling. The streetlamp outside cast ominous shadows on the walls, and Angela traced these shapes with her eyes. She stroked Jasper beside her and listened to him purr. His body vibrated under her touch, and she liked to feel the rise and fall of his ribcage as he breathed.

"Okay," she said at last, sitting up in bed and putting on her slippers and bathrobe before she stepped out into the hallway. She crossed to her parents' room, cracked open the door, and peeked inside. They were there as usual, the dark storm cloud of souls surrounding her father. She watched for a long moment, not speaking. Then she turned away, leaving the door ajar, and walked down the hallway toward the main staircase. Jasper kept pace at her side.

Reaching the bottom of the stairs, Angela turned and headed for the dining room. She pulled out the chair at the head of the table and climbed up into it. Facing the hallway, she could see the bottom of the staircase. She reached forward and placed her palms down on the wooden table. Jasper jumped up onto the dining table surface and sat down to one side.

"Alright, you can come down now," Angela whispered. She thought maybe she should be afraid, but she wasn't. She felt strong, peaceful. And with Jasper beside her, she wasn't alone.

Angela waited patiently in the dark. She knew they had heard. She could feel them coming, even if she couldn't see them yet. She closed her eyes, visualizing the dark cloud emerging from her parents' room, approaching the stairs. Jasper moved closer, brushed against her hands, and looked out into the hallway. When Angela opened her eyes, she saw the souls reach the bottom of the staircase as they descended.

The grouping hesitated in the hallway. Jasper crouched low, gauging the situation. He walked to the end of the table, coming within a few yards of the shadows, and sniffed at them. The cat raised his front foot and pawed at the air, then studied the strange jumble of figures. Narrowing his eyes, he turned and walked back along the table to Angela, where he resumed his place, sitting beside her.

The shadowy cloud approached, stopping at the threshold of the dining room, hovering. It was a stand-off. She cocked her head to one side as the group expanded horizontally, filling the double-doorway. As the cloud thinned, distinct forms slowly took shape. Not quite ten men stood before her, their outlines murky, their faces gray and worn.

"It's okay, you can come in, one at a time," Angela said with genuine hospitality in her voice. Jasper jumped down into her lap and peered over the top of the table as the first hazy figure approached.

The spectre advanced slowly, fluidly, skirting the edge of the table and coming to rest a few feet from Angela's side. The shadow floated on the air, towering over her. She peered up into the shade's face and made out the features of a young man. He wore the same clothes she saw in her Daddy's Army pictures and sometimes on television, too. She saw in his ghostly eyes that he was sad and afraid. Jasper's tail twitched.

"It's okay," she said to him. "You don't have to be scared. There's no one to hurt you here."

The shadow bowed his head. Angela thought he was crying. She remembered what Michael had told her about these souls.

"Bet you want to go home?"

The shadow slowly raised his head, his face displaying all of the horrors of war he had seen. He showed her the broken and mutilated bodies, the split skulls, the burning villages, dismembered animals, the defiled corpses of soldiers and civilians alike. But Angela was not afraid. Instead of recoiling, she reached out to this lost spirit with her heart. She cried tears of compassion for his pain and loneliness. The images flickering across his face faded, his visage reflecting the heavy burden of shame and trauma.

"That's all over now," she said to him. "You don't have to live there anymore."

The shade's eyes sparkled with moisture. Angela thought she saw a faint smile cross his gray lips as he stepped back and allowed the next shadow to enter.

Angela was their confessional priest. Finally they had someone who could see and understand them, a living being before whom they could lay down their torturous yokes. One by one, the shadows revealed themselves to this small child, at last finding relief from endless grief. The souls had separated into individuals again, no longer magnetized by each other's pain and fear.

Angela sat at the head of the table, surrounded by these sad spirits standing on either side. Jasper stood steadfast in Angela's lap, regarding these shades.

"It's time for you to go home," Angela said confidently, despite the confusion in the faces around her. "It's alright, you can do it. My friend Michael says you can go home anytime you want to, but you need to look around first. See?" Angela pointed to the hallway, which had filled with a bright, white light that sparkled and shimmered. Jasper saw the light and yawned. He climbed back up on the table and lay down.

"That's the way to go, right there. It's always there. You just have to look for it."

One by one, the shadows filed out into the hallway. Angela could sense their fear but felt the excitement as well. Stepping over the threshold, each one was absorbed into the light, the dark forms disappearing into its brilliance. As the last shade prepared to cross over, he turned to face Angela once more. From across the room, she could see his eyes. He was smiling. He turned again toward the light and stepped into it.

Angela closed her eyes. She was sleepy. She stretched out her arms and yawned. When she opened her eyes again, the light was gone. So were the shadows.

"Hmm," she said quietly to herself as she tapped her small foot against the leg of the chair. She inhaled sharply and sneezed. She climbed down out of the chair, pushed it back toward the table, and reached up to pet Jasper. "I'm going back to bed now."

Angela walked softly out of the dining room and climbed the stairs to the second floor. Jasper remained behind. Michael stepped out of a dark corner and placed his hand on the cat's head. "Good work, Jasper," he said.

Chapter 17

12 July 1973
London

Robin sat beside his wife's hospital bed as she nursed their daughter, nearly twenty-four hours old.

"You know we should have done this sooner," Alice chastised her husband.

"We tried that," Robin responded, looking over the list in his hands. "But you were convinced we were having a boy."

"Oh, is that what it was?" Alice shot her husband a playful, sideways glance.

"Yes, that's it exactly. Anthony Harris Michaels will simply have to wait." He winked at her, then read over his list. "Alright, so it's Phoebe, Angela, Rose, or Grace." He looked up again, regarding mother and daughter together. "I like Rose."

Alice pulled the soft blanket away from the baby's face to gaze once more upon her delicate features. "Rose. Yes, I like Rose, too."

"That's it, then. Rose Peabody Michaels." Robin smiled, chuckling quietly as he crossed off the unused names. Alice regarded him suspiciously.

"Rose Peabody Michaels." Alice smiled, stroking the few strands of fine hair on her baby's tender head. "R-P-M," she pondered for a moment, then her eyes grew wide. "Wait, RPM? Rotations per minute??"

"Yes," Robin beamed in satisfaction.

"No." Her tone was firm.

"Yes," he insisted, slipping the list and his pencil into the breast pocket of his shirt.

Alice shook her head in disbelief. "Robin, you would honestly use your own daughter for this kind of amusement? This is a child's name, not a working title for some pop ditty."

Robin leaned forward in his chair, placing one hand on Alice's thigh and the other on his daughter's head. "I know. I know this is real. Alice, if she's got any of me in her, she is going to love this. Trust me. Please."

Frowning, she stole her gaze from her husband's entreating eyes and looked down again on her infant child.

"Please, Alice." Robin's voice was soft but insistent. He leaned down and kissed the top of his daughter's head. "Sweet Rose," he whispered softly to her.

* * * *

Hours later, as Alice slept, Robin spent his first moments alone with his daughter. He sat with her in a chair by the window.

His hold on her was delicate. He was afraid he might break her. She was so tiny, so pink. He listened to her breathe and thought his heart would break from tenderness. He held her up to the window and pointed out the trees and the sky. He tried to explain what clouds were made of and told her of the hours they would spend together, lying in the grass as they watched these great wisps float by idly above.

As Rose drifted in and out of sleep, Robin pulled a few worn pages from his pocket and held them up for reference as he softly sang her song, the gentle and vulnerable melody written in the wee hours of the morning, months earlier:

Heaven's herald of your coming

The wheels of fortune do spin
A dream of ethers embodied
Into flesh the eternal spirit rushes in

A touch, a kiss, rhythm of life immortal
I step up, onto this circle I walk
I tremble, I am undeserving
To be blessed by this magic, miracle that is

Faithful and steadfast is my pledge
My joy is in your simple sighs
This is my promise
To see the world again through your eyes

Compromise me, bend me to universal will
Intrude into this existence, set me free
Show me the new path, the new light
Create in me a better man to be

Your rays of light penetrate my darkness
Your splendour breaks open my soul
I hear your tender whispers on the wind
Your touch all wounds console

Faithful and steadfast is my pledge
My joy is in your simple sighs
This is my promise
To see the world again through your eyes

I will climb the highest mountain

Hang over the perilous precipice
Tame my wild diversion
If only for your smile

Faithful and steadfast is my pledge
My joy is in your simple sighs
This is my promise
To see the world again through your eyes

Compromise me, bend me to universal will
Intrude into this existence, set me free
Show me the new path, the new light
Create in me a better man to be

Robin peered down into Rose's face, her new eyes closed against the world as she rested, her head nestled against his chest. He ran his fingers over her tiny hands, and he wept.

Chapter 18

October 1973
McLean, Virginia

"Granddad?" Angela stood beside her grandfather's chair. "Could you help me with a story?"

Donald Francis lowered his newspaper to find his granddaughter's glistening green eyes peering up at him. He smiled and folded the paper.

"You have a story to tell, little Angel?" Granddad patted his knee and invited her into his lap. Angela accepted his assistance climbing up into the chair.

"It's a big story, and I don't want to forget," she explained as she touched the lapel of his wool blazer.

"Maybe if you tell me the story, I can help you remember. We can even write it down, if you'd like."

"Okay," she responded with a shy smile. "I mean, yes, please."

"Go ask Grandmum for a pad of paper and a pen," he suggested as he eased her back down onto her feet. "I'll be right here, ready to hear your story, when you get back."

He watched proudly as his granddaughter scampered out of the living room, hearing her small shoes on the hardwood in the hallway, quietly calling for her grandmother. It was a delight to have her all to themselves as Mark and Marie spent some time alone together. He listened for any sounds from the napping Anthony upstairs.

Angela reappeared with a pad of lined paper and a pen in her hands. She ran excitedly to her grandfather's chair and handed these simple treasures to him.

"Why, thank you, young lady." Granddad lifted her once again into his lap. With the paper balanced on one knee and his granddaughter sitting on the other, he held the pen in his fingers, ready. "Now you can tell your story, and we can write it down, so no one will forget."

"Okay," Angela beamed. She kicked her heels against the bottom of the chair cushion. "Okay. The story happens in a place that's far away, a long time ago. And so it's not like today. And then, and there was a king there, and... only he wasn't the king yet. 'Cuz, because an old man put a sword in a rock. A big sword. And he had magic, he used magic and stuff to do it."

"Magic?" Granddad asked.

"Yes. It's special magic. Good magic. He was a good guy," Angela explained excitedly. "And he made this big sword go into the rock, because there was this contest. And all of the people came to the contest, and they tried to pull it out. It was in a, in the rock. But everybody, they couldn't pull it out. And he made this other man, somebody else, go to the rock, so he could, to try and pull it out. Only, and he could do it. And he pulled it out, because he was the real king. And then, and his name was Arthur."

"King Arthur?"

"Well, after that, then he was the king. But before, he was just Arthur."

"Right." Granddad scribbled on the paper, trying to keep up with her. "Where did you hear this story, Angel?"

Angela frowned and played with the hem of her dress. "Umm, I think maybe it was a dream. Nobody told it to me."

Granddad touched her cheek and smiled. "Okay." He looked back at the pad of paper. "Did the old man have a name? The one with the magic?"

"I'm not at that part," Angela responded impatiently.

"I'm sorry. You tell the story the way you want to."

Angela clasped her hands in her lap and thought. "I have to go back to the start. I forgot to tell some things. Okay, so... See, Merlin is a wizard. And he did magic for people, for kings and people. And then, he could make it look like you were someone else. So, if, like if I wanted you to think I was Mommy instead of me, maybe Merlin would do a magic thing, and then, and then I would look like Mommy. But it's really me, but you don't know that."

"I understand."

The emeralds in Angela's eyes sparkled as she told her story, her grandfather listening attentively and taking down every word of the tales she recounted: the whole history of legendary Camelot.

* * * *

Angela was down for an afternoon nap. For the third time, Donald Francis read over the story his granddaughter had told. He adjusted his glasses as he scanned the words in his own handwriting.

His wife entered the study, drying her hands on a kitchen towel. "What are you studying there, honey?"

Donald sat back in his chair. "Iris, how old were you when you first heard the story of King Arthur?"

She looked at the ceiling. "Oh, I don't know. I was ten years old, perhaps? Let's see. I remember reading some of those stories when I was a schoolgirl, and a friend wrote a short story about Camelot in high school. Is that what you're reading now?"

"I don't know what I'm reading," he responded.

Iris peered over her husband's shoulder, glancing at the words in front of him. "Yes, that's Camelot all right. But that doesn't sound like you. Are you writing this story?"

Donald pulled off his glasses and laid them down on the desk. "No. Angela was telling me a story. She wanted me to write it down."

Iris gestured toward the papers. "And this is the story she told you?"

"Yes." He rubbed his eyes. "I was thinking maybe she had heard this somewhere, maybe they've been reading her these stories at bedtime. Or she saw something on television. But look at this." He collected the stack of papers and handed them to his wife. "Look at the detail. It's as if she saw all of this happen first hand."

Iris shuffled through the pages, frowning as she scanned through her granddaughter's story. "Was Gwynevere blonde? I don't remember. Dark eyes, too. You must have interpreted some of this for her, Donald." Iris rested a hand on her husband's shoulder as she returned the pages to his desk.

"No, this is precisely what she said. Sometimes she had to repeat parts of it, to make sure I wrote it down correctly. She had me read it back to her until I got it right."

"Well, something happened. You must have paraphrased for her when you wrote it down, inserting your own familiarity with the story. Angela will only be five next month, not twenty-five." Iris dismissed him with a wave of her hand and walked out of the room.

Donald stared at the pages in front of him as if they might disappear before his eyes. He touched his own handwriting on the paper and then looked to the ceiling, where his granddaughter slept in the room above.

* * * *

Chicago, Illinois

"I don't understand what you're trying to tell me."

George looked at his old friend sitting on the floor in his hotel room. Imbolc was just over half-way through their first U.S. tour, promoting their new CAMELOT album.

"I'm not sure I understand it myself," Robin responded.

It was 1:30 in the afternoon, following a disappointing show the previous evening. Robin had come knocking on his door an hour earlier with a wild look in his eyes and some crazy story about his first psychedelic experience in the wee hours of the morning.

"I told you not to get mixed up with that stuff," George chided from his perch on the bed. "Now look at you."

"No, I'm alright." Robin got up on his knees and looked about the room. "I am in my right mind. I know what I saw."

George sighed and crossed his legs. "Look, you've never done this kind of thing before…"

"And I don't think I'll be doing it again," Robin shot back.

"Good." Still in his pyjamas, George stretched his arms out to his sides, trying to wake up. With time changes added to the concert schedule, George feared he might lose his own grip on reality. "Listen, Joe and Danny might do that sort of thing. That's fine, as long as it doesn't interfere with the band or the tour. But you…" George gestured to Robin, now on his feet slowly pacing the beige carpeting. "You're not like the others, Rob, in case that's a surprise to you."

Robin paused, stopping to look at his feet. He wiggled his toes inside his socks and studied the movement.

"And I'd say you're feeling the effects of it still. What was it you took again?"

"Mmm. No." Robin faced George and rested his fists on his slender hips. "No, I'm quite clear. But you could say I see things differently now. I…"

He became distracted by the sounds of traffic in the street below and crossed to the window. Pushing aside the sheer curtains, he pressed his palm against the glass and looked out at Chicago.

"What happened, what I saw, was not completely outside the realm of my experience," he continued. "It was just more… vivid. More intense. Ah, it was, it was so real! Not the way it comes in dreams. I could touch all of it. Right in the middle of everything, though I felt so powerless. Like I was just an observer. Some casual spectator in this colourful torrent of activity…" His voice trailed off as his gaze softened.

George rose from the bed and poured a glass of water. "Robin, you had a drug-induced experience that combined working too hard with missing your family."

He walked to the window and faced Robin, handing the glass to him. Robin accepted it unconsciously, not even looking at George.

"You saw the entire story of Camelot play out in front of you," George recapitulated. "And all of us were the characters in the story, right?"

"Mmm," responded Robin, still looking outside.

"So Alice was Gwynevere. Hardly surprising, considering you told me yourself you had seen the whole album unfold one night as you watched her sleeping. So there's no mystery there."

Robin pressed his hand firmly against the cool glass, listening vaguely.

"And there was a little girl, with the same hair and eyes as your own. Probably Morgan le Fay. I'd say that's Rose. You were picturing your own family, because you miss them."

Robin shook his head. There was a piece that still wasn't congealing.

"A stranger, a man you didn't know, stepped in as Merlin," George continued. "That could be anybody. It could even suggest Gilbert Treanor as our new manager when Cecil retired months ago."

Robin raised the water to his lips. He grimaced at the taste, not sure what he was expecting. Looking about the room, he spotted the night table and put down the glass.

"No, that's not it. Not Merlin." Robin hunched forward, resting his hands on his knees. "Gareth. Gareth was Merlin." Robin stood up straight and touched his friend on the shoulder as he passed, beginning to pace the room again.

"Okay, so Gareth was Merlin. Another mystery solved."

Robin frowned and continued to shake his head. "There was still this man. And that girl was not Morgan. There's simply no way. She was, I believe... Yes, she was telling the story. Everyone else was just acting it out. Or perhaps she was verbalizing what she saw happening. I don't know. But I do know that man. Who was that?"

He stopped, facing a wall as he searched his mind for the key that might unlock the entire vision. Watching his friend's back, George knew better than to disturb Robin.

Robin spun around quickly, his eyes on fire. "I've got it! That man," he announced proudly, "that man was Michelangelo!"

"Michelangelo," George repeated.

"Yes! It was Michelangelo, with the child. I told you this wasn't just the Camelot story! He has no place in there if it is." Robin nearly leapt across the room, using movement to place the image. "Michelangelo was standing with the little girl, as though he were some kind of... guardian for her."

"Robin," George interjected. "I hate to interrupt your reverie. Michelangelo certainly does not appear in the story of Camelot. But we do have our song *My Michelangelo* which we've been playing sporadically throughout the tour, remember? I still say this whole thing is just a manifestation of putting too much of yourself into the concerts and being away from home. And I'm sure the drugs helped as well."

Robin looked hard at George, considering his words. After a long moment, he filled the room with his confident voice. "No, that little girl was not Rose. I've seen her before. I know I have. I know it."

A long, slow breath escaped his lungs as he sat down on the bed, cradling his head in his hands. George sat down beside him and rested a reassuring hand on his shoulder.

"Robin, not everything has to be of earth-shattering significance, you know." George's voice was low and soothing. "You cannot always squeeze pertinent meaning out of every little thing. Just let it go."

Robin disagreed, but kept these thoughts to himself. He would spend hours and days more piecing together this puzzle. He dug his fingers into his thick hair and tugged. "Part of this... I saw Alice betray me. Even if she was Gwynevere... I don't know who it was. I couldn't see his face."

* * * *

Late that night, following another concert, Robin struggled for restless sleep.

He hadn't eaten until nearly 2 a.m., still full of energy from the show. Spilling his room-service soup on the floor as he jumped up from his seat, he had pounded his fist on the table and exclaimed, "No! It was me! I was the one telling the story. She... We told the story together. She and I!" Then he had looked around the empty room and slowly sat back down. Perhaps George was right, he thought to himself, wondering if the effects of his drug adventure truly had worn off.

Gareth had suggested a telephone call to Alice in London might settle his nerves, though Robin had caught her as she was dressing the baby in the morning. Hearing his daughter's cries from across the Atlantic only spiked his anxiety. During the brief conversation, Robin hadn't mentioned Danny's escapades with women he picked up from who knew where.

It was 4 a.m. as he lay in bed. Finally managing partial dream state, Robin's body and mind relaxed as he faced that same small figure. The little girl with the brown hair and emerald eyes emerged from the mist and walked toward him. She looked up at him and smiled, taking his hand into her delicate fingers.

"Please," she said in her soft voice. "Tell me another story."

Chapter 19

20 May 1999
New York City
10:03 a.m.

The necessary introductions had been made. Everyone had copies of the proposal and of Westone Publishing's documents. It was show time.

Jeff nodded to Angela. "You're on."

Angela took a deep breath and glanced quickly at her notes. She looked back up at the blank faces across the table and felt a wild spasm of panic in her stomach. She cleared her throat, forcing the anxiety from her system. Feeling a gentle radiance spreading through her chest into her fingers, she placed her hands over her notes, covering her words. She smiled at the three Westone executives.

"Gentlemen, you've read the proposal." She was surprised by the cool confidence of her voice. "I won't waste any time reiterating what has already been stated. But I will discuss in greater detail how we came to this undertaking, and how it has brought us to you this morning."

She noticed the raised eyebrows of the senior executive and the intrigued smile subtly betrayed at the corners of his mouth.

"We live in a country where we pretty much have whatever we could possibly desire," Angela continued. "Need is no longer an issue for the majority of Americans. Survival is practically assured. We enjoy an incredibly high quality of life, one constantly changing for the better. We also have a great deal of what we don't want, simply because we've come to believe that ownership is not the sign of success, but is success itself."

Jeff cleared his throat. Angela acknowledged his warning against becoming too political.

She looked carefully into the eyes of the men sitting across from her. "Have you ever been on the Carousel of Progress attraction at Disney World?"

"Mmm," the two junior executives grunted in concert. Sitting between them, their boss nodded and smiled.

"That's an incredible vision, the way Disney presented his hopes for the future. Increasingly complex—and useful—technology would improve lives and give families more time together. Everyone is happy in those vignettes. While a number of Disney's predictions were fairly close on the mark, the social aspects today are quite a bit different."

Angela got up from her chair and walked toward the head of the table. "Do you mind if I stand?" she asked. "I feel better on my feet this morning."

* * * *

"Now, smile for the camera, Robin," Mary K teased as she stood in the shadows behind the lighting equipment.

Robin grimaced in response, at the precise moment the camera shutter clicked, unintentionally ruining the shot.

"Come on, Robin," Mary K goaded. "You can do better than that, wasting film."

"Sorry about that, Vivienne," he offered meekly.

"It's alright," the veteran photographer replied. "You sure you don't want any more make-up on him?" Vivienne asked over her shoulder to Mary K.

"No, we want to show the mature Robin Michaels. We want to see the man, not the rock-and-roll persona. No more make-up. I think he looks great. Grounded."

Robin laughed. "Oh, God, is it that bad?"

Vivienne adjusted the lights to take an unflattering hot spot off of Robin's brow. Considering her subject, she stood in front of him and smiled. "When was the first time you did this?"

"Ooh, ah," he thought. "I don't really know. Twenty-five, not quite thirty years ago? Good lord."

"I told you you're getting old," Mary K cracked as Vivienne crouched down a few yards in front of Robin's chair.

"I like this backdrop for you, Robin," Vivienne commented as she snapped a few shots. "The deep teal color really brings out your eyes."

"Ah, yeah, green," Robin responded vaguely as he smiled for her. "Good colour."

"So, what's next? What are you working on now?" Vivienne continued to make conversation with him.

"Mmm, back to England tonight," he replied thoughtfully. "And I suppose, back to the studio tomorrow, or the weekend. There's, umm, I'm scoring the soundtrack for an IMAX production, working with another composer. Miragio is doing a series. You know, METROPOLIS, about cities around the world, ancient and modern. There's also OCEAN, SPACE, and RAINFOREST. They've got some great musicians, umm, composers lined up. FOOTPRINT is the working title of the one I'm on. The story is... It's an overview of human history—through sound and image only, no narration—to mark the turning of the century. The next millennium. It's pretty cool."

"I thought you were working on a solo album, Robin?" Mary K asked.

"Oh, yeah," Robin recalled. "That, too. Oh, and, umm, there's a new CD, multimedia CD-ROM, also, in the works," he explained as Vivienne hovered, almost dancing to the rhythmic clicking of the camera shutter. "Mythology."

"Mythology," Mary K repeated.

"Yeah. Mythological interplay across cultures. We're still mapping that one out, so there's not much I can say about it." Robin stopped and gave his warmest, most genuine smile to Vivienne. "Unfortunately."

Vivienne looked up and grinned. "That was it. That's the one. Thanks, Robin." She set her camera equipment down on a worktable and switched off the fill lights.

Mary K stepped forward with a towel to wipe the powder and sweat off of his face. "You know, the sun goes into Gemini today."

"Gemini?" Robin climbed down from the elevated chair. He accepted the clean towel and dabbed at his forehead and cheeks.

"The twins. Maybe that's why you feel pulled in so many directions at once."

"Oh. Is that how I'm feeling?" Robin handed the towel back to her and smiled.

"Maybe. I don't know. I really don't know much about that stuff. Astrology. I thought maybe you did, that it would mean something to you."

Robin shook his head. "Not really my bag."

Mary K took his arm and led him out of the photo studio. "Well, if it's not today, then soon. My friend, Roger, is a Gemini, and his birthday is Monday."

* * * *

"Restlessness," Henry Peters, the senior executive, directed to Angela.

"Yes," she responded emphatically.

"Restlessness is the cause of rampant capitalism?"

"Well, yes, in part," she explained, pacing assuredly. "For centuries, survival was a primary focus. We labored and toiled and struggled just to stay alive. It's a deeply ingrained part of our make-up. Life wasn't always as certain as it is today. Of course, there exist today places in the world where this is still the case."

Angela looked to her partner and found Jeff wearing an interested frown.

"Most of us don't have to worry about this. So we've got this excess energy, that would have gone into that struggle. Now it has no place to go. So people fill their lives with all sorts of activity, or inactivity, as the case may be. We have holes in our souls, and we're trying desperately to fill them."

"Holes in our souls?" one of the junior executives asked incredulously, raising his eyebrows as he glanced to his boss.

"I like it," Henry replied. "That's why markets like self-help and new age have taken off, not only book publishing, but seminars, aromatherapy, spa resorts…"

"Yes, exactly," Angela congratulated the elder businessman. "There is a quest for meaning in our lives, conscious or not. We've experienced it ourselves." Angela gestured around the table, pleased to find most everyone nodding thoughtfully.

"We're looking for individual significance within an increasingly global environment," she proceeded. "Just look at the number of personal sites on the World Wide Web. People want to fill the void. They want to prosper as human beings, not just cogs in the machine. We all want to change the world. We're told to think globally and act locally. There is no more local a target than our individual selves, so this is where so many of us start to manifest the changes we see as necessary in the world around us."

Angela leaned forward and rested her hands on the conference room table, connecting with each pair of eyes as looked around the room.

"People want to find themselves," she stated clearly. "I have no interest in telling them where to go or what to do. I am absolutely interested in offering alternatives and possible pathways back to center. In short, what I want to do at this stage is help people discover themselves and happily stumble upon meaning in their lives."

She gestured to the proposals on the table. "And, yes, there is a plan."

Chapter 20

February 1974
London

Imbolc had been locked in the studio for four hours. With no windows, the recording space felt even more like a prison. Their results-oriented manager, Gil Treanor, had made sure they were properly fed but not coddled in any way. Their scheduled release date was two weeks away, and the band had only completed two out of ten tracks.

After scheming how they might escape from the building, the five had sat around grumbling about how Cecil would never have pulled such a stunt, conveniently forgetting that their former manager, in his own frustration with their routine creative blocks, had several times come close to this very scenario.

Joe sat at a large folding table, building a fairy fortress with the remnants of their lunch. George had used the entire supply of sharpened pencils as darts, lodged in the wall behind Gareth's drums. Biscuits had been provided a short time earlier, and Gareth sipped steaming coffee as he sat on the couch and mused on his life's direction. Robin was curled up on the floor, asleep.

An hour or so earlier, Danny had talked his way out of captivity on the promise of a prompt return following a secret errand necessary to the creative process. The others had no idea what he was after and doubted he would come back to the studio at all.

Gil had let him go without much argument. Their manager was uneasy with his ultimatum—lay down at least one final track to earn release from the studio. He feared a worried wife, girlfriend, or parent might call the authorities, resulting in his being charged with wrongful imprisonment.

George leaned across the drum kit and retrieved one of the pencils stuck in the soundproof padding. Joe watched him step behind his keyboards. George scratched his head with the tip of the pencil.

"Do you have something, then?" Joe's voice broke the thick silence.

George stared at the black and white keys. "I don't know. Mostly, I'm just bored out of my skull." He slid the pencil into the back pocket of his blue jeans. "I suppose playing crap is better than playing nothing at all."

"You go right ahead." Joe fit another crust of bread into his food castle. "Let us know when you hit upon something."

George stretched his hands over the cool keys and felt their delicate promise beneath his fingertips. Closing his eyes, he took the plunge. He played a single middle-D, the gentle note surprising his eyes back open. He released the key and stepped away from the instrument, shaking his head.

"That's it?" Joe asked from across the room. "That's brilliant. That's the whole album, right there. Good work."

Gareth sighed and covered his face with his hands. "This has got to be one of the most mad days of my life. Completely useless. When did we become such sorry bastards?"

"I don't know what you're complaining about. I'm a genius over here. Just look at this." At the table, Joe opened his arms wide to showcase his edible fairy kingdom.

Gareth got up from the couch and walked over to consider Joe's work. Bits of sandwiches were stuck together with mustard and some mashed peas to form the main walls, while carrot sticks were held upright in their sentinel posts with spots of jam. Joe had fashioned a castle gate out of a few straws and a collection of pitted olives. A ring of beans outlined what appeared to be a moat, and somewhat removed from the fortress, Joe had used chips to construct a balustrade structure which oddly resembled Stonehenge.

Gareth shook his head. "I'm speechless, Joe. I have no idea what the hell this is."

Joe sighed angrily. Without a word, he stepped over to the coffee service. He carefully lined up the paper cups, upside down, one by one, in a long row. He walked around the table to sight the row from each end, making sure the line was perfectly straight. Gareth watched as Joe assumed his place behind the table, standing solemnly with the cups before him. He took a deep breath, lifting his chest in preparation, and then with a loud grunt brought his fist down on the first cup, flattening it. He stepped to the side, raised his fist, and brought down a crushing blow on the second. Each successive paper cup crumpled under his pummeling, one by one, as he moved down the line.

"Christ," Gareth sighed audibly, returning to his seat on the couch.

Danny burst into the room. "Lads! I'm back."

"Just in time," George commented. "You were missing all the excitement."

"Where did you go, anyway?" Joe demanded, kicking the crumpled cups across the floor.

Delighted mischief spreading across his face, Danny reached into his coat pocket for a small paper bag, which he held up for the others to see. "In here lads," he explained, "is the key to this album. We're all set."

Joe stomped over to Danny and grabbed the bag from him. Looking inside, he frowned. "What the hell is that?"

"LSD," Danny replied.

"Yeah, okay." George stepped across the room and reached into the bag. "Anything to get out of this rut." He placed a tab on his tongue as Gareth looked up at him. "What?" George responded to Gareth's raised eyebrows. "I'm about to lose my mind in here."

"You'll definitely lose your mind on that stuff," Gareth crossed his arms over his chest.

Joe took a tab for himself. He held it carefully between his fingers, studying it, then opened his mouth.

"Good man," Danny commented. He turned to Gareth on the couch. "Gareth? Care to join us on this little trip of discovery?"

"Thank you, no." Gareth turned his back to the others and lay down, stretching out to the full length of the couch. "I think Robin had the right idea when he went to sleep."

"Right." Danny spotted the singer on the floor and tiptoed lightly over to him. Kneeling down, Danny got his arms underneath Robin and lifted him up. "Robin, wake up. There's something very important going on, and we need you."

Deep in sleep, Robin did not welcome this intrusion. "What?" he slurred. He squinted at the light of the room, then closed his eyes again, leaning against Danny's shoulder.

"No you don't." Danny propped Robin's head back and pulled gently on his jaw to open his mouth. "We need you to help us out with something here."

Gareth sat up just in time to witness Danny slide an acid tab onto Robin's tongue and then press his mouth shut.

"That was not a good idea," Gareth bellowed.

* * * *

Arlington, Virginia

Marie's face was pale and worn. She had been up all night with her daughter, who had become suddenly very ill. Though the doctor reassured her that everything would be alright, that the penicillin would bring down the fever and control the infection, Marie still took Angela's temperature every hour. She removed the thermometer from her daughter's mouth and checked the reading. Jasper watched, his tail twitching.

102 degrees.

Marie had contracted scarlet fever herself when she was about Angela's age. She knew her daughter wasn't in any real danger. Such childhood illnesses would come and go. Before long this would be more an annoyance than a concern. Soon, Angela would be laughing and dancing again.

But this evening, they were both so tired.

Mark finally persuaded his wife to get some rest herself. Marie dragged across the hallway and accepted his help getting into bed. Angela had been blissfully unconscious the majority of the day while her body fought off the invading illness. Jasper was constantly at her side.

But then Angela awoke, not quite sure of her surroundings. She was in her own bed, but the room was fuzzy. The walls moved like waves in the ocean. Some colors were bright and sparkly, while others were very dull and threatened to drop out of sight altogether. She sat up, feeling disconnected from her body in a strange, shifting kind of way. Two men stood together at the foot of her bed. They were glowing.

"Hello, Michael," Angela said cheerfully, her words sticking to her ears like strawberry syrup.

Michael smiled and nodded. Without a word, he stepped back and disappeared into the shadows.

The younger man moved closer and sat down beside her. Jasper regarded the visitor suspiciously, then crouched down to see what would happen. The man appeared confused but unconcerned. He threaded his fingers together and rested his hands in his lap. He looked around the room, glanced down at his hands, and then met Angela's eyes.

"I don't know where I am," he admitted.

"Your voice sounds funny," Angela stated.

He laughed. "I suppose you're an American. I'm English. You hear my accent. I hear yours."

She gazed curiously into his clear, green eyes. "Why are you glowing?"

Robin looked again at his hands, having wondered the same thing. There was a light source inside of him, as best he could tell, and he could practically see through his hands, his wrists, his feet… He felt incredibly light, if he had any weight at all. Was he even breathing? He hadn't walked but had instead flowed across the floor to this child's bed. His last certain memory was lying on the dingy carpet of the studio floor. How had he gotten here? Who was this little girl? None of this much bothered him.

He saw her hands were flushed a delicate pink, and he noticed the feverish luminescence reflected in her face.

"You're glowing, too," he commented.

His words hummed in her skull like a pair of gentle bumble bees. She raised her hands to her face, feeling as though she were moving through stale water. Her cheeks felt like warm lead under her sluggish fingertips.

"That's 'cuz I have a fever," Angela responded.

"That's okay," Robin smiled. "I'm on acid, apparently."

* * * *

It was close to eleven o'clock when Mark headed to bed. He stopped outside his daughter's closed door and heard her soft voice.

"I think I need to go to sleep now. It's morning there? Is it time to wake up? Are you going to sing when you wake up? Just tell them you were only droozing. Thank you for the cookie. Goodnight, sweet dreams…"

Mark turned the knob quietly and pushed open the door. "Sweetheart? Are you awake?" She must have been talking to the cat.

Poking his head into the room, he found Angela fast asleep, the soft glow of the nightlight illuminating her angelic face. Jasper lay curled at her side.

Mark stepped into the room to confirm that, indeed, Angela had a streak of chocolate smeared across one cheek. In her hand she clutched a partially eaten cookie as she slept.

* * * *

London

Robin awoke in his own bed.

Confused images of intensely vivid dreams swarmed through his head, swooping in both ears and pounding tiny fists against his eyes from inside and out. He sat up under the covers and shook his whole body, trying to pull himself together.

A car horn sounded from the street below, the sudden, shrieking noise shattering the crystalline structure of his skull, sending shards into the warm, red gelatin of his baby brain. He felt his jaw drop down to his navel as he took a deep breath, the great caverns of his lungs filling with the howling winds of the desert as his bowels descended to his knees.

He shut his eyes tight and tapped a hand against his brow. "No, no, no, no, no," he muttered, feeling the spongy impact of his fingers against his face. "No, no, no." He tapped out a familiar rhythm against his forehead. Da-da-da-da dum-dum dip da-da dum dip-dip dum. "I'm only droozing…"

Robin opened his eyes.

He looked out the bedroom window. At least half the day must already be gone. Becoming more aware of his surroundings, he realized he was still fully clothed. He ran a hand across his unshaven face, feeling the tiny razors of stubble slice into his overly sensitized skin.

"Wait a minute."

Robin felt across his chest with both hands, searching for his shirt pocket. Inside, he found two carefully folded pages, filled with lyrics in his own handwriting:

Droozing—Written by Robin and an angel

Clouds of colour hover over me
Shedding rain drops of purest silk
The sunlit edge of the wanderer's brow
Presumes an axis of the global tilt

Sky of purple
Water free
Don't wake me
Don't shake me
I'm only droozing

Mine is a green glow quiet
Comfortable feather bed rest
Creeping, crawling under the covers
I build my fevered scarlet nest

I hear the sounds of early morning cries
Below wood beams and slate and tile
Cover me, the ground is so cold
I must walk this long and lonely mile

Sky of purple
Water free
Don't wake me

Don't shake me
I'm only droozing

Steal into the kitchen, little one
Reach up, strain for the top shelf
Sweet morsels of reward, sticky fingers
The chocolate smile of a hungry elf

Touch my brow, so hot, so hot
This evil I fight beneath my skin
Cool my face with a tender voice
I see the sameness of you within

Sky of purple
Water free
Don't wake me
Don't shake me
I'm only droozing
I'm only droozing

He read through the pages several times, trying to understand what he had in his hands. Robin simply stared at the words and chord progressions, looking first to one page and then to the next.

"What the hell is this?" he asked his handwriting.

Chapter 21

May 1977

Arlington, Virginia

"Mommy, Anthony's soul is sick."

"What?" Marie looked up from her magazine into the concerned face of her eight-year-old daughter.

"He's sick, on the inside," she explained calmly.

Marie rose from her chair on the sun porch and made her way through the house to her son's bedroom upstairs. Angela trailed behind.

Anthony had come down with a baffling fever two weeks earlier. Though the doctor had finally controlled his temperature with antibiotics, no particular infection or biological agent had been found. In the past few days, the fever had returned, accompanied by rashes and constipation. The doctor had indicated this might be the beginning of a chronic condition.

Marie found Anthony napping on his bed. Trying not to wake him, she knelt down next to her son and brushed the bangs out of his eyes. She held the back of her hand against his forehead to check his temperature. Angela stood at the end of the bed.

"No. He's not that kind of sick, Mom," Angela insisted.

Marie frowned. "He doesn't have a temperature." She looked into Anthony's face. "Why do you say he's sick? Has he vomited?"

"It's his soul that's sick," Angela replied patiently. "He's sick on the inside."

Marie patted her daughter on the shoulder. "You keep an eye on him. I'll check again after he's up. If he's not looking well, then we'll call the doctor, alright?" She got back on her feet and walked out of the room, leaving Angela alone with her brother.

Angela sat down on the bed next to Anthony and laid a gentle hand on his head. Through the softness of his hair, she could sense his brain's electrical impulses under her fingertips.

"She doesn't understand, Anthony," she whispered. "She doesn't know you're angry. That's why you're sick. Don't worry."

Anthony's fingers tensed in his sleep. Angela bent down to kiss his cheek.

* * * *

Marie sat down again with her magazine and tried to read. But as her eyes scanned the glossy pages, her mind was full of her children.

Several years earlier, Angela had begun talking about someone named Michael. Marie assumed she had created an imaginary playmate, but the fantastic stories about him continued, and Michael began to sound more like a cult guru than a child's imagination.

Marie felt her daughter lived in more than one world. Her dreams were incredibly vivid, her recounting of them filled with exacting detail. A year earlier, the seven-year-old had expounded upon soul theory at the breakfast table, explaining the process of reincarnation and the interconnectedness of souls. Interconnectedness of souls! Where had her daughter learned such words, much less been exposed to these concepts?

Her parents monitored her television viewing and helped Angela choose her reading material. They steered her away from C.S. Lewis and Madeleine L'Engle, suggesting instead Value Tales, Eloise, and Judy Blume books—anything to ground her in reality.

Anthony was a more down-to-earth child, incredibly normal compared to his sister. But this mysterious illness had struck so suddenly. Marie hadn't slept the previous night, anxiously imagining late night emergency room visits and mounting medical bills.

Marie pressed her face against the cool pages of the magazine. Why couldn't her children be ordinary?

*   *   *   *

Late at night, Angela crept into her brother's room. The blue nightlight on the bookcase illuminated her way across the floor as she stepped over building blocks and toy trucks scattered on the carpet.

Sitting down beside him, she put her hand on his shoulder and shook him awake. "Anthony," she called gently.

The five-year-old rolled onto his back and opened his eyes, looking up at his sister.

"I think I can help you," she told him

He propped himself up on his elbows.

Angela laid her hand on his knee. "Your soul is sick."

Anthony nodded in agreement.

"I know what to do," she reassured him. "Just keep looking into my eyes, without blinking. Okay? As long as you can without blinking."

Her brother complied, his eyes growing wide as he struggled to keep them open.

"Tell me what you see."

His eyebrows knitted together. So many shapes and colors danced across his sister's face in the dim light.

"Your face is purple," he mumbled. "Now it's green. Oh, you had horns, but they're gone. Now... You have funny spots, like a big cat."

"Okay, that's good. Keep doing it. Keep telling me what you see," she directed.

"There's a big swirly thing, red and purple, and some blue. You look like a frog," Anthony started to giggle. "Now you're all white. You look just like an angel."

Angela smiled. "Keep seeing that as long as you can. You can blink again."

Anthony's shoulders relaxed as he released the tension in his eyelids. He still could see the radiance of his sister's face, shining through the darkness. He felt very sleepy. He blinked repeatedly.

"Are you tired?" Angela asked.

"Yeah." Anthony sank down into his pillow.

"That's okay. Keep your eyes open as long as you can," she advised. "Then you can close them and rest, like you're going to sleep."

Anthony blinked, more and more heavily. He yawned as his eyelids slowly sank and stayed closed. His breath deepened.

"He's asleep," Angela said.

"Not quite asleep," Michael commented, stepping up behind her.

* * * *

"I don't understand," she said as Michael helped her into her bed, where Jasper was curled up waiting for her. "What happened with my brother?"

Michael pulled the blanket up to her waist as she leaned against the headboard. "He was carrying a lot of pent-up anger and hostility from past experiences." He sat down at the foot of the bed, and the cat brushed up against him. "Since he didn't have any outlets in this life, because he had made a decision against external violence, those energies were instead attacking the self, on the inside."

"I knew he was making himself sick," Angela said proudly. "What happens now?"

"He's going to sleep for awhile. He'll be tired. He'll take a lot of naps."

"Why?"

"He's recharging," Michael responded. "He let go of a lot of destructive energy that was hurting him. Now he has to fill up those holes again."

"But why was he so mad?" she complained. "He's only five. But he didn't like when I took one of his cookies after dinner."

Michael laughed. "It had nothing to do with cookies." Michael interlaced his fingers and pressed the tips of his thumbs together. "Anthony had some experiences in other lives that were never resolved. There were some things he didn't release. Sometimes, right before we die, we look back over our lives. And sometimes, like with Anthony, there is an uneasiness, unfinished business or a need for revenge. We may vow as we're dying that we're going to get that revenge, no matter what it takes."

"What for? What did he think he was going to do?" Angela asked.

"That doesn't matter anymore," he replied. "He had gotten that destructive energy stuck in his soul frequency—"

"What's that?" she interrupted.

"The vibration of your soul," he replied. "Every soul has its own vibration. Its own rhythm. Your brother's rhythm had gotten corrupted through holding onto emotions he didn't need anymore. So it sat inside, waiting, until there was a trigger in this life."

"So maybe it was the cookie," Angela suggested.

Michael smiled. "Okay, maybe the cookie. And maybe something else. But it's gone now. You helped him release that."

Angela glanced down at her hands. "How did I know what to do?"

He touched her chin and looked deeply into her eyes, radiating affection. "Sometimes Spirit works through people, to get things done."

"You mean, God?"

"Sure," he answered. "We're all Spirit anyway, but we forget. Sometimes someone opens up and Spirit can work through that person. Tonight, Anthony couldn't see me. That's not his path. But you were there. So it came through you."

"He said I looked like a frog!" Angela protested.

Michael laughed again. "That's a clearing process. He was seeing layers of himself, reflected through you, until he could get to a place of light. You were just a mirror."

"So, then," Angela said with a sleepy smirk. "He's the frog."

Michael smiled as she lay back into her pillow. He touched her brow lightly, and she yawned. "It's time for you to forget about me for awhile, little Angel."

She sniffed, fighting sleep. "Why?"

"There are some things you have to do without me," he explained gently. "But don't worry. You'll never be alone."

Angela blinked. She wanted to stay awake so he wouldn't leave, but her eyelids were growing heavier.

"You'll see me again, Angela."

She sighed and drifted off to sleep, her memories of Michael slipping away.

Chapter 22

November 1977

Phoenix, Arizona

Robin didn't know where he was from one day to the next anymore, and he no longer cared.

Imbolc had been on tour since February, with only a two-week break to recapture what was left of their sanity. Robin had lost count of the countries they had visited, though he was confident they had crossed the equator at least twice.

It had been eighteen months since they lost Joe in an automobile accident. Though they had never been easy companions, Robin still missed his friend. He was suspicious of Imbolc's quick recovery. After a month's hiatus to mourn, the band was back at work. Robin ignored the stone his stomach and tried to make their new bassist feel welcome. Every night on stage, he looked to his right, expecting to see Joe's red hair bouncing in rhythm with his bass guitar. Show after show, Robin was greeted by Allan's excited grin instead.

One day bled into another, no difference between day and night. Weeks and months passed, and he rarely slept in the same bed twice. Robin had expected a rigorous pace going in, but was wholly unprepared for the fantastic nightmare his world had become.

Newly divorced, George had transformed into an altogether different person, one Robin didn't much care for. He had become a true party animal, and there was an outright contest between George and Allan over who could bed more groupies before the year was out. The roadies wagered not only on the final score but on tallies for any given country or city, and they regularly preyed on the hopeful girls not chosen by Allan or George.

Robin couldn't bear the sight of either one of them, merely tolerating them at group meetings and other social events. One or the other was nearly always high or hung-over, and Robin couldn't get used to the endless stream of pretty faces passing through. Robin resented their behaviour, casting the band in a bad light and compromising the tour.

And the constant exposure to Danny was eating at him. It had been two full years since the affair, Danny's careless involvement with Alice. In the studio, Robin had put aside his personal feelings. Although convinced he had forgiven and forgotten, Robin still wondered if he were in denial. Out on the road, with the whole world turned round on its head, in such close quarters with the other lads, he was in a new level of hell.

He focused on the music, but playing the same sets over and over as they moved about the planet wore on him. He tried to reclaim the original passion behind each song, to infuse his vocals with genuine feeling and presence. In those moments, firmly within the music, with his feet beneath him, he clutched the microphone as his only lifeline, each note pouring from him as though it might be his last.

Concert tickets were not inexpensive, and he wanted to give fans in every city a show they would not soon forget. But as the tour dragged on, Robin found he was forgetting his own lyrics.

It was November, and he was somewhere in the American Southwest, drained and hollow. Tonight's show had been another personal disappointment, though the fans had gone home happy. After a few hours commiserating with Gareth at the bar in the hotel lobby, he was most certainly very drunk.

Pissed. Shit-faced. Three sheets to the wind. Robin entertained colourful descriptions of his current chemical state as he rode the lift to his floor. Hammered. Blasted. Wasted. At least Gil had reserved the same room numbers from one hotel to the next. No worries about forgetting. Shit-canned. Tipsy. Plastered. Gareth had come up an hour earlier to ring his wife, and it had taken Robin that long to regain his bearings.

Toasted. Sloshed. Lit. Sauced.

The others teased Gareth for being on such a short leash, given his frequent calls home, but Robin envied this strong connection. Though Alice and Robin had begun the year strong, the strain of the tour was felt on both sides of the Atlantic.

Alice had traveled with the group through Europe in April, and it had been absolute magic. With her at his side, Robin had felt invincible, despite a few awkward moments with Danny. They had made love every night and greeted each dawn together, as though the grueling tour schedule were a second honeymoon. When she had announced she was pregnant, his world was finally making sense in ways that both reassured and excited him. The tour would keep him away during her pregnancy and delivery, but he was certain he could work something out to honour professional obligations and also celebrate these personal joys. He was so thrilled with the bigger picture that the small details did not concern him.

Elated. Enthusiastic. Happy.

But then Alice had miscarried, at home alone, while he was so far away. Australia. July, just weeks after Imbolc had returned to the road following their short break. Alice and Rose moved in with Priscilla and her children. Robin's family was in London, and he was everywhere else.

Late nights alone in so many hotel rooms found the twenty-five-year-old convinced of his failures as a husband and father. Four months remained on this god-awful tour, and Robin was seriously considering running screaming into the deepest, darkest cave he could find once it was all over. If he could hold on that long.

Demoralized. Disgusted. Raw.

He wanted to get off this carnival ride.

The elevator doors slid open, and Robin stepped cautiously onto the green and almond carpeting of the hallway. He stood there, wavering, as he tried to remember where he had last seen his room key. Absentmindedly, he dug through his trouser pockets and ambled slowly toward where he thought his room should be.

Also wandering the hall was a small, slim girl with long hair. She appeared blurry; Robin squinted to get a better look at her. She walked patiently along, studying the room numbers, then doubled back. She stopped in her tracks when she saw Robin.

He blinked. His head was swimming. "You look lost," he said.

"Nope, I'm in the right place." She had a gentle smile, and her strawberry hair glimmered in the dim light. Robin thought she looked honest. "I'm just waiting."

Robin glanced at the doors on either side, not certain which was his. He looked back at the girl. She was about twenty, he guessed. "It's pretty late. Did you get locked out?" Maybe her girlfriend was in one of these rooms with Danny, Allan, or George, he thought to himself, while this faithful friend waits in the hallway. Trusting. Loyal.

He started to wobble. She stepped toward him. "Are you alright?" She reached out to steady him, but Robin regained his balance.

He straightened his spine and smiled slightly. "I'm afraid my ship has set sail."

She raised her eyebrows at his remark. "You're drunk."

"That, too."

"Do you need help getting to your room?" Her hands were on his elbow.

Robin was beyond making decisions. His throat was dry. His head hurt. It wasn't so much alcohol as pure exhaustion. Dead tired. Wiped out. Empty. "I'm not sure I know which is my room, to tell the truth."

"Let me see your room key."

She took the key from his fingers and looked at the numbers printed on the dark plastic. Robin stared down at his hands, still feeling her touch. Had the key been in his hands this whole time? What city was this, anyway?

"Here you go. Your room is right here." The young American tried to lead him a few doors down, but Robin stood his ground. She smiled up at him reassuringly. "It's okay. My name is Julianne. I don't bite."

He was touched by her sweetness. Warm. Welcoming. Present. He relaxed. "Sorry. I appreciate your help. I'm Robin."

"I know." Taking him by the arm, Julianne led Robin down the hallway and unlocked the door to his room.

Open. Vulnerable. Lonely.

* * * *

It was past 10 a.m., and Robin crept into the hotel dining room. He felt as though his skull were being bludgeoned repeatedly with an ice-cold sledgehammer. He spotted Gareth at a table well away from the windows and made his way over. Looking up from the menu, Gareth could see immediately that Robin was a nervous wreck.

He waited for his cousin to sit down, then handed him the menu. "What's the trouble with you this morning?"

Robin sighed heavily. "I've got to get off this damned tour."

Chapter 23

December 1977
Tulsa, Oklahoma

Alice was nearly frantic on the other end of the telephone.

After talking to her husband, Priscilla had handed the receiver to Alice, who hadn't heard from Robin in weeks. He no longer returned her calls. There were no more postcards from the different airports and hotels. He had ignored her telegrams.

It was late morning. Gareth sat at the small desk in his hotel room, doodling on the stationery as he talked to his cousin's wife, many time zones removed. Robin lounged on the bed and stared at the television, cycling through the channels over and over with the remote control. He tried to ignore Gareth's conversation with Alice.

"Is he alright? Is he sick?"

"Alice, he's fine. Really. He's fine."

"Gareth, you've got to tell me what's wrong," she pleaded. "This isn't like him. Can you go to his room and get him for me? Can you put him on the phone? Please."

Gareth cupped his hand over the receiver.

"You've got to talk to her Robin," he whispered. "It's two weeks to Christmas, and you know they're all flying into Dallas to spend the week with us. Stop torturing her like this. Talk to her."

Gareth held the phone out to his cousin, but Robin kept his eyes on the television.

"No," Robin responded firmly.

"Gareth? Gareth, are you there?" Robin winced at the tinny sound of his wife's voice emanating from the telephone.

Gareth returned the receiver to his ear. "Yes, I'm here, Alice. Sorry, minor interruption. I'm not going to be able to get him for you just now, I'm afraid. But I'll tell him you called…"

"No!"

He sighed. Gareth hated getting caught in the middle of what seemed a stupidly simple matter. "I'll talk to him, Alice. I promise."

Robin turned off the television and got up from the bed. He walked to the window and drew apart the sheer curtains just enough to peer down on the small park across the street. A light snow was falling. Indeed, two weeks until Christmas.

Gareth rang off. He drummed his fingers on the desk as he studied Robin's back.

"You realize you've invented this problem, Robin?"

"Not entirely," he responded flatly.

"You're not giving her a chance. You're making up her mind for her."

Robin turned away from the window and sat down on the bed. He pressed his palms down on his thighs, bracing against his own demons.

"I just don't know who I am anymore, Gareth," he said at last. "I've lost my grounding. I'm floating. Nothing feels real. I can't stand that."

Gareth relaxed in his chair and listened, even though he wanted to throttle Robin, to shake some sense into him.

"I've betrayed my marriage. There's no redemption for that. I can make the excuse that I was too intoxicated that night with Julianne to know what I was doing. But it was more than sex. She listened to me. She comforted me. And in the morning, when the alcohol was out of my system… Well, I don't have much of an excuse for that."

Gareth leaned forward. "I'm sure Julianne is a lovely person," he said gently. "But she was there waiting for you, for the rock star. She had an idea of what she was doing."

"No, it was more than that. She wants more than that."

"I thought you weren't going to call her."

"I wasn't, but that would just make me a bad person," Robin admitted. "We've talked a few times. I'm just not the sort who can have a one-night stand. I didn't think I was, but then there was that girl in Denver. I can't believe this. I don't even remember her name." Robin looked down at the floor and kicked his heels against the bottom of the bed.

"You want to know what I see?" Gareth clasped his hands in front of him. "I see a man away from his home and his family, working under strenuous conditions that have taken a toll on everyone. He hasn't been there for his wife and his child like he thought he should, and they haven't been present for him, either. In a moment when he was feeling a bit shaky, he accepted some comfort. He felt bad about it and so now has decided to plague and harass himself with more questionable behaviour, to prove to himself and everyone else that he is just as rotten a person as he believes himself to be. Don't make yourself into a self-fulfilling prophecy."

"Mmm," Robin responded.

"Robin, I'm not suggesting you lie to Alice, but you don't have to blurt it out the very next time you talk to her, if that's what this is about. Just talk to her, for the love of God. You'll know when it's the right time to tell her."

"She would never forgive me. I can't blame her for that."

Gareth was on his feet. "You don't know that, Robin. You can't make that decision for her."

Robin looked up at his cousin, towering above him, then slowly shook his head.

"I don't think you give Alice enough credit." Gareth knelt down in front of Robin. "She loves you. You love her. And you forgave her for the same transgression."

"Did I?" Robin's jaw tightened. He flexed his fingers to relieve the tension. "I thought I had. I thought I had let that go. But now, I just don't know."

Gareth sighed. "A marriage is not a contest, Robin. It's not about who loves the most, or how deeply you can hurt each other."

Robin buried his fingers in his hair. "I'm just so bloody tired. So tired." He closed his eyes against the tears.

Gareth rested a hand on his shoulder. "Why don't you go back to your room and get some sleep. We don't go on 'til eight, so you've got some time. Then you're going to call Julianne, and anyone else you need to, to say it's over. You won't be calling again. And you won't."

Robin looked up at him. "You make it sound so easy."

"It is that easy," Gareth responded. "Just get yourself through today. Everything will look different tomorrow."

Robin glanced away as he thought. He nodded. "Yeah. Okay."

"Good lad." Gareth smiled. "And then tomorrow morning, you're going to call your wife and daughter."

Chapter 24

January 1978
Washington, DC

Here I am. Capital city of the New World, Robin thought to himself as he walked along the frozen grass of the National Mall. Washington was not what he expected. It's much lower to the ground than I would have imagined, he finally decided, stepping onto the pavement approaching Jefferson Drive.

None of the others had cared to join him on this afternoon's excursion. Perhaps they had had their fill of American cities during the four months they had been touring the continent. But this metropolis was not at all like the "cities of sin"—as Gareth called Los Angeles and Las Vegas—they had experienced previously.

There was something different in the air here, Robin surmised, feeling a charge of energy snake its way up his spine. He crossed the street and hiked up the block toward the National Air and Space Museum.

* * * *

"Now, I want everyone to look around and make sure you have your partner," Mrs. Thompson announced loudly to her class of third graders. The twenty children were not paying much attention to their chaperones as they gawked at the exhibits and the crowds inside the front entrance of the museum. Angela's mouth hung open, gazing in wonder at the flying machines suspended overhead. She felt Lucy grab her hand.

"We're only going to spend an hour in here," the teacher continued. "And we're all going to meet right back here at exactly 2 o'clock. Make sure you stick with your partner, and be back here by 2. Alright?"

There was a vague murmur of agreement as the students filed into the expansive main corridor of the gallery. Lucy and Angela wandered aimlessly, dodging international tour groups and marveling at their many languages.

"I want to see Skylab," Lucy announced, spotting the space station. She lead Angela to the staircase. "My brother says you can actually walk through it!"

"That sounds neat!" Angela let go of Lucy's hand as they climbed the stairs. "What do you think it's like to live in space?"

"Well," Lucy began with authority, "you're weightless, of course. You have to eat out of plastic bags, so the food doesn't go floating all over the place."

"That would be messy," Angela commented.

"Yes. And you have to strap yourself down to sleep, for the same reason."

Angela imagined being strapped down. The image made her uncomfortable. "You mean, like wearing a harness or something?"

"More like a sleeping bag that hangs on the wall," Lucy explained.

Reaching the top of the stairs, they headed toward Skylab. There was a long line of people ahead of them.

"This is a popular exhibit," Angela said as they took their place at the back of the queue.

"The line moves quickly," Lucy reassured her.

* * * *

Robin pressed his way through the succession of Skylab compartments with the rest of the museum visitors. He was surprised the station was so small. It looked bigger from the outside, he thought to himself, but the equipment must take up a fair amount of space.

He couldn't imagine living in quarters so cramped. Being on tour for months on end was no treat, either. At least the scenery was always changing, even if the personalities weren't.

"I think I'd lose my mind in here," Robin muttered as he entered yet another tight, dimly lit section of the station.

The elderly woman ahead of him turned and smiled. "But just think," she said to him. "They were living in the stars!"

He nodded politely as they continued on. Emerging at last, he inhaled deeply into his lungs and released the air slowly, grateful once again for freedom of movement. He stretched his arms wide, nearly smacking another tourist in the face.

Hearing his stomach rumbling, Robin patted his ribcage. "Right. Lunch."

* * * *

Lucy was a wealth of information about the American space program, educating Angela about Skylab itself as well as life in space. Listening in awe, Angela was proud that her friend was so smart.

The pair stepped out of the station and into the main museum gallery. "I'm going to go into space one day," Lucy confided to Angela. "Only the Russians have sent a woman into space, and that was a long time ago. But NASA will change that. I'll even join the military if I have to."

"Do you think you'll go to other planets?" Angela asked, imagining her small friend in a bulky space suit with heavy boots and a big, gold helmet.

"Sure," Lucy replied confidently. "We've already been to the moon. We'll go to Mars next. Maybe like five years from now."

Angela nodded.

"What do you want to be when you grow up?" Lucy asked.

"I don't know," Angela shrugged. "There's lots of things." She thought of her flute lessons and imagined playing with an orchestra. Her face brightened. "Maybe I'll be a reporter for TV, and I can interview you about your space travels!"

"Yeah!"

Angela looked around. "I'm thirsty. Do you see a water fountain?"

* * * *

One principle instilled by St. Anthony's that Robin had never been able to escape—besides the rigid sense of honour and duty—was the ritual necessity of washing up before eating. It was an impossibility for Robin to sit down to any meal, even on a picnic or at a fast food restaurant, without first visiting a wash room. He had exasperated Alice on enough occasions looking for an available sink that she had started carrying individually wrapped towlettes in her purse.

But Alice wasn't here. The public restroom would have to do.

Although the wash room was crowded with men of all international descriptions, there was no queue for the sinks. Robin ran his hands under the warm water and washed the front and back of each, paying close attention to his fingertips. He rinsed off and looked for the paper towels. The dispensers were all empty, and he had never trusted those electric blow dryers. He shook the excess water from his fingers and wiped his hands across the front of his shirt.

Back in the main gallery, he stooped over the water fountain for a long, slow drink, enjoying the cool sensation that spread from his throat to his chest with each swallow. He was aware of someone standing behind him, but chose to take his time anyway.

* * * *

Lucy tapped her foot impatiently on the carpet and checked her watch. They had already spent half of their allotted hour in Skylab, and now they had to wait for this guy at the water fountain.

She looked at Angela and raised her eyebrows. "I guess not everyone is in a hurry, the way we are," Lucy said loudly, hoping the slowpoke in front of them would hear.

Angela tugged at Lucy's sleeve. "Maybe there's another water fountain," she suggested, beginning to walk away.

The man finally stood up and moved on. Lucy grabbed Angela's arm and pulled her back. "See? It worked," she gestured to the fountain proudly.

Angela smirked at Lucy and leaned forward to get a drink of water. But when she touched the fountain, she jumped back suddenly, shaking her hand vigorously.

"What's wrong?" Lucy asked in alarm.

"Shock!" Angela exclaimed. "It shocked me."

"Are you okay?"

Angela looked down at her fingers. "Yeah," she responded. "It didn't hurt."

Lucy stepped up to the fountain and cautiously touched the metal basin. Feeling nothing out of the ordinary, she reached for the spigot and depressed the button, starting the water flow. "It's okay now," she said over her shoulder.

Angela touched the fountain again and let the water run for awhile. She did not feel that same, sudden charge, but there was still a faint hum, deep within the metal. She shook her head, then bent down to drink.

Chapter 25

July 1979

Henley-on-Thames, Oxfordshire

Rose Michaels had just turned six. On summer break from school, she stayed home with her father while her mother went to work in Reading.

Alice was becoming a savvy investor. Using Imbolc royalties, she was building a modest portfolio that would eliminate Robin's accumulated debts within two years. Her own earnings went toward payments on the family's new country house.

Upon Robin's departure the previous October, Imbolc had disbanded, despite growing revenues and pleas from fans. Not quite twenty-seven, he was unofficially retired. Alice went to the office, and Rose went to school. With the house to himself, Robin sat around for the first month, bored out of his skull, before inventing household projects.

Allan and Gareth had formed a new band, Eclipse, and George was trying his hand as an independent producer. Robin sank deep within, floundering in shadowy doubts—the same pattern as before. But at least then he had had the fledgling Imbolc to give him grounding.

Robin was adrift, with no idea what to do with himself. Eclipse released a debut album, produced by George, to positive reviews and healthy sales. Imbolc's runaway success had astonished him, but Eclipse threatened to be even bigger. Had he made a terrible mistake?

All of his notes, instruments, and costumes had been packed away in a dark corner of the attic. Save for the upright piano in the living room, there were no artefacts to remind Robin of his former life. He was hibernating. He would reinvent himself, craft a new world and a new life.

Alice was again supporting him, despite Imbolc's royalties. He lacked motivation. He couldn't focus for more than a few moments at a time. He delved into world mythology and paranormal studies, then waxed cynical on the nature of man as related to the global petroleum market. He would build himself up with a brilliant new idea, another personal revolution, only to feel mired down again by impossible details the next day.

By late spring, he had painted every room of the house at least twice, experimenting with every colour of the visible spectrum, and he had re-tiled the kitchen floor. He studied international cuisine and treated his family's tastebuds to a new corner of the globe each week. Discovering he was a complete disaster when it came to household plumbing, he had gone to work in the garden instead, to get his hands dirty.

Robin had engineered a collection of themed areas in the yard, including the Green Man's vegetable patch, Rose's Sanctuary, Gwynevere's Butterfly Haven, and Morganna's Herbal Cauldron. Neighbours frequently stopped in to marvel at his amateur work and to accept the clippings and transplants he offered. Many suggested a new career in landscaping and even tried to hire him, but he always declined.

Robin sat in a folding chair outside the back entrance, admiring his efforts. He had pulled up what few weeds had sprouted and mixed in fertilizer where it was needed. Arms folded loosely across his chest, Robin breathed easily. He listened to the birds and tried not to think about what he might possibly do for the rest of the day.

Rose ambled from the house clutching a piece of notebook paper. She climbed into her father's chair, throwing her slender arms around his neck. Smiling, Robin welcomed her embrace. She pushed her face against his and gave him a sloppy kiss on the cheek.

"Ah, thank you," he responded gratefully. "What was that for, little Rosebud?"

She settled into his lap. "Because I love you, Daddy. Want to see what I drew for you?"

Rose waved the wrinkled paper in front of Robin's eyes. He caught hold of the drawing and held it up for them both to admire.

"This is lovely, Rosie," he commented appreciatively, recognizing the shapes and colours of the flowers he had planted in Rose's Sanctuary. A distinct, rocky outline loomed in the background. He ran his finger along the jagged range his daughter had drawn. "Are these mountains here?"

"Yes," Rose admitted. "I was tired of drawing clouds. Clouds are boring."

Robin smiled and tried to suppress a laugh. He loved having Rose home for the summer. It gave him someone to play with.

Rose pressed her back against his chest and extended her legs to twirl her bare toes. Robin combed through her fine hair with his fingers. Golden blonde at birth, Rose's hair had been so much like Alice's, but more recently was darkening, showing the vaguely auburn highlights she could only have gotten from her father.

She grabbed hold of Robin's hands and pulled them out of her hair. Rose rested her head against her father's torso and sighed. Robin closed his eyes and felt his daughter's breath move through him. There was nothing he loved more in this world than being a father. Sometimes, not even music, he thought to himself.

"Daddy?" Rose asked in her strong, little girl voice. "Would you tell me that story again, about the talking drums, from last night?"

* * * *

It was well-past Rose's bedtime when Alice returned home. She entered quietly, careful not to disturb the dimly lit household. She left her briefcase by the front door and made her way to the kitchen. She grabbed a cold sandwich from the refrigerator and took a few bites as she walked through the house. There was a single light on in the living room, illuminating Robin's figure as he leaned over the writing desk in the corner, tapping his foot in a steady rhythm and scribbling across the pages of his notebook.

Alice stood in the doorway and smiled. Her husband was working again.

She had missed him. While she was increasingly busy with work, Robin had channeled his restless depression into flowers and herbs. They had both been too tired to speak more than a few syllables to each other at night in bed, much less to touch.

She stepped quietly across the floor and stopped behind him. Resting her hand on the back of his neck, she felt his body relax into her fingers.

"What are you working on, Robbie?"

Robin stared down at the notebook and smiled. Leaning back in his chair, he looked up at his wife.

"It's a story," he responded, happily noting the pleasure in his own voice.

"A story? Not music?" Alice looked over his shoulder at his written words.

"No." He flashed his trademark, mischievous grin. "Rose's bedtime stories. We'd both grown weary of the standard story books, so I started making them up."

Alice smiled at the excited calm in her husband's eyes. "You're writing them down. That's good."

"She asked me today to tell her again the story from last night. That's when the idea struck me." Robin rested his hands lovingly on top of his notebook. "These are Rose's stories. I don't want to lose them."

"And there are other children who might like them as well."

Robin pulled Alice down into his lap, resting his hands on her hips. "Yes, there's that aspect, too."

"Do I get to hear the story?" Alice leaned closer to her husband and kissed him lightly on the lips.

"Mmm," Robin smiled. "You want me to tell you a story, Miss Alice?"

Robin wrapped his arms tightly about her, nuzzling her neck tenderly.

Chapter 26

20 May 1999
New York City
10:32 a.m.

"Cool." Robin spotted Mary K's grape iMac as they entered her office.

She sat down next to the computer and smiled at him. "I thought you'd get a kick out of this."

Robin leaned across the desk to get a better look at the iMac on the computer table. "Zip drive. Ethernet. Funky little mouse you've got there."

She laughed at the sparkle in his eyes. "Come on, Robin, if one of these arrived new in the box right now, you'd have no idea how to set it up."

"Nah, I'd figure it out," Robin reassured her as he took a seat. "But it would probably shut down the second I touched it."

"Is your multimedia shop an all-Mac operation?" Mary K uncapped her pen.

"Generally, yeah," he responded. "Mmm, we've got a couple, some other boxes. Our servers, they're running UNIX. I don't know the specifications. Ahm, I could have one of the technical folks get that information to you, if you need it for the article."

"Please. That'll fit nicely into how Robin Michaels is launching into the 21st century." Mary K scribbled a reminder to call Robin's office the next morning.

"Why did you choose purple?"

"Excuse me?" she looked up from her notepad.

He gestured to her iMac. "Oh, grape. Why did you choose that flavour?"

Mary K looked at her computer. "I don't know. I just like it. Is it important?"

Robin shook his head. "Not really. I just like that this kind of power is so common now, to the point you can even pick out the colour, like you're buying an automobile or a sofa, or an appliance for the kitchen. That makes me happy."

She held her hand over her mouth to suppress a laugh.

"Yeah. Giggle at me all you want, Mary Katherine," Robin admonished, pointing at her computer. "That's a good company there. Empowering people. Tools to interact with a world opening up more and more, after having been segmented and separated for so long. We live in a world seeking to embrace itself."

Robin felt the familiar, passionate tingling in his solar plexus. He leaned back and lifted his hands, punctuating his words. "Look at the music industry. Not too long ago, there existed these barriers, holding in the world's music, with very little exposure or cross-pollination. The Americans had American music. African music pretty much stayed in Africa," he touched the corners of her desk, emphasizing the distance. "The West had never heard of Tibetan overtone signing. But now it's like floodgates opening up, with so many incredible musical traditions pouring forth. That's huge!" He relaxed into the chair, his face charged. "You don't have to speak Swahili or Cantonese to feel the emotion in the singer's voice, to absorb rhythm and melody. What you'll find, as you immerse yourself, is that each individual has a voice. All across the globe. That's key."

"Right." Mary K nodded with a smile.

* * * *

Standing at the front of the room, Angela rested her hands on the table. "It used to be, if I were just an average Joe, probably working the land to eke out an existence," Angela speculated, "I'd get up before dawn, tend to the livestock, work the crops I'd be raising to feed my family and trade for goods like clothes and shoes... That would be my day. Every day, pretty much my whole life. Not a whole lot of choices. If my parents were farmers, I'd be a farmer, too, or maybe I'd be apprenticed to a local tradesman. Anything outside of that—wars on other continents, the discovery of new lands, new religions springing up, identification of planets—wouldn't have had much bearing on my life."

Angela rested her hands on her hips. "But today, there's almost this moral, Western imperative to know precisely what's going on everywhere all the time, and to take action on constantly changing facts and figures. There is no possible way to keep up. Information is the commodity of our age. And it's just exhausting!" She nearly laughed, defensively holding up one hand. "I know, it sounds like I'm lecturing."

The men around the table smiled. "Go on," Henry prompted her.

"Basically, what I'm saying is that we live in a world of choices. We're launched out onto this sea of opportunity, with the mission of being the best people we possibly can be, to leave the planet a better place than when we came into it."

"It's a good philosophy," Henry commented.

"Sure," Angela replied. "But where do you start? We're very privileged people, generally speaking, and one of our greatest treasures is choice. You don't have to go into the hardware business just because that's what Dad and Granddad did. You can be a nuclear physicist instead. Just because Mom taught third grade in Iowa doesn't mean I can't be a ballerina in New York or a journalist for CNN. There aren't a whole lot of rules anymore. While that's tremendously exciting, it's also pretty uncomfortable."

Catching her eye, Jeff broke in. "It used to be that professionals and workers across the board took a job right out of school and remained with the same company for the duration of their careers. There were exceptions, but that's pretty much how it worked. Nowadays, people not only switch jobs every three to five years—more often, sometimes—but they're changing careers completely several times over."

Angela flipped through her copy of their proposal as Jeff spoke. "Page twenty-seven," she said quietly to the group.

"Say I'm awash in a sea of confusing choices and infinite possibilities. I could be in my forties or fifties, still trying to figure out what—and who—I want to be when I grow up. How do I decide? Who's going to help me with that?" Jeff pointed to the open page in front of him. "This is the tool."

"Well, it's one tool," Angela commented.

Jeff looked to her and nodded, grudgingly.

"Yes." Henry glanced over the next few pages. "I remember this catching my attention. People looking for an outside definition of themselves, to provide a framework and boundaries for their lives."

Angela frowned. "Mmm, that's not how I see it. It's more about empowerment, a starting point for self-discovery. To make meaningful sense of myself as an unique person inside the larger world, a world that more and more seeks to embrace itself. And from there, seeing how I might best interact with and integrate into that world. To find and use my individual voice, my own song."

"You're both pretty much saying the same thing," Jeff suggested.

Angela squinted at him. "Not really."

* * * *

"So you can take that same concept, and look at it either figuratively or literally."

"I don't understand," Mary K said, frowning slightly.

"Okay." Robin leaned forward and clasped his hands together. "It's very much along the lines of that book you gave me on soul twinning. The idea of searching for wholeness. You can see that as an individual quest to integrate all aspects of the self, or as a more universal longing for wholeness—whole society, whole culture, whole planet."

"Whole soul," Mary K offered.

"Well, yeah," Robin admitted. "That's generally what it's been about for me. This isn't entirely new, of course. But the underlying theme of this current project incorporates these different levels—a hierarchy of unity and wholeness—the goal of completeness and how it motivates and shapes our feelings and actions."

"How are you bringing that into play?"

Robin scratched his chin and looked to the far wall. "Ah, I have no idea." He laughed. "No, I'm working on a couple of different avenues, incorporating some earlier work, you know, sampling my own songs, to give a snapshot of the entire journey. The journey up to this point."

Mary K stopped taking notes, letting the tape recorder handle the load. She rested her chin in one hand and looked admiringly at her friend.

"You're going to be making music on your deathbed, aren't you?"

"Mmm, yeah, probably." Robin paused to collect his thoughts. "I really love music. Not just from, well, a professional standpoint. Obviously. I mean, it has such tremendous power, to unlock so much within each of us. It can be quite effective therapy. It's completely intangible. You can't put your hands around it, yet music is something that's been with us from the beginning, the appreciation for and natural response to rhythm and melody. Very primal. It's incredible to me, a very powerful experience, to be living my life in exploration of this medium."

Chapter 27

May 1980

Henley-on-Thames, Oxfordshire

It was nearing 10 p.m. as Robin finished washing the dinner dishes. Rose had been put to bed, and Alice was in the living room waiting for him.

Anxious about a potential confrontation, Robin had busied himself with various chores, putting off Alice as long as possible. Even after their years together, he hadn't expected his marriage to be so volatile, but at least it wasn't boring.

Robin carried the dish towel through the hallway and into the living room, drying his hands as he approached his wife. She was on the sofa, her back toward him, tension visible in her shoulders. Stepping around behind her, he felt a mix of fear and excitement, as though he were traipsing along the open mouth of an active volcano.

"Robin," she began before he even sat down. "We need to have a talk."

"So you've said." Robin settled into an upholstered chair facing her, ignoring the space she had left for him beside her on the sofa. He would maintain a safe distance until he knew what was on her mind.

Alice folded her hands delicately in her lap. She pushed her long hair behind her shoulders and straightened her spine. "I want to know your concerns about scoring this film. I want to know where you are, to sort through what may be on your mind."

Robin smiled incredulously. "Is that what you've been so worried about?" He almost laughed. "You made such a big production about needing time with me, I thought you were going to tell me you or Rose had some terminal illness!"

Alice pursed her lips impatiently. "I'm sorry if I gave you any cause for alarm."

Robin leaned forward in his chair. "Alice, I'm happy to talk to you about this. I'm taking my time, weighing my options. We can go into that. But I need you to talk to me. You've got your defenses up about something."

She dropped her gaze, looking down at her hands. She had trimmed her fingernails after dinner and had cut them too short. Her fingertips felt raw and exposed. She pressed them against each other, testing the sensitivity.

"I need to know if you plan on working again, Robin," she said in a low, shaky voice. "Before, it was a matter of when. When you would go back. Not if."

She raised her eyes to meet his. Seeing his face full of sincere concern, Alice nearly burst into tears. Regardless of his faults, Alice reflected, Robin has always had an incredible aptitude for honest listening.

Alice smiled at herself. "You know, I really don't mind working. Yes, sometimes I resent being the only one bringing in any real money, even with your royalties. I didn't think I would have to work. When the band finally started doing well, I thought that was it. We were all set. But, I have to tell you, I like the strength my job gives me. While I dislike that you and Rose are dependent on me, you couldn't do this without me."

Alice brushed away the tears before they could spill down her cheeks. The saltwater stung her pink fingertips.

"I appreciate that you need time, Robin." She got up from the couch and took a deep breath. "You're a creative person. You're brilliant and talented. I'm just not like that." She coughed to stifle the rising emotion and began to pace the floor. "I don't understand that process, after all these years with you. I don't pretend to know what that's like for you."

She stopped to look out the back window onto Robin's gardens, eerily lit by a single lamppost. The yard was littered with his amateur sculpture, strange shapes and angles that didn't appear to represent anything in particular. Silent sentinels from another dimension, standing watch in the yard. Tonight, in the twisted shadows, Alice thought they looked more like the Horsemen of the Apocalypse.

"Sometimes I wonder what I've gotten myself into," she whispered.

"I don't know what you're wanting me to say to you," he said in mild exasperation. This wasn't the first time they'd had this conversation, and each repeated episode felt charged with ever deeper reserves of panic and anger.

Alice turned around to face him. "What is it that you want, Robin?" she demanded. "For the past year-and-a-half you have wallowed inside this cocoon. You try one thing, then another. First it was the house, then the garden. You started writing children's stories, and that was so positive. But you gave that up, too. And now there's this," Alice gestured to his sculpture garden outside. "I just don't know what you want, Robin. Yet I keep providing you space to work this out for yourself." She sighed. "I'm worried, Robin. I wondered if you'd ever pull yourself out of this. Then Reggie called—two months ago now—about working on his movie, and you still won't make a decision!"

Alice planted her fists on her hips and clamped her lips tightly, afraid to say any more. She looked up at the ceiling, avoiding her husband's eyes. She didn't want to see how her words had struck him. Still in her business clothes, her high-heeled shoes pinched her toes, and her calves ached.

Robin sank back into the chair and crossed his legs. She was right. He had taken advantage of this self-imposed exile for too long. His sabbatical, begun without any specific intention, had become a prison. He had no structure, no discipline. The generative passions were boiling over inside, with no external framework in which to create. She had named it. He was floundering, not thriving.

He cleared his throat. Alice turned her back on him.

"You want me to take this job," he said.

"I think it would be good for you." Alice looked down at her uncomfortable shoes. "It would be good for us."

"It would be good for me to get back in the studio," he agreed. His lungs felt heavy in his chest. He didn't like being chastised. He didn't like being told he was a bad little boy. But he also didn't like being the cause of tension in his own home. It was time to reclaim his life, although that's precisely what he thought he had been doing all along.

* * * *

Robin sat alone in the garden shed behind the house, still reeling. Alice had retired to a long bath and then to bed, after they were done with each other. He had even kissed her forehead and told her they would get through this, though he didn't know how. He had sat in the living room, listening to the water running through the pipes above his head. Somehow, he had gotten his body into motion, and had gotten out of the house.

He used to come outside at night to sit quietly in the grass and commune with the powerful energies he felt in the air. He even became nocturnal for a time, fascinated by the shift in consciousness. He had imagined harnessing the sleeping world's psychic vibrations and channeling them into his own creative work. Whatever work that might be.

Tonight, he sat on an upturned bucket and tried not to cry.

It was over. That terrible conversation. She had said what she needed to say, having held it for so long. He didn't ever have to hear that again. Now the healing could begin. He would spend this one night thinking, agonizing, integrating. And then he would forget, he told himself. Forever.

"Argh! God!" He kicked at the rakes and shovels leaning against the wall, sending his garden tools crashing to the floor.

She had been unfaithful to him. Again. It was years ago, but she had kept it to herself. Tonight, Robin's wounds were fresh. She had been so angry with him, leaving her alone while he went on tour. The grueling schedule had taken the band to all corners of the globe, and she had been jealous.

Jealous of his success. Of the attention paid to him, first by the music industry, then by the fans—the girls in particular—and at last, by the whole world.

At least when they had been struggling, she was his focal point. She was his support, his solace. And she had given him Rose. Alice had been the goddess of his world. He had needed her. But then the band's fortunes were changing. Desperation turned to recognition. She had been furious with him for succeeding, and she raged against herself for finding out just how badly she needed him. And she had told him none of this.

She was addicted to that lifestyle. She needed him to be who he was then, though she hated him for it. And now, she missed his rock star world. She missed being an insider floating on the periphery. She needed him to leap back in again.

Jumping to his feet, Robin lunged for his work bench, angrily sweeping the surface with both arms as tools flew across the shed. He kicked blindly at the paint cans in the corner, the colourful contents spilling onto the floor. He spun wildly, searching for something to destroy. He ripped at spare electrical cords. He tore the garden shears and several trowels from their wall mounts and threw them down, silently hoping to strike and injure himself. He wanted to do damage, to everything in sight.

Alice had been thankful for that miscarriage. Thankful! She had feared being further trapped in a marriage that produced so much turmoil. And she had worried the child wasn't Robin's.

"Aaaaaahhhhhhrrrrrrrrrrrrr!" He growled from the base of his spine, kicking out at anything and everything within reach.

Now he understood why she had been so accepting of his own confession of infidelity. Why she had wept with him when he broke down under his own guilt. Why she had wrapped her arms around him and kissed him, telling him everything was going to be alright. Telling him that she forgave him.

She had continued her own affair for a full year while he was away. And Alice had given him a name.

Terry Roberts. His former bandmate from St. Anthony's. The hapless bastard had finally taken his revenge on Robin for gracelessly separating from The Wombles, and for his success with Imbolc. Robin had broken up his band, so Terry had taken a stab at breaking up his marriage.

He sent his fist into the plywood wall. Robin stepped back and shook off the searing pain. As the blood trickled down his wrist, he examined his split knuckles and the deep gouges across the back of his hand. Soft tissue damage only. Damn. He wanted to punish Alice by hurting himself.

No, not Alice. God. He wanted to rage against God.

Robin collapsed over the empty work table, his knees giving out beneath him. He pressed his head against the wood surface, the desperate grief pouring out in strangled sobs.

* * * *

The approaching dawn found Robin hard at work. The yard had become a dumping ground for his tools and supplies. He had begun by pitching the smaller items out onto the grass from inside the utility shed, then dragged out the larger pieces, as many as he could carry at once. The sheer volume of what he had stored in that small space amazed him.

Robin leaned his weight into the workbench, inching it closer to the door. His tired muscles protested as he grunted with each breath, but he was grateful for the physical release of his aggressions. Once across the threshold,

Robin unceremoniously turned the bench end over end out into the middle of the yard.

Glancing back, he saw his footprints in the grass, the shape of his shoes imprinted in pink, yellow, and white on the crisp, green blades. He had stepped in the wet paint on the floor of the shed.

Robin ran through the plan he was formulating in his head. Reinforced walls. Generous storage capacity for equipment. A cooling unit was vital, and he would require significant electrical voltage. And soundproofing, of course. He had never constructed anything of the kind before.

He regarded the storage unit he had built with his own hands.

"Down it goes."

Running an electric saw from an outlet in the kitchen, Robin stepped carefully over the debris in the yard and deftly wove the electrical cord between the sculpted stones, preparing to rip into his precious shed, constructed just as impetuously as it was being destroyed. Before he powered up, he looked up to his daughter's bedroom window and considered the hour. Not wanting to disturb his sleeping cherub, he lay the saw down in the grass. He would wait until she was awake and off to school. No need to bother her with this madness.

His gaze panned along the upper floor of the house, coming to rest on the window of the bedroom he shared with his wife. Robin frowned.

"To hell with Alice," he muttered to himself. "I hope she doesn't sleep for a week."

Chapter 28

4 September 1982
New York City

Robin's head was pounding. Even with the curtains pulled closed, the shards of sunlight filtering into the sterile hotel bedroom pierced through his eyes into his skull like so many steak knives.

Glancing at the bedside clock, he made out that it was some time after 8 a.m. He pushed himself up to a sitting position on the side of the bed, resting his feet on the soft carpet. He held his head in his hands. Thirty years old and a day. He felt like an old man.

Larissa stirred on the other side of the bed. Rising to his feet, he fought the lingering effects of last night's party and slowly found his balance. The throbbing in his head was now joined by the urgent ache of his bladder, and his eyes burned.

Stepping carelessly on the clothing scattered about the floor, Robin headed for the bathroom. He deliberately ignored his bedmate.

* * * *

Robin stepped out of the shower into a small room of steam and tile. After drying off, he rubbed at the fogged mirror to look at himself. He rested his hands on the edge of the marble sink basin. "What the hell are you doing, old boy?" he asked his reflection.

He could hear her calling him from the living room of the hotel suite. He had come to New York City for many reasons. To help complete the final mix for the new Eclipse album, to meet with director Nathan Pratt to discuss a film scoring project, to give both Alice and himself some solid geographical distance.

He had been in the studio. He had had his meetings. He had even begun work on a few new songs dancing around his head. But somewhere along the way, he had become some kind of playboy, indulging a lifestyle of vapid decadence he had only vaguely imagined before. So here he was, shacked up with a supermodel, racing along from one mindless party to the next until dawn, awaking each morning or afternoon more bloated and hollow than the day before.

He looked deeply into the mirror, poring over every detail of his body. He hardly recognized himself.

Larissa was calling him again. He bowed his head in resignation and reached for the terrycloth robe on the back of the door.

Robin ran his fingers through his wet hair and padded barefoot across the taupe carpeting of the bedroom, stopping just past the threshold of the living area. Stark naked, Larissa stood by the kitchen counter, holding the telephone out to him.

"It's for you, Robin," the nearly six-foot nineteen-year-old said in her sultry, Southern accent.

He accepted the receiver reluctantly. "It's your wife," she whispered to him, kissing him softly behind his ear as she reached under his robe and patted his testicles. He flinched at her touch, immediately invaded by the sweet scent of her hair.

Robin held the telephone receiver against his chest as he watched Larissa saunter toward the bedroom, playfully tossing her long, blonde hair over her bare shoulder and slowly swinging her hips. Once inside, she turned and winked at Robin, then closed the door between them. He sighed in relief.

"Yeah," he said at last into the telephone.

"Robin." He could hear the tension in Alice's voice, accentuated by the gentle crackle of the transatlantic connection. There was a long, painful pause.

"Good morning," he said, alarmed by how low his voice had dropped.

"Who is she, Robin?"

An uncomfortable tightness spread across Robin's chest. He quietly wished for a sudden heart attack, anything to avoid this conversation. "Larissa. Larissa Troy." He nearly choked on the words.

"Ah, yes, the American fashion model," Alice's voice rasped. "We've seen photos of the two of you here in the papers. I just wanted to hear it from you."

Robin leaned his full weight onto his elbows on the countertop. "Right."

"How old is she again? Seventeen? Eighteen?" Alice was straining. "No, nevermind. I don't want to know."

"No, I suppose not," he replied quietly.

There was another long pause. Robin frowned, thinking of the mounting cost of this call. He heard Alice take a sharp breath on the other side of the ocean.

"Your daughter wanted to tell you happy birthday, Robin. She's standing right here. Thank God she didn't place the call herself. She didn't have to talk to that, that girl."

"Alice…" Robin picked up the telephone base and paced the floor, wandering as far as the cord would allow him to stray. "Alice, please don't do this."

"What? Me?" she exclaimed in mock surprise. "I'm not the one gallivanting about. Publicly! I have a child to raise, after all." Her voice caught in her throat. Robin maintained his silence as she coughed.

"Robin, I'm sorry," her voice softened. "We won't do this now. Here's Rose. She wants to talk to her father."

Robin leaned against the counter again, his face buried in one hand as he kept the phone to his ear. It was only his daughter's voice bridging the distance that kept him from bursting into tears.

"Happy birthday, Daddy!" Rose's greeting exploded into her father's head.

"Good morning, sweetheart. How are you doing?"

"I'm sorry this is a day late," she offered with sincere regret. "We tried calling yesterday on your real birthday, but I guess you weren't there."

He most certainly hadn't been. The past twenty-four hours were a colourful blur of various intoxicants and more parties. "Umm, no, I'm sorry. I wasn't here," he responded. "Some friends took me out."

"Oh." The disappointment in her voice sent slivers of guilt shooting up under his fingernails. "I hope you had fun with them."

"It was nothing to get excited about, Rosie." He forced himself to smile, to sound more cheerful. "I would have much preferred talking to you."

She giggled on the other end of the phone. That was easily Robin's favourite sound in the world.

"I know I have to ring off soon, because this is an expensive call."

"Don't you worry about that," Robin told her. "Just hearing your voice right now is worth everything I own."

"I miss you, Daddy," Rose said quietly, nearly whispering into the telephone. Robin imagined Alice's reaction, standing beside their daughter.

"I miss you, too, sweetheart," Robin said as he heard Larissa step into the shower. "I'm going to see you again very soon, alright?"

* * * *

The remainder of the weekend with Larissa was nothing more than a collection of tense and unsatisfying moments. She had distractedly flipped through magazines or watched television while Robin and Alice fought over the telephone, so he had started retreating into the bathroom with the phone and closing the door. Larissa pursued her own activities. Robin paid a handful of visits to personal acquaintances and spent hours wandering through Central Park and sitting in small coffee shops, pretending to read the newspaper.

Larissa was rarely in bed waiting for him in the evenings that followed, but she was always there in the morning. He frequently awoke to find her long, slender limbs wrapped about him, her head nestled against his chest. He would lie awake, listening to her breath rise and fall as she slept, feeling the warmth of her body against his skin. He wondered what affection they might possibly share, complete strangers in the same bed. Even in this emptiness, he was thankful he didn't have to wake up alone.

Robin had run out of work to do in New York. It was time to decide. Either he would remain in America to launch new projects and establish a permanent settlement abroad; or he would return home to work with old friends, the musicians and engineers he knew and trusted, and try again with Alice to figure out what to do.

Robin was only mildly surprised by Larissa's casual anger as she watched him pack up his belongings not even a week after the birthday bash she had thrown for him. Barely wearing a short sundress, she lounged on the bed while he shuffled around the room, retrieving a pair of shorts from a dresser drawer, a jacket from the closet, and a handful of socks from beneath the bed. She toyed with her thick, wavy hair and twirled her toes. He muttered to himself about where other items might be located.

"Did we send out any laundry this week?" Robin balled up a few shirts and stuffed them into his valise.

Larissa looked out the window at the grey afternoon sky. The forecast called for rain, but there was only darkness. "I sent out some things on Tuesday. I didn't realize there would be such a hurry." She examined the opal polish on her nails. "I'll make sure your items are sent to you in England."

Robin couldn't tell if she were truly upset with him or merely annoyed. While this had not been a deeply emotional relationship, they had found a kinship despite the difference in their ages. Even though he was returning home to his family, not knowing her thoughts at this moment disturbed him. Regardless, he wasn't sticking around to find out.

He checked his watch. He was right on time. He made another pass through the suite, scanning for anything he may have inadvertently left. All clear. Coming back into the bedroom, Robin closed his suitcase and sat down on the end of the bed.

"I won't go with you to the airport, if that's okay," she said, her arms crossed over her chest.

"No, I wouldn't have expected you to." Robin checked the inside pocket of his jacket for his airline ticket.

Larissa bit her bottom lip. "You'll be late."

"No, I've got plenty of time. Well, not plenty. But I'm on schedule."

"Well, thank God for that!" Larissa exclaimed, throwing her hands up in the air. He caught her gaze and held it for a long moment before she looked away.

Robin placed a hand on top of her bare feet. "Larissa, I don't know what to say to you. I honestly believe I would have lost my mind in New York by myself. You've been a, a wonderful companion, and I've enjoyed my time with you."

Staring at his hand resting on her feet, Larissa frowned at his practical tone, then looked up and smiled, wiggling her toes under his touch. "Yeah, it was pretty fun, huh?"

Robin returned her smile and gave her toes a squeeze. "Yes, it was." He got up from the bed and stood beside her, leaning down to give her a quick kiss on top of her head. "I'm on my way out now. Take care of yourself."

"Give me a call when you'll be in town again," she replied, touching his hand quickly as he stepped away from her and walked out the door.

Chapter 29

August 1984
Cozumel, Mexico

Angela's summer vacation was coming to an end.

She would return to St. Barbara's for her sophomore year of high school in September. Already done with her summer reading, she had brought Kurt Vonnegut's WELCOME TO THE MONKEY HOUSE to read again during her family's week in Cozumel.

Friday. One more day in this beautiful place before returning to Fredericksburg. Sitting in the shade of a few strategically planted trees on the beach, Angela scanned the watery horizon. Marie lay on a lounge chair reading magazines, while Anthony and Mark threw a Nerf football back and forth in the gentle surf of the Gulf of Mexico.

Beside her book, Angela had a journal ready for any insightful entry. She felt the sand shift underneath her beach towel as she drummed her toes. She pulled her knees up to her chest and wrapped her hands around her ankles, sitting alone in a quiet daze.

She felt her mind and soul out of phase with her body. Or perhaps it was just the opposite, she thought to herself, out of alignment all these years, only now assembled properly. Her fingers and toes tingled, and she could feel a steady current buzzing along the length of her spine. Whatever Raina had done to her, it was having a lasting effect.

The family had met Raina Marron and her husband on their first night at the hotel. During dinner, Raina had initiated a fascinating metaphysical discussion that had Angela spellbound. Hearing simple truths spoken with such confidence, Angela opened up like a sponge, wanting to absorb more.

The previous afternoon, Angela had come in from snorkeling to find her mother lying peacefully on the bed while Raina hovered over her. Grimy from sunscreen and salt water, Angela dropped her mask and fins and walked across the tile floor to stand beside her mother. Not looking up, Raina smiled.

"This is energy healing, Angela. Remember, we talked about this?" Raina lifted her hands from Marie's shoulders and placed them together on her solar plexus.

"Mom, are you sick?" Angela looked down into her mother's relaxed face. She had never seen Marie so serene.

"Not at all!" Marie laughed, her eyes closed. "Raina is a Reiki healer, and she has generously offered me this session with her."

"I'm really not doing much myself," Raina explained. "Just using my body as a channel, for the energy to flow through me into your mother's body. The energy goes where it needs to, to loosen tight muscles, heal any injuries, release any pent-up tensions or emotions."

Angela pulled up a wicker chair beside the bed and sat down, watching. Raina again lifted her hands and placed them on Marie's abdomen. She kept her fingers very close to each other, as if they were stuck together with crazy glue.

"Where does the energy come from?" Angela almost whispered, not wanting to interrupt.

Raina looked at Angela and smiled. "That all depends on your belief system." Her lips betrayed a wry humor, and she winked at Angela.

"Where do you believe it comes from?"

"I believe the energy comes from the God Source, the great reserve that powers the entire universe. This same energy holds everything together, the cells in your body, molecules, atoms, all particles of matter. I'm just harnessing that energy, and focusing it."

Angela crossed her arms, clasping her elbows. "How do you focus the energy? Do you have to do something special?"

Raina was pleased with Angela's interest. "Not really. There are symbols you can use, for some extra juice, or to send the healing to someone who is not present—distance healing. But really there's nothing to it. It's more about intention than anything else."

Raina moved to the end of the bed, placing her hands on Marie's knee and ankle.

"What kind of symbols?" Angela shifted in her chair to follow Raina's work.

Again, Raina smiled. "I'll tell you what, Angela. When I'm done with your mother, I can show you, if you'd like."

Raina and Angela had spent the remainder of the afternoon in this same spot where the fifteen-year-old now sat. Raina explained the history, theory, and mechanics of Reiki. The system was straightforward, simple, and yet so incongruent with the physical world. Although she had listened skeptically, Angela didn't hesitate to accept Raina's offer of training. She could judge for herself once she had this heat in her own hands.

Raina was a Reiki Master. She offered healing at the holistic center she ran with her husband in Arizona, and she only gave attunements to those she individually selected.

It was unusual for Raina to attune one so young, but she clearly saw the old soul in the youthful body, struggling with a difficult incarnation. She knew Angela needed to integrate her spirit to continue her life's work, even if Raina's own wisdom couldn't see beyond this immediacy.

After an early breakfast, Raina again led Angela to this quiet spot on the beach. They had spread several beach towels on the sand. Angela sat facing the ocean, her feet flat on the ground. The morning sun cast long, cool shadows across the beach as Raina knelt in front of Angela.

"I want you to close your eyes. Listen to the sound of the waves, and breathe deeply. Concentrate on your breath. If you find yourself drifting, bring yourself back by finding your feet." Raina touched Angela's bare toes. "Feel your feet against the soft towel. Feel the sand beneath. Ground yourself with your feet."

Raina placed her hands on either side of Angela's rib cage. "You can also bring yourself back to present awareness through the mechanics of your breath. Feel the air on the back of your throat as you inhale. Feel your diaphragm working as your lungs expand. Focus on pushing the air back out as your lungs deflate and rest."

Raina dropped her hands into her lap. "And listen. Don't forget to always be listening." Raina smiled and Angela giggled lightly.

"So while you're finding your feet and finding your breath, and listening to the ocean," Raina continued, placing her hands over her own heart, "I'm going to be passing the attunement to you. This will align your emotional and ethereal bodies with your physical body, just like we discussed."

Angela watched Raina's dark eyes intently. It was fascinating and exciting, this talk of spiritual energy and ethereal alignments, but it still sounded like science fiction.

"Let go of those gears turning in your head, Angela," Raina smiled as she looked deeply into the young girl. "Don't worry about what does and does not make sense. You've got the rest of your life to make up your mind about all of this. Right now, I need you to be open and receptive."

Angela took a deep breath and relaxed her shoulders.

"That's better. I'm going to place symbols in your auric field. This will open up your energy centers in a way you may not have experienced before. You may feel strange sensations in your spinal column, or in other areas of your body. It's a different for everyone. Some people have an entire past life regression during the attunement, and others feel nothing. Just accept your personal experience without expectation or judgment."

Angela nodded. Raina took a deep breath and smiled. "I'm ready to begin."

"Okay," Angela answered softly. She closed her eyes and brushed her hair away from her face, securing the long, red-brown strands behind her ears. She wiggled her toes, feeling the terrycloth towel and the warm sand beneath.

Angela was aware of Raina's movements around her, though she tried to stay focused on her feet and lungs instead. Raina pressed Angela's hands together between her own. Angela listened to the gentle rhythm of the waves rolling into the beach. She could hear Raina's faint whisper, then felt her breath as she blew on Angela's fingertips.

So where's the experience? Angela thought to herself. When I bite into a York Peppermint Patty, I get the sensation of a Reiki Master... No, stay focused.

Angela let go a quiet sigh. She felt the light pressure of Raina's hands on her shoulders. Her touch was warm, getting warmer. Hot. She felt as though the sun were shining directly into her spine. Her back was a solar panel drinking in the light and energy that Raina offered.

Then she saw colors. Against her closed eyelids, her field of vision exploded into a sea of vivid blues and greens, swimming with the rhythm of the surf. Her pulse quickened as electricity hummed through her body. Angela tried to keep her breathing steady and slow. She saw characters, elements of another language, fading in and out against the kaleidoscope of aquatic colors.

Her scalp tingled as Raina traced symbols across the top of her head. A light vibration traversed the soles of her feet and the palms of her hands. Angela stretched her toes, anchoring her feet, even as diffuse orange and yellow balls darted like fish in the blue-green ocean against the inside of her eyelids.

It was nearly 10 a.m. when they finished. Raina suggested that Angela walk alone for awhile along the beach, to ground herself and get used to having all of her bodies in alignment, moving together in phase. She also recommended that Angela spend some time practicing her symbols, tracing them in the sand.

Angela wasn't hungry when her family came to collect her for lunch. She felt spacey and disoriented. She couldn't think straight. Or was she thinking too much at once? She skipped lunch. Curling up under a beach towel even in the August heat, she slept. According to the watch in her knapsack, it was 3:37 p.m. when she awoke.

Her hands were on fire.

The heat had awakened her. Intense heat. She sat up and looked at her hands. They weren't flushed, and there was no pain. Yet Angela felt flames dripping from her fingertips.

Remembering to be mindful of her breath and her feet, Angela felt a warm quivering in her toes. She placed her hot hands gently on top of her head. The electric warmth spread across her scalp, down into her face and neck. A soothing vibration rumbled through her. She looked out on the water as she changed hand positions, squinting against the light reflecting off the sea.

Her first self-healing complete, she sat now with her tingling fingers resting on her ankles, still feeling the quiet pulse flowing through her. Though fully conscious, she felt she might drift off to sleep at any moment. She couldn't remember ever being more relaxed, yet she was also about to jump out of her skin.

Angela released a deep, sighing breath and closed her eyes, listening only to the waves rolling into the shore.

* * * *

She sat at a picnic table by a beautiful blue lake. The sun was shining, and she could hear birds singing in the distance. Instead of worrying about sunburn, she felt energized by the sunlight. One by one, blurry figures of muted colors approached from behind, walked around the table, and sat down facing her. Some were more vivid than others. Each smiled and in turn expressed genuine gratitude, then got up from the table and walked down to the water's edge. As they stepped in, the figures melted into the water, the colors gradually dispersing as they blended their beings into the lake, one by one. Angela climbed on top of the wooden table to watch them. The table wobbled and creaked under her feet, but she wasn't concerned about falling. Angela had excellent balance.

"Oh! I see what you're doing!" she exclaimed as the last figure melted into the water.

The sound of her own voice awakened her. Talking in her sleep again.

And again, her hands were on fire.

She fumbled in the dark for her watch. It was just after 2 a.m. She could hear the deep, sleeping breath of her brother across the room. Angela pulled on a sweatshirt, tiptoed to the door, and made her way to the beach.

She stood expectantly on the shore, out of reach of the water, her hot hands pulsing. She shook her head at the crazy idea that something had called her here, that something in the water needed her healing. She was nervous about wading into the ocean alone at night, but she couldn't shake the pull she felt, drawing her into the surf.

She stepped into the gently breaking waves, the water lapping up around her knees, splashing her pajama shorts. To control her pounding heart, she took several deep breaths. She stretched her arms out to her sides and opened her chest, trying to purge whatever was beckoning her. Looking up into the heavens, Angela felt the warm release of tears on her cheeks. Her mind and body relaxed. She traced three symbols in the water—to open as a channel for healing, to promote emotional and psychological release, and the third to enable distance healing.

She waded deeper, feeling the water soak into her clothing as it came up to her waist. She drew in her arms and rested her hands over her heart, whispering a spontaneous prayer. "God, make me an instrument of your grace. Send this energy through your healing waters. Great mother ocean, we come to your shores to heal our wounds. In your deep blue depths, I am home, I find release. Mother mother, wash me over."

Her palms lightly touched the surface of the water. She smiled at the tickle of the ocean's rhythm against her skin. She closed her eyes and felt the energy build.

In a tremendous flash, a great wave of lightning coursed through her body, entering simultaneously through her head and feet, meeting in the center of her chest and shooting out through her hands into the water. Though nearly knocked off her feet, she was held in place by an invisible force. She expected to see the water glowing around her, but all was still. Her entire body was pulsing. She was a conduit, pumping the energy into the water from... from somewhere.

"Robin." She heard her own voice echo in the chamber of her skull. She frowned, her mind racing, but she was interrupted by a surprising response: "I am here." The answering voice was gentle, confident, masculine, and definitely not American.

"Robin." The name again resonated within her. Another wave of energy swelled, and as it spiraled through her spine, she saw a face, softened by red-brown hair, a piercing pair of brilliant green eyes gazing out at her. She wanted to reach for him, but as the last surge ebbed out through her fingertips, the image was gone. All she could hear was the sound of the surf.

The rise and fall of her breath matched the rhythm of the waves. She was in a daze, trying to pull back into focus. Slowly, she turned away from the night's horizon and walked through the cycling salt water toward the shore. Soft sand sticking to her wet skin and clothes, Angela sat down a few feet from the water's edge and looked out again where the sea met the sky. She rested her elbows on her knees and laughed.

"There is a song," Angela smiled, speaking to the stars. "There is a song in me, but I don't know how it goes."

Chapter 30

August 1984
Corazón de la Paz Resort
Playa del Carmen, Mexico

Robin's life was in shambles.

Standing on the shore, under the scintillating canopy of the clear, star-lit sky, he felt incredibly small. Warm waves lapped gently over his toes. Robin stood on the threshold, not quite sure what lay on the other side.

He had run away to Mexico. There was no solace for him at home.

They had celebrated Rose's eleventh birthday on July 11, just the three of them, at her favourite Italian restaurant. Robin and Alice had hardly touched their food, while Rose devoured her spaghetti and meatballs. She talked enthusiastically about her summer activities, which boys liked which girls, and the coming school year. She had blown out a candle propped precariously in a scoop of strawberry ice cream. Robin and Alice had spoken few words to each other, the silence not altogether uncomfortable.

After dinner, her parents kissed her and sent her off to bed. Alice retired to the master bedroom; Robin had slept in the guest room. Rose's dinner was the last family function they would attend together.

Robin was spending half his nights at the studio, mixing his latest solo album, PRISM. There was so much emotion he finally let spill out into his work, threaded together by the ever-present turbulence beneath the surface. He didn't know where he felt more raw and vulnerable—at the studio, or at home.

He worked long hours. When he woke in the morning—often on the studio floor—his first thoughts were of the album, once he had banished the hallucinatory sprites of the night's dreams. His diet consisted almost exclusively of coffee and the spoils of the ground floor vending machines. He frequently skipped meals—either through forgetfulness or sheer obstinance—and he was losing weight.

Alice seldom caught sight of her husband at home. He kept odd hours and often stayed away for days. When she did see him, she was astonished by the pale wraith he had become.

Rose visited her father in the studio nearly every afternoon. She made cassette copies of his reels and finished tracks to listen to on her new walkman, and she made her father go out walking with her, to get him outside in the sunlight.

Toward the end of July, Alice came to see him.

She had arranged for the moving van to relocate Rose and herself to a flat in London. They had already been over the separation agreement, the schedule of visits with their daughter, and the division of the household. Still, Alice fought back nausea as she gave her husband her new address and telephone number in the city.

Robin looked at the piece of paper she had put down in front of him on the mixing console. He saw her handwriting, the numbers, the name of the street, but he couldn't make sense of it. The roar in his head deafened him, protecting him from anything Alice might say. He brought a weary hand from his lap and touched the paper, tracing the ink that spelled out his daughter's new home. He dropped his hand back into the chair.

His hands clasped between his knees, Robin lowered his head onto the console, resting his brow on the sliders and knobs.

Alice couldn't stand to see him so drained, so defeated. She thought he might burst into sobs, but he remained silent. She looked out the window. A gentle drizzle had begun. Alice held her hand against her mouth, forcing back the tired arguments, desperate compromises, curses, and pleas she felt welling up inside.

Robin had not moved. Closed eyes, shallow breathing. Alice reached to touch him, running her fingers lightly across the back of his head, knowing this would be the last time she felt the softness of his hair. His spine relaxed. His breath deepened. Within minutes, he was asleep.

Robin awoke, alone in the studio. Night had fallen, and the building was deserted. The other artists and engineers had gone home to their families. On his forehead, he felt the indentations of the sound board controls. Finding his family's new address and phone number still on the console before him, he folded the paper and slid it into his back pocket. After a quick trip to the bathroom and a disappointing visit to the vending machines, Robin went back to work.

* * * *

On August 10th, Robin returned home.

He had spent the entire week living in the studio, immersed in his work, producing less than satisfactory results. He had enjoyed dinner with Rose the evening before, cleaning himself up as best he could for her sake. When he dropped her off at the house afterward, he declined her invitation to come inside. From his car, he watched her walk through his own front door. He sat there longer than he realized, looking at the closed door and surveying the light coming through the windows. Finally, he spied Alice's figure looking down on him from the master bedroom. They held each other's gaze for a long moment before he shifted the car into gear and slowly drove away.

The next afternoon, Robin stepped across the threshold into an empty house.

He dropped his bag on the bare floor just inside the front door and walked into the living room, hearing the hollow echo of each step now that most of the furniture was gone. Alice had left the older of the two sofas they had owned together. There was a single upholstered chair, two half-empty bookcases, and an antique side table. She had arranged the remaining pieces for him, even laying down the area rug from the guest bedroom. He spotted the stereo cabinet, complete with all of its components, standing next to the television on a small work table.

He walked slowly from room to room, surveying the depletion of his home, all according to the massive lists they had drawn up to divide everything as fairly as possible. While he mentally ticked off each item, nodding in agreement with Alice's handling of the disbursement, his heart was stunned into silence. Numb. The walls were now bare, save for a few pieces of artwork from his family. In the upstairs hallway, Robin paused before a drawing Rose had made when she was seven: the brilliant sunrise she had seen in her mind's eye when she had heard her father's song, *Morning Kiss*. He touched the frame delicately, pretending to adjust it. He caught his reflection in the glass, a shadowy visage cast over such a beautiful scene.

Rose's bedroom was completely empty.

His last stop was the master bedroom. He stood in the doorway, not daring to cross. Alice had left nearly all of the bedroom furniture. Their dresser, their wardrobe, the laundry basket. She was starting a new life, and she wouldn't want the emotional baggage. He looked at the bed they had shared. The night table from her side was missing.

He sat in front of the television, completely oblivious to what he was watching as he ate Chinese take-away from the carton. There were a few lights on in the house, but he sat mostly in the dark. He probably would have gotten drunk, but in this confused fog the thought never occurred to him. The thirty-two-year-old had been a bachelor for all of four hours, and he was desperately addled.

Sitting in a folding chair just a few feet from the television, Robin picked mindlessly at the lukewarm chicken and broccoli and drank flat soda from a jar. Absorbed in the flickering eye candy on the screen, he was comforted by the vague shadows on the walls of the sparsely appointed room.

A familiar sound echoed through the house, and he was slightly alarmed it took him a few moments to recognize the ring of the telephone. He hurried to the kitchen and picked up the phone.

"Hello...?" he answered tentatively.

"Dad?" It was Rose. "I wasn't sure you would be at home. I rang the studio first, but you weren't there."

"No, I'm here sweetheart. I'm ho—.... I'm at the house."

"I'm sorry I didn't get to say goodbye before we left. There was so much to do, and we were helping load the furniture and boxes. But we're in the new flat now. Mum says I can paint my room any colour I'd like."

"Of course you can, Rosie." Hearing the simultaneous dread and excitement in her voice, he felt the skin tighten across his brow. She sounded so far away.

"Did you get something to eat?" She was worried about him, all alone in the house with no one to look after him.

"Yes, all taken care of. You needn't fret over me. Dad will be alright. So you're settling in, then?" He leaned against the kitchen counter and looked through the window at the dark night outside.

"Yes. I thought it would be a tiny place, but it's not. My room is great! I have a window over a small garden. And we're just two blocks from the tube. It's such a big city, but everything seems so close. I wish we'd always lived in London!"

Wincing, Robin sniffed at this comment, unintentionally disrupting his daughter's enthusiasm.

"I miss you already, Daddy." Her voice was softer now. Robin pictured her winding the telephone cord between her fingers, as she had always done.

"I miss you, too, Rosie." Robin fought the threatening break in his voice. "I suppose I'll have to get used to living alone for awhile."

There was a great gulf of silence, neither father nor daughter knowing what to offer in comfort to the other.

"Once I get more settled myself, you'll be coming back to visit, and I'll come to the city to see you. It won't be so bad."

"Right," Rose responded more cheerfully. "Mum's in her room putting her clothes away. Do you want to speak to her? I can put her on for you."

"No. Not tonight, love. It's late." Robin had no idea what time it was, but he didn't want to subject Rose to further strain. "You run along and finish unpacking. You're going to have a great time in your new place."

"Alright, Dad. I love you." There was a smile in her voice as she said this, the words he most needed to hear from her.

"I love you, too, Rose. Thanks for ringing your old man."

Robin rang off, walked into the front hallway, and lay down on the floor, within sight of the overnight bag out of which he had been living for the past week. Listening to the muffled sounds of the television, he stared at the chandelier directly above. He studied the facets of crystal, the curves of metal, shutting out all thought as he mentally traced the many pathways within, without, and through the light fixture.

Robin was greeted by the morning sun reflecting off the chandelier, sending shards of broken light into his face. He picked himself up off the floor, grabbed his bag, and walked out. As soon as he had reached the studio, too early on a Saturday for anyone to be about, he picked up the telephone and called his travel coordinator's home number.

How long ago had that been? Days? Weeks? Robin had at last emerged from his stunned stupor and discovered himself on a rustic Mexican resort property called Corazón de la Paz, outside of Playa del Carmen on the Yucatan Peninsula. He had been dozing on a beach chair under a thatched parasol, facing the crystalline water of the Gulf of Mexico. Sipping chilled fruit punch, he was suddenly clear, enjoying this anonymous refuge from the turbulence he had left behind in England.

There were no phones at Corazón de la Paz, no way for anyone to reach him. Not his producer, not his manager, not Alice, not Rose. No old flame would catch him off-guard, hearing the news of his marriage's demise. No tabloid reporters would prey on him in this raw state, desperate for some juicy comment.

But now, standing on the beach in the wee hours of the morning, Robin was consumed by anxious emotion, having gained an unreliable edge of clarity through geographical distance.

He felt the soft, white sand between his toes. He thought on the lyrics to his own *Ocean Fever*:

Walk me down to that ocean, feel the sand shift under my feet
I can feel that fever chill, taste the salt breeze so sweet
Captured eyes ever wandering, scanning the distant horizon
What calypso gaze might mine meet?

Mother, mother, wash me over
My anxious moments your love replace
Cleanse me of my conscience
Let me drown in your embrace

A shiver rushed up his spine as the melody in his head mixed with the sound of the Mexican surf. Singing quietly to himself, he waded into the warm water, letting the ocean soak through his clothes to his skin.

"Fight the good fight, only to surrender to an uneasy peace," he sang in a whisper, feeling the wet sand below the surface squish under his feet. He waded in up to his hips. "Push on against the wall, where whispers become pleas."

Loosening his knees, he moved his body with the rhythm of the waves, feeling the gentle pull of the waning tide. "Run away, I come to your shores to heal my wounds. In your deep blue depths, I am home, I find my release."

Robin looked up into the perfectly clear sky and laughed aloud. He saw a shooting star and made a wish: May I indeed find that release. His hands relaxed at his sides as he sang, full-throated, to the heavens above. "Mother, mother, wash me over. My anxious moments your love replace. Cleanse me of my conscience. Let me drown in your embrace."

He surveyed the watery horizon as he whispered again, "Let me drown in your embrace."

The music gradually faded from his consciousness. All he could hear was the surf. He was chest-deep in the water, the waves rocking him back and forth, back and forth. He closed his eyes and bent his knees, letting the water touch his chin.

"What if..." he said silently.

"Let me drown in your embrace," the surf whispered back.

It was so tantalizing, so close. He could surrender, he could release. Everything that tormented him lay far away on a distant shore. The stars sheltered him. He was safe in this darkness. As long as he was in the water, he would have peace.

Robin sank even deeper, tasting the salt on his lips, feeling the sting in his eyes. The water in his ears distorted his hearing as each wave lapped over him. "Great mother ocean," he murmured, his entire body relaxing into this warm, wet embrace.

A bolt of lightning shot through his body. He stood immediately upright in the water, trembling. Every nerve ending was on fire, but there was no pain. He looked to the sky, perfectly calm. No storm brewing. This staggering surge again pulsed through in steady rhythm. Had an electric eel brushed up against him? Every cell in his body responded, opening up to receive this incredible vibration that encompassed him. It was coming from the water itself.

In a flash, he saw the girl's face. He was in her presence. Without moving a muscle, he touched her warm, brown hair. He felt her breath. He heard her voice: "Robin." He gazed deeply into her emerald-green eyes. He was engulfed in pure, white light, penetrating every pore. An electrified peace settled over him. He forgot everything. He had left the ocean behind and was swimming in energy.

Before he could make sense out of what was happening, he found himself back on the shore, collapsed on the sand, coughing up salt water. His lungs and sinuses burned. He lay down in the sand, the grains sticking to his wet skin, clothes, and hair in a protective layer. He looked back up at the sky, unchanged from moments before.

"What in God's name was that?" he demanded from the stars. He received silence in reply. "Yes, that's it exactly," he said to no one in particular as his mind raced ahead.

Sitting up, he dug into his pockets and found only soaking wet pieces of scrap paper. He tried to shake off the sand as he struggled to his feet, then ran through the darkness back to his cabana. His notebook was waiting on the desk, with a sharpened pencil ready beside it. He threw open the windows, filling the room with the sound and smell of the nearby surf.

Taking a deep breath, still dripping wet, Robin sat down and wrote *The Voice*, his love song to Spirit.

Chapter 31

19 August 1984
In Transit

Sunday. Time to go home.

The Harris family reluctantly packed, enjoyed a casual breakfast on the hotel veranda overlooking the water, and then boarded a small plane back to mainland Mexico. The four now waited at the departure gate in Cancun, on their way to Miami.

Anthony and Mark were restlessly bored, playfully wrestling each other in the plastic chairs as they invented ingenious new card games. Marie smiled sleepily as she watched them. Anthony looked so much like his father, both tanned to a golden bronze, while she had freckled all over.

With two flights still ahead, they would be home for dinner.

Marie reached an arm around Angela, who sat reading beside her. Pulling her daughter closer, Marie kissed her on the forehead. Engrossed in her book, Angela was barely aware of Marie's affections.

"I thought you had finished your summer reading," Marie commented.

"This is one I want to read." Angela turned the page and hunched down. She had been deliberately distant and disconnected since her strange experience in the water. Safely sequestered within her book, she wouldn't have to think about it until she had some quiet time to herself.

"We'll be boarding soon," Marie said more to herself than anyone else. "I can't wait to sit down and just sleep for awhile."

Angela grunted in response, sitting cross-legged in the hard, plastic seat.

* * * *

In the Cancun airport, Robin stepped away from the coffee stand, taking a moment to shove his change into his pocket. He wasn't sure if he had just been ripped off, as he couldn't remember the exchange rate between pesos and pounds. He was grateful for the lukewarm coffee and stale pastry, having eaten nothing the previous day as he sat at his desk, furiously composing. He would sound the song out properly in the studio. He was looking forward to going back to work.

He had not yet considered his electric experience in the ocean. He would think about it when he got home. As it was, he had rolled out of bed and barely gotten all of his crap in his bag in time to leave for the airport.

Not looking where he was going as he balanced his pastry on top of his styrofoam cup, Robin stumbled and splashed a small puddle of coffee onto his shoe. He caught the danish just before it landed in the lap of a well-tanned man sitting with his son.

"Sorry about that," Robin mumbled, offering a weak smile and avoiding the other man's eyes.

"No problem," the stranger responded distractedly before returning to the card game he was playing with his son. "Anthony, you can't do that, and you know it."

Robin found an empty seat close to the gate's main door. He would be the first person on the plane if it killed him. He would strap on his sleeping mask and bury himself beneath a blanket. He would wedge his body against the window before anyone else was onboard, turning his back on the world and dropping out.

"Good morning, ladies and gentlemen, and welcome to American Airlines flight 445, service to Miami," the attendant's voice came across the loudspeaker. Robin was out of his seat and at the head of the queue before she had finished her first sentence.

"First Class?" she said to him with a smile.

"Yeah." Robin handed her his rumpled ticket. He crammed a napkin into his empty coffee cup and tossed it toward a small wastebin by the door. He missed.

"I'll get that for you, sir," the attendant said pleasantly. "You're in seat 3D this morning. Have a nice flight, Mr. Michaels."

Robin hurried through the door and onto the plane, not waiting around to find out if that woman—or anyone else—had recognized him.

* * * *

"Thank you for waiting, ladies and gentlemen. We are now ready to begin general boarding for flight 445 to Miami."

Marie roused her family from their seats, made sure everyone had their belongings, and herded them toward the growing line at the gate. Angela was still reading.

"You'd better watch where you're going with your nose in that book all the time," Marie chided.

"Mmm," was her only response.

Mark handed the boarding passes to the attendant at the gate. "All four of you together?" she asked blankly as she counted. "You're seated together in row 23, seats A and B, and seats E and F."

It was a full flight. People pushed their way onto the plane, trying to secure various pieces of luggage and sombreros in the overhead compartments. Marie smiled at the man in First Class, already zonked out as everyone else paraded in. She hoped to do the same as soon as she sat down.

* * * *

The Miami airport was a zoo. Angela guessed the entire population of the Western hemisphere must be returning from vacation, all routed through the same Miami terminal.

Mark and Marie had gone ahead to a fast-food restaurant across from Gate 6, where their plane to Washington, D.C. would board in another ninety minutes. Angela paced in front of the newsstand, waiting for her brother to come out of the men's room. She looked at the magazine covers and scanned newspaper headlines without registering what they said. She stared absently at the tabloid journals, laughing that people took such publications seriously. She read the story titles and smiled.

"Alien babies," she said, quietly amused.

She looked over her shoulder again for her brother, but there was no sign of him. He had gotten sick on the plane. He probably needed some time to clean himself up.

Angela turned again to the news rack. She was stepping toward the major U.S. newspapers when one of the tabloids caught her eye. There, on the end of the rack, was a face she recognized. There were those same features, that brown hair, those eyes. Angela froze. It was the man she had seen in the ocean.

"Calling It Quits: Robin Michaels and Wife Split for the Last Time."

"Robin," Angela whispered in disbelief.

She felt a tap on her elbow. Startled, she spun around to find her brother standing next to her.

"Okay, let's go."

She just stared at him, her mouth hanging open.

"What? Did I scare you?" Anthony laughed at his older sister.

"No, I just..." Angela stammered. She looked back at the magazine, then turned to Anthony. "It's nothing. Let's go. You feeling better?"

They had walked no more than a few yards toward the gate when Angela asked her brother, "Anthony, who's Robin Michaels?"

Anthony frowned. "I don't know. That new kid who moved in down the street?"

* * * *

Robin stopped at the water fountain between the restrooms. God, this place is a nut house, he thought to himself as he watched the throngs of people moving past. Spotting a newsstand, he plunged through the streams of human traffic and somehow made it safely to the other side. He grabbed a soda from the refrigerated shelves and picked up a Snickers bar. Not the best lunch, but he needed to get something into his system. Besides, he knew he would be well-fed on the British Airways flight to London.

Standing on queue at the register, Robin took stock of the world's news, broadcast across so many front pages and glossy covers. Scanning the tabloids, he was stunned. There, on the front of THE UNDERCOVER PLANET, was a photo of himself with Alice and Rose.

Oh, God, not Rose, he agonized. He was immediately nauseous, almost dizzy. He had never gotten used to these invasions of privacy, even if this vicious dribble was the price of success. But now they had plastered a photo of his daughter across the front cover, with copies being sold in who knew how many languages worldwide?!

"That will be $1.49," said the young man behind the cash register.

Robin was oblivious, gaping at the photo and accompanying headline.

"Sir?"

Robin looked up at the youth. "I'm sorry. How much did you say?"

"It's $1.49 for the drink and the candy bar," he repeated.

"Right." Robin dug into his pockets and deposited the contents onto the counter. He had produced a mixture of international currencies and hurriedly sorted through the coins and paper bills to find the proper combination in U.S. dollars.

The cashier laughed. "You must travel a lot, huh?"

"Mmm. Yeah," Robin responded distractedly. By some miracle, he had the exact amount in the proper currency. He handed his money to the cashier, collected the rest from the counter and stuffed it back into his pocket. He picked up his drink and candy and stepped aside for the next person in line. And he stared a few minutes longer at the paper.

"At least the photo is good and fuzzy," he muttered. Anyone outside their close social network would have a difficult time recognizing Rose from that photo.

Turning away from the newsstand, Robin was again pulled along the corridor toward the departing gates. He wondered what headlines might be waiting in London. It was precisely this sort of thing that had him flee the city in the first place, to take a country home to protect himself and his family from the constant media attention.

Absentmindedly, he fell into step behind an adolescent brother and sister, no doubt American. He wondered why the world was interested in him anyway. There were plenty of other people to spy on, people ever more fascinating than himself. He knew Alice and Rose, in their London flat, would no doubt see these same papers everywhere.

The American teenagers in front of him veered left into a McDonald's restaurant. Jarred, Robin watched as they were absorbed into the fast-food feeding frenzy. He was struck by the girl's hair.

"Wait a minute." There was something familiar about her hair, if she would only just turn around so he could see her face. She had been right in front of him, and only now did he pay attention. Robin took a few steps toward the restaurant, just in time for a collision with another traveler.

"Hey! Watch where you're going!" the man said brusquely before disappearing down the corridor.

Robin looked again into the restaurant, but the girl was gone. He shook his head. "There is just too much going on here today."

Glancing at the clock on the wall inside the restaurant, he realized he had no idea where he was supposed to be. He reached into his back pocket for his boarding pass. British Airways, Flight 779, Gate 6. Looking up, he found Gate 6 directly in front of him, but the board announced that American Airlines Flight 895 would be departing for Washington, D.C.

Robin's head hurt. "Crap," he cursed under his breath. "I'm in the wrong bloody terminal."

Chapter 32

May 1985

San Francisco, California

Robin bent down and quickly kissed Marianne Sommers' cheek when he reached her table at the restaurant in downtown San Francisco. He was late, but he would redeem himself with charm. "I haven't seen you since your family moved back to the States!"

Marianne regarded him with a smile, gesturing for him to sit down. "The past fifteen years have been good to you, Robin."

His eyes grew wide as he took his seat. "Good lord. Has it been that long?"

She nodded cheerfully. "Almost. Robin, this is my cousin, Mary Katherine Baker. Mary K, this is Robin Michaels."

Robin reached across the table to shake her hand. "Hello, good to meet you."

"Thank you. Likewise," Mary K responded politely.

"I was just telling Mary K about how you and I knew each other when we were in prep school. We were penpals."

"Penpals!" Robin burst out with an amused grin. "Marianne, you were my sweetheart."

Marianne winked at him. "I'm glad you could join us today. What are you doing out here, anyway?"

"Mmm. Meeting with some media developers," Robin responded as he opened the menu and perused the selections. "Picking their brains a bit. What in the world is a fontina-rosemary grit cake? I swear, you Americans have the strangest culinary habits."

The two women giggled. Robin looked up from his menu and smiled.

"Robin, Mary K is a journalist," Marianne commented.

"Really?" He glanced to Mary K as he reached for his water glass. "What's your area?" He took a sip.

"Music." She looked him directly in the eye. He liked that.

"She's looking to get her foot in the door with ROLLING STONE," Marianne suggested.

Robin glanced back and forth between the two, his mischievous grin growing wide. His gaze settled on Mary K. "You'd like an interview, then?"

"Yes." Mary K was self-assured, confident. Robin liked that, too.

"You don't mind, do you, Robin?" Marianne asked coyly.

Robin turned to his boyhood sweetheart and patted her wrist. "How could I possibly mind being ambushed by two beautiful women who are buying me lunch?" He noticed the gold wedding band on Marianne's finger and withdrew his hand from hers. He turned to Mary K. "When would you like to start?"

"Well, if you're not doing anything this afternoon..." she suggested.

"Aggressive," Robin commented to Marianne. "As it so happens, I'm not previously engaged. I would be happy to give you an hour or two." Robin basked in the glow of pleasing both his old friend and this new one so easily. "In fact," Robin announced as he unfolded his napkin with a flourish, "why don't we get started now?"

Marianne smiled at her cousin, who produced a notepad and pen from her purse.

"Well, my marriage was an absolute disaster, but I suppose you already know about that," he launched in voluntarily, deflecting questions before they could be asked.

* * * *

After a lingering lunch, Marianne had driven Robin back to his hotel, where he now sat in the bar with Mary K, completing their interview.

"I have to tell you, Robin," Mary K confessed as they sat across the table from each other, "I've really enjoyed your latest album. It's full of honest emotion. And while I know you well enough now to appreciate how intensely personal that material must be, it's still delivered in a way that is immediately accessible, to people who don't know you at all."

"Mmm."

"I didn't much care for *Sticks and Stones*, however," she admitted.

This comment sparked something within, and Robin smiled. "Yes, that's a fairly angry song, although I tried to inject a softer element as well. Obviously, it's about the barbs and jabs we all take at each other, in our most intimate relationships," Robin waxed. "The pushing and pulling that goes on. We use verbal onslaughts as a defensive barrier against those closest to us, since they are the ones who can do the most damage. But it also concerns the labels we place on ourselves, whether we've learned these from our parents, our schoolmasters, or wherever. We put ourselves down. We're all convinced we're just frauds on the inside, waiting to be revealed and humiliated."

"There is one song, from this current album, I've wanted to ask you about."

Robin raised his eyebrows in anticipation.

"I want to know about *The Voice*."

"Mmm. Yes. *The Voice*." Robin heard the Mexican surf in his head, considering what he might say. "What would you like to know?" he finally asked in return.

"Well, it's a deeply spiritual song."

"Yeah, that was a new vehicle for me, expressing some of the churnings that had been going on for awhile." Robin grew quiet as he thought. Mary K kept her pen poised, waiting.

"I was in an incredibly raw place when that came to me. Very emotional time. My family had at last disintegrated, which I'm sure in the end will prove a positive thing for all of us, but it was very trying then. It still is," he admitted.

Mary K nodded sympathetically.

"I had run away from home, more or less. No." Robin shook his head. "Rather than giving my personal experience writing that song, I'll tell you what I've come to realize since then, as a result."

"Alright," she agreed.

"Okay, we're all generally taught that, 'In the Beginning, there was the Word.' You'll pardon the Christian reference. This isn't so much religious as inclusively spiritual. But sound, music, is a vibration, a force which essentially brings matter to life. Mmm. Maybe that's not quite how I want to put that." Robin reached for his scotch and soda and took a long drink. "I'd like to think each of us has that connection, that 'still, small voice' within. God. Intuition. Call it what you will. It's our connection to something greater than ourselves. What's unfortunate is sometimes we have to get all worked up and broken down within some crisis before we can even hear it speaking to us, much less make any kind of sense of it." Robin leaned back and looked up at the ceiling. "So that song, obviously came out of turmoil in my own life. It's about finally accepting the self as something more than just an organic machine. That moment of understanding there is so much beyond what we can touch, taste, hear, smell, see. And we're, each person, a part of that. All you have to do is listen. It's a beginning."

Robin watched as she jotted down his words. God, it was good to have someone to listen, he thought to himself. Even if it's her job.

Mary K lifted her pen and read back over what she had just written. She smiled, then looked up at Robin. "So this is your beginning as a spiritual person."

Robin smiled broadly. "Mmm, I hope so. No organized religions, though, for me, please," he laughed. "I've always, sort of, danced around the whole concept of religion. I'm fascinated by the psychology, though at the same time, I feel that same yearning, within myself, for something greater, something beyond…"

The gears in Robin's head spun suddenly. Robin had a good chuckle at himself. "You know, when I was a child, years ago, I had this, mmm, I suppose you'd call it an imaginary friend. Michael. I remember pretending he was some kind of master, or guru, and he had chosen me especially to pass along his wisdom."

He heard the scratch of her pen on the paper. "Hey, that's off-the-record, okay?"

She crossed through a few lines. "Sure." She looked at him, trying to make out his exact features in the dim light of the lounge. She wished she could get a better look at his eyes. "Whatever happened to Michael, then? Was he successful in that mission?"

"Oh! I could never answer that question," Robin roared with laughter. "I don't know what became of him. I guess I grew up. Funny idea, that. Me, as a grown up."

* * * *

Robin studied the woman as she slept. Her skin glowed just beneath the surface; her energy was not particularly strong.

Her hair was deliciously dark. Robin wanted to see her body, buried under the blankets. She shifted in her sleep and moaned slightly. Robin felt an excited ripple move through him as he closed the distance between them.

His astral form hovered beside her. She was drawing him in, though something at her core produced an immediately negative reaction within his own system. He ignored this instinctive warning and whispered to her without words.

"What is your name, dear one?" he asked, sending his presence into her dream. "I'm Robin Michaels. I suppose you've heard of me?"

She sighed peacefully, her eyes dancing beneath closed lids. For this moment, Robin told himself, let this woman be the sleeping goddess. Let's see what happens.

"What do you dream of?" he addressed her. "Turn toward me, so I can see you."

She rolled over in her sleep, facing him. He ran his hands of light over her body, feeling her energy, completely unlike his own. She moaned again, a smile on her lips.

"You like that, do you?" he whispered to her.

"WHAT ARE YOU DOING?" a voice commanded behind him.

Startled, Robin flew to the perimeter of the room. Turning to face this intruder, he found himself confronted by an incredibly beautiful creature with skin the colour of clay and hair that reminded him of the deep blue-green of the sea.

The sleeping woman turned away, oblivious to the drama in the corner of her room.

"Who, who are you?" he stammered, not wanting to anger this imposing presence.

"I am Isis," she responded coolly. "I am your advocate, Robin." She towered above him like an Amazon goddess, her amethyst eyes blazing.

"I don't understand."

Isis gestured to the woman. "Your game of energy seduction is amusing. It entertains you."

He felt himself a schoolboy, at St. Anthony's once again, caught red-handed. "Energy seduction?" he asked meekly.

"You have no right to meddle thus," she reprimanded. "You have no idea how dangerous such a practice is."

"This is real?" he asked in disbelief, glancing around in alarm. He was in a stranger's bedroom being scolded by some interdimensional being for what he thought was merely enjoyment of a good dream.

"Everything is real, Robin." Her tone softened into a smile. "This is happening. We are having this conversation. It's not a dream." Isis gestured to the sleeping figure. "Her name is Donna. This is not the first time you have visited her. Or others like her."

Robin was dumbstruck. His mind raced, trying to recall any previous encounters. There were only vague shadows of dreams, but perhaps these had not been dreams at all.

"You are on a path of awakening, Robin," Isis offered patiently. "Sometimes the skill comes before the wisdom."

"The skill?"

"You are projecting your consciousness, though in a limited fashion," she explained. "Be careful what you do with your energy, especially out of body. This woman is attracted to your music. Her fantasy called out to you. In your response to this open doorway, you don't know what you may have inadvertently triggered, not only within her, but within the larger energy plane."

"Umm," he mumbled. "I still don't understand."

Isis nodded. "You will."

In an instant, Robin was back in his darkened hotel room in San Francisco, floating just off the floor not far from a lump on the bed — his own sleeping body. Moving closer, a gravitational vortex opened. Swept up in the stream, he was deposited back inside his body and lost himself in sleep.

* * * *

Henley-on-Thames, Oxfordshire

At the end of the month, Robin was finally home after a longer than planned stint in California and a spontaneous holiday with Rose. His manager delivered his accumulated mail to his home in one large box, just in time for his arrival.

Robin avoided the box for several hours, busying himself with laundry and then taking a nap. Hands on his hips, he studied the cardboard box in the hallway and sighed. "Right," he said finally.

He tore open the top and found most of the letters and parcels had been carefully sorted. He felt immediately guilty for not dropping his manager a single postcard from his holiday. Needing a lift this dark, drizzly afternoon, Robin plunged into the fan mail.

He spread the envelopes on the floor, quietly appreciating so many people choosing to reach out to him. One particular envelope caught his attention. It was large and formal. He recognized the stiff, crisp paper often used for official announcements. He wondered how this one ended up with the fan mail. He didn't recognize the return address in San Jose, California.

Robin was sure his heart stopped in his chest when he read the engraving on the enclosed card: The honour of your presence is requested at the marriage of Donna Baylor Cox and Robin Ashcroft Michaels... Attached was a sticky note: "Shall we set the date, love? The ring is awaiting your payment authorization at Tiffany's, and the dress is to die for! I'm nearly done packing for the move to England. Yours always, Donna."

Sitting on the floor, Robin steadied himself against the wall. What in the world was this? He didn't know anyone named Donna. Reflecting on his limited exploits during tours and other functions, he was certain he had not happened upon this woman. Though he had been overtly propositioned by fans before, he had never encountered anything like this.

He tried to catch his breath. Something else slipped out of the envelope and slid across the floor. Reaching for it, Robin turned over the woman's photograph. She was completely nude, save for strategically placed copies of several of his albums. "Oh, God," he sighed. "I simply don't have time for this kind of—"

He looked closely at the face in the picture. He felt his energy flood out of his body and into the floor. He heard the voice of Isis, from that strange dream of the goddess, the warning he had so quickly dismissed, attributed instead to the effects of California cuisine: "You have no idea how dangerous such a practice is. You don't know what you may have inadvertently triggered…"

Robin let the wedding invitation and photograph slip to the floor. Conscious of the prickly fingers of anxious dread creeping across his skin, Robin buried his face in his hands.

Chapter 33

October 1985
Fredericksburg, Virginia

Angela sat alone in St. Barbara's School chapel on a dreary afternoon. The Peacemakers meeting had concluded with the half-dozen students discussing how to boost human rights awareness on their small campus. They had even tried visualizing world peace in a group meditation, though Angela had been too distracted and too cold to focus.

Her friends had all returned home, though she still had forty-five minutes until her Dad would be ready to leave. When her father had joined the faculty of St. Barbara's English department, his children had been guaranteed placement at the exclusive coed prep school. Angela didn't mind having her father teaching her friends' classes, but she disliked not being able to go home right away at the end of the school day.

Brian and the varsity squad were on the field now, wrapping up their soccer match against Collegiate School. When they were dating, she had never missed a game. Then she didn't mind waiting for her father to grade papers or meet with students after school. She had been the unofficial mascot of the boys' soccer team. Brian would wink at her from the field, turning to smile at her as he ran past. He was handsome and strong. Angela had liked being his girlfriend.

She listened to the chilly rain beat against the chapel windows and pulled her sweater close around her shoulders. Sitting on the hard wood of the pew, she gazed up at the large, ominous cross suspended over the altar, casting long shadows across the polished floor. It was never a question of faith, which Angela had in abundance. It was a matter of religion, which she didn't trust at all.

Tracing the carved wood of the heavy cross with her eyes, Angela wondered at the accidents of history. If Jesus had faced a different form of execution, would Christians worship another symbol? She tried to imagine a noose or an electric chair over the altar instead. A distasteful shiver ran up her spine.

She cleared her throat, hoping she wasn't coming down with a flu. Her feet were ice cold. She slipped out of her loafers and curled her stocking feet beneath her. Sitting cross-legged in the pew, she rested her hands on her knees and closed her eyes. I'm going to try this again, she thought to herself.

Deep breath filled her lungs. She straightened her spine against the back of the pew. She shut out the endless stream of thought. "Please," her mind whispered.

"Yes," a voice inside responded. Angela was startled to hear any reply so clearly. A glowing light shone against her closed eyelids, warmth spreading through her body.

"Yes," she said aloud, fighting to sit still as her excitement grew. A scene took form in her mind's eye. She was sitting in the grass with a tall, beautiful woman with hair the color of the sea. This woman took Angela's hands into her own and smiled.

"Don't be afraid, Angela," she soothed her, though her lips never moved.

"I'm not afraid," Angela replied proudly.

The woman leaned forward, gazing deeply into the girl's face. Angela blinked, amazed by the radiant amethyst orbs of her eyes, framed by the warm brown of her skin.

"You walk alone, Angela."

Her fingers tightened in the woman's hands. The lovely lady smiled.

"Do not be angry with Brian, for not loving you the way you think he should," she counseled. "It is no tragedy that you have parted. The only tragedy is the hurt you carry in your own heart."

Angela felt fresh tears spring from her eyes and spill down her cheeks.

"Your tears heal, Angela." The woman's voice was pure music. "They carry the pain and the toxins out of your body and your heart."

Angela looked down, ashamed. She felt this wondrous being embrace her, and she rested her head against her angelic breast. Angela's breath softened as the woman stroked her hair and patted her shoulder.

"You will not find yourself through relationship to others," the woman advised. "Your path is to find yourself through relationship to Spirit. You are in tremendous growth. You will not settle into your true self for years yet. Be patient with yourself."

The angel held Angela gently by the shoulders. "Boys and men will pass through your life, but you will find love in the divine." Her violet eyes smiled, exuding marvelous light. "You are learning to look within yourself now. You are learning to journey."

A question grew on Angela's face. The woman touched her chin lightly with her fingertips, then spread her arms wide. "This, Angela. This is a journey. When you are unsure, seeking wisdom, come to this place within yourself. Quiet the body and the mind, and look within."

She leaned forward to kiss Angela's forehead, in the middle of her brow. A great radiance passed through the space above Angela's eyes, and her mind flooded with light. The weight of her body disappeared as her being filled with quiet joy.

Angela's chin dropped sharply against her chest, waking her. She blinked as she looked around the dark chapel, the cold again encroaching. The rain outside continued. "Mmm," she groaned, again pulling her sweater up over her shoulders. She had fallen asleep. What had she been dreaming about?

She checked her wristwatch. 5:30. Dad would be done by now and was probably already waiting for her. She stood up and stretched, stiff from the rigid pew. Angela climbed the few steps toward the chapel entrance, pausing to look back at the cold cross before grabbing her bookbag by the door.

Chapter 34

September 1986
London

Robin, per usual, was running late.

He had taken the train into London for the meeting of studio investors he had been invited to attend. Of course, there had been some mysterious technical failure on the train. It seemed all Robin need do was pass nearby any kind of machine, and it automatically shut down.

Finally making it into the London station, Robin had run for the underground. He was partially thankful for the rail delay, as he had missed the usual commuter crush on the subway cars. Watching the stops flicker past, he laughed at his own dumb luck.

I'm a fortunate fellow, he thought as he stepped off the car and made his way toward the exit. No matter what happens, everything manages to work itself out.

He wasn't surprised that he had gotten lost walking from the tube stop to the office building. He had spent years of his life in this city, but he was damned if he ever felt comfortable in London. It finally occurred to him to stop and ask for directions. The clerk at the bank office indicated he was only a half-block from where he intended to be. Indeed he had passed the very building at least a half-dozen times as he wandered. He stepped back out onto the pavement, shaking his head. "If my own head weren't already attached to my body..." he cursed under his breath.

Robin dashed inside the building containing the offices of Wexler Reed Associates and rode the lift to the seventh floor. He stepped out of the carriage onto the soft peach carpeting just as his meeting broke for lunch.

"Robin!" a familiar voice called out from the end of the hallway. Robin turned and found Manuel Dixon waving to him.

"Ah! Good morning," Robin responded, making his way down the corridor. The other attendees filed out into the hallway from the conference room.

"We were beginning to worry," Manuel commented as he shook hands with Robin.

"Ahm, sorry I'm running a bit late," he apologized. "There was a delay coming into Paddington."

"No worries. You're just in time for lunch," Manuel replied. "You can join us?"

"Mmm," Robin nodded in the affirmative.

"Alright, well," Manuel said, looking around at the group. "The accountants and legal types have gone ahead to the restaurant. But I believe you already know Dirk Sprewell, formerly of Mandala Records?"

"Yes, your reputation precedes you," Robin said with a smile as he extended his hand to the elder gentleman. "It's good to finally make your acquaintance."

"Thank you, Robin," Dirk responded politely. "I've been looking forward to talking with you as well."

"And, of course, Erin Josias," Manuel continued.

Robin turned to her and smiled. "How is the new Eclipse album coming then?"

"Going well," she nodded as she shook his hand. "But don't be surprised if you get another call from the lads to lend your talents. At this rate, the band should change its name to Imbolc Revisited."

Robin and Erin laughed together as an unfamiliar woman stepped into the corridor. Robin noticed the pleasant curves and shapely face of the short red-head before him, so dissimilar to the leggy, fragile actresses and barmaids who normally caught his eye.

"And this is our representative in the real estate world," Manuel introduced her to Robin. "Gwendolyn Pruett."

Gwendolyn extended her hand to him. "Not in the music industry. I'm just a normal person," she confessed with a smile.

"Thank God for that!" Robin laughed as he shook her hand, feeling the softness of her fingers.

* * * *

Including the accountants, lawyers, and bank representatives, there were eleven in the lunch party. Robin and Gwendolyn sat together at the far end of the table while she helped catch him up on the details of the meeting.

"So the group has settled on a property in Winchester," Gwendolyn told him.

"Winchester," Robin repeated.

"Yes. Far enough to avoid the frenetic energy of London, while still easily accessible from Gatwick and Heathrow," she explained.

"Ah, right." Robin took a delicate bite of pasta, exercising his best table manners. "But where in Winchester?"

"On the River Itchen, and actually outside of the city, to the south."

"Outside. Good," he commented. "And on the water, as well."

She nodded. "The property owners hoped to renovate for business offices," Gwendolyn said. "We were fortunate to get in before too much work had been done. It's an old mill factory, and one warehouse is still standing, though it's in pitiful condition. A few structures may need to be torn down."

Robin tried to exercise his intelligence, to impress Gwendolyn and further engage her conversation. "What's the property been used for recently?" He kicked himself under the table.

"Well, of course, the mill closed down some years ago," she responded. "The main building was used as a banquet hall for a time, and more recently as some kind of retreat center. But the property has been standing empty for some time. The owners were happy to be rid of it." She nodded toward Robin's prospective business partners. "Your group stepped in at just the right time, I'd say. Lucky."

Luck. Robin smiled. "I'm not exactly a member of the group just yet," he confided. "I think we're still sort of auditioning each other."

She looked toward the other end of the table as Manuel and Erin laughed loudly. "I don't know much about music, as a business," she said to him quietly. "But from talking with the others, I'd say this is a solid venture. An expensive proposition, to be sure. The property itself is not a huge investment, considering it's not in any usable condition. But the renovation and construction work, that's going to take some capital."

Robin smiled. "I think that's why they're interested in me."

Gwendolyn regarded him in silence. Robin laughed.

"I know," he conceded with a quick laugh. "I don't exactly have a reputation for financial supremacy. But some old seeds have borne fruit." Robin dabbed at the corner of his mouth with his serviette and leaned closer to Gwendolyn. "Eclipse and some of my own releases since the split have revived interest in the old Imbolc albums." He paused for a sip of cola. "So we negotiated a rather attractive contract for re-releasing the older material, with a few 'greatest hits' type of arrangements. That in turn has made my solo work more valuable. It's an interesting process, and I can't say that I entirely understand it." Robin sighed. "So I'm suddenly flush, and looking for something worthwhile to do," he explained with a satisfied grin.

"That's a good turn of fortune."

Robin smiled. "Oh, I'm not a big power player, or anything like that. But this seems a decent investment. Something to put toward my daughter's future. And in the background, I've always wanted to run a studio the way I think it should be handled, with other competent professionals," he gestured toward Erin, Manuel, and Dixon, listening in on his conversation.

"Of course, I have no idea what kind of an executive I might make!" he exclaimed boisterously, eliciting a smile from his colleagues. "That could itself go down as one of the most glorious disasters of all time."

The others at the table laughed with him. Basking in the amusement, Robin caught Gwendolyn's eye and winked.

* * * *

A week later, Robin enjoyed Gwen's company as she showed him around the Winchester property. She had taken him through the more viable buildings, explaining in vague layman's terms what the rest of the group had planned. He would have to consult the contractors for more detailed information.

"You can see it's a sizable property," Gwendolyn said, scanning the surroundings. Outside, not far from the river, they were treated to the sounds of the rushing water.

Hands on his hips, Robin surveyed the area with a satisfied smile growing on his lips. He hid his sensitive eyes beneath dark glasses, but they sparkled all the same. He inhaled deeply, each breath escaping with a quiet hum that resonated through his torso. The ground under his feet felt solid, and exciting. This was good. Very good.

He faced the main building, a large brick structure that shyly turned away from the water. The dirty, broken windows revealed only empty darkness inside. Robin smiled.

"You know what I see?" he asked, nodding toward the building.

Gwen responded with a smile.

"Windows, lots of them. A whole wall of windows. Let the light in. Great views of the water and the rest, especially from higher above," he explained, gesturing about. "That side of the building should be entirely glass. Or mostly."

Gwen teased him. "And who's going to clean all of those windows? You?"

Robin smiled. He liked this one. He liked her a lot. He wasn't usually attracted to plump figures, though he had spent breakfast thinking about the sway of her generous hips when she walked. She stood next to him and smiled. His buxom strawberry-blonde.

"And over here," he pointed to the desolate field bounded by the three buildings still standing, "corridors, connecting buildings between these others. Functional arcades."

"Full of windows," Gwen commented, playing with him.

"Well, yeah." Robin shrugged. "And you'll want something nice to look at, from those arcades, instead of just this dead mess." He frowned at the sparse patches of dry weeds in the dusty ground.

* * * *

"You want us to build what?" the contractor asked from across the table.

"A pond," Robin restated. "We're building an organic facility. It's should be a peaceful place, with something nice to look at."

"You've already got the river on the other side," the lead architect commented.

"Right," Robin responded. "That's good, too. Keep that."

At the head of the table, Erin suppressed a quick laugh.

The contractor dropped his pencil onto the table in frustration. "Do you have any idea what's involved in that sort of thing? You don't just arbitrarily go dig a hole and fill it with water."

Robin leaned back in his chair. "I suppose that's why we've hired you fine people." He looked around the table at his partners, appreciating their quiet patience. He realized he was testing everyone's reserves. He was grateful they had at least convinced him that transparent plumbing was very likely a bad idea.

The architect scanned the list of "suggested requirements" Robin had offered over the last three hours. "Alright," he commanded the group's attention. He ticked off each item with his pencil. "We've got glass walls reinforced with steel, facing out toward the river and facing inward on the courtyard, which is now apparently going to be a pond."

Robin nodded in agreement.

"There will be a series of tiered, arcade-style buildings to connect the three larger buildings. We will explore the feasibility of using the existing underground tunnel system as passageways. The cafeteria walls should be curved. Drives and other outdoor passages will be lined in either brick or stone."

Robin listened with distracted attention. He couldn't tear his thoughts from the previous night with Gwendolyn, the sweet taste of her mouth and the delicious disorder of her hair this morning. As the architect continued, Robin just nodded and smiled.

"The reception area of the main building will accommodate several lounging areas as well as..." he read his own handwriting and almost shook his head. "As well as floor and wall space for the display of artwork, with as much natural light as possible. The facility will contain as few flat rooftops as can be managed. All buildings will be climate controlled, for the care and maintenance of production equipment, so each room will be individually monitored."

He looked up at Robin, then scanned the faces of the rest of the group. "Of course, we've already been over the structural designs of the larger buildings, including the offices, studios, and dormitory. Is there anything else?"

"Ducks," Robin commented.

The contractor and architect both glanced at him with raised eyebrows.

"There should be ducks on the pond, with benches around, for people to sit," Robin thought out loud, gazing through the window to the overcast sky. "Benches under those... those weepy trees." Robin tried to demonstrate weeping willows with his hands.

The contractor cleared his throat. "Landscaping and animal control are an entirely separate matter," he commented, barely masking his impatience with this impossible artist pretending to be a businessman. "So we're done then, yes?"

"Solar power." Robin blurted out.

The architect pursed his lips. "Solar power?"

"Yeah. For the studios. All of it."

The architect sighed. "We couldn't possibly power the entire facility through solar energy. The drain is much too great, and there simply isn't that much light."

"Mmm. Well, not the whole place, of course," he backtracked. "See what you can do. Ahm, how about hydroponics? Water power. The river is right there..."

"Hydroelectrics. Right," the architect nodded his head. "I'll look into it."

"And, there could even be, mmm, a kind of fountain system. Cascading, a waterfall sort of thing, cascading down the tiers of the connectors, the glass arcade. People are inside, underneath the running water..." Robin looked far away and smiled. "That same system can feed and circulate the water within the pond!"

Quite pleased with himself, Robin looked toward the end of the table, where Erin Josias quietly shook her head.

"I don't think so, Robin," Manuel interjected.

Robin frowned, his lips hinting at a grimace. "Okay. But what about a transport system running through those tunnels, instead of just walking corridors. A people train."

"What do you think you're building?" the contractor challenged him. "Disneyland?"

"Well, no," Robin defended immediately, then thought a moment. "Umm, actually, yes."

Chapter 35

14 February 1987
Fredericksburg, Virginia

Angela sat alone on the frosted grass. The neighborhood was still. She could just make out the gentle sound of the river below. With only a few distant street lamps intruding, Angela enjoyed this winter wonderland. She pulled her heavy coat close and listened to the laughter from inside Sandra's house. It was just after midnight, on Valentine's Day.

Sandra's parents were out of town, and she had invited her uncommitted girlfriends to a sleepover. While other girls received flowers and boxes of chocolate from their boyfriends, the "Footloose Fredericksburg Five"—alternately, the "Rappahannock River Goddesses"—would spend the weekend celebrating their singlehood.

Angela and Ryan had split up just after the New Year, their volatile relationship lasting only six months. Newly single, Ryan had quickly turned his attentions to Angela's classmate, Bianca, and would no doubt spend the romantic holiday with her. Angela was impatiently grateful to join her friends for a distracting weekend of empowering activities.

After school let out, the girls threw their overnight bags into the back of Sandra's family station wagon and made a quick stop at the grocery for sodas, chips, and sweets. It was twilight by the time they got to the house. Toting matches and tapered candles, the five hurried from Sandra's house on Caroline Street and in the waning light tentatively descended the slick incline of Rocky Lane to the Rappahannock River.

It was cold on the water, where a gentle breeze carried the smell of the murky river to shore. They kept warm on their own nervous excitement, alternately giggling and holding their breath as Sandra lit her candle and passed the flame to her friends, one by one. They shared an uncertain silence, holding their candles on the riverbank, listening to the water rushing by, before they broke into mostly forgotten songs from childhood.

In the middle of an enthusiastic chorus of *I'm Bringing Home a Baby Bumblebee*, the group spied a patrolling police car creeping along Sophia Street behind them. Though there was nothing improper about their Valentine's Eve vigil, they quickly clambered back up the moss-covered stones to the warm refuge of Sandra's home.

The tribe had gathered around the kitchen counter to munch on chocolates and licorice, and Josie suggested a visit to Battlefield Park to roam the old Confederate trenches, thrilling the others with the possibility of encountering the restless dead. The haunted city's homes dated prior to the American Revolution, and the Civil War had only increased the supernatural population. Sandra's house itself was reported to be haunted. Hanging around the kitchen with her friends, Angela felt the presence of... something. She shook it off, as always, and turned her attention to the conversation.

As Kim, Josie, Angela, and Sandra crunched hard candy and licked melted chocolate off of their fingers, Carter checked her watch and thought of the leather pouch stashed in her overnight bag. Interrupting, she advised staying in and ordering pizza in advance of their special ceremony.

Hours later, sitting alone in the winter grass, Angela watched the frozen crystals of her breath escape her lips and spread themselves thin on the crisp air. Entranced.

She had never tried drugs before. She hadn't had the interest. She had felt a moment of hesitation when Carter produced the small collection of magic mushrooms. But escaping into the steady rhythm of the drums they were all beating, Angela put her misgivings aside, embraced her adventurous spirit, and opened her mouth.

The initial nausea passed quickly, although Kim had spent at least an hour hovering over the yawning mouth of the toilet. Crossing her legs beneath her in the grass, Angela felt she might float away, untethered, still bewitched by the persistent beat. There was only a single drum now, probably Carter's. Angela looked up into the stars and laughed.

"Hmm," she hummed peacefully, the vibration travelling down her throat into her solar plexus, finally radiating out through the base of her spine and into the ground. She imagined a network of energy branching out beneath her, keeping the ground warm and alive. "Well, God," she said to the sky with a smile, "looks as though I've finally got you all to myself." She laughed again. "Trouble is, I've forgotten what I wanted to say."

Angela closed her eyes and rocked herself from side to side, ignoring the numbness slowly spreading across her hindquarters and thighs. "What to say, what to say, what to say," she sang quietly. "So many words, and nothing to say."

"Would it be easier if you tried talking to me?" a distantly familiar voice asked out of the darkness.

Angela hummed and smiled at the sound of his question. Slowly opening her eyes, she turned to the subtly luminescent man sitting in the grass with her.

"Ah, so here you are," she remarked with a wise wonder that seeped through her pores. She regarded the wan and slightly bloated musician. "You're not looking so good this evening, even if you are just a vision."

He stretched his arms in front of him and nodded. "Slight food poisoning, I'm afraid," he explained in his English accent. "Nothing serious, but it's a powerful nuisance, the fevers and vomiting."

Angela raised her eyebrows and tipped her head to one side.

"It's just as well," he smiled, patting his padded belly. "Might help me lose this extra layer I've put on." He pulled his knees to his chest and clasped his arms around them. "What are you doing out here in the cold dark?"

Angela placed her palms flat on the ground, feeling the tiny ice crystals begin to melt beneath the warmth of her hands. "I thought I'd write a new song for my band, since I'm feeling so groovy. But of course, I don't have my guitar." She leaned back and pulled up her knees, imitating her friend. "And I don't seem to be much inspired. So I was thinking about what to say to God. That's when you showed up out of nowhere," she gestured toward him.

"I hope I wasn't interrupting." He gazed lazily at her, his eyes softly penetrating.

"Nope." She tilted her head playfully from side to side, then looked deeply into his face. They were sitting together inside a prism of energy, the grass beneath them a sea of frosted green. A light smile tickled the corners of her mouth and was reflected in his face. "Who are you, anyway?" she asked.

He nodded and tried not to laugh. Without a word, he lifted a finger to the outside corner of his right eye. Brilliant green, glowing. His sly smile was infectious.

A warm wave of reassuring light passed through her, leaving a tingling residue dancing along her spine. She leaned closer to get a better look at his sparkling eyes, then smiled broadly as she sat back again. "Mmm," she sang drunkenly. "Yes, to see myself behind another pair of eyes, my own soul smiling back. What a clever way to know God."

He reached behind his back and produced a flute, pulling it straight out of the frozen ground. Finding his finger placements across the shining surface, he raised the instrument to his lips. He looked at Angela and raised his eyebrows. "I'm ready when you are," he suggested. "You just have to tell me what you want me to play."

Angela smiled and hugged her knees close, her eyelids drifting shut as she watched brilliant colors dance across the darkness. Somewhere, many miles away, she saw this same man bundled up in bed, trembling with fever. A woman with red-blonde hair lay next to him, wide awake as she watched him. "Be my Valentine," she heard his voice, not certain if these words came from the other side of the ocean or from this glowing avatar in the grass. The distant woman kissed his hot brow. Angela opened her eyes and smiled at her radiant twin, softly playing the melody she already knew by heart.

* * * *

The mushroom experience was a fantastic blur. When she awoke, curled up on the couch, Angela had hazy memories of dancing in the stars to the careless lilt of an ethereal flute.

She leaned back into the generous cushions and held out a hand to keep the room from spinning. Angela found she was clutching the small notebook she always carried in her coat pocket. She read curiously through the scribbled notes on melody and chord progressions. She had even gone to work on the guitar tablature and bass line. Angela shook her head in disbelief. Her individual efforts had never been so detailed.

The lyrics were in her own handwriting, a song unlike anything she or anyone else in the band had ever written.

Unveiling (child of light)—A. Harris & R: 2/14/1987… wee A.M., time? ya ya

Open my eyes against this darkness
Peer out through tattered holes
There are chinks in this armour
Breakdown of ego control

Recognition now.

I will starve out the snake
Coiled so tightly round my spine
The shudder run through me, I quake
The subtle bodies starting to align

Premonition vow.

Slip off the mask, unveiled
Slide out of this skin, and see
Living too long in shadows underneath
On my own shores, a refugee

Build a bridge, stone by stone
Build a ladder to the skies
Climb out of self, reach out, reach out
Touch the light in my own eyes

I step out from beneath the veil
Standing bare, I am revealed
Child of Light, natural wonder
The staff of life to wield

Magician endow.

Slip off the mask, unveiled
Slide out of this skin, and see
Living too long in shadows underneath
On my own shores, a refugee

I am an angel of understanding
No longer martyr to my own whim
Bend to spirit force expanding
The twisting turning fission begin

Ignition. Ignition.

Angela frowned. "Armour?" she whispered aloud. "What's with the British spelling?"

There was some commotion on the floor. Angela looked past the coffee table to see Kim stirring in her sleeping bag. Sandra lay several feet away, undisturbed. Josie was curled up on the love seat, while Carter was nowhere in sight. Angela cautiously raised herself to her feet and padded down the bare floor of the hallway. She was still wearing yesterday's clothes.

Carter was in the kitchen brewing herbal tea. She smiled at Angela and nodded toward the notebook she held tightly in her hands.

"You wrote a good song last night," Carter said pleasantly before turning to the cabinets in search of ceramic mugs. "You were singing it in your sleep."

Chapter 36

June 1987

Fredericksburg, Virginia

Angela fidgeted in Ruth Ruby's parlor as she waited. Josie was treating her to this consultation as a fun graduation present. Angela was still uncomfortable, imagining herself a few minutes in the future, sitting down with a psychic to have her fortune told.

Perhaps it's just as well, Angela thought to herself as she flipped through an outdated fashion magazine. The eighteen-year-old was preoccupied with heavy choices. Maybe this psychic woman had some wisdom for her.

The office door opened, and Josie emerged in an excited glow. Ruth's divining had obviously tickled her fancy. Angela felt a tightness spread from her chest down into her stomach. Very likely, this woman would simply tell her what she thought she wanted to hear. Alternately, the idea of anyone looking into the depths of her soul made her nervous.

"Your turn," Josie grinned at her. Ruth stood in the doorway.

Angela got up from the worn sofa. Ruth held out her hand in greeting.

"Good morning, Angela," Ruth said cheerfully. "I appreciate your patience in waiting. Please, come in."

Angela glanced back at Josie, who had settled onto the sofa with the same magazine. Taking a breath, Angela unclenched her jaw and followed Ruth inside.

Sitting at a round table against one wall, Ruth motioned for Angela to take a seat opposite. She looked deeply into the girl's eyes, and smiled.

"You're not sure you want to be here," Ruth offered sympathetically.

"My friend's idea," Angela motioned toward the door.

"That's okay," Ruth told her. "I've been doing this about twenty years, advising people spiritually. I'm more of a counselor than a fortune teller, if that helps. I have different ways of receiving the wisdom I impart to clients. Different mediums use different tools. You'll see people using Tarot cards, or reading palms. Others use rune stones, pendulums, astrological aspects. There are many ways to get to the same truth."

Angela blinked, trying to keep her skepticism on a tight leash.

"I use several methods," Ruth continued. "I wait to get a sense of the individual before deciding how to proceed. So, just make yourself comfortable, physically or otherwise. Can I get you a drink of water?"

Angela shook her head. "No, thanks."

"Alright. Do a quick inventory. Run through each part of your body, and ask what it needs to be as relaxed as it can be right now."

Angela cleared her throat as she self-consciously ran her awareness from the crown of her head, through her chest and abdomen, and down into her feet. She wiggled her toes, then leaned down to slip off her shoes.

Ruth smiled. "Good. Anything else?"

Angela gently rocked her weight back and forth in the chair. She adjusted her spine, trying to find the right position, but she couldn't get comfortable. Angela rose from the chair and sat down cross-legged on the floor. Ruth's face brightened.

"Is this a problem?" Angela asked, looking up at the counselor. She leaned against the small loveseat behind her.

"Not at all." Ruth took a seat on the carpet facing Angela, their knees almost touching. "You like to get grounded before you go to work. I like that."

Ruth again looked into Angela's eyes and took a deep breath. "Alright." Her eyelids closed slowly as she concentrated. "Okay, yes," Ruth said, nodding slightly. She opened her eyes and held both hands open to Angela.

"I'd like to try an intuitive soul reading with you, Angela," Ruth said to her. "Unless you had something particular in mind?"

"No," Angela responded. "What's a soul reading?"

"Place your hands, face down, on top of mine," Ruth directed as she rested her own hands, palms upward, on her knees.

Angela complied, feeling a cool tingle at the touch. Ruth closed her eyes again, breathing deeply.

"What I'm doing is reading your energy. I'm getting information from your soul field, through what I already know about my own. Reading the similarities and differences, listening to the guided wisdom you're carrying, but may not be aware of." Ruth opened her eyes and lifted one eyebrow. "That sounds like a lot of baloney, doesn't it?"

Angela laughed nervously. "I don't know. This is all kind of new to me."

Ruth smiled at Angela's denial. "Okay," she announced. Ruth scooted back a few feet and leaned against her desk. She looked at Angela squarely. "So you've come to a fork in the road, and you're worried about making the wrong decision."

"Mmm," Angela responded tentatively. "Yes."

"Okay, what you need to know, before you go any further trying to figure this out," Ruth counseled, "is there is no way to do this wrong. Do you understand that? You cannot do it wrong."

"I guess," Angela replied hesitantly.

"No," Ruth shook her head. "You've got to hear this, and understand. There is no right and wrong in this life any more than the only colors you see are black and white. If there's an opportunity for learning and growth that wants to present itself, and you're not ready to go that route, don't worry about missing out on that one. It will just come back again later on in a different form. Do you understand?"

"I think so."

"Okay." Ruth frowned as she pieced together the words for Angela. "You also need to know that you don't have to do everything yourself. You've divided your workload. I can't give you the specifics. What you've got is one half of the focus, one half of the perspective. You'll get the other when the time is right. That could be later this afternoon, or after you leave this body at the end of the journey. But just know that you're right on track. Okay?"

Angela nodded and squinted slightly, not understanding at all.

Ruth tapped her fingers on her knees. "The decision you're facing right now…" She looked up at the ceiling. "Ah. You're worried about taking a chance. It's a big one. Something, a creative pursuit… Is there something musical?"

"Yes," Angela replied, surprised. "I'm in a band."

"Mmm," Ruth nodded. "What's the name of the band?"

"Michelangelo."

"Ah. Yes. Okay." Ruth shifted her position, centering her hips beneath her. She looked hard at Angela, scanning her body. "Your solar plexus, and your throat. You're the singer?"

Angela nodded silently.

"I see the dilemma. You know in your heart what you need to do. And you've got to give yourself more credit there; get better at listening on that level. You're concerned about letting the band down. There's some fear of abandonment there."

Caught off-guard, Angela's eyes filled with tears. "Yes," she replied softly. "I'm supposed to start college in the fall, but we've just gotten this offer… Our demo finally made it to an executive at Geffen. I really don't know how. I never thought this kind of thing would happen."

"Pay attention to that," Ruth interrupted. "Sit with how that surprise feels. That's one way to tell what you might want to do, whether that pathway was part of your original plan. Even if it's not, you can still go explore that for awhile."

"This band, to me, this was just something fun to do," Angela confided. "I love music, sure, but I never thought of it as a career." She scanned the walls and the ceiling, opening to raw trust. "These guys, they were already in college or just graduated. I'm the baby. I'm the only one facing this. We've been offered this contract, this recording deal, and it's pretty good. The other guys, they're just elated. This is what they've been waiting for! But me... I'd like to go to school. I had a different life in mind."

Ruth nodded and thought quietly. "I don't think you want to go that route, either, Angela. You may decide to try it out for awhile, but I'm not getting that this is where you're meant to end up. Besides, you've already done that before."

Angela looked at her quizzically. "I don't understand."

"The celebrity thing. You've already done that. You don't need to find that out again, living that kind of a public life," Ruth smiled inwardly, then peered into Angela's eyes. "Yes. But you do have music and rhythm all around you."

Angela felt an uncomfortable excitement growing in her chest.

"You're not exactly geared toward working behind the scenes, you know, anonymously," Ruth continued. "People are going to know who you are, through your work. Do you keep a journal, do any kind of writing, that sort of thing?"

"Sometimes," Angela responded vaguely.

"Well, that might be one avenue," Ruth suggested. "You're a teacher. I don't mean you have to have a classroom and teach algebra or grade papers. But you are someone who imparts knowledge and wisdom to others. That's happening regardless of what you choose to do with yourself. And there is music around this."

Ruth looked again into Angela's eyes and giggled. "Oh! But you are just so stubborn! Deliberately willful. I love it!"

Angela made an effort to smile. Her skin was beginning to itch from the inside out.

Ruth laughed out loud. "You're the kind of person, if the Universe told you one thing, you would go do the exact opposite, just to prove a point."

"I don't know about that," Angela commented quietly.

Ruth leaned forward. "I want you to listen to me on this one," she said very seriously. "You're having this love-hate relationship with Spirit. You used to be a lot more open, and it's your choice whether to get back to that place. But you're going to keep feeling this inner anxiety, this private struggle, until you stop fighting God."

Angela almost laughed. "I'm not fighting God. I'm not even religious!"

"Religion and spirituality are not the same thing. There's a big difference. Big difference. Anybody can be religious, going to church or synagogue or temple or whatever every week. Religion is external; being spiritual is personal. A person can be one and not the other. Do you understand?"

Angela nodded anxiously. This was not at all what she had anticipated.

"So tap into that," Ruth advised. "Work out your suspicions and your skepticism. That's only coming from the outside, anyway, what you think the outside world is saying about what and who you should and should not be. Let go of all that garbage. You don't need it, not this time. Just take a deep breath, and get rid of it. It's that easy. Let go of the fear. And trust. That's all. Trust yourself. Trust God. Trust the Universe."

Angela blinked. Her breath was coming faster, her heart pounding.

Ruth felt Angela's anxiety and smiled. "Just trust."

Chapter 37

20 May 1999
New York City
11:07 a.m.

"So your multimedia is going well?" Mary K asked as Robin stared out the window behind her.

"Hmm. Yes," Robin muttered, pulling himself back into focus. "We've had a lot of fun with that, providing interesting tools of exploration to people. We're still only in our infancy with this technology. It's amazing, what we can do now that we only imagined before. And so we've got some very exciting things in the works, new projects, some interesting new directions. I think you'll be pleased to see what Segue turns out next, several new titles on the verge of release."

Mary K smirked as Robin rambled, infused with his own enthusiasm.

"Robin," she held up her hand in reassurance. "Remember you're preaching to the choir here. I'm already sold on what you're doing."

Robin coughed and laughed. "Right. No sales pitch, then."

"What's been your biggest challenge producing these CD-ROMs and other projects?" Mary K's pen was poised above her legal pad, awaiting his response.

"Ah." Robin leaned back in his chair as he looked to the ceiling. "I'd have to say the biggest problem I've been having is mistaken identity."

Eyebrows raised, Mary K looked across the desk at him, waiting for her interview subject to continue, though he was perfectly content with his response and looked about the room, anticipating her next question. Finally, she asked, "Would you care to elaborate?"

Robin looked back at her. "Hmm?"

"What does that mean, 'mistaken identity'?"

"Ah, well, you know, there are quite a few of us, old rockers, into this area these days," he offered. "There's, ah, David Bowie, of course, and Sting, Peter Gabriel, and some others, working in mixed media, multimedia, producing enhanced music CDs, CD-ROM games and experiences, web-based environments, using the Internet as a distribution channel. That sort of thing. Of course, we're all English, so we all look alike. Or so you Yanks say."

"Uh-huh." She scribbled his words across her pad of paper.

"That was supposed to be a joke," Robin suggested.

"Hmm?" She glanced up from her notes, then looked down again.

"That last bit. You didn't laugh."

Mary K smiled at her friend as she wrote. "I was busy trying to keep up with you." She put her pen down and leaned back in her chair. "There, now I can laugh at you all you want."

"Oh, good."

She chuckled and turned to the computer. "I've been looking at one of your CDs this morning."

Mary K clicked her mouse a few times to bring up a colorful interactive screen of mixing controls bounded by musical instruments in the surrounding border.

Robin leaned forward to get a better look. "Is that GLOBAL NOMAD?"

"Yes. I know this is an earlier one, but I'm fascinated by it. Especially the traveling adventure—I felt like Indiana Jones!" She clicked around the interface. "And here I am mixing different instruments from all around the world, creating my own music. And I can find out more about the origins of the instruments and the music samples. Before you arrived, I was learning about Tuva, in Southern Siberia. I'd never even heard of Tuva."

Robin sat back in his chair. "Yeah, I like that aspect, too. We were fortunate to have the cooperation of a lot of artists across the planet with that one, enabling us to include a variety of music samples."

Mary K turned to face him.

"But GLOBAL NOMAD is more limited than I had originally hoped, especially with the mixing—the screen where you are, where you were just then," he pointed to the purple computer. "We had to speed up or slow down a lot of the samples, to the same tempo, so people can put them together. I had hoped for something more sophisticated, for the user to choose the tempo, the timing of the percussive rhythms, to make those kinds of decisions himself. But in 1995, that was simply not meant to be."

Mary K glanced over her notes, touching her chin thoughtfully. "You never did tell me where you got the name for your company, Segue."

"Oh!" Robin laughed with a broad smile. He pushed back in his chair, the front legs lifting slightly. "That's, well, that's all about me, I'm afraid."

"Explain."

"My friends, people I've worked with, have complained that the way I work, the way I think, really, just seems a mess of isolated fragments, that I jump from one unrelated tangent to the next with no clear pathway. But it somehow all works out in the end, happily enough." He laughed again and leaned back further, balancing precariously on the back legs of the chair. "I'm just one massive segue waiting to happen."

She smiled at his enjoyment. "I see."

"When it came time to figure out what to do next, what direction to take, it was a huge jumble of possibilities. Some could work, some were a bit dodgy, you get the picture. No surprises there. But no logical connection, to bring it all under one roof, to base a company on my scribbled notes on bits of paper." He rocked the chair gently back and forth. "The way to bring it into focus, then, was to model the new enterprise after my own odd personality."

"Segue," she commented.

Robin nodded and smiled. "Segue!"

He leaned back a bit too far. Feeling himself tipping over, Robin gripped the arms of the chair and lunged forward too late. Both he and the chair swung backward and crashed to the floor, Robin knocking his head against a corner table in the process.

"Robin!" Mary K dashed over from behind her desk and helped him up to a sitting position on the floor. "Are you alright?"

He shook his head to reorient himself. "Yeah." He glanced at the turned-over chair. "Oh, man, that was quite a ride."

He touched his scraped scalp, just above his brow. Withdrawing his hand, he found a few spots of blood on his fingertips. "I'm getting too old for this."

"Oh, God," Mary K exclaimed in distress. "You're bleeding."

She jumped to her feet and grabbed a handful of tissues out of the dispenser on her desk. "The last thing I need, Robin, is for you to kill yourself during this interview."

Robin laughed as he climbed back to his feet, reaching out to the corner table to steady himself. "Perhaps, but at least then you'd have one hell of a headline."

* * * *

On the other side of the building, Angela's business meeting had adjourned for a short coffee break.

The Westone executives had excused themselves to check voice mail and e-mail messages. Angela stood before a small serving table against the wall, pouring a cup of tea. Jeff stepped up beside her.

"I'd say it's going well," he offered. "You're doing a great job with these guys."

Angela laughed, pushing the tea bag around in the hot water with a wooden stick. "I'm just grateful to be forming complete sentences this morning. I also didn't realize I would be the only woman in the room."

Jeff fixed himself a cup of coffee. "Ah, don't sweat that stuff. You're giving them a lot to think about. That's good."

Angela faced him squarely. "Jeff, I want a sound studio. At the new facility."

He was still getting used to her sudden flashes of inspiration. "Sound studio?"

"Yes," she responded confidently. "A recording studio for music. Music as therapy."

"Okay...?" he replied tentatively.

"Just trust me on this one."

"Could this be the 'next big thing' you alluded to at breakfast?" he asked, almost teasing her.

She smiled. "Yeah, maybe." Angela reached for a packet of sugar, then suddenly dropped it to the floor as the throbbing sting hit. Reaching out, she steadied herself against the wall and raised a hand to her forehead as a sharp pain shot through her skull. She winced.

Her partner grabbed her elbow to support her. "Angela? Are you okay?"

Opening her eyes, she stepped away from the wall and from Jeff. "Yeah. I just, suddenly, there was this pain." Bringing her hand down from her brow, Angela expected blood on her fingertips, but there was none. "I don't know. It's gone now."

"Do you want some Tylenol or something?"

Angela shook her head. "Thanks. I'm okay."

Chapter 38

September 1989
Charlottesville, Virginia

"That's good. Just keep your eyes closed. Those eyelids are feeling heavier as you breathe more deeply with each breath," Adam counseled.

Angela felt every inhale surge through her body, almost lifting her from the floor. Though the twenty-year-old college junior was acutely aware of her surroundings, she was floating inside her own skin, slowly detaching from her senses.

"Good, Angela. Now, how are you feeling?"

Angela was slow to respond, not sure she would have use of her vocal chords. "I'm fine. Good." Her voice was deep and full. She felt its vibration in every pore.

"Alright, we're almost ready to begin. We'll take a moment here to change our music..." Adam motioned to Susan to switch off the Enya album, whose last song was fading to its conclusion. She put in a new tape. Angela smiled as the familiar strains of Dead Can Dance filled her dormitory room.

I don't know what I would do without music, Angela reflected. Her own world music broadcast earlier in the evening on student station WUVA 92.7 FM had her in a mellow mood, and she was happy to continue this groovy state well into the night.

Susan had arranged this pathworking session with Adam, a practicing pagan and aspiring shaman. The intention of tonight's journey was to consciously connect Angela with her guides and to ground her on her path. Feeling fairly directionless, as did most students, Angela was naturally curious at the suggestion of this ritual. She could use as much focused assistance as she could get.

"Okay, Angela, I want you to visualize now. You're walking alone along a gentle, dirt path, leading you farther into the woods," Adam suggested. "You hear only natural sounds. This is a peaceful, relaxing experience for you."

Angela took another deep breath and envisioned tall pine and oak trees around her. She imagined herself barefoot and tried to feel the earth beneath her feet.

"You can see a clearing ahead, not too far away. You're approaching now. Green grass, sunlight filtering through the trees. This is a sacred place." Adam's voice was almost liquid as he guided her. "There's an animal there waiting for you. Can you see?"

Angela stepped into the sanctuary of trees. She glanced around for her expected contact, but she was alone. "No," she frowned. "I'm here by myself."

"That's okay," Adam reassured her. "Just take a deep breath, and let it go."

"Wait, here it is." Angela saw a small fox enter from the right. It skittered into the clearing, its orange-red tail a brilliant flash in the patches of sunlight. Spotting Angela, the fox turned toward her, his nose twitching. He regarded her cautiously, then lay down in the grass, inviting her to do the same.

She walked toward the small creature and sat down.

"I have come to give you a message," Fox said to her.

Angela was startled. "He's talking to me!" she said aloud.

"That's fine," Adam encouraged. "Just listen to what this guide is telling you."

"Don't let your preconceptions and prejudices play tricks on your imagination," Fox advised.

"Okay, I don't know what that means," Angela responded.

Fox smiled at her. "You will. You put your loyalties in the wrong places. To experience harmony in your heart, first let go of the heavy heresy of your head."

Angela was confused. Fox rose from his resting place, stepped toward her, and pressed his nose against hers. In a split-second, he had disappeared into the woods.

"He's gone," she complained to Adam.

"That's alright. You have the message you needed. Store it away in a safe place. It's time to move on. There's another path leading away from the clearing. Do you see it?"

Angela got up from the grass. To her right, where the fox had entered, there was a small trail. "Okay, yeah."

"Good. As you follow this path, you'll notice it's growing wider with every step. The trees are beginning to thin. Up ahead, you see the path is leading you to a house."

She gazed into the distance and saw a lodge not far away.

"Keep walking toward the house. There's a party going on inside," Adam's voice directed her. "You don't have to knock. Go on inside. You've been invited. Everyone is expecting you."

Angela climbed the wooden steps to a wrap-around deck. She heard animated voices, and through the window, she saw a lively cocktail party underway. Reaching for the handle, Angela opened the door and stepped inside.

The main room was packed with people, all strangers, each turning to smile in welcome as she passed. She walked to the center of the room, looking for any familiar face.

"I'm inside," Angela told Adam. "But I don't see anyone I know here."

"There is someone in this room who wants to talk to you," he told her. "Just look around, see who grabs your attention."

Angela scanned the surrounding faces. She noticed a man in the back corner, standing alone, unlike the others engaged in loud conversation. He was looking directly at her, smiling.

He waved her over. The crowd parted, making a pathway for her. As she approached, she studied this strange character, noting his colorful clothing and longish, dark hair. He was sipping a bright red beverage from a paper cup. There was something intensely familiar about him.

Angela extended her hand in greeting. "I'm Angela. Have we met before?"

Refusing her handshake, he laughed. "In a manner of speaking."

She smiled at his accent. "You're a foreigner. Irish?"

He winked at her. "Close. I'd offer you a drink," he said, indicating his cup, "But you can't have any of this."

"Why not?" She tried to see what he was drinking, but he kept the cup in motion, deliberately defying her.

"Because they don't make it in the States!" He roared with laughter, quite pleased with himself. He finished his drink in one large gulp.

She crossed her arms and regarded him suspiciously. "Who are you?"

He looked at her lazily and smiled. Angela was struck by the intense depth of his eyes. Green.

"I am Master Robin of Thither and Yon." He dropped into an exaggerated bow before her, then straightened again with a flourish of his hands. "I play the fife and drum," he practically sang.

"Okay," she responded warily. "What are you doing here?"

"Well, technically," he began, playing with his fingers, "I'm everywhere you are. Except, of course, that I'm not."

"Are you a guide for me?"

"No," he responded flatly.

"Thank God."

He again erupted into laughter. "The blind leading the blind, that would be. I'm an earthly sort, as you are." He indicated the crowd behind her. "This is an odd party, don't you agree?"

"But I'm supposed to meet a guide here." Angela looked around to see if anyone else wanted to talk with her, but they were all absorbed in their own conversations. She turned back to her companion and observed his clothing. "You look like a court jester."

He smiled broadly. "A rainbow has wept over me. I'm afraid I'm not much help to you right now, am I?"

Angela shook her head. "I have no idea what I'm supposed to get out of this impossible conversation."

She felt a hand on her shoulder and turned to find Adam in her vision. "It's time to move on," he said gently. "There's someone waiting for you in another room."

"This guy is a nut case," she confided, indicating the character behind her.

Adam pointed out a hallway on the other side of the room. "Go down that corridor. It's the first door on the left."

Angela obeyed. Reaching the door in question, she pushed it open, revealing a remarkably beautiful woman, her skin a warm terra cotta. Her waist-length hair, hanging loose down her back, was the color of the ocean. Clad in a flowing silk gown of pale lavender, she welcomed Angela with a loving gaze and the gentlest of smiles.

"Come in." Her voice was music. "My name is Isis." She had amethysts and stones of lapis lazuli for eyes.

Angela stepped into the room. "You don't look like Isis."

The ageless woman smiled again and nodded. "It's a name you can understand, one you can remember. What did you think of your companion outside?"

Angela shook her head and sighed in incredulous frustration. Isis laughed, a sound like the tinkling of crystal.

"It can be difficult to get a clear line of communication, when you're both awake," Isis offered. "You were just as much of an enigma to him as he was to you just now."

"I find that hard to believe."

Isis laughed again as she crossed the room, floating over the floor. She came to rest at a lectern on which rested a very old, very large book. "I want to show you something," she said, opening the volume.

Angela stepped up beside her, only now aware of her great height and the shimmering translucence of her skin. Standing next to Isis, Angela felt her own body buzzing in sympathetic vibration, just below the surface. She looked down at the pages in front of her and saw a great swirling of color, as if someone had spilled metallic paint onto the ancient papyrus. Dominated by shades of bluish purple, the pages also contained deep aquas and greens, with occasional bits of fuchsia and pink. The colors swam and eddied about under the direction of Isis' long, slender fingers.

"What is it?" Angela asked in amazement.

"A map of your journey," Isis explained. "Few have access to this during their lifetimes. You will always remember having seen this. You will always remember exactly what it looks like, though you may never consciously know what it means."

"It looks like the star chart for an unformed galaxy," Angela offered.

Isis placed a loving hand on Angela's head, touching her lightly. Angela felt her body fill with the subtle energy of an intensely bright but invisible light.

"Go now," Isis whispered softly. "And keep this vision of your path."

Angela blinked, and was suddenly back in the hallway, leaning against the closed door. She could hear the cocktail party as she stood alone in the dim corridor.

"Okay, I'm finished with that room now," she said aloud to Adam.

"Angela, I want you to continue down that same hallway, away from the party," he suggested. "There is a room at the very end of the hallway. Inside is another guide, the last one you'll meet today."

She walked quickly toward the open door ahead of her. Stepping into the brightly lit room, she was surprised to find a familiar face awaiting her.

"Oh!" She exclaimed aloud. "It's Michael!"

Angela was beaming, happy to see her old friend again. Michael embraced her and held her tightly. "I'm glad you haven't forgotten me."

"I wasn't sure I had remembered you at all," she admitted. Searching her memory, she laughed. "I'm not sure what from childhood was real, and what was pure fantasy."

"Your mind doesn't know the difference," he advised. He tapped the top of her head. "Whatever's in there is in there for a reason. Whether real or not, it's the material you work with. And who says imagination isn't real?" He laughed.

"I guess I should have known you would show up here, even though none of this has been what I anticipated."

Michael motioned toward a pair of chairs by the window, and the two sat down.

"What did you expect to find?"

Angela squinted and looked at the ceiling. "I really don't know. I guess I thought it would be more magical, you know? More mysterious, dramatic. Although that guy at the party seems to have those bases covered pretty well."

"He's in somewhat of a chaotic state these days," Michael confided. "There's quite a bit of change he is embracing."

"Well, what's he doing here? I thought I was going to meet all of these great guides to help give me a clue about what I'm supposed to be doing."

Michael smiled at her impatience. "You're never going to get all the answers you want at the same time, Angela. It's not going to happen the way you want it to, and as long as you hold that expectation, it will continue to be one of your biggest obstacles. Wisdom comes in pieces, so you can make sense out of the little bits before getting caught up in the global whole. That's what she showed you down the hall, you know. She showed you the big picture, and it was too much for you to understand."

Angela sighed and crossed her ankles. "Yes."

He leaned closer to her. "You're getting an awful lot of information all at once here. It's going to take awhile to digest it. Be patient with yourself. With Spirit also, but with yourself in particular. Just sit with all of this, for as long as it takes. Years from now, you'll still be processing what you've seen today."

She gestured toward the door. "So, who are all of those people at the party?"

"They are companion souls, some incarnated, some not. Their paths have, will, and are touching your own. As you move up the energy ladder, time and individuality blur together. Those are human inventions, necessary to live your lives on the physical plane you create. Ultimately, neither exists."

Michael got up and stood by the window. "Your friend out there, for instance. He has privately convinced himself he is the reincarnation of Michelangelo Buonarroti."

"The artist?" Angela asked.

Michael nodded.

"Well, is he?"

Michael turned to face her. "Everyone is the reincarnation of everyone else. And everything else. And the pre-incarnation, as well. There aren't discreet divisions the way you think of them, though there are closer affinities. This will become more clear, although I can see this isn't making much sense to you now."

Indeed, Angela was listening with a growing frown. "Maybe I'm just tired."

He placed a hand on her shoulder. "It's late at night for you, for your body. You've had a full day, and you have attempted to absorb quite a bit here. Don't worry. This is only the beginning."

Angela looked up into his eyes, growing steadily brighter. She felt herself drawn into them, closer and closer, as they reached out to embrace her. Abruptly, she was aware once again of her physical surroundings, sitting on the floor of her dormitory room, lit only by a handful of candles. She could hear the music playing nearby. She opened her eyes to the inquisitive faces of her friends.

* * * *

Angela spent the next hour relating to Adam and Susan all she had seen and heard during her pathworking experience. They had turned on a desk lamp now that the real work was over. Adam was encouraged, and at the end of her story, he asked, "And what do you make of all of that?"

She was stunned by his simple question. "I don't have a clue in the world."

Adam laughed. "I've only gone through the pathworking once myself, and that was enough. You could spend the rest of your life trying to figure it all out. But I can offer my own perspective on a few points, if you'd like."

Angela was relieved. "Please."

Susan flipped the tape over as Adam took a long drink from a glass of water.

Adam cleared his throat and rested his hands together in his lap. "Alright. The fox can represent innocence, loyalty, cleverness, camouflage. Any and all of the above. You can look it up in books about animal totems. You'll know intuitively what his appearance signifies to you. What was interesting about your fox is that he dashed in, then stopped everything and sat down in the grass with you. He invited you to be still, to slow down, before he imparted his wisdom. What does that say to you?"

Angela chewed the edge of her thumb as she considered. "That maybe running around all the time will only accomplish so much?"

Adam smiled and nodded.

"So you might try meditation or yoga, something requiring more relaxed concentration than activity," Susan suggested.

"Okay, I'll tell you about the people you saw in the house," Adam continued.

"Thank you," Angela responded emphatically.

"Not everyone has the same experience, so there's no exact formula. It sounds like the second and third guides were actually two different aspects of your Higher Self, your soul's connection to the Divine. And one of these you had encountered before?"

Angela nodded. "Honestly, I guess I thought Michael had been an imaginary playmate or something, if I even remembered him at all. He just made me feel safe when I was afraid and alone, and very small."

"I would say Michael is your advisor, and the woman, Isis, is your advocate. He's going to be easier to talk to because he's closer to your plane of existence. He is you, of course, but at a higher vibration. Does that make sense?"

"Umm…?" Angela looked to Susan for support, but she just shrugged.

"Don't worry about it," Adam said. "Isis is more on the ethereal side, and Michael is more mundane. That's about all I'm trying to say."

Angela stretched her arms out to her sides, stifling a yawn. Susan gathered what was left of the candles into a canvas bag.

"As for that other person, the fife and drum guy…" Adam began.

Angela threw her hands up in the air and laughed. "Yeah!"

"It sounds like he may be earth-bound, incarnate," Susan offered

"You mean a living person?" Angela asked. "That's weird. Why would he be hanging around my pathworking party?"

"Or perhaps someone who has just recently passed, or a 'lower angel,' as they say," Adam commented.

"Oh, is that what they say?" Angela asked sarcastically.

"Mmm, yes." Adam checked his watch. It was well past 2 a.m. He got up from the floor, and Angela followed suit. She extended her hand to him, which he shook readily.

"Thank you, Adam," she said sincerely. "I appreciate your doing this, especially so late at night. I'm sorry I'm so tired."

"This can take a lot out of you, give you a lot to think about," he replied. "I would follow Michael's advice. Just sit with this. You don't need to figure it out overnight. Or even at all."

Adam opened the door and stepped into the hallway. Susan gave Angela a warm hug.

"Get some sleep," Susan told her. "I'll call you in the morning."

Angela locked the door behind them. She changed into a big tee-shirt and boxer shorts and switched out the Andreas Vollenweider tape for Peter Gabriel's PASSION, an early birthday present to herself. As the music rose from beneath her feet and filled the room, Angela tilted her head from side to side and yawned loudly. She was glad her roommate was spending the night with her boyfriend. The last thing she needed right now was more contact, human or otherwise.

She stretched her arms high over her head and let out a long, audible sigh, releasing tension from her body. She bent her knees and bounced gently as she brought her arms back down, then rested her hands on her hips. She looked around the room and clicked her tongue against her teeth. She was exhausted.

"Right," she said at last. "Bed."

She shut off the music, turned off the lamp, and crawled into her standard-issue, twin bed. Within thirty seconds, she was deep in sleep.

* * * *

Gloucester, Gloustershire

Robin's hands were still stained blue, green, and pink.

Rose had been visiting for the weekend, and father and daughter had launched a tie-dyeing project that had quickly grown out of control. In the colourful excitement, every pair of Robin's socks had gone into the mix, as well as several shirts, a pair of trousers, and his underwear. The cat himself had barely escaped.

Regarding himself in the mirror, Robin admired the blinding kaleidoscope of his oxford shirt. Beneath his white denim jeans, now splashed through with swirling patterns of aqua, his cotton briefs were green and purple. His socks were a subtle swarm of yellow, orange, and pink.

"All I need is a big hat and some pointy shoes," he said to his reflection, "and I can take a position as court jester." What a way to re-enter the real world after being out on tour, he thought silently.

It was Sunday evening. Gwendolyn was downstairs in the kitchen. Although he had been living with Gwen in her Gloucester townhouse for more than a year, he still wasn't comfortable. Obligations at the studio in Winchester kept him away for days or weeks at a time, and now that construction had begun on his own house on the New Haven property, Robin felt increasing pressure regarding the future of the relationship.

One thing was certain, Robin reminded himself as he slipped into his leather sandals. Gwendolyn will be furious when she finds out we dyed her new sheets.

Strolling into the kitchen looking like a fashion experiment gone awry, Robin found Gwen at the sink drying her hands, finished with the dishes. He stepped up behind her and kissed her quickly below her ear.

"Thanks for your patience this weekend," he said quietly, slipping an arm around her waist.

Sinking into his embrace, she turned to face him with a smile, but was caught off-guard by his clothing. "Good lord."

Robin chuckled and stepped back to be admired, spreading his arms wide. "What do you think?"

"That I don't want to be seen in public with you any time in the near future." She hung the damp dish towel on a lower cabinet. She nodded toward a jar of scarlet-coloured liquid sitting on the stove. "Do you want any of that, or should I store it away?"

Robin picked up the jar and studied its contents. "Gareth's bramble scrumpy." He turned the glass in his hands and held it up to the light. The beverage glowed a rich ruby colour. "Well, he was good enough to send it. I suppose we should give it a try."

Gwendolyn produced a small saucepan and placed it on the stovetop. Robin looked to her, questioning.

"Aren't you supposed to serve it warm?" she asked.

"I, I really don't know." He retrieved a coffee mug and a drinking glass from a cabinet. "I'll try it both ways and let you know."

"I'd warn you against spilling any on your clothing, because it would stain." She gestured toward Robin's outfit. "But I don't think it would make much difference."

Laughing appreciatively, Robin struggled to unscrew the lid of the glass jar. "I'm going to try working tonight," he grunted with his effort, at last breaking the seal. "I won't be to bed until late."

"Good luck," she winked. She left him in the kitchen and went upstairs.

* * * *

It was nearly 3 a.m., and the music simply wasn't coming. Robin had carefully set the lighting in the study and had shut the door against any noise, though the window was cracked open to allow the air to circulate. He had the entire night, the entire world, to himself. Everything was perfect. But it would not come.

Some nights were simply like this, and Robin resigned himself in frustration to not having complete control over his own creativity. He preferred the night, when the rest of the world was sleeping. With popular consciousness at a minimum, with everything so quiet, he had greater access to the mystical realms and could tap into the psychic flood of dreams that filled his neighbours' nocturnal minds. Or so he imagined.

He reached for the glass on his desk and swallowed the remaining bramble scrumpy. He winced at the raspberry cider's bite and groaned to clear it from his throat. "That's just awful," he complained.

Robin pushed his chair away from the electronic keyboard on the desk and turned to a stack of books he had been accumulating. Atop the pile, Irving Stone's THE AGONY AND THE ECSTASY had a bookmark buried deep within, though Robin chose a large volume of photographs instead. He opened MICHELANGELO: THE MAN AND HIS WORK to a random page and studied the artist's Pieta for the hundredth time. He ran his fingers over the sinewy muscles of the crucified Christ and the draping folds of Mary's dress.

"My God," Robin whispered in his awe. "That's a master at work."

He lay the book in his lap and looked to the ceiling, his fingers resting on his lips. He wondered how he could possibly harness that kind of raw yet refined power. He closed his eyes and allowed his thoughts to wander.

Michelangelo. Michael Angelo. Angelo Michael. Angela Michaels. "Thank God we chose Rose instead," he murmured, drifting off to sleep.

* * * *

Robin was in a room full of strangers at some kind of party. Everyone was elegantly dressed, and here he was in his tie-dye fantasia, his fingers and nails still stained with colour. He found himself in an empty corner, away from the loud conversations. He looked out the window at the trees casting magical shadows in the sunlight.

He took another sip of the bramble scrumpy and studied the paper cup in his hands. Where had this come from?

A hush came over the room. Robin turned to see the entrance of a young woman, moving effortlessly through the party, not stopping to socialize. Gazing casually about the room, she came to rest in the middle of the gathering. Robin was transfixed by her presence and could not tear his eyes from her face, so very familiar.

It was a long moment before he realized her gaze had met his. He smiled meekly, penetrated to his core by her eyes. "Emeralds," he whispered as she approached.

She extended her hand, introducing herself, but he was so shaken by her touch, he could not make out her words. Finally, he stammered, "Do I know you?"

She smiled broadly. "I'm here to meet you." The lilt of her voice tickled his ear drums.

"Me?" Robin was dumbfounded. "But I'm just a musician." He felt like an adolescent idiot, struggling for every word. Who was this woman?

She reached for the cup in his hands. "May I have some?"

He immediately pulled the drink from her grasp and swallowed the remaining contents. The bitterness stung his throat. "Believe me, you don't want any of that."

He looked again into her eyes, glowing green prisms. The reddish brown halo of her hair shimmered in the light filtering through the windows. "Are you an angel?" he mustered the courage to ask.

An expression of gentle amusement swept over her face, and he felt lightly engulfed by her mirth. "Not exactly," she responded with warm laughter in her voice. "I have my feet on the ground. At least, that's the idea."

He felt his body filling with enchanted delight, staving off the impossible questions swimming through his head. He wanted to run away from this odd party, and take this intriguing woman with him. But he was afraid that if he tried to touch her, or merely said the wrong thing, her image would shatter, and she would disappear into thin air.

Caught up in these thoughts, Robin blinked, and she was gone. There was the vague memory of a smile offered in farewell, but he was left with a dull emptiness in the pit of his stomach. He looked at his dye-stained hands and crumpled the paper cup in his fist.

"I wish…" he whispered, alone in the corner. "I wish I could have touched her eyes."

Suddenly, he was trembling. The room was shaking. It was an earthquake. Looking out the window, he saw the woman standing alone in the grass and heard her calling him. "Robin. Robin."

"Robin. Robin, wake up." Gwendolyn was standing next to his chair and shaking him, trying to rouse him from sleep. "Wake up, Robin."

He opened his eyes to the morning light casting long shadows across the study. As he sat up in his desk chair, the book of photographs in his lap slid to the floor.

"It's nearly seven in the morning." Gwen knelt down to pick up the book. "I suppose you've been down here all night. And you slept in those clothes."

He looked down across his body and squinted his sleepy eyes against the assault of colour. He rose from the chair slowly, feeling every muscle and vertebra protesting.

"Are you on your way out?" he asked as he made it to his feet.

"Yes, I have a breakfast meeting." Gwendolyn retrieved her briefcase from the top of the bookshelf. "When are you leaving for New Haven?"

Robin shook his head, still fighting for full consciousness. "I'll get myself put together and will depart shortly. I'm expected for lunch. I'll be back on Wednesday. Wednesday evening. Probably."

"Probably." Gwen smiled sadly. "Drive safely, alright?"

She gave Robin a quick kiss on the cheek and squeezed his hand.

"I'll call you tonight," he said, patting her hip.

She walked out of the room. Robin stood next to his desk, feeling he might float away, up through the ceiling. He held onto the chair and wiggled his toes, reminding his feet to stay put.

Chapter 39

December 1989
Florence, Italy

Angela wandered through the halls of Florence's Academia Gallery with Susan and several other students lucky enough to be invited to spend winter break at their sociology professor's home outside Cortona. The small group had taken the bus down to the Camucia rail station the previous morning, headed for a long weekend in Florence. After a lazy morning meandering through the landscapes of the Boboli Gardens, they now found themselves in the company of Botticelli's paintings.

"This is incredible!" Susan exclaimed as she and Angela stood before the brilliant oils. "I mean, Viva Italia! At Christmas! And our parents let us come!"

Susan jumped excitedly, spilling a handful of currency onto the marble floor. Bending down, she briefly studied several bills before stuffing them back into her coat pocket. "I just need to get used to all this Monopoly money."

"That's not play money," Angela reminded her friend. "That's lunch."

"Right. 75,000 lira for a Coke!" Susan laughed.

"I don't think that's the exact exchange rate," Angela responded wryly.

Susan beamed, her exuberance oozing out through her pores. "Angela! Look!" Susan gestured to all the walls at once, spinning herself around.

Angela laughed, placing a steadying hand on Susan's shoulder. "Yes, I know," she said appreciatively. "We're in Florence. We're in the Academia."

"Yes!"

"And you'd like to see the David?" Angela asked.

"Umm, yeah," Susan responded coyly.

"Then we need to keep walking." Wrapping an arm around her friend's shoulder, Angela guided Susan slowly through the gallery, pausing in awe in front of each work.

* * * *

Robin stood before the David, his jaw nearly on the floor. "My God," he whispered.

Gwendolyn was making her own way through the gallery. She knew that for Robin, this trip was more about some secretive research than it was a true vacation. She was enjoying herself all the same, and hoping Robin might loosen up a bit.

Standing beneath this sculptural masterpiece, Robin felt exceedingly small.

"What the hell was I thinking?" he demanded under his breath. He felt himself shrinking with each passing second as the colossal figure of Michelangelo's David towered over him.

Feeling a gentle hand on his shoulder, Robin turned slowly, expecting Gwen. Instead, he met the face of a man he felt he should recognize.

"Take a walk with me, Robin," suggested the man with glistening green eyes, his greying beard making way for a warm smile.

* * * *

Robin sat with the familiar stranger at a small table on the piazza, sipping coffee. He wasn't sure how they had gotten here, nor how long ago. It was unseasonably warm, the brightening sun casting a vital glow over the wintering city. Robin studied this man across the table, trying to remember when they had encountered each other before.

"You're not going to be able to recall that information, Robin," he offered with a smile.

"Hmm?"

"You're thinking that you know me, but you cannot place me within the context of any conscious memory," he elaborated.

"Yes," Robin admitted self-consciously, leaning his elbows on the white metal table.

"But you do know me," he suggested.

Robin's face betrayed the turning mental gears. His eyes narrowed, then brightened into an excited, confident smile. He pointed at the man. "Michelangelo!"

The stranger shook his head. "Robin, you have got to let that go. For your purposes, the work of Michelangelo is a small device, to get you in the right place at the right time. The artist himself is not a significant influence in your life."

Disappointed, Robin sank back into his chair. "Alright, then, tell me who you are."

"My name is Michael," he stated simply.

"Michael. Michelangelo. What's the difference?" Robin threw his hands in the air.

Michael leaned forward. "Hear this, Robin. I'm a part of you, and you're a part of me."

Robin felt the dull thud of Michael's words as they rained down on his defensive armour. He smiled blankly, then looked around, trying to find an escape route.

Michael laughed. "I'm not a deranged fan, Robin. And if you were to run, where do you think you would go? You haven't moved a single step from the gallery."

"Oh, come on," Robin protested as he got up from his chair. But turning to walk away from this obviously deluded fellow, he noticed for the first time that the piazza was deserted—an impossibility in mid-day Florence. His surroundings were completely static. The light filling the square was hazy, ethereal. He turned back to face Michael.

"Am I dreaming?"

"Not exactly." Michael motioned for Robin to sit. "You could say you're having a vision."

"A vision?" Robin slowly sank back down into his chair.

"Something like that."

"But...why?" He felt like a child as the simple question crossed his lips.

Michael smiled affectionately. "Well, to start, you simply hadn't been paying attention. I've been trying to get through to you for years. Occasionally something would make an impression, but even then you were integrating unconsciously. So, now that you've managed to get yourself here, I thought I'd take you aside and invite you to pull back the veil. To awaken."

"Uh," Robin responded vaguely, shaking his head. "I don't know what any of that means."

"Don't worry," Michael suggested. "It will begin to make sense in time."

Robin peered into Michael's eyes. "Are you sure you're not Michelangelo?"

"Quite." Michael rested his hands in his lap and leaned back in his chair. "I gave you the song, *My Michelangelo*, you know. And that suggestion was used again to get you here. You are in Florence, Robin, on this very spot on this exact day, for a particular reason. Do not doubt this."

Robin frowned. "And you're sure you're not a psychotic stalker?"

Michael laughed. "What do you think, Robin? It's time to awaken. Are you ready?"

Robin sighed. "I don't understand."

"To your spirit. To yourself." Michael looked into his eyes with sincere tenderness. "Are you ready to wake up?"

"Robin. Robin?" Gwendolyn was standing beside him. The David loomed again before him the moment he became conscious of her voice. He was standing in the gallery. He had never left.

"Hey. Wake up."

He turned to her in a sluggish daze, as though he truly had fallen asleep, standing up, eyes open.

"You alright?" Gwen asked with a concerned smile.

"Um, yeah," he answered, recovering himself. "Did you get to see everything?"

Gwendolyn chuckled. "Not quite everything, but enough. I'm ready to move on. You?" She nodded toward the sculpture.

Robin glanced back up at the magnificent marble. What had he just been thinking? He grasped at a vague image of a man at a café... then it was gone. He turned to Gwen. "You fancy a bit of coffee?"

She smiled in agreement and turned to head back to the gallery's main entrance. Robin was a step behind when he suddenly found his feet rooted to the floor.

There, just now approaching the statue, was a face that made time stand still. She was young, probably a student. Rich brown hair, with hints of red. And her eyes! He caught a quick flash of them before she turned away to admire a framed oil painting.

Robin was nearly hyperventilating. "I am here." The feminine voice inside his head rocked him to his core. Completely shaken, he was sure his skeleton was about to collapse within his skin. He broke into a sweat, though he rather liked the sensation reverberating through his body.

He was desperate for her to turn around, to see her eyes again. He stood his ground, hoping to plant himself in her path. But she and her friend crossed on the far side of the room, missing him completely. He watched her circle the David, marveling at the work.

"Robin?" Gwen had returned to retrieve him, placing a hand on his elbow. At her touch, a shiver ran up Robin's spine. He shuddered, unintentionally shaking off the vibration coursing through him. A large student group crowded around the statue, and he lost sight of the girl. The world was still again.

"Right," he sighed. He turned with Gwen and walked away, feeling as though he had been hit by a freight train.

* * * *

Angela approached slowly, in complete awe of the calculated strokes of the chisel, the intimate understanding of human anatomy that had produced such a powerful figure. She gazed up at the statue, her eyes tracing every line and curve of David's limbs.

"Now, that's the master at work," she said to herself quietly.

There was a disturbance, a vague movement in the air. She felt the floor vibrating subtly beneath her feet. An earthquake? She looked around in confusion, the light itself dancing across her field of vision. The trembling was coming from inside herself.

Someone spoke her name. Was that Susan? No, it was a man. She heard nothing but the fading echoes of his voice. Angela scanned the gallery, searching for a familiar face, not knowing what to expect. Her entire world crystallized into a prism of haloed light as she saw the side of his face. He was turning away, retreating down the hallway.

Susan placed a hand on Angela's shoulder. "Angie? Are you okay?"

At her touch, the pulsation ceased. She was surrounded again by the nuisance of the crowded gallery. He was gone, disappeared into the mass of tourists.

Angela took stock of the space around her. Everything was perfectly normal. What had just happened? She saw the concern in Susan's eyes and smiled.

"I'm fine," she lied. "I just got dizzy there for a second." Angela gestured toward the statue. "I didn't expect it to be so big! I feel like a tiny dwarf next to this thing."

Chapter 40

October 1990

Winchester, Hampshire

It had only been a few months since Robin had moved into his new home on the perimeter of the New Haven property. He liked the snug cottage feeling, and visitors were surprised to find a full second story hidden beneath the sloping roof.

Robin stood barefoot in the kitchen, enjoying the cool ceramic tile beneath his feet. Clad only in his bathrobe, he composed ridiculous pop tunes as he cooked breakfast.

"Talk about... mmm, yes. Shake me. Double-up, double-down. Pop music!" Robin sang as he turned the bacon and slid a few pieces of bread into the oven for toasting. "Da-da-da-da. In control. Hey! Everybody now."

He heard the shower come on upstairs and smiled. He took a step back from the stove top and looked about. "Alright. Plates, plates, plates."

Opening one of the wooden cabinets, Robin pulled down two plates from his mismatched fiesta collection. "Beans and bacon on the plates," he sang, swinging his hips and tapping the spatula as he served. "Ba-ba-ba, ba-ba-ba-ba bacon!"

He was happily outdoing himself, though he regretted not having fresh fruit for hand-squeezed juice. He would have just made a big mess out of that. An attractive autumn bouquet of grasses and small flowers from his yard sat on the breakfast table next to an open window. Open-air dining.

Robin admired the table he had set. Much better than the miserable burnt mash he had forgotten on the stove in Alice's apartment so many years ago.

He heard footsteps overhead and giddily anticipated Alice's reaction to his efforts. Despite last night's argument, these past weeks had been wonderful, better than he could have imagined.

When they delivered Rose for her final year at St. Barbara's, he had noticed something different about Alice, something playful and endearing. Within a week, she had phoned to invite Robin into London for dinner. They had easily fallen into step again.

There were visits back and forth and a long weekend exploring St. Ives and the Isles of Scilly. It wasn't that same, blissful blush he had known when they were first courting. But her companionship was comfortable, encouraging. Her presence quieted the persistent doubt that had plagued him since Gwendolyn's exit. After the unwieldy defeat of their divorce, Robin basked in this potential redemption.

He stood in the open doorway and looked out on the nearby woods and the small stone circle he had constructed his first weekend in this house. He envied his daughter with a kind of sentimental dread. St. Anthony's. St. Barbara's. What's the difference?

When building this home, he had specified a bedroom for Rose when she came to visit. They would need a larger place now, Robin reasoned. He was tied by his partnership in New Haven, several hours by train from London, where Alice had built a successful career of her own. But he was confident some agreeable compromise could be sorted out.

Robin walked across the porch and stepped down onto the grass, the moist, green blades sliding between his bare toes. He felt the light spring of soil beneath his feet and almost laughed. After the marriage had ended, he had been afraid of commitment, wary of all relationships. But there was no more trepidation. Alice, his anchor, had returned.

"There you are," came Alice's voice from behind him.

Robin turned and smiled at her, standing in the kitchen doorway. He mounted the stairs to the porch and reached for her. She wrapped her arms around his waist.

"No fair," he murmured into her neck, kissing her ear. "You got dressed."

"Yes, well..." She pulled away from him and stepped back into the kitchen. "You really didn't need to go to such trouble over breakfast."

"It was no trouble." He walked behind her, his hands on her shoulders. "I wanted to do it."

"It's just, I don't think I'll have time this morning..." Alice faced him, her expression unsure. He looked past her into the front hallway. Her suitcase stood ready by the door. His smile quickly shrank from his lips.

"I don't understand." He looked squarely into her face, transfixing her with his eyes. Alice turned her head and stepped away.

"It's time for me to say goodbye, Robin," she said, staring at the floor.

He crossed the few metres to the breakfast table and took a seat, motioning for Alice to do the same. "Let's just sit down and talk about this."

Alice crossed her arms over her chest and leaned against the wall. "No," she said firmly. "This is not going to work. We want different things."

Robin shifted in his chair to face her, waiting for her to continue. Alice sighed and released her arms. She took a few steps closer to her former husband.

"I've had a wonderful time with you, Robin, these past weeks. Really I have." She gazed into those gorgeous green eyes she knew so well. His hair was more grey, thinning at the temples. Every one of his thirty-eight years showed in his face. Alice thought he looked incredibly sexy, even in a frumpy robe. She offered him her most intimate smile.

"I think we both needed this, to reconnect and remember the good things about our relationship." She paced easily in front of the table. "But that wasn't enough to save our marriage. Not then, and not now."

Robin sat back and looked out the open window. "I thought we had moved past all of that."

"In some ways." Alice sat down across the table from him. "But you and I, we're in different places now. Perhaps we always have been."

She looked down at the table, then followed Robin's gaze out the window. She closed her eyes. "Leaving you was the most difficult thing I've ever done in my life."

Robin brought his attention back inside and studied her profile. "I know," he almost whispered. He watched the sunlight dance across her blonde hair, duller now than when they had first met, but still beautifully familiar.

Alice looked into his eyes and felt her heart leap into her throat. "But I had to do it. It was the right thing, for all of us."

"That was years ago," he entreated. "Everything is so much different today."

"I agree," she nodded. "And I like it. I have a life of my own I never had before. I'm not constantly caught up in the emotional drama our lives together had become."

Robin sighed. "It doesn't have to be that way, Alice. We've already started over. The past few weeks have shown that we're not the same people we were. We've both grown so much since then."

"Yes, we have." Alice reached across the table, and Robin slid his hands into hers, trying to smile as he looked into her brown eyes. "But that doesn't mean we've grown closer together."

Robin tightened his grip around his ex-wife's fingers as he looked down at their joined hands.

"When we were talking last night," she said gently, "it was so clear that we had come back together for entirely different reasons. There's no denying it any longer. You want to rebuild our marriage. I don't."

Robin got up from the table and walked across the kitchen floor. "Is it so wrong to want that, Alice?" He raised his voice, the anxious hurt bordering on anger. "To want a home and a family? A normal and stable home life. After all, we have a daughter together."

"And she's beautiful, Robin. I thank God for Rose every day of my life. But you and I simply don't belong together. I've loved this time with you. Honestly. It's wonderful to know we can be like that again. We've had a lot of fun. But having an affair is a much different proposition than having a relationship."

Robin felt bolted to the floor, a torrent of cold lead shunting from his heart down into his feet. "An affair?"

Alice got up from her seat. "I think I'd better go now."

"Is that what this has been to you?" he demanded. "An affair?"

Alice spun on her heel, her back toward him. She remained calm, unwilling to replay the old tapes they had recorded together, over and over again. She cleared her throat and placed her hands on her hips. Slowly, she turned to face him.

"Robin, I think you need to stand on your own two feet just now."

His face was blank, with a hint of incredulity at the corners of his mouth.

Alice took a step closer. "You and I were together for a long time, beginning when we were very young. Even during our separations, when we weren't physically together, there was still this connection, something to fall back on. Even so, you spent that time surrounding yourself with other relationships."

She could see his defenses going up as he set his jaw and crossed his arms over his chest. She smiled reassuringly.

"I'm not trying to start an argument with you. I'm just concerned about you."

"So concerned that you've decided to leave me," his voice was hard, uncompromising.

"Robin, I want you to listen to what I'm saying," Alice soothed. She didn't want this message to get lost in another altercation. "You've really never been alone. You've never tried life on your own. I think maybe it's time you tried doing that."

"I don't know what you're talking about," he protested, stepping several paces away, facing the kitchen door. "I'm alone all the time. All I'm trying to do is open up a bit more, for a real partnership. I thought that's what you wanted." He turned back to Alice, challenging her.

She clasped her hands in front of her chest and bowed her head. "You're always holding that space open, waiting for someone to walk in. While there's nothing intrinsically wrong with that... Ask yourself, honestly, how much of you wanted to be with me, and how much just didn't want to be alone? It hasn't been that long since, since you and Gwendolyn split. That was a significant relationship for you. Maybe you were reaching out to me again for stability and reassurance."

"Alice..." Robin was exasperated. He had no idea what he wanted to say.

"I'm just suggesting you spend some time alone. See what that's like. It might be a good idea to concentrate on just being you right now. Find out who you really are, by yourself, apart from everyone else."

Robin had his hands on his hips, eyes cast downward. Alice knew there was nothing more she could say to him that would penetrate.

She closed the distance between them and took his hands into hers. "I love you, Robbie. You know I always, I always have. And I'm very proud of the work that you're doing. I want you to know that."

Robin interlaced his fingers with hers. "I know," he said quietly.

"Goodbye," she whispered, her eyes filling with tears. Squeezing his hands tightly, Alice leaned close to kiss him on the cheek. "Thank you, for everything."

Robin stood staring at the floor as she moved away from him. He felt the familiar, dull ache in his chest as the door closed behind her.

* * * *

Not even an hour had passed when Robin stepped out of the shower. The hot water had beat onto his scalp and coursed down the contours of his body while he imagined this grey pain washing away down the drain.

He pulled on his most comfortable clothes—loose-fitting trousers, a cotton jumper, well-worn leather sandals—and stared at himself in the mirror for a very long time.

* * * *

Breakfast had long since grown cold. Robin carried the plates outside and set them down in the grass as an offering. Jasper the cat was out here someplace and would no doubt make good work of the bacon. Robin had lost his appetite.

He shoved his hands deep into his trouser pockets. The sun shone brightly, and the air was heating up. Such beautiful weather, Robin thought to himself, scanning his horizon. Such a beautiful day.

"Might as well make the most of it, old boy," Robin said to himself as he shifted his weight between his feet in the grass.

Robin breathed in the cleansing sunlight, then came back inside the house and wandered into the living room. He stood before the hearth and looked at the photos of his daughter, his parents, his brother and sister, and of himself, Alice, and Rose together. He cleared his throat and kicked his toes against the hardwood floor.

The exposed stone wall supported instruments and artefacts from across the globe. His gaze came to rest on the flute, suspended above the mantle — that same, tired instrument from the pawn shop that had enraged Alice. The flute he had taught himself to play.

He reached up to touch the cool metal, trying to remember when he had last felt its weight in his hands. His mind swam with the images and sounds of the Green Man. He smiled.

Robin lifted the flute from the wall and ran the fabric of his jumper across to dust it off. With fingers carefully poised, he raised the instrument to his lips.

Chapter 41

November 1992
Bowie, Maryland

It came in sharp, stabbing pains, as if someone had plunged a dagger deep into her abdomen and was slowly twisting the blade. Angela stumbled through the strange hallway and closed the bathroom door quietly before switching on the light.

Soaking a washcloth in the sink, she regarded herself in the mirror. Her face was completely white, her eyes dull and hollow. She held the cool cloth against her face and bent over the sink, taking heavy, thick breaths. She gasped as her knees buckled, another searing spasm attacking. She sank to the floor.

It had been only minor discomfort at first, easily dismissed. Angela had assumed she had eaten too much Thanksgiving dinner, or perhaps something on the menu wasn't agreeing with her. She put the cramping out of her mind. She hadn't wanted to worry Carl's family, who had welcomed her into their home for the holiday.

Asleep in his boyhood bedroom, Carl knew nothing of his girlfriend's distress. She was grateful they weren't sharing a bed. She honestly didn't want anyone with her now.

Angela pressed her face against the cool floor tiles under the sink and curled her body into a tight ball. Here it comes again, her mind screamed in silence. She clenched her fists and tightened her jaw against the pain. She imagined dropping this torture on the floor and dashing down the stairs, out into the night. But that sharp stabbing came at her again, striking her pubic bone and ripping upward into her belly.

She clamped her hands over her mouth, whimpering pitifully. The last thing she wanted was to wake anyone. The embarrassment of being a sick stranger in her boyfriend's parents' house would be worse than the pain. She would get through this. It would pass. Angela braced her bare feet against the base of the toilet.

Her eyes were closed tightly, her breath coming in quiet gasps. The trauma had temporarily subsided, allowing a moment of peace. But she knew it was coming again. Another wave might strike at any second.

With desperate tears, Angela prayed. She dismissed guilt, knowing she only sought God when she was in need. But she did need now. In this shallow valley between the sharp peaks of pain, fear was creeping in. She knew what was happening, having denied her situation for weeks. So much hope and terror had been bound together, joy and panic flooding her simultaneously. She hadn't said a word to anyone, not even to Carl.

"Oh, God," she whispered in her smallest voice, stray tears running over her lips. "Please. Please help me get through this."

Angela took a cautious breath, giving her muscles a tenuous instant of rest. A gentle warmth slowly seeped into her, running the length of her spine, spreading into her limbs. She opened her eyes. The small room was filling with soft light. She blinked. The light grew brighter.

She pulled herself from the floor and sat up, leaning against the warm coils of the radiator. She felt calm and comforted. Safe. Angela sensed an unmistakable, invisible presence somewhere within this subtle glowing.

Managing another deep breath, she felt the oxygen course down into her toes. "Okay," she whispered.

"It's in your hands, Angela," a quiet voice inside suggested, echoed in the rhythm of her heart. "Your hands."

She lifted her hands from the floor and looked curiously into her palms. A golden, glowing light pulsed just beneath the skin. She could feel the heat flowing into her fingertips. "Okay," she replied, not caring if she might be hallucinating.

Angela reached for a towel on the wall rack and spread it out beneath her on the cold floor. Pressing back against the radiator, she pulled her knees close. She flexed her fingers to encourage the energy flow, feeling the next ripping wave threatening.

"Mmm," she grunted, her first impulse to again fight the pain. Angela inhaled deliberately and rested her palms on her slightly rounded abdomen. Searing pain dulled into uncomfortable throbbing, and she could feel movement beneath her hands. Her skin tingled under her fingertips. She closed her eyes and concentrated on steady breathing.

"Thank you," she whispered fervently, desperately grateful for the release from pain. She felt a great flood beneath her hands, rushing downward, out of her body.

A deep sob rose in her throat, a silent, mournful moan as she felt the passing. Opening her eyes, she was embraced by the sticky wet smell of her own womb. Looking down onto the dark towel, tears again sprang to her eyes when she saw the tiny gelatinous mass within a pool of blood.

"Oh," she choked. Controlling her sobbing, she touched the dying cells that would have been her child. "Goodbye, little one," she whispered, tears streaming down her cheeks.

* * * *

Angela lay awake the rest of the night, staring up at the ceiling, never moving, barely blinking. Her mind swam with impossible thoughts, long forgotten regrets, uncertain fantasies about the future. The fragile prospect of life.

"I know this is stupid," she whispered in the dark, conscious of a stray tear trickling into her ear. "But I can't help feeling morbidly panicked, as if this were my only chance."

She chased her thoughts, her breath quickening with immediate emotion. "I know this is for the best. I know that," her anxious voice strained. "It would have been a disaster, for everyone. For me, for Carl… especially for the child."

She swallowed hard, fighting back the rush of reactive grief. Separate fact from feeling, she reminded herself impatiently. She breathed deeply and forced her mind into quiet. Her muscles relaxed. Angela felt herself finally drifting into an exhausted sleep.

The sky was lightening with the coming down. "You already have a child," a familiar voice. "You have a daughter. Rose."

"Mmm," she murmured unconsciously against the pillow.

Chapter 42

March 1993

Hastings-on-Hudson, New York

"What would you say is your biggest regret?" Mary K asked gently.

Robin looked into a far corner of the room. "Being a better parent," he said strongly. "I don't much like to focus on the regrets of my life, because I cannot change the past. I am who I am, for better or worse. I can still make headway in certain areas, take advantage of the time and opportunities that remain. But I wish I had been a better father, that I had been more present for my daughter as she was growing up."

He reached for his drinking glass. "There's so much Alice and I went through, and I'm sure… Well," Robin took a sip of water and swallowed quickly. "I don't think there's any way a child can NOT be affected by the relationship between the parents. It's a symbiotic unit, parents and child together."

Her tape machine clicked off. Mary K raised her hand, asking Robin to hold his thoughts. She ejected the full cassette, wrote a number on it, and then put a blank tape in. Robin shifted his weight in the generous chair, feeling the supportive padding conforming to his shape. Mary K made a few notes and hit the Record button.

Robin looked through the window of her apartment onto the Hudson River. "How long have you been living here?"

"Not quite two years," she responded, looking up from her notebook.

"What's the name of this town again?"

"Hastings-on-Hudson. I like it here," Mary K commented. "Nice people, good distance from the city, still close enough to commute."

Robin nodded, listening to one of the trains on the Metro-North line go rumbling past along the river below, heading back toward New York City.

"Good view," he offered. "I like the sound of the rails below."

Mary K smiled. "You were talking about parents and children, your own relationship with Rose".

"Right." Robin leaned back and collected his thoughts, threading his fingers together in his lap. "I've always had it in the back of my head that my own, mmm, romantic involvements, learning through relationships, would have an effect on my daughter. That's a fine line to walk. You want to provide a strong role model for your child, while also needing to live your own life and work through your own stuff."

He paused, glancing out again toward the water. He imagined what summer would look like with sailboats on the Hudson.

"I figure I'm doing the best I can," Robin said quietly, the late winter sun highlighting his eyes. He turned back to Mary K. "The best gift I can give Rose is to live my life as honestly and as openly as I can. That means making mistakes—huge ones sometimes. God knows I've had my fair share. But it also means integrity, trying to be the best person I can be every day. So I can reach the end, hold up the years of my life, and say, 'I've had a good run.'"

"Let's talk about those big mistakes," she suggested.

Robin smiled uncomfortably and leaned forward, resting his elbows on his knees. "Ah, yes, I knew we'd come to this again."

"Don't feel you have to cover everything at once, Robin," Mary K reassured him. "It's not as though this is our only meeting. That's the great part of writing a book, instead of just an article."

"Yeah, it takes a hell of a lot longer."

"Do you want to stop now? Take a break or something?" she offered.

"No, that's alright," Robin backed off. "I'm sorry. I guess I'm a little tired."

"We don't have much longer this afternoon anyway. I really appreciate your making time for this, your availability by phone and correspondence," she told him.

"It's not completely selfless. I do get a cut of the profits, if there'll be any. I'm still trying to figure out," Robin started to laugh, "why anyone would be interested in reading about such a sorry sod."

"Robin!" Mary K exclaimed with a surprised smile. "You don't give yourself nearly enough credit, you know that?"

"Hmmph," Robin pondered. "Perhaps."

"Would you like to continue?"

"Mmm, yeah," he responded tentatively. "You know, Mary K, I'm glad I never asked you out on a date."

"Oh, thank you very much, Robin," she replied flatly.

"No, I meant…" he stammered. "Sure, I thought about it, when I first met you. But, what I was trying to say is, I'm glad that we're friends."

She smiled sweetly. "Me, too. Of course," she gestured toward the notebook in her lap, "it's been a profitable relationship for me!"

"Right," Robin chuckled. "But I don't think I'd be doing a book project, I can't think of anyone else who could've convinced me to agree to a biography."

"An authorized biography," she corrected him.

"Mmm." She had hit a sore spot. Robin rubbed his palms on the tops of his knees, then leaned back. "So, let's talk about those mishaps of mine."

Mary K nodded and held her pen poised over her notebook, glancing quickly at the tape recorder to make sure it was still running.

"My relationships with women," he mused. Robin took a deep breath and sighed. "Ah, you could say I've always been looking for the other half of myself. It's odd to think of it that way, since each of us is complete and whole, within ourselves, if we'll allow ourselves that realization and actuality."

"So you feel you're only half a person?" she asked.

"Mmm. No, not exactly. It's not a matter of incompleteness," he attempted to explain. "I know who I am. I'm not looking for anyone to fill any kind of emptiness inside of me. I, well, I'd like to think I've gotten that part worked out for myself. Rather, it's a matter of a complement... Umm, I suppose how a pair of Siamese twins might—is that a politically correct term? Siamese twins?"

Mary K shook her head. "I don't know."

"Joined, conjoined twins? How they must feel, having developed in the womb together." Robin wove his knuckles together in demonstration. "Physically connected, then to be separated—through surgery or whatever—into two completely separate bodies." He pulled his hands apart, emphasizing the distance between them. "They are separate people. Individual beings. They don't need each other to survive, to be whole. But there has been a splitting apart of what was once a single unit."

Mary K nodded. "So you're looking for your twin. In a manner of speaking."

"Mmm. Yes," Robin affirmed. "And it occurs to me, well, I've always assumed this was a romantic partner. Actually, I've not thought much about it, at this level of detail. I suppose it could be another kind of pairing."

"But it is a woman," Mary K offered.

"Yeah, that's my feeling. Or my own feminine side, embracing that part of myself. But, umm, anyway, that's not really what we were talking about," Robin brought himself back into focus. "Alice and I married very young. December 1971. I was nineteen years old, if you can believe it. Alice was a bit older, twenty, but we were both just children."

"Was it a rocky marriage from the beginning?"

"Not really." He thought a moment. "I don't know what it was. It was nice. Fun. But it was also a real struggle. There was no money—and I mean NO money—and we were still figuring out who we were individually, playing at being adults, trying to build what we thought was a healthy partnership. Honestly, we had no idea what a marriage was supposed to be. The rules had changed since our parents' generation. I still don't know what that's supposed to look like, which may account for some of my more recent, umm... failures? Adventures." He rubbed his chin, his gaze turned inward. "Maybe it's not something you're supposed to figure out, ever. Perhaps it's a matter of meeting a reasonable and compatible partner and drawing your own roadmap. Together."

Mary K turned the page in her notebook. "Do you think you'll re-marry, Robin?"

"Oh!" he exclaimed in surprise. "I don't know. I never thought about it in such final terms." He tapped the arms of the chair with his fingers, unconscious of the familiar percussive pattern. "Certainly, that was the plan with Gwendolyn, toward the beginning. But my work, and the persona that seems to go along with it, always manages to intrude. Or perhaps I let it intrude. I've found some women seem to like that, however."

Mary K smiled. "Yes, you've enjoyed a string of famous beauties, haven't you?"

He laughed and shook his head. "Not as many as you would think. There is a certain attraction to that whole celebrity, rock-star thing. I'm overwhelmed by the sheer ridiculousness, absurdity, of it all. Those in the public eye naturally gravitate toward each other, to someone who understands what it's like to be under constant surveillance. So, yes, there have been connections with some well-known people, but not very involved."

"Why not?" Mary K challenged him. "These are beautiful women, Robin."

"Mmm, yes. Of course, that only goes so far, doesn't make two people compatible. And, I think there was a certain expectation level. Umm, you know, man of the world, that whole rock-and-roll mystique…"

"What are you talking about?" Mary K interrupted.

"What's the term? I think I must be a lousy lay."

"Robin!" Mary K nearly fell out of her chair laughing. "I am NOT putting that in this book."

"Oh, sure, go ahead," he said, waving toward the tape recorder. "Umm… Ah." He was still laughing. "Okay… Well, I meant that, in a one-nighter kind of capacity."

"I see," Mary K choked, her eyes glistening with tears.

"Once I get to know someone, in an emotionally intimate relationship, well, then I can be quite creative."

"Thanks for sharing that information, Robin," she said, still recovering.

"Oh, my pleasure." He could feel the heated flush spreading across his face.

"Okay. So the main issue in your relationship with Gwendolyn was your celebrity status?" Mary K asked, wiping her eyes.

"No, I wouldn't say that. It was a combination of factors, as it always is." Robin wrinkled his nose, fighting a sneeze. "I think with Gwen… Ultimately, it wasn't a solid match." He sniffed hard, finally eliminating the tickling in his nostrils.

"Do you want a tissue?"

Robin shook his head. "Gwen was a wonderful influence. There's no doubt about that. She was a refuge, a stable bit of normalcy in my crazy world. Sometimes, I look in the mirror and understand I'm not a normal person. Maybe I can't have a normal relationship. But that period with Gwen was probably the most steady I've been. I was doing more soundtrack scores, environmental music, that sort of thing, during our first few years together, so when I did travel, it was generally only a week or two, to complete some mixing or do some extra recording. It was nothing like what Alice had to put up with."

"You mean your touring schedule?" Mary K clarified.

Robin nodded. "Yeah, that was really brutal sometimes."

"How long were you on the road?"

"Oof," Robin sighed and raised his eyebrows. "Well, during the Imbolc tour, the last one. Mmm. 1977, 1978. I think we were going for about fifteen months. All over the globe. It was madness. We had released two albums in the space of a single year, which in itself was, well, I don't know how we managed that. That was TROUBLED DAYS and EXPERIENTIA, the two albums. And then while we were on tour, 1978 it must have been, there was that unauthorized band biography…"

"THE IMBOLC EXPERIENCE," she commented.

"Right. That was… a revelation, on some fronts," Robin confided. "An outright embarrassment on others. That publication definitely put some strain on Alice, our relationship. I'm guessing Danny was the one who disclosed those details, about the affair they had." He looked down at the floor and sighed.

"Is it still difficult for you to talk about?"

"It's not my favourite topic of conversation, obviously." He ran his hands through his hair, which wasn't offering the same resistance it used to. He looked back up at Mary K. "I hadn't wanted to know any more about that. As far as I was concerned, they had a relationship, and then it was over. That was enough for me. I just wanted to move forward. But here I was faced with all the particulars of their involvement, the secret meetings, the pet names, the drug usage… the private details that should have remained between the two of them. And not only was it there for me to see, but for everyone else as well. Our friends, our families, the whole world."

"And you discovered later that Alice had another affair, with a prep school friend of yours," Mary K prompted. "And your own infidelities…"

He nodded. "Mmm. It was generally not a good time." Robin reached again for his water and took a long drink, nearly emptying the glass. "But to get back on topic, no, there weren't those same pressures when Gwen and I were together. I wasn't recording solo albums, just lending a hand to Eclipse — what generally became of Imbolc after the split — doing some film scoring and such. And working at New Haven, of course. Probably the most normal my life has ever been."

"So what happened?" Mary K looked at her friend and frowned. "I'm sorry, Robin, to have to ask you these questions."

"No, it's alright. We were on this subject anyway, I believe. Ahm…" Robin looked around the room and ran his tongue across his teeth. "Well, I started recording again. I went back into the studio to work on my own material. That's a fairly intense process, really absorbing. It took my focus away from the relationship. That was difficult for her. And then, I discovered I had really missed my own music. I had needed a break from it, I suppose, but when it was time to resume, there it was again, in full force. And once the new album was complete—"

"That was EPIPHANY, right?"

"Yeah, there was a lot of me, my buried self, that came out in that one, a lot of hidden fears and desires," he elaborated. "I think she felt threatened by that process of unburdening and revealing, when it was happening outside of the confines of our relationship. Then the tour was being planned. It was too much for her. No, it was too much for us as a couple. We stuck it out as best we could for that shorter concert run — it was only five or six months, fairly limited — but when we came back together again…" Robin shook his head. "Different people in different places. I'm very glad for those years with her. She gave me a safe place to work out some things for myself, which I don't think I could have done alone. I'd like to think I was able to give her some of that in return. And she was more tolerant of my spiritual explorations than I would have expected."

"Where are you with all of that?" Mary K winked at him. "These days, that is."

"Ah," Robin chuckled. "I'm afraid I still subscribe to the religion of the month club."

Mary K smiled appreciatively.

"Actually, no, that's not where I am." He leaned forward in his chair and crossed his ankles. "I pretended to be Buddhist for awhile. I still like those ideas. The philosophy involved appeals to me. But I don't know that I have the discipline, the way my life works right now. I do meditate. The idea is that it's a daily practice, but it's more like once a week. I know it's about making time, and ultimately, I'm the one in control of my schedule and commitments. I've got a lot brewing on this one, actually, and I'm not ready to talk about it quite yet. I'm confident it will all fall into place when the time is right. Until then, I'll just keep wandering."

Mary K checked her watch. "I'll have to return you to your hotel shortly."

Robin nodded. "One more, then? I'll try not to take so long in my answer."

She smiled. "What do you consider your greatest accomplishment?"

A broad grin spread across his face, and he enjoyed a private chuckle. "Well, I'd like to think I'm still on the upswing, that my greatest achievements and best work are still ahead of me, not behind me." He crossed one knee over the other and took a deep breath as he thought.

"Ah, in terms of what I've already done, I'm quite proud of New Haven Studios, although I still ask myself whether I'm an asset or a detriment to that operation!" Robin burst out laughing and scratched the back of his head. His hair was indeed thinning. He would take another careful look in the mirror before going to bed.

"I'd like to think I've pulled together some decent music over the years, managed to have some positive influence through different efforts. Not just musically, perhaps socially as well, helping to raise consciousness about the world we live in. I honestly feel if I can't leave this planet a better place, then what's the point in my being here?" Robin watched Mary K nodding as he spoke. He didn't envy her having to transcribe these audio tapes, listening over and over again to his babbling. He just hoped he was half-way interesting.

"And of course, Rose," he said genuinely. "I'm very excited to know that she is out in the world, and simply amazed I had anything to do with that."

Chapter 43

March 1995
Reston, Virginia

Angela walked alone through the windowed hallways of the multimedia studio in the early morning. While some producers and designers had worked through the night, most everyone had yet to report in for the day.

She had been specifically invited, but she couldn't remember by whom. Pausing by one of the many windows, she looked out on the gray, wet day. A woman outside was unloading a car in front of the building. She dragged cardboard boxes of supplies from the back of the vehicle and placed them on a dolly on the brick drive.

Angela continued on, coming to a large room full of workstations. Vivid wisps of color hung from the ceiling like brightly decorated kites. The computers hummed. Someone had suspended a bicycle on the wall.

She was drawn to one particular monitor, displaying a multimedia interface in the design process. On the left side of the screen were slider bars to control the environment. On the right was a text list of musical instruments. Angela leaned down to study the layout.

Several people walked through but took no notice of her. Sitting down at the computer, Angela manipulated the design on the screen. Simple changes, she told herself. Make the environment more manageable. She moved the control graphics to the center of the screen. To replace the text listing, she found a folder of clip art and used a graphics of drums, horns, and guitars as placeholders, constructing a musical border.

Angela leaned back to admire her work: a colorful, organized picture frame of an interface. She smiled at the screen. And I'm not even a designer, she thought to herself.

Suddenly, she was standing outside, by a body of water, part of the same studio facility. She wasn't concerned with her spontaneous transport. Instead, she looked around, sensing there was more than multimedia being created here. She felt good in this creative refuge, glad she had decided to come. She stood at the edge of the pond and gazed across the clear water as a misty rain began to fall on her face and hair.

Angela awoke in her own bed, hours before the alarm was set to go off. She sat up in the dark, missing the gentle kiss of the English rain. Just a dream. Though she had never even seen a photo, she knew instinctively it had been Robin's studio.

She looked at the clock. Given the time difference between Virginia and Great Britain... Yes, it was the start of the business day on the other side of the ocean. Angela laughed. What was she thinking? That she had actually been there, an astral projection, in real time?

"This is too much," she said to the darkness. "I've really got to find something else to think about."

Angela fluffed her pillow and lay down, refusing to consider the matter further.

* * * *

Segue/New Haven Studios
Winchester, Hampshire

Robin had spent the night sequestered in the Loft—the attic "writing and reflecting" room he had designed for himself in a remote corner of the Segue/New Haven compound, across the pond from the main buildings. It had been awhile since he had worked through the night. There were many late hours in the studio in his younger days. Reminiscing on those prolific nights, he marveled at his stamina then, conceptualizing and producing some of his best work and actualizing several of the most profound epiphanies of his life.

With this dawn, Robin had looked down on the long table against the wall, where he stored so many files, books, gadgets, and other paraphernalia. The flat filing cabinet. Gauging the disappointingly small pile of new score sheets, he shook his head. Despite his best intentions, he had succeeded in sleeping more than working.

But he had watched the sun rise over the water, through his three walls of windows. He loved this room. Rain was already threatening, but at least it was warming up. There was such peace in this place, if he would remind himself to stop and take notice every so often.

Outside, he made his way along the pavement to the main building before the regular crew started to arrive. He stopped to help Betsy cart several boxes of office supplies inside from her automobile. Why did it always have to be so wet here?

After visiting his executive office, where he conducted his portion of New Haven business, Robin decided to circulate. It was his occasional habit to visit the studios and production suites, not so much for a surprise inspection, but instead to check in with everyone and offer encouragement.

Wandering the hallways, he wondered what his employees thought of him. Not one for business books or management seminars, Robin tried simply to treat each person as a human being and trusted them to know more about their work than he did.

He stepped into the "Vision Room," as the designers called their communal work area, and admired the banners and colourful streams fabric and paper suspended from the ceiling. Spying Arthur's bicycle in its wall rack, he knew his chief designer was around someplace. He stopped by Arthur's computer to take a look at what he was working on.

Segue's first multimedia CD-ROM title, GLOBAL NOMAD, had been largely assigned to the junior designers, though Arthur had saved the "Musical Toolbox" for himself. He was pushing for an interactive interface offering a choice of instruments from around the world and a selection of rhythm tracks, so the user could create a unique musical melange. In truth, given the limitations of these new technologies, there would be a fixed number of possible combinations. This restriction frustrated Robin, but he maintained his enthusiasm and looked forward to testing these barriers again in the future.

It was still early in the process, but Robin was happy with what he saw on Arthur's computer monitor. With appropriate illustrations to replace the placeholder clip-art, Robin could already envision the final product, appreciating the intuitive ease for the end-user.

"Good morning, Robin," came Arthur's voice from behind him. Robin turned and smiled his felicitations to the tall, slightly overweight designer as he approached.

"I like what you've got here, Art," Robin offered.

"It's not nearly ready for anyone to see," Arthur defended the rough sketches of his work. "I came in early to map out a few possibilities."

"Especially the layout, that's good," Robin continued as Arthur reached him. Facing the monitor, Robin pointed to the outer perimeter of the interface. "The border of instruments around the central controls is a nice idea. I think people will like it."

Listening to Robin and surveying the interface on his screen, Arthur's expression grew into a confused frown. Even the colours were different. He leaned over his workstation and clicked through a few windows, trying to figure out what had happened to his original work.

"Alright, what's this, then?" Arthur mumbled.

"Is there something wrong?" Robin asked.

Arthur stood back up and gestured to the computer. "That's not my design. I hadn't even begun designing. I was still assembling the raw materials. Somebody's been mucking about on my computer."

Robin raised his eyebrows at Arthur's agitation, then settled into a subtle smile. "Are you suggesting someone broke into the studio and designed our interface for us?"

Arthur laughed and scratched his head. "Yeah, the multimedia elves."

"I've heard of those." Robin patted him on the shoulder. "Keep up the good work."

Robin headed back toward the main reception area. Arthur sat down at his computer and stared at the interface design. "I'll be damned."

* * * *

Robin stood at the beverage bar in the cafeteria. He poured himself a cup of coffee, mixing together several of the exotic blends offered this morning. A few visiting artists sat at small tables scattered about, indulging their own caffeine fixes and nibbling on fruit and pastries provided by New Haven.

Stirring some sugar into his coffee, Robin looked out the window at his pond. One of the things he loved best about this facility was the sheer number of windows with real views of something worth looking at.

Spotting a young woman standing at the edge of the water, Robin stepped closer to the glass. She looked familiar. Drawn to her shimmering, spectral image, he felt himself grow lighter, as if in a dream. Perhaps the morning humidity was distorting his vision of her. He could hear her heartbeat, across this distance, and he felt his own rhythm adjust to hers. He watched this old friend scan the New Haven buildings and then look again over the water. He was certain she could walk out across the pond's surface, if she wanted to.

A friendly hand clamped down on Robin's shoulder. "Morning, Master Robin."

Robin turned to greet Samuel Benedict, his recording engineer, newly returned from a holiday in Portugal. "You're looking well. Got some colour in your skin, eh?"

"I'll tell you all about it over lunch. Right now, I'm just trying to wake up." Sam sipped his coffee and gestured toward the window. "I can't say I missed this rain."

"Sam, do you know who that woman is?" Robin gestured behind him toward the pond.

"What woman?"

Robin turned back to the window to find that his misty morning muse had disappeared. "She was just there," he stammered. "She was standing there, by the water."

"I heard Bonni Carpenter came in last night," Sam suggested, standing behind Robin, still studying the scene outside. "Maybe that's who it was. I've got a meeting with her and her musicians in an hour, to talk about her recording schedule for the week."

Chapter 44

20 May 1999
New York City
12:15 p.m.

"So I always thought there would be some great moment, some epiphany, that would mark a turning point in my life," Robin rambled. "I always expected that. I think everyone does, to one extent or another. And I can't say it ever happened. Maybe it did, and I missed it. Maybe it was happening all around me all the time, and I just didn't see. Perhaps I was focusing so much attention waiting for 'the big one' that I missed the true revelations along the way."

Mary K checked her watch.

"Here I am, going on forty-seven years in this skin," he continued. "Still waiting to grow up." Robin enjoyed a quick laugh at his own expense.

"It's after twelve, Robin," she advised. "I've ordered lunch to be brought in. Nothing special. Soup, sandwiches, maybe some muffins. I hope that's alright."

He smiled. "Sounds perfect."

"I know how you feel about being recognized in public, so an elegant restaurant is out of the question." Mary K got up from her desk. "I thought since you've been around so many people this week—the graduation, the Amnesty symposium…"

"Yes," he agreed. "I could use a little anonymity right now."

She stepped around the desk and leaned back against it, facing him.

"I have to tell you, and you can put this in your article," Robin gestured to the notepad on her desk. "Sometimes I wonder what my life might have been like if I hadn't been a public figure, if the music hadn't succeeded. Or if I had stayed in school and pursued a more traditional career. I can't imagine I would have been very happy, but there's something to be said for some honest privacy every now and again."

Mary K offered a sympathetic smile, and he laughed.

"And as much as I'm enjoying my time with you today, Mary Katherine," he said loudly, "I can't wait to get on that plane tonight and go home."

"It's a long day for you, I know," she conceded. "I was surprised you agreed to spend so long with me. I'll go check on lunch."

She made her way toward the door. Robin got up from his chair to follow her out.

"I think I'll wander a bit, if that's alright," he suggested. "I'd like to wash up."

"Just don't get lost again," she teased.

* * * *

Henry Peters, head of Westone's new ventures division, sat across the massive conference table from Angela and Jeff. Behind him, a wall of windows revealed more office buildings across the street.

"I like the way you've tied this together," Henry commented. "I wouldn't have thought to combine these different lines, and that was the major question about this proposal."

Jeff studied the two junior executives Henry had brought to the table. He tried to read their facial expressions, to gauge what resonated and what didn't. They had obviously given input prior to today's meeting, but their faces were blank. The only thing Jeff could discern was that they were listening intently.

"The viability of these different efforts working in harmony," Henry continued. "But your center, Angela—I think I know well enough that one was entirely your idea…"

Angela smiled in acknowledgement.

"It's intriguing. There are centers and retreats springing up all over the place. My daughter has an ashram about an hour from home that she visits periodically. But you're coupling that same retreat focus with a production facility."

He met Angela's confident gaze. Henry smiled.

"This isn't just a business decision," he admitted. One of his colleagues cleared his throat. Henry looked at his juniors with a stern smile. Mike Ralston and Bill Washington. They hadn't been in this business—or even out of school—long enough. He used to be just like them, more concerned with projected revenues, business cases and analyses, all contributing to the bottom line. They didn't know what it was to simply take a chance on a good idea. He would show them the courage to do just that.

"You mentioned people wanting to fill the holes inside," Henry said to Angela. "I've seen that. I don't want to keep throwing products at people to help them feel better for just a few minutes at a time."

Angela responded softly, "That's why we're here."

"Come down and take a tour of the facility," Jeff interjected, "once we've broken ground and begun renovations. You'd be welcome any time."

Henry acknowledged Jeff with a nod. He turned back to Angela, once again finding confirming reassurance in her eyes. "Alright. Let's get to work."

Jeff's face brightened confidently. Angela felt an electric charge race through her solar plexus.

Mike checked his watch. "I think it's about that time," he suggested.

Henry glanced at the time and agreed. "A working lunch then." Mike rose from the table, headed for the door. Bill moved his chair closer to Henry's to confer with his boss.

"We'll be bringing lunch in," Henry told Angela and Jeff from across the table. "Should be ready by now."

Bill placed a stack of papers in front of Henry, and the two began sifting through them. Holding a steadying hand to her chest, Angela turned to Jeff and smiled, breathing a sigh of relief and excitement.

"Oh, my," she said quietly.

Jeff placed a hand on her shoulder. "I'll told ya, kid. This is happening. Affinity Harbor. It's real."

"Let's rethink that name," she confided. "It gets the idea across, but it's a mouthful."

Jeff laughed.

Mike was a few feet from the door when it opened from the outside. A casually dressed, middle-aged man poked his head into the room, obviously lost.

"Pardon me," the man apologized in a subtle English accent.

"No trouble," Mike smiled. "Can I help you find someone?"

"Ah, mmm," the man stammered as they stepped into the hallway. "I'm here doing an interview with Mary Katherine Baker. I was just wandering a bit…"

"Go to the far end of this corridor, then take a right, and she's six doors down," Mike gestured toward the opposite end of the long hallway. "I can show you."

Mike closed the door behind him.

Sitting with her back to the door, Angela was oblivious to the interruption, the gears in her head turning. "There's so much to be done, Jeff! All of the contractors and landscaping. That warehouse will have to be completely rewired to support the multimedia studio, not to mention the other spaces. And the plumbing!"

"Easy, jets," Jeff cautioned with a smile. "Everything in its own time, remember?"

Chapter 45

August 1995
Reston, Virginia

"Angela, I want to help you write a book."

Angela blinked at the suggestion, sitting in Cheryl's living room on this warm summer evening. In the year since their accidental meeting at the bookstore, Cheryl had quickly become Angela's closest confidante.

"Aren't you going to say anything?" Cheryl poured herself a glass of iced tea from the heavy pitcher on the table between them.

"I just..." Angela was suddenly conscious of the air from the ceiling fan moving across her skin. "No, you mean it the other way around. You want me to help you."

Cheryl sat back into the papasan chair and smiled. "No. I mean I want to help you." She took a long, slow sip of tea, savoring Angela's mystified reaction.

"But I'm not writing a book," Angela replied.

"Not yet." Cheryl's voice was smooth and confident.

Angela regarded her friend, sitting cross-legged in the round womb of her chair like some kind of mother-buddha-goddess. "Cheryl, do you want to tell me what you have in mind, or is this something I'm supposed to discover for myself?"

"Actually, you already have your material. You've had it for some time," Cheryl explained. "You're getting ready to embark on a special journey. A leap of faith."

"Oh? I didn't realize that's what I was doing," Angela responded sarcastically.

Cheryl smiled patiently. "We both know there are no accidents, right?"

Angela nodded in concession.

"Okay, then. Some things that seem totally random when they occur can begin to make sense down the road when you see them all coming together. Yes?"

Angela sighed, surprised her defensive walls had sprung up so quickly. "Yes."

"How long have you been practicing Reiki now?"

"I am not writing a book about Reiki!" Angela protested.

"That wasn't my question, Angie."

Angela slipped off her shoes. She pulled her feet underneath her and leaned against the generous arm of the couch. "Since I was sixteen. I haven't been doing it a whole lot all this time. But it was about eleven years ago."

Cheryl nodded. "Okay. Awhile back you admitted it was good that Reiki showed up in your life when it did, because it got your spirituality out of your head and into your body. Right? It grounded you at an early age, even if you then chose to ignore it."

"Yeah," Angela acquiesced. "Maybe."

"Alright. Well, you've got an opportunity now, Angela. And don't you start rolling your eyes at me," Cheryl warned, wagging a finger at her friend. "In my meditations lately I've gotten a strong message about this. It's time for you to get it into your fingers."

"Into my fingers," Angela repeated flatly.

"Yes." Cheryl placed her empty glass on the table. She relaxed back into the papasan cushion and looked up at the ceiling, choosing her words. "You have been using writing as a means of creative self-expression for some time. This talent is no mistake. It's cathartic for you. And you and Fred are publishing your magazine."

"Mmm," Angela reminded herself that she had never known Cheryl to be wrong. Quieting her mind, Angela made a conscious decision to listen.

"This book is going to come through you. You've been feeling it already. Restless, seeking an outlet, not sure what to do with the energy brewing inside of you."

"That's nothing new," Angela laughed. "Everyone feels like that."

"No. With you, it's a little different. Sit with this. You'll find there's been a definite shift, within the last year, within you. You've been getting ready."

"Getting ready to write a book I don't know anything about," Angela commented.

Cheryl looked into her friend's eyes, radiating a tranquility that almost unnerved Angela. "You just don't know that you know," Cheryl said with a smile.

"Alright," Angela shrugged her shoulders. "What's this book about, anyway?"

Cheryl inhaled a deep breath and looked around the room. "The subject will come to you in pieces, but still more quickly than you might imagine."

Angela shifted on the couch, waiting. Cheryl focused inward.

"First, you're going to focus on chakras," she offered.

"Chakras."

"Meditations on the chakra system. Exercises to attune with the chakras, get connected with them, open them up. Activate the energy flow. And don't worry," Cheryl laughed before Angela could protest. "You know more about this than you think you do. You won't have to work too hard. It will come easily."

Angela sighed, trying to put aside disbelief. Cheryl caught her eyes and winked.

"For the most part, you'll be channeling this material."

Angela laughed out loud. "Channeling! I don't think I'd be much of a channel. I don't want to be a channel, for anything." She dismissed the idea with a wave of her hand.

"Just sit with this, Angie," Cheryl suggested. "You don't have to do this if you don't want to. But consider it a gift, before you let fear and skepticism talk you out of it." She closed her eyes. "You'll also be writing about soul twinning. Twin souls."

* * * *

"I don't want this, Michael!" Angela shouted within her meditation, turning her back on her guide. She kicked at the dirt with the toe of her sandals. "It's nuts. It makes me feel like I'm nuts."

Angela turned around to face Michael, who smiled on her sympathetically.

"I'm not, am I?" she asked desperately. "Tell me I'm not a fruitcake."

Michael placed his hands gently on her shoulders. "These are easy answers, Angela. You're the one making this difficult for yourself."

Angela looked away to a small grove of trees not far from the dirt road where she and Michael stood. She could hear the inviting babble of a brook running beyond. She took a deep breath and sighed.

"Look," she said. "I know I've created all of this for myself. So how do I get out of it? How do I make this all go away?"

"I think we need to sit down," Michael responded.

He took her hand and led her through the trees to a patch of thick grass jutting out over the water. They sat down on the ground, facing each other.

"First of all, I want you to keep breathing," he advised.

Angela nodded and smiled, fighting the tears. "Okay."

"None of this is a surprise, Angela," he began quietly. "If you want to, you can turn your head and look the other way. But this truth will remain. This is a part of who you are. You cannot make that go away."

Angela looked down into the water running beside her. She wanted to shout. She wanted to cry. She wanted to curl up in a tight ball and go to sleep for a long, long time.

She squinted at Michael. "Are you sure I haven't lost my mind?"

He laughed good-naturedly and took her hands into his.

"You're concerned that you have stumbled upon an unhealthy obsession, that you have invented these connections, and that if you seriously contemplate this specific soul twin, you will fall into a fantasy world from which you will never escape," he stated calmly. "Is that about right?"

"Damn straight!" Angela exclaimed, beginning to laugh. "Some girls in school had a birthday party for Prince out on the bleachers. They didn't know him, not even remotely. They were out there, dancing around, eating cake. I remember thinking how ridiculous that was, what a waste of energy. Although I guess if you like the music… But there are people who are totally off their rockers, completely obsessed with an actor or singer or somebody famous, believing they have some special claim, some secret connection between them. That they are destined to spend their lives together."

"Now, there's the distinction," Michael interrupted. "Ask yourself, honestly, are you in love with Robin Michaels?"

Angela pulled her hands from her guide's grasp. "How could I possibly? I don't even know the bastard."

Michael smiled gently into her eyes, urging her to move deeper.

"I don't know," Angela shook her head. "All sorts of crazy things occur to me. Sure, I have that fantasy. No, a fantasy is something you enjoy, right?"

"Usually," Michael agreed.

"I don't like that idea. It makes me feel creepy. No, I'm not in love with him. Even if I did have those feelings, it wouldn't be real. It would just be an attachment to an idealized version of who I thought the other person was, who he should be."

Michael nodded.

"Mostly, it's more that I imagine a possible partnership, creatively. If anything." Angela fidgeted, pulling on her fingers.

"Okay," he commented. "And you know, Angela, you already have that."

Angela raised her hands defensively. "Don't start with me."

"Who do you think Sir Robin was in that pathworking you did in college?"

"Oh, God!" she exclaimed, clutching her stomach. "Please, no."

"Angela. Angela, look at me."

Lifting her eyes to meet his, she felt the tightness in her chest pulling her focus away from her journey experience. Michael's image began to blur.

"You're losing your concentration," he warned. "Find your feet. Bring yourself back."

Turning her awareness to her physical body, Angela wiggled her toes under the light blanket on the bed. She let the tension drain from her shoulders and her hands. Returning her attention inward, she rejoined Michael beside the water.

"There's a lot of emotion coming up with this. And doubt," Michael advised. "It's trying to disconnect you from this experience."

"Can you blame me?" Angela asked, almost laughing. "Let me see if I've got this straight." She extended her hands as if spreading cards on a table. "Robin Michaels and I are soul twins. We share the same soul. We share creative responsibility and credit, for all of his work, and all of my work. We are, essentially, the same person, just split, in different bodies, which explains all of the strange coincidences. And I'm not crazy."

"Yep, that's about it," Michael confirmed simply.

"I'm sorry, Michael," Angela shook her head. "But that's nuts!"

"I thought we just established that it's not?"

Angela crossed her arms over her chest, drumming her fingers on her elbows.

Michael pressed his palms together. "You're not the only one, Angela. Soul twinning is not rocket science. Do you imagine every single individual that has ever lived on this planet, or that is living now, is host to a unique and exclusively separate soul, completely distinct from any other?"

"Well, yeah," she responded emphatically.

"That's not how it works. Once you let this idea sink in, you'll begin to make these connections for yourself," he counseled. "This happens all the time. Most people are unaware, since it would distract from worldly experiences to have this in their consciousness. But some, like yourself, do integrate this knowledge into earth-bound journeys. Soul twinning is not only common, it's the rule. With few exceptions."

"So all those crazy obsessed fans, they're just acknowledging twinship?"

"No," he replied. "Some people feel the need to look outside themselves for definition of who they are. They may feel a connection, but often they are searching externally for the recognition they need to give to themselves."

Angela raised her eyebrows, silently questioning.

"No, you're not in that place yourself," Michael reassured her. "There are others like you, sharing a soul with those choosing more public lives. Everyone comes into body with different challenges. One of your big ones is faith. You are a teacher, Angela. You guide others through the example of your own life, not just your words. To do that, your path involves the conscious integration of spiritual truth. You have to walk the talk."

"Great." Angela wanted to end the journey. Usually these experiences were not so emotionally charged, nor so long in duration. She felt tired and discouraged.

"You could say you're more highly concentrated in this lifetime," Michael revealed.

"What is that supposed to mean?" she inquired wearily. "You make me sound like a laundry detergent."

"You think souls only distribute themselves between two bodies at a time?"

"Oh, man," she replied with a frown. "You mean there are more?"

"There are infinite possibilities, Angela," Michael offered. "You are the only two incarnations for this soul at this time, in this reality. But think on other potential scenarios, for your book."

Angela blinked. Her visual field was wavering. She was falling asleep.

"That's more than enough for tonight," he acknowledged. "Take what you can with you. Save the rest for later." He reached forward and touched her third eye center with his fingertips. "Now, go to sleep."

Angela felt herself being sucked backward, pulled away from her journey as her consciousness retreated back into her body. She felt the familiar blanket covering her skin and heard the crickets outside. Angela rolled onto her side and drifted into deep slumber.

Chapter 46

September 1995
Reston, Virginia

Robin awoke to find himself flying.

"Ah! I'm out of body," he exclaimed without words.

He was somewhere in the atmosphere, moving fluidly through frozen crystals and suspended gases. At the smallest thought, he instantly descended in a controlled fall toward the surface of the planet, where he hovered over a large metropolis. Probably New York City, he thought, given the pattern of lights marking a long coastline.

"New York, New York," he sang to himself, vibrations of sound and light moving through him.

He felt another presence approach. A being of incredible radiance was pulsating all around him. Robin regarded this visitor in awe.

"What are you looking for, Robin?"

"Truth," Robin responded, before he could formulate thought.

"You are on a path of reconciliation. You will see much, but will understand little."

"Why?" he asked.

"You are not fully conscious, Robin," answered the voice of sound and light. "Your physical body is asleep. Your mind is asleep. There is no conscious integration in this moment."

Robin reflected on finding himself in the clouds moments before. This must be another flying dream. Robin gazed down on the brightly lit city. He could feel all of the people there, minds working, hearts beating. He might remember a fraction of this when he awoke.

"What can I do?"

"What would you like to do?"

"I would like to know myself," Robin responded without hesitation.

In a flash, Robin found himself in a darkened bedroom. He could plainly make out the glowing, sleeping form in a bed not far from where he floated. His own energy pattern began to shift in response to this new presence. He drew closer, seeing the same sequence alignments in the light body he was approaching.

He stopped suddenly. "No," he said firmly, resisting the natural pull to the woman's side. "This is wrong. Interference means trouble." In a gravitational tunnel, he stood his ground against the force pulling him forward.

"This is your twin, Robin," came the voice of the gentle being, somewhere nearby. "This is yourself. Reconciliation. Trust, Robin."

An invisible magnet drew him to her. These two energies belonged to each other. He saw her light through her skin, her spirit active even as she slept. Electric pulses moved through him, in harmony with those visible in her soul pattern. They were coming closer into alignment in a completely unconscious process. In his own excitement, his curiosity and inherent connection to this other outweighed any fear.

She would not wake. Robin was sure of this. He molded his light body to fit her form. Her heartbeat locked with the rhythm of his own, many miles away in his English bed. Her breath moved through him. He sighed and felt her vibration deepen.

* * * *

"Why do you keep fighting me?" he asked her as they sat in bright orange beanbag chairs by the river running through her parents' basement.

In her dream, Angela picked at the fraying holes in her blue jeans with a fork. "I don't know, Robin," she responded flatly. "Maybe if I had a better idea of where we were all going, I wouldn't be so difficult."

"I can't tell if I have any demands or requirements." His dark business suit changed into a reflective prism of color, fluctuating with every emotion and thought that passed between them. "But then again," he continued, "I'm a big idiot."

Angela laughed. "I thought that was my job!" Falling into his smile, her own expression grew somber, and she pointed a stern finger at him. "I don't want any part of any kind of crazy life you've built for yourself."

Robin nodded and dipped one bare foot into the stream flowing across the red cement of the cellar floor. The outside door stood open, and Robin watched the dark green ivy creeping quickly down the stairs. He leaned forward, reaching for her. "Give me your hands," he whispered plaintively. "I want to touch your fingers."

Angela reached toward him. Her hands slipped easily into his. "How could I forget this?" she said, tears growing heavy in her eyes. "Robin," she murmured in her sleep.

* * * *

Ron Blakeman walked into Angela's bedroom, having used the spare key she had given him a few weeks before. He tiptoed across the floor, trying not to wake his girlfriend. It was well past midnight, and he was supposed to have been here at nine. He would make it up to her in the morning—breakfast in bed, or perhaps a fancy champagne brunch on the water—before he headed back into the office for the weekend.

Sneaking past the bed to the bathroom, Ron turned on the light over the sink. He reached for the door, glancing at the shadows thrown across the bedroom. His jaw dropped.

Ron stepped back into the bedroom and looked hard at the shape of his sleeping girlfriend, and the man curled up with her.

He stomped angrily across the floor and hit the wall switch for the overhead light. "What the hell is going on?" Ron demanded loudly as light filled the room.

Angela sat up groggily, shielding her eyes with one hand. "Ron?" she yawned.

Ron stared at her, dumbfounded. Save for Angela, the bed was empty.

"Alright, where is he, Angela?"

She tried to shake the sleep out of her head. She was having difficulty waking, though she felt peacefully energized.

"Where's who?" she asked, still squinting against the light. "What time is it?"

* * * *

Winchester, Hampshire

Feeling the sun on his face, Robin stretched his arms and legs under the blankets. He kept his eyes closed, not quite ready to face the day. His body was waking. He tried to return to sleep, chasing the blissful dream that had so sweetly encompassed him. Where had he been, again?

Bonni cleared her throat beside him. Sleep wasn't coming anyway. Robin opened his eyes and found his occasional girlfriend glowering down at him. "Well," she said warily. "Talking in your sleep again."

With a quick groan, Robin sat up in bed beside her. He looked into her angry eyes. "Hmm?" he asked in sleepy confusion.

"And just who the hell is Angela?"

Chapter 47

December 1995
Reston, Virginia

Angela glanced at her notes for reassurance, though her fingers danced across the computer keyboard, shaping so many of the details she was still learning herself.

"While the word 'twin' is commonly used to describe a pair of identical beings, twinned souls can manifest as a single pair or as a larger group. There is no rule dictating how many separate incarnations — bodies and personalities — the soul might assume simultaneously," she wrote. "However, even though these concurrent incarnations stem from the same soul source, each will carry its own nuances of the soul's inherent frequency—i.e. each incarnation of the same soul will exhibit a unique energetic fingerprint."

She rested her fingers while the gears in her head turned. She still needed to explain how souls split off from the God Source to begin with. She had no idea how to address energy manifestations in different incarnations across history. She didn't understand it herself. She laughed. "That's if you believe in linear time."

An idea flickered out of nowhere. Angela smiled.

"Music provides an excellent example of how this works," she typed. "Members of related soul families—a soul family being a group of related souls and their incarnated twins—will vibrate at complementary frequencies producing pleasant harmonies, similar to a musical chord of sympathetic notes played together. Subtle dissonance within that harmony may be the result of historic karma. Originating from the same soul source, soul twins vibrate at different levels within the same frequency, such as middle C and high C on the musical scale—while these are different keys on the piano, they are still the same note, one simply at a higher vibration."

Angela reached for her glass of juice and took a hurried sip. "I'm definitely going to need some diagrams." She could feel the spiraling energy inside, a restless excitement that didn't allow many breaks.

"Individual nuances of the notes in our musical example can be heard in the Eastern vocalization of overtone singing, practiced by many Buddhist monks. Singers spend years learning to enhance the subtle shades of each note, so the nuances can more easily be heard by the untrained ear. The resulting impression that the singers are vocalizing more than a single note at a time is similar to the soul giving the appearance of living more than a single life simultaneously. Both are illusions."

"Oh, boy," Angela said quietly. She hadn't thought through these musical analogies beforehand. "Of course it would be musical," she laughed. "My twin is musical."

"The nuances on the same note are similar to the lives of the soul. While in separate bodies, the twinned soul develops these enhanced tones," she mumbled aloud, pressing the computer keys in rapid succession. "And through the individual experiences of each twin, these vibrations move in and out of phase with one another."

Angela looked at the words on the screen and frowned. "Now, what does that mean? Da-da-da-da," she sang to herself, trying to jog her memory. "Oh, right."

"When out of phase, the level of dissonance—or difference in vibration—between the individual incarnations of the soul can be felt when two or more twins come into close physical proximity," she wrote, hardly pausing to consider her words. She would edit for clarity later. "Two soul twins in perfect energetic alignment with one another—having not developed the enhanced tones or nuances—will automatically stimulate the rising kundalini within each other. But a pair of twins who have moved out of phase with each other—having developed the enhanced overtones and undertones of the original soul frequency—may experience other physical symptoms when encountering one another."

She took another quick sip of juice and returned to typing as she swallowed.

"One example of the 'out of phase' experience is the sensation of electrical sparks, indicating the twins are not far off of their inherent vibrational patterns; i.e. their energetic fingerprints are still almost identical, with minor variations between them. As the twins are shaped by independent life experiences, coming within close physical range of each other will produce more profound effects, including dizziness, disorientation, nausea, and even a buzzing sensation that can be mistaken for a mild earth tremor, though it can only be felt by the twins in question."

She wondered how common such events really were. "Once this thing has been published," she said to herself, "I'll have a better idea whether I've just pulled this right out of my ass."

"Soul twins also oscillate back toward the pure frequency of the soul. Twins will occasionally establish a kind of energy orbit around each other as they move in and out of phase, similar to closely matched biorhythm patterns—perfectly synchronized at some points and off-balance, to a large or small degree, at other times. (Note to Angela: find out how this compares to twin stars)." She took a second to scribble this same note on a scratch pad, then returned to the keyboard. "This relationship is common among the 'perfect pair' soul twins, as discussed earlier, since their individual vibrations are more closely matched at the outset. (Note to Angela: reference 'fraternal' vs. 'identical' birth twins? 'General' soul twins operate in parallel, while the perfect pair will experience true synchronization.) Coming together, the perfect pair will naturally spark the kundalini energy in each other, regardless how far out of phase they might have grown. However, if they are significantly out of phase, the resulting energy may not be completely pleasant, indicating further work needs to be done to bring them closer together."

"Angela, come to bed." Ron stood behind her, leaning down to kiss her neck.

She smiled and reached up to pat him quickly on the cheek. "Not just yet." She continued to type, no pause in her rhythm.

Ron studied the otherworldly glow on her face from the computer monitor in the dark room. "I'm glad you asked me to stay over," he said sleepily. "But I kind of figured that meant you would be there with me."

"Mmm," Angela commented.

Ron pulled a chair from the small dining table across the floor and sat down beside her. He glanced again at the side of her face and the determined smile on her lips, then leaned forward to read what she was typing.

"What is that?" he asked, squinting at the screen. "Kunda-what?"

"Kundalini," she replied.

"Yeah, okay. So what is it?"

"Just a second…" Angela typed with a speed that astonished her, her fingers moving deftly across the keyboard. Reaching a stopping point, she dropped her gaze from the monitor and let her hands fall to rest in her lap. She turned to her boyfriend and smiled.

"Kundalini is the rising of energy through the chakra system," she said simply.

"Mmm."

"Though it doesn't always have to go that way."

"Doesn't have to go what way?" he asked.

"Up."

"Oh," Ron responded blankly.

"It's okay," Angela smiled sympathetically. "You're not interested in this."

"No," he protested. "I just don't understand it. I have no idea how it fits in with everything else in the real world."

"Yeah." Angela felt a twinge of anxiety in her stomach.

"Okay," he encouraged softly. "So try explaining some of it to me."

Angela wrinkled her nose and looked at him sideways, grinning. "What do you want to know?"

Ron sat back in the chair and raised his eyebrows. "Umm…?"

Angela pushed her chair away from the computer and faced him. She could feel her energy returning.

"Why don't you just tell me what you believe," he suggested.

"Ha! We'll be here all night and into next week, Ron." She winked at him slyly, then gestured toward the computer. "That's part of what this process is, to get straight on what I believe, and to express that in concrete terms."

She looked into his eyes and found a gentle smile waiting for her. "I told you before," she shook a playful finger at him, "I'm not like you. I'm not a normal person. But I do applaud your efforts for trying to have a normal relationship with me."

"Ah, thanks." Ron grinned. "So what kind of abnormal person are you, then?"

"If I had to describe myself… I heard the term once, spiritual promiscuity…"

Ron chuckled and shook his head. "And I'm just a disillusioned Catholic."

"Right." She enjoyed the way his humor put her at ease. "I like that expression. I understand what it means, flitting from one thing to the next, trying to find my own place. Some people take this piece from one religion and that bit from another, to create a religious casserole to fit their individual needs for that moment. But there's no nutritional value. I'm after something that's… well, not quite so superficial. I'm trying to find my grounding. There's so much judgement, doubt, the immediate suspicion of anything remotely spiritual. That's happening internally, and now here I am opening myself to the outside world to judge me. Assuming that's what would happen."

"Maybe not," Ron offered. "Why don't you try telling me? See how that goes."

Angela glanced at the small clock on her desk. "Ron, it's 1:30 in the morning. Do you really want to get into all of this?"

He stretched his arms out to his sides and yawned. "Tell you what. Give me another twenty or thirty minutes, and then we'll call it a night."

* * * *

They had sat together for the next hour as Angela explained the individual chakras, taught him a meditative breathing pattern, and danced around the idea of soul twin theory. Angela was relieved when he finally went back to bed. Discussing all of this still made her nervous.

The apartment was quiet again. "Oh, gee," she lamented humbly. "How am I supposed to write a book if it's so difficult for me to just sit down and talk to one person about it?" She closed her eyes and bowed her head, resting her brow on her desk.

"Just relax. Get your ego out of it," her inner voice advised.

"Oof, yeah." She leaned back in her chair and faced the computer screen. "Easier said than done. It's my name on this. People are going to think I'm nuts."

"So write under a different name. The universe doesn't care."

"No." Remembering Ron in the next room, she lowered her voice to a whisper. "I don't want to hide. If I'm going to do this, then I'm really going to do it." Feeling the frustrated tears rising, Angela looked out the window onto the dark, wintry street. "I still think I'm totally nuts. I want to give myself over to this, really. But I'm afraid. Even after everything that's happened. I'm still afraid. I'm a big, fat idiot."

She wiped the corners of her eyes. "I'm afraid I'm just another fruitcake. Maybe this whole thing is a huge waste."

"Are you trying to walk on water?" came the response.

She looked up and the ceiling. "What was that?"

Angela got up from her desk and paced the room. She was almost angry. Agitation. Why?

She stopped in her tracks, her gaze coming to rest on the computer several yards away. She walked quickly to the desk, sat down, and opened up a new text file.

"Okay," she said in a determined voice, her fingers poised over the keyboard. She closed her eyes and took a breath she could feel in her toes. She began to type.

Walk on Water
By Angela Harris

I find myself alone in the garden, my own folly having brought me here
I think I am following, walking in grace
But I understand I have been fighting, raging from the moment I was born

Sometimes we are shown a plan, a path we are urged to take
And we laugh
We hem and haw
We shuffle our feet
In pretended humility, we come up with our own plan
"That's not how I would do it"

This is my name
It must be my game
It's my way or the highway
I will walk on water, you'll see

No room for benevolence

Off on our many roads we wander, tearing off to impossible distances
So far off course, off kilter, off center
What is this external validation?
I bite, I kick, I scream in the darkness
"Show me the way!" I cry out
As I keep stomping out my own candles and ripping my roadmaps to shreds

Walking too many miles in these shoes
To find that I'm only just standing still
These circles I dance around and around
Never seeing the direct path back to myself

Always so close, all I have to do is reach out
But I am so afraid to embrace my own blindness
I push this cup away again and again
Unable to taste the sweet nectar through invented bitterness

Days pass, months and years
And all I've done is wear holes in my soul
Looking down, this I can see
At last the ego mantle crown tumbles to the ground
Bowed head and worn feet

Cast off the shackles of personality
Lay myself bare under divine sight
Share those universal eyes
Shining emeralds, sparkling bright
There is nowhere in this expanse, enough darkness to put out that light

To see plainly, without fear or convention
Smite the blackness in my own heart first, release the hurt I hold so close
Find the sparkling seeds of forgiveness and sow them deep
This is the harvest most bountiful

Who is the savior in this life?
Who will obliterate these chains once and for all?
I find the key, deep within my heart
And, somewhere, the courage to be my own messiah

Coming clean, purified by fire, taste the kiss of that holy water on my lips
Climb out of the mud to this higher ground, leaving my barbs and boxes behind
"Wonderful, wonderful," my body sings out through its pores
The torch is lit, the road is clear

And seeing that crown of thorns left behind
Will I stop to pick it up, saying,
"I will walk on water, you'll see"
Once more?

Within thirty minutes she was done. She read back over her words. "Ouch," she commented. "I don't know. This is either fairly decent, or that's got to be some of the worst writing I've ever done."

"And why do you suppose you think that?" she asked herself silently.

Angela leaned her elbows on the desk and rubbed her eyes. She disliked being so critical of herself. She wanted to drop her defenses to the floor and walk away from them. But it was precisely at such moments that her armor clung more fiercely than ever. Would she ever reach a sufficient level of achievement, in any area of her life, when she could breathe more easily and say, "Yes, well done indeed"?

"Mmm, mmm, mmm," she clucked to herself. She looked at the clock. It was past 3 a.m. She leaned back in her chair and yawned. "That's it. I give up."

"That's a good beginning. Surrender," the familiar, intuitive voice suggested. "When are you going to start taking your own advice?"

* * * *

Angela was in the clouds, flying above the earth with faceless friends. She felt such joy and freedom, soaring in this collective light. Seeing a barbecue below, she dove toward the earth and hovered above the brick patio. The people at the party were her parents' friends, the parents of classmates, and others she didn't recognize.

She knelt on the patio while the people watched. She easily plunged her hand through the bricks as if matter were non-existent, the consistency of air. When she brought her hand back to the surface, she held an assortment of gemstones, mostly emeralds, gleaming in the sunlight. Angela was delighted. She smiled and held her hand up, displaying the magical stones for all to see. The adults stood by, unimpressed. They crossed their arms and frowned in stern, skeptical judgement.

Again, she reached into the ground, feeling no resistance, and pulled out another handful of sparkling gems. Behind her, she heard the comment, "The molecules are too thick, and we haven't the time. This trickery has no place in the waking world."

Angela had to push her fingers into the earth and pulled out fewer stones. She collected them in a pile in her lap, shifting her weight to keep her emeralds, rubies, and sapphires carefully guarded.

She heard murmuring around her as the party guests conversed with each other.

"I heard your uncle has pancreatic cancer. How horrible," said one voice.

"My nephew is a stock trader. Last weekend, he bought a new Mercedes!"

Angela kept reaching into the earth, finding more resistance with each effort. She pushed hard against the bricks, feeling the abrasions on her fingers.

"Everyone knows that's just a bunch of hooey." One older man scowled down on her. She hammered at the bricks with her fingers, her hands bloody, trying to reach the treasures below, but she could no longer get to them. Angela's hands were stuck in the bricks.

* * * *

It was past noon when she awoke, alone. Ron had left a note on her pillow, again gone to the office to catch up on a few things and work out a project plan for an extensive network installation, even though it was the Saturday before Christmas.

Angela got up and began her regular morning routine. Brushing her teeth, she glanced at the newspaper headlines. She needed music this morning. Good music. She pulled a CD off the shelf and popped it into the stereo, looking forward to the familiar strains of *The Voice*. She waited for the music to move her feet and fill her soul.

But this morning, Robin's song hit too close. Her feet were rooted to the floor. His voice struck her ears and her heart powerfully, and she doubled over in unexpected emotion and anxiety. She pulled herself toward the stereo and immediately shut it off.

"Dammit, Robin!" she yelled at the empty room. "Now I can't even listen to your stupid music anymore. Thanks a lot."

She stomped across the floor toward the bathroom and turned on the shower.

Chapter 48

March 1996

Reston, Virginia

"Are you done yet?" Cheryl asked impatiently as Angela sat before the computer at seven on a Friday evening. "I thought we were going out to play."

"We are, don't worry." With a few mouse clicks, Angela uploaded revised files to her personal web space. "Just a couple more things to do."

Cheryl pulled up a chair and looked at the screen. "What are you doing, anyway?"

Angela smiled, waiting for the file transfer to complete. "Just updating my web page."

"Can't that wait until tomorrow?"

"Actually, I should have posted this last night. I slacked off," Angela admitted. Her computer beeped with the successful upload. She turned to Cheryl. "I try to stay on top of this, so folks have the links they need for research and campaign information. There have been some updates to Amnesty International action items and the Women's Alert Network. Even if this were a full-time job, I don't think I could keep up with it."

Cheryl smiled and placed a supportive hand on Angela's shoulder. "I'm sorry I was pushing you."

Angela shrugged and turned back to the computer.

"I'm really glad I know you," Cheryl offered. "I think it's great you invest so much of yourself trying to help other people. You're a pretty groovy lady."

Angela laughed as Cheryl winked at her.

"Alright, do you mind if I check a few other things quickly?" Angela asked. "This is for work, though, not for global peace or anything like that."

Cheryl chuckled. "Sure."

Angela loaded America Online into her web browser and navigated to several chat rooms. "My manager asked me to check in over the weekend, to make sure the chat is functioning properly."

Cheryl pulled her chair closer. She and Angela watched the conversation in the herbal gardening chat room scroll up the screen. Users were discussing appropriate planting seasons for parsley in different North American regions.

"Okay, this one's kind of boring," Cheryl commented.

Angela closed that window and entered a chat on Siamese cats. "This one's running alright, too."

"How about we go look in on your friend," Cheryl suggested.

"My friend?"

"There's got to be a chat room on Robin Michaels, right?"

"Oh," Angela responded. "Sure, we can go there." Angela entered a few keystrokes, and the Robin Michaels chat room popped up on her screen.

> IMBOLC4EVR: I don't understand people who get involved with this action or that one, just trying to be like Robin. These people don't have a clue. Intentions in the wrong place.
>
> TARANTULA: Agree. Hypocrisy.
>
> PRISMATIC: But you must admit RM has done a good job raising awareness. Not too many would otherwise have a clue about these issues around the world. You can say RM has jumped on the celebrity bandwagon... Doing the popular thing of supporting causes.

"Hey!" Cheryl exclaimed. "I want to talk to these folks. Can I?"

"Sure." Angela got up from her chair and let Cheryl take her place in front of the computer.

Cheryl stared down at the keyboard and began carefully pecking at the letters. She hit Return, and her message appeared on the screen.

> AH1243: So what if Michaels is politically correct for his own purposes? If fans around the world get involved just to be more like their idol, then good for Robin, getting people motivated through his own conscience. If intentions are off-base to begin with, their hearts will come into place after they get started.

"Hey, who is AH1243?" Cheryl asked.

"That's you," Angela replied. "That's my screen name."

"Okay, just checking."

Cheryl typed in a few more comments. "Hey, you didn't start your action work just because of this guy, did you?"

Angela sighed impatiently. "Cheryl, I was a founding member of Peacemakers in high school and was on the board of the Amnesty International student chapter in college."

"Okay, okay," Cheryl backed off. "You don't have to get defensive."

"I'm going to change my shoes," Angela remarked as she walked out of the room.

Cheryl continued to read the chat comments as they scrolled up the screen. A new personality entered and caused quite a stir amongst the other chatters. "Mmm, who's this person?" Cheryl asked the screen.

MRSROBIN: Just stopping in to let everyone know the move is ON. Took a leave of absence from work and will relocate at the end of the month.

PRISMATIC: Don't you think you're going overboard, Sarah? (I will NOT refer to you as 'Mrs. Robin') You're uprooting your entire life for some fantasy.

TARANTULA: Don't do it.

MRSROBIN: It's not like that. I just can't get this out of my system. If I don't do this now, I'll never know.

VERT: Sarah, think about this. Is Robin Michaels just sitting around his house waiting for you to show up? This man has a life. Quite a full one. He gets fan letters every day from women just like you, asking him to marry them or sleep with them or whatever. You saw the photos with Bonni Carpenter. He's not hurting for company.

"Ooh!" Cheryl exclaimed. "This is juicy!" She pecked at the keys again as the conversation sped up the screen.

MRSROBIN: Yeah, I saw. I'd be lying if I said I wasn't upset. Only makes me need to do this more. I can't just keep waiting for him to find me. I have to go to him. It's the only way.

AH1243: Are you just going to go to his front door, ring the bell, and expect him to say, 'Oh! There you are!'??

MRSROBIN: I could do that. I'm not thinking about that just yet.

PRISMATIC: THINK ABOUT THIS! How crazy this is, Sarah! I understand you love the music, how you admire his work, or even be titillated by his personality. You've never met him, never had contact with him. How can you say you love him? Or that he has got to love you? You're just a small step from stalking.

TARANTULA: What are you going to do for work, for money? Won't you just have a tourist visa?

MRSROBIN: My company has a British office in Portsmouth, not too far from his studio. I'll have a job. And I have had contact with him. I just can't keep still waiting for him to settle with the wrong person.

VERT: Having a dream about him doesn't count as 'contact,' Sarah.

"You're convinced you're the right person?" Cheryl spoke aloud as she typed.

"What are they talking about now?" Angela asked as she stepped back into the room.

* * * *

Sitting in a quiet corner booth with Cheryl at a coffee shop, Angela was close to tears. "How can I not question this? I mean, I've heard about this before. I kept saying, 'Oh, no. That's not me.' But what if it is? What if I'm just being manipulated like this other woman?"

Cheryl shook her head. "I don't know, Angie. I still think you need to look at this more objectively."

"Cheryl, perfectly sensible women do some pretty crazy things because of situations just like this," Angela shot back. "I'm sure Sarah is a completely normal person, leading a completely normal life, except for this one thing. I can't believe I ever considered this! Thank God you're the only one I've told."

"Alright, I'm going to tell you something," Cheryl put her coffee mug down on the table and clasped her hands in front of her.

Angela took a nervous breath and waited, reassured by the warm cup in her hands.

"Whenever someone lives in the spotlight, they're going to attract a certain amount of attention, obviously," Cheryl began. "This attention is an investment of energy. When we pay attention to someone, even from far away, totally removed, we send our energy out to him. So from an energetic standpoint, celebrities are strong. They're infused with other people's energy from all over the world."

"Mmm." Angela stared at Cheryl's fingers.

"And what happens within this energy field is not completely up to them, as it carries the intentions and influences of the people who sent out that energy," Cheryl continued. "Mostly, it's a matter of how awake, aware, that celebrity is. He or she can use the energy to do good things, or for more nefarious purposes."

"So Robin's been using the energy to manipulate people and make them crazy," Angela interjected. "Great. That's just great. My God, I've got this book going to press! So much time and energy, completely wasted. It's all been a lie."

"Maybe that's not what's going on," Cheryl insisted. "That could certainly be the case, yes, or part of it. He was young when fame came to him. I can't imagine he was too conscious then. He had people all over the world absolutely adoring him. It would be understandable if he took advantage of that, to whatever extent. But that doesn't mean that's where he is now."

Angela rested her chin in one hand and stared dejectedly into her coffee mug. Cheryl reached across the table and touched her elbow, trying to engage her.

"From what you've told me about Robin, I'd say he's a pretty good guy," Cheryl offered with a smile. "It's true that once that kind of manipulative energy gets injected into the field, it's out there, whether anyone likes it or not. It doesn't just clear itself up overnight. But think on your experience."

Angela sighed. "I just can't say my experience has been all that different."

"Oh, no?" Cheryl asked in surprise. "Angie, the man was partnering with you in pathworking before you even had a clue who he was. Look at the similarities in your lives. He shows up in your journeys and works with you."

"And he shows up in dreams, just like with Sarah," Angela complained.

Cheryl sighed. "Well, of course that's going to happen. Remember how we talked about separating fact from emotion?"

"Yeah," Angela responded unenthusiastically.

"Here's a good time to put that into practice," Cheryl advised. "I don't have any answers for you on this one. My feeling is no, you're not disillusioned like Sarah, though you do have a tendency toward emotional attachments to foreseeable outcomes. You are part of a twinned soul, with this man. Don't you think this happens to other people, too? There are other people in the world, experiencing exactly what you are, and not having any explanation for it. You're more awake than that."

"And if I'm totally wrong?" Angela questioned. "What if it's not Robin Michaels, but somebody else? Someone masquerading as Robin, just to get in my head and mess with me?"

"Angela, everything happens the way it does for a reason," Cheryl tried to console her. "You're the only one who can answer these questions for yourself. And even then, you might never know. But you do control how you choose to feel about it. Even if you're wrong, it hasn't been a waste."

* * * *

"I'm getting tired of this, Michael," Angela complained to her guide in journey state. "I thought once I finished the book, this would all be over with. I want that freedom! The book is out of my hands; it's gone to press. But this is still tugging at me."

Michael sat across the rough wooden table from her, in a tight space hewn out of rock deep underground. "I can't tell you anything new, Angela. We came into this space for protection, to reassure you that you weren't being influenced by outside forces. But the message is the same. Robin Michaels is your soul twin, like it or not. You can say you've both been manipulating each other since the very beginning."

"What do you mean?"

"Your influence on each other, guiding each other to progress along individual paths," he explained. "Call it manipulation, but it doesn't carry the same negativity."

Angela rested her forehead on the coarse tabletop.

"You wouldn't have been given this information if not to serve a purpose," he told her gently. "You've only lived a portion of your life thus far. Consider that when you put it into perspective. Who says you have to have it all figured out, ever?"

She looked up at him from underneath her bangs. "Will this ever go away, Michael? I just want to live a normal life. I'm feeling like that's pretty much impossible."

"Haven't you wondered why you're so afraid of the possibility of this being true? Of meeting him?"

"I don't want to think about it." Her frustration was making her angry.

"He's the one person in this world who can hurt you the most," Michael revealed. "Keep in mind you have the same power over him. It's a good idea to be separate until you're both more awake. You can also love each other the most."

"Oh, man!" Angela looked away. This was simply too much.

"Fact and emotion, Angela," he advised.

Angela cursed under her breath.

Michael placed his hands flat on the table. "Angela, look at me."

She turned to look deeply into his eyes, challenging him.

"This is an opportunity, one that's going to keep coming back until you make peace with it. Faith has been a challenge all your life. You like tangible things. You like to put your hands around a belief and know that it's real. You can't do that here. You're just going to have to accept this and learn to live with it."

Chapter 49

September 1996
Winchester, Hampshire

Robin sat alone in his living room on the periphery of the New Haven compound, far from any major roadway. In the fading light of day, he rested. Through the open window, he listened to the breeze in the trees, the singing birds and crickets, and the occasional scurrying in the woods nearby.

Each evening before he retired, he vowed to walk the single kilometre to the studio the next morning, to control his expanding waistline. But he generally awoke late or became distracted by something in the house and ended up driving in.

This evening, Robin needed time alone. The television was dark, and the stereo was quiet. He had even resisted the wave machine. Sitting still, he could just make out the distant babbling of the River Itchen.

Robin switched on a lamp to again consider the poem that had so disturbed him.

"To see plainly, without fear or convention," he read aloud. "Smite the blackness in my own heart first, find the sparkling seeds of forgiveness and sow them deep."

He skipped ahead and back again, reading at random. "Cast off the shackles of personality, lay myself bare under divine sight, share those universal eyes."

Robin sighed. Resting the literary magazine on his lap, he again gazed out the window. The poem was all about releasing personal expectations and embracing a higher purpose. Not surprising, nor uncommon. He saw this new consciousness arising all around him. Or had it been there all along? He himself had been working on a similar theme in one of the tracks intended for his new album.

"*Walk on Water*, by Angela Harris," he read aloud from the top of the page.

When he had first read these words, a creeping paranoia suggested that somehow, someone had gotten into his workroom, had spied what he was drafting, and this poem was the result. A quick glance at the magazine issue date checked that suspicion. *Walk on Water* had been published at the beginning of 1996, the poem likely written months or even years earlier. He had been crafting his song for only a few weeks.

Comparing his lyrics to her poetry… They were more than curiously similar. Exact phrases and rhythms of words were consistent between the two. How was this possible?

"Coming clean, purified by fire," he read. "Climb out of the mud to this higher ground, leaving my barbs and boxes behind." He put the magazine down again.

"She's going to think I've plagiarized her," Robin muttered.

He closed his eyes and felt his feet on the floor. The way to clarity, he knew, was through disengaging. He tensed his toes, then released. He slowed his breathing.

Was this some lasting consequence of his haphazard paranormal experiments in years past, when he had entertained himself with astral projection? That had been a distracted struggle in itself. He had landed in unpredictable places, never completely in control. Sometimes he had even moved between planes of existence, interacting with magical beings, communicating via thought and feeling, traveling as pulses of light.

Other experiences were more mundane, landing at a random hot dog stand in Texas in the middle of the night or finding himself in the midst of early morning Tai Chi in a Chinese square. Occasionally, he visited his fans across the globe. Especially women. Following these exploits, he got a big laugh out of surges in fan mail—"I had the strangest dream about you"—though he doubted any of it had been real.

It had been some time since he had meddled thus.

This woman... Who was she? Had she snuck into his mind, seen inside his secret world, and excavated his ideas before he himself was aware of them? He was no longer a well-known musician, compared to the likes of Bruce Springsteen, Tina Turner, or Elton John. His life had been quieter these past years. It was entirely possible this poet had never heard of Robin Michaels.

At least my stuff rhymes, he thought in silent amusement, eyes still closed in meditation. Hers doesn't at all.

Let go of thinking, he reminded himself. Quieting his mind, he set himself adrift...

"There is no true ownership of words or ideas, Robin," spoke his inner voice.

He opened his eyes, a bit startled. He reoriented to his surroundings, feeling as though he had fallen asleep in the chair.

Mulling over this bit of wisdom, Robin smiled. He had been a great proponent of copyright enforcement. It had seemed the right thing to do, though he quietly wondered how any one person could own a sound or an image or a word. Such intangible things.

He liked the aboriginal idea that people belong to the earth, rather than the other way around. But that hadn't stopped him from investing in property. One of these days, he kept telling himself, I'm going to get better at walking the talk.

"Authorship and ownership are two different things," Robin whispered as he looked out at the twilight sky and saw stars beginning to appear. He sighed. He wouldn't figure this out tonight. He would simply have to be patient. Perhaps he would never understand this inexplicable coincidence, though he felt an inner hint at something deeper.

"Ah, well. Chalk up one to the collective unconscious."

Robin got up and walked to his desk. He switched on his PowerMac and sat down, wiggling his fingers to warm them up. He reached into the drawer for a blue letter envelope. When he sent mail in these distinctive envelopes, his regular recipients recognized him before even checking the return address. Robin liked that.

He opened his word processor and began to write.

Chapter 50

October 1996
Reston, Virginia

Angela entered the Momentum Workshop through the basement door. Beneath the house Fred shared with his roommates, the space was entirely theirs, except for the laundry area. She was early, per usual, and she heard Fred in the kitchen above.

When MOMENTUM had been a simple quarterly release of only a few pages, she and Fred could knock out an entire issue in little more than a weekend. But with bi-monthly delivery — and with submissions and queries on the rise—they now met every Saturday and occasional weeknights to tackle the business of their burgeoning literary magazine.

Angela dropped her knapsack onto the worktable and stared at the two large boxes confronting her. One was filled with material to be considered for upcoming issues; the other held fan mail and subscription notices. She loved what they were doing, but just looking at these two boxes made her tired.

Fred had already booted up the two computers on a folding table against the wall and had begun laying out the next issue's front page. Thank God for Quark, she thought to herself, remembering leaner days using the most basic word processor.

Angela sat down and sifted through the poems, essays, and articles, always happy to see new authors contributing. With the advent of e-mail distribution in addition to hardcopy publication, designers were sending in multimedia files. By this time next year, MOMENTUM would be producing at least two CD-ROM issues annually.

Fred jogged half-way down the steps from the kitchen. "Good morning! Do you want anything to drink?"

"Hey, Fred," Angela responded as she read. "I'll take some tea, thanks."

"K-O." Fred headed back up the stairs.

"Oh! Fred!" Angela pulled a paper bag from her knapsack. "I brought bagels, in case you hadn't eaten."

"Angela, it's eight in the morning on Saturday," Fred called down from the top of the stairs. "No one in their right mind is up before nine, much less eats breakfast. I think we've got some jelly or something in the refrigerator."

"Good." Angela liked Fred. They worked well together. She pulled a notebook out of her bag and opened it to the current issue's checklist. They had already committed a generous amount of material, with not much space remaining. Choosing only a handful of submissions from this large stack would be difficult. When they paid their contributors in copies, there wasn't as much interest. But with subscriptions increasing, they could offer modest compensation, attracting even more submissions. Even with the never-ending workload, it was exciting to watch the growing success of their labor of love.

Fred appeared with a jar of jelly and set a mug of herbal tea in front of his partner.

"I know what you're thinking," he began.

Angela reached for the tea and smiled. "Okay, tell me what I'm thinking, Fred."

He leaned on the table and nodded toward the boxes. "You're thinking it's a good thing we've started publishing every other month, but maybe we made that move too late. We're so swamped with people sending us stuff that we'll never be able to read through it all to even choose what goes in. Much less take a vacation, ever."

Fred stopped to gauge Angela's reaction. "Not exactly what I was thinking," she replied. "But close. Continue."

He rested his hands on his hips. "So we need some help. Especially if we're thinking about CD format next year. Which I want to do. I'm really excited about that."

"Good." Angela glanced through her calendar for the remainder of the year. Every Saturday until Christmas was committed to MOMENTUM. Ron was not happy, but with his own workaholic schedule, her boyfriend didn't have much room for complaining.

"Who do you have in mind, to help out?"

"I've thought a lot about this." Fred began to pace. "We're making some money now, but really only enough to pay contributors and cover publication. And going toward debts, like the CD burner. We'd have to get creative with the budget to hire someone."

"Yep," she replied. "So you want Yvonne to give us a hand?"

Fred was surprised, expecting an argument. "Well, yeah. I mean, she's good at proofing, layout, FileMaker databases, and she really believes in MOMENTUM…"

"When can she start?"

"You're okay with this? I thought, because she's not a writer or an artist…"

"Fred," Angela interjected, "Just because Yvonne doesn't write haiku doesn't mean she's not creative. Her talent lies in another area. If she's willing to assist, why would I have a problem with that?"

He shoved his hands into his pockets. "She was nervous you'd think she was only interested because she's my girlfriend, and that she'd flake out."

Angela laughed. "She can start anytime. We need the help. Is she upstairs?"

"No, she didn't sleep over. Mike and John were having some kind of dinner party, so we stayed at her place."

"No wonder you look so put together this morning," Angela teased him. "Usually I find you in your pajamas with a bad case of bed head."

Fred self-consciously ran his fingers through his hair and smiled. "I'll tell Yvonne. She can be here next week. Then maybe Ron could start coming in…"

"Right." Angela pulled a stack of submissions across the table toward her. "Ron… he's not really the artsy type. We're lucky to have him troubleshoot our systems."

"Even if he hates Macintosh."

Angela laughed. "Yep."

Fred walked across the concrete to sit in front of the computers. He pulled up the table of contents for the next issue.

"Anyway, he's at the office most weekends, or working from home…" She sighed and tapped her pen against the table.

Fred turned around in his chair to face her. "Angela, I know you don't want to hear this, but what's the point of living with someone if you never get to see them?"

Angela pointed her pen at him as a warning. "Don't start with me."

Fred shrugged and turned back around.

"I'm sorry, Fred," she offered. "I just really don't want to talk about it."

"Okay, let's talk business then," he said over his shoulder, facing the computer screen. "We got a couple of fan letters in the mail yesterday…"

"Yeah?" Angela reached for the second cardboard box. "Where?"

"They're in there. Two envelopes, close to the front, paperclipped together."

She found the letters and pulled them out of the box. Looking at the return address on the top envelope, her mouth dropped open. "Rita Chamberlaine?! THE Rita Chamberlaine? Are you kidding me?"

Fred laughed. "I thought you'd like that. See, you were right. Not only did the web site boost subscriptions, but it's easier for people to find us in general. She enclosed a check for a year's subscription."

Angela only half-listened as she read the three short paragraphs from the poet and author of such classics as BOTTLED WATER, WEST OF THE MISSISSIPPI, and RUDY'S LEATHER. Chamberlaine congratulated them on their efforts to give a voice to unknown artists and offered encouragement for future success. General praise, but Angela was thrilled.

"And we've got some new international subscriptions, too," Fred continued. "Which might explain that other letter."

Angela returned Chamberlain's letter to its envelope and turned her attention to the blue envelope paperclipped beneath. She saw the U.K. postmark and felt a shock of electricity zing through her system.

* * * *

To the Editors of MOMENTUM Magazine
Reston, Virginia

Dear Sirs:

I am writing to commend your work on MOMENTUM Magazine. I understand that it has been in publication for two years now, and I congratulate you on your success.

My daughter, who attended college in Virginia and now resides in the area, brought your magazine to my attention last year, so I have been an anonymous subscriber for some time. I have enclosed a bank draft to continue receiving your publication.

In a recent issue, I was struck by the works of Cynndara Galbreath of Wales and Ernesto Cooke of Belize. Their unique viewpoints added a very rich flavour. I was also riveted by Angela Harris' *Walk on Water*, finding expressed in her words so many of my own truths. I look forward to reading more from these and other authors.

My own work in music has allowed me the great privilege to be exposed to different cultures through rhythm and melody, and I have been fortunate enough to get to know some of these international artists personally. I am happy to see that MOMENTUM is also reaching out to artists around the globe. I encourage you in your quest to seek out and lend an ear to the many voices across the planet who have so much to say.

Keep up the good work.

Sincerely,
Robin Michaels

*   *   *   *

Sitting across from Angela in a booth at Martha's Midtown Grill, Cheryl read through the letter.

Angela scanned the dimly lit restaurant, noting the differences in the silk flower arrangements from one table to the next. She bounced her knees anxiously under the table. She rearranged her silverware. She rested her chin in her hand and drummed increasingly complex percussive patterns on her cheek with her fingers.

Cheryl reached a hand under the table and grabbed hold of one of Angela's frantic knees. "Stop it!"

Angela fell still and leaned back against the red vinyl upholstery.

Cheryl smiled at the letter, then returned it to the envelope. "He's very polite."

Angela dug her fingers into her hair. "He and I both went to prep school. We know how to write letters. It's one of the things they teach you there."

"Well, it's a very nice letter. I don't see why you're so upset about it. He's just telling you what you already know."

"That Fred and I are running a quaint little magazine that makes no money?"

Cheryl smiled at Angela's sarcastic frustration. "No. That you are giving voice to each other's thoughts and feelings. Because you're the same person."

Angela pressed her palms against the table and fought an anguished growl in her throat. Cheryl covered Angela's hands with her own.

"This kind of thing happens all the time, Angela. It doesn't have to be such a burden. You're the one making that choice."

"I know. I know that." Angela bowed her head. "I've got to figure out what to do."

"What to do," Cheryl repeated inquisitively.

"Yes." Angela withdrew her hands and dropped them into her lap. "What I'm going to do about this letter, what I'm going to do about this whole thing."

Cheryl smiled. "Who says you have to do anything, Angie?"

Angela stared into her friend's warm face, then sighed loudly and looked away. There was an entire hive of angry bees trapped under her skin, threatening to consume her from the inside out if she didn't find the key to unlock this gated door. It was the same feeling she had had all along, since the pieces had begun to fall into place.

The waiter appeared with their drinks, telling them to expect their sandwiches shortly. Angela took the plastic straw between her fingertips and poked at the ice floating in her cola.

"I don't see why you have to put so much pressure on yourself." Cheryl poured a packet of artificial sweetener into her iced tea.

"Oh, come on. Like you wouldn't get worked up about something like this."

Cheryl crossed her arms over her chest and chuckled. "I think you've bought into the western romance of the soul, and that's what's causing your problem."

"The what?"

"The western romance of the soul," she repeated, then took a sip of tea. "At least, that's what I like to call it. We live in this intense media culture constantly telling us what society thinks about this or that. We're exposed to different viewpoints, but most of the options still fall pretty close together."

Angela sipped her drink and listened, trying to be patient. Her jittery feet tapped on the floor.

"There are movies, and books, you name it, all saying that somewhere out in the world, there's someone for everyone, one perfect soulmate. They've been making millions off of this, and we keep buying it."

"I don't believe that Robin Michaels is my 'one perfect soulmate,' Cheryl," Angela remarked, hoping no one was eavesdropping.

"But there's a part of you that's terrified maybe he is."

Angela looked down at the table. She reached for the packets of sugar and Nutrasweet and began to construct a house with them.

"That's where the nervousness is coming from, Angela. You've bought into the idea of the soulmate, whether you like it or not." Cheryl watched her friend's growing sugar structure on the table. "If you were to change your own ideas about this, then there would be nothing more to worry about."

Angela looked across at her. "I don't understand."

Cheryl smiled broadly. "You yourself have been careful not to use the word 'soulmate' in this context. Why do you think that is?"

"Because that would make me some kind of psycho fan," Angela responded. "And that's not me."

"Okay. Why else?"

Angela placed one too many sugars on top of her delicate structure, and all of the packets collapsed into a small heap. "I don't know. It just doesn't feel like that."

"And what does it feel like?" Cheryl prompted.

Angela looked into her friend's encouraging eyes and felt a dull ache in her chest. "Listen, Cheryl, why don't you just tell me whatever it is that you're thinking? I'm sorry I'm so short this evening. I'm trying to make sense out of this, but at the same time, I can't believe I'm taking any of it seriously. I am not this nutty."

"Alright," Cheryl ceded. "You don't have to keep this same framework. You're working with a set of restricting definitions that say because of A, B must also be true. Because you've got this connection with Robin, then he must be your soulmate."

"Or I must be nuts."

"That's also a possibility," Cheryl smiled. "You're struggling against a concept, and it's getting in the way of the truth. All you have to do is change your mind."

* * * *

Angela sat cross-legged on the ground under an elegant tree with long, twisting branches. She gazed out on the brilliant green grass, heard the forest birds singing, and felt the delicate mist of the early morning air. She knew she was dreaming.

Instinctively, she looked up and found Michael balanced on a branch a few feet above. "Are you ready to hear the truth?" he asked bluntly.

"I think so," she nodded, feeling a sudden adrenaline rush.

Michael dropped down from his perch and sat in front of her. "You're so tenacious," he said. "Stubbornly so. You get an idea in your head about something, and you won't let go of it, even if that idea is hurtful to you."

Angela smiled and dropped her hands in her lap.

"It makes it difficult for you to get a clear picture about things," he continued. "You keep trying to throw familiar walls around everything, put everything in a box. So when something new comes along, and you don't know what to do with it, this razor sharp mind of yours distorts it to fit some predetermined category and not be threatened by it any longer."

"Yeah, okay."

Michael smiled, his expression full of love and understanding. Angela was warmed to her core by his eyes. She felt her body and mind relax as her defenses fell away. Maybe she wasn't ready, but she would at least make the effort. Looking beyond Michael, over his shoulder, Angela could see Robin, standing in the distance, smiling and waiting.

Chapter 51

20 May 1999
New York City
1:12 p.m.

"I hate to put it in these terms, but spirituality sells," Angela nearly grimaced as she answered Henry's question. In the spirit of the new partnership, he had moved across the table, closer to Angela and Jeff. He bit into a tuna salad sandwich and listened.

"People are looking for that. They want to be better human beings living more fulfilled lives," Angela explained. "We're talking about not only producing tools to help people find that wholeness within themselves, but also providing this safe space to use them and experiment."

"This idea of the retreat bothers me," Mike Ralston interrupted.

"Yeah, she had to sell me on that one, too," Jeff commented with a smile.

Angela took a quick sip of iced tea before continuing. "As an example, there are people exploring music and sound—its potential to unlock memories, boundaries, just so much. Music is such a powerful force, very primordial. We'd be giving these therapists and artists an external marketing outlet for their work, while also bringing in clients to experience these new tools in an environment designed especially for that process, where they'd have access to the people doing the research. You see?"

"So there'd be workshops. What kind of calendar are we looking at?" Henry asked.

Jeff cleared his throat. "Initially, we'd offer a series of core workshops to repeat each quarter, with variations to accommodate returning participants.

Starting with the first year, there would be an annual symposium or open house, with workshops and seminars running concurrently. Writing and journaling workshops, seminars on musical therapy, that sort of thing, attracting a larger group of presenters and professionals to the center, and stimulating interest in products and services."

"Will MOMENTUM be making its home in this new facility?" Bill Washington asked.

"Mmm, we haven't really talked about that," Angela said as she looked to Jeff.

"I think it would make sense, certainly," Jeff commented. "Of course, Angela is only one half of the magazine's ownership. She has a partner to consider."

Angela shook her head. "It's a tiny thing, really. I don't think we should be taking up space in the new place."

"Actually, I wanted to talk with you about MOMENTUM, so it's just as well Bill brought it up," Henry said. "It's not tiny, though small, yes. It's a quality publication with potential. What's interesting is that Westone had been studying your magazine, with an eye toward sponsorship or outright acquisition, when you came to us with your proposal."

"You're kidding me." Amazed, Angela looked to Jeff and found his confident smile waiting for her.

* * * *

"So, off the record, what's the current buzz in your world, Robin?" Mary K asked just as he took a bite of his sandwich.

Grinning, Robin chewed quickly, trying not to laugh, as he would certainly choke himself. He swallowed and reached for his glass of water.

"Sorry about that," Mary K apologized.

"No, it's okay." Robin put the glass down. "We're just making conversation, eh?"

Mary K nodded.

"Well," Robin relaxed his shoulders. "I can tell you I may shortly acquire New Haven Studios in full."

"Really?" she exclaimed in genuine surprise.

"We're still working out the numbers there," he told her. "You know I've been slowly buying up bigger chunks of the enterprise."

She shook her head. This was indeed news.

"Yeah, I started out as an equal partner, I guess. But I still had these royalties coming in, and I didn't know what to do with all of it." Robin chuckled at himself. "All that time Alice and I had been totally broke. I felt pretty bad about that, that the money really started coming in relatively soon after we split."

"You weren't that bad off those last few years together, were you?" Mary K asked.

"No, of course not," he replied. "We weren't struggling like we had before. But there were still issues. I took a big piece to establish a trust for Rose, which has already transferred over to her. I gave away a lot of it, you know, to different causes."

"Right."

"And I kept investing in New Haven. There wasn't a plan behind that, at first," he admitted. "But when I saw how easy it would be to gradually buy out my partners... They didn't really fight me on that, either, since New Haven was not initially quite so profitable as we'd hoped. So they are transitioning into being more executive management types."

"Oh, God, Robin," Mary K laughed. "They're your employees!"

Robin shook his head and smiled. "No, I don't tell them what to do. They tell me."

"Somehow I don't think it's quite that simple, Robin," Mary K surmised. "I know you a bit better than that."

"Well, yeah, maybe," he smiled bashfully. "I can collaborate on projects, but ultimately, long-term, it's got to be my show. Mmm. That explains a lot, doesn't it?"

Mary K just nodded and smiled. "Alright, let's get back to work."

Chapter 52

June 1997
Reston, Virginia

"Tell me more about how you started the magazine," Mary Katherine Baker asked Angela as they sat together in the Momentum Workshop, still in Fred's basement.

"Well, Fred and I met during our first year at the University of Virginia," Angela began, resting her chin in one hand. "We were on the same hall in our dormitory. So we were friends in college, and we both worked on the campus literary magazine for awhile. After graduation, we went our separate ways for a few years, but I suppose the fates-that-be saw to it that we both ended up here in Reston." Angela took a breath, suppressing an unintentional yawn. "We started MOMENTUM in 1994 mostly just as an outlet for our own writing. But we had friends, and friends of friends, interested in contributing—not just writing, but artwork as well. At first, we couldn't offer any kind of compensation. Fred and I were funding the printing and mailing out of our own pockets. We started paying folks in copies, and once we'd built up a respectable mailing list, we started offering paid subscriptions. I guess that was toward the end of 1995. But of course, that meant we were more accountable for getting it out on time!" Angela laughed.

Mary K smiled as she scribbled Angela's words in her notebook.

"I guess Fred already told you a lot about that," Angela conceded.

Mary K nodded as she finished writing, then looked up at Angela. "Sure, he gave me his run down. But I want your perspective. How did you begin writing?"

Angela smiled. "A lot of people ask that question, and I'm afraid I don't have a simple answer. I don't know when it started. For awhile, I suppose it was more journaling than anything else, getting out my thoughts and feelings, especially when I was a teenager." Angela grew quiet, allowing the journalist the opportunity to catch up with her.

"And then it became, mmm, kind of cathartic," Angela proceeded. "You know, a way to process through some of the more painful moments of my life."

Mary K nodded sympathetically and waited for her to continue.

Angela looked her directly in the eye. "I'd rather not talk about that, if you don't mind."

Mary K smiled. "Not at all." She flipped through the preceding pages, scanning her notes. "Tell me, Angela…" she said, still looking at her notebook, then glancing up to meet the gaze of her subject. "Tell me more about your book, ANGEL OF UNDERSTANDING?"

"Yes." Angela sat up enthusiastically. "That's been quite an experience. It's just coming out, you know."

"Finished it last night," Mary K admitted. "I was really unprepared for that one!"

Angela laughed. "You and me both! I can't even tell you where the title came from. With my previous poems, character sketches, the occasional short story, I never thought I'd be writing non-fiction. Especially something so, ahm, 'new age,' for lack of a better term. When you consider how uncomfortable I am just talking with anyone about this stuff, well, it's a wonder I ever put those words on paper."

Mary K held her hand up. "I'll tell you right now I'm not very knowledgeable about all of this," she confessed with a good-natured laugh. "But I really liked the way you took the chakra system… Chakra system? Am I pronouncing that correctly?"

"Yes."

"Okay, the way you took this energetic system and explored different meditations and ideas surrounding each chakra center, not only in terms of the individual, the individual person," Mary K gestured to herself, "but how you then expanded that into how all of these separate, seemingly contained systems actually connect with everyone else's. How one person's energy can physically, psychologically, psychically, whatever, affect the energy of a completely different person."

"Yeah," Angela commented. "I didn't know how I felt about that myself until I sat down to write about it."

"And how these influences can be felt across great distances," Mary K said, spreading her arms wide, "all across the globe, through what you're calling affinities."

Angela nodded and smiled at Mary K's understanding.

"I'm glad you mapped that out, with illustrations of how that all works, because it's pretty complicated stuff."

"It is, when you're first exposed to it," Angela responded. "I think you'll find—at least, this was my own experience—that the longer you sit with it, the more it makes natural sense. It's really not all that complex. It's simply another viewpoint, another way of looking at the world. And the universe."

"Okay, so how did you personally come up with or run across the idea of these affinities? I think you also used the term, 'soul twin'?"

Angela smiled nervously and looked away. She cleared her throat, then turned back to Mary K. "Okay." She tried to disguise the anxiety in her voice. "Even though this makes total sense, and I know deep down that it's absolutely true, I still think I sound like a flake sometimes."

Mary K laughed. "Not at all!" she exclaimed reassuringly. "Angela, I interview a lot of people, and I've met some real loonies. You're one of the sanest, most reasonable people I've had the pleasure of talking with."

"Well, thank you for that, but I also know it's your job to get me to talk," Angela smiled wryly, looking up from beneath her eyebrows. "Anyway, from speaking with other people over the years, hearing a lot of stories, and from some of my own experiences, I understand that this idea of affinity, soul twinning, happens all the time. I met one woman who had developed a mathematical formula—I think she used biblical references, and maybe some other sources—to explain precisely how many souls there are in the universe, and she had this big hierarchy chart mapping out just how the, umm, God Source, or whatever you want to call it, divides itself again and again, forming different groupings and soul families, monads, to populate this planet—and some others, depending on whom you talk to—in a structured and meaningful way."

Mary K frowned as she listened. "But you're not buying into that."

Angela pursed her lips. "I don't think her way is wrong. I'm just not focused on the what and how. I'm more interested in the why of it, and even then it's hard to make it stick. I think her way is well thought out. It's just one of many ways of looking at this."

"You said you had some personal experiences with soul twinning?" Mary K asked.

"Hmm," Angela laughed. "I know people like to have examples. It makes it easier to understand some things. But I think if they can grasp the principles involved, and then look to their own lives, they will find their own examples, their own evidence, there."

"Mmm," Mary K nodded.

"Okay." Angela stared into the distance. "Say there's you, and then there's someone named... Marvin Smith." Angela looked quickly back to Mary K. "You don't know anyone named Marvin Smith, do you?"

Mary K shook her head. Angela laughed.

"You never know with me. I can pull some pretty wild synchronicities right out of a hat sometimes," Angela explained. "Okay, so there's you, and there's Marvin. You've never met, but you share the same soul. You live complementary lives, working through the same lessons, if you believe life's a school, that life's about learning lessons and then moving on. Let's say you're on completely different parts of the planet. You're in... Wyoming, and Marvin... lives in Australia."

"Australia. Okay."

"You and Marvin are different people. You have different bodies, different names, different identities," Angela continued. "But if you were to sit down and compare the details of your lives—the big things and the little ones—you would find not just striking similarities, but absolute, incontrovertible parallels. Even though you're separate people with individual experiences, you've essentially been living the same life, sometimes through similarity, sometimes through opposition."

"Explain that last," Mary K requested.

Angela smiled. She looked around the work table, reached for a nearby soda can, and set it down between Mary K and herself. "Alright, from where we're sitting, you and I can both see this soda can, right?"

"Mmm-hmm," Mary K nodded.

"So we're looking at the same soda can. If we lean forward," Angela leaned toward the can, with Mary K following, "we can both see the top of the can. We agree that it's silver, with a tab to open it. This is where we have the same, or similar, perspective of the same thing."

"Okay," Mary K responded.

"And leaning back again," Angela sat back in her chair, "well, now I can tell you the ingredients and nutritional value of what's in the can, because I can see that printed here on my side, while from your side, all you can say is that the can is purple."

Angela looked into the journalist's eyes. "We're looking at precisely the same thing, but we're seeing it differently. You and Marvin share a soul, the same objectives and goals, but you may approach some lessons—like looking at the soda can—from different perspectives. But if you turn it around," Angela rotated the can 180 degrees, "you can see you've been looking at the same thing, climbing the same mountain, all along."

"Huh," Mary K commented, allowing Angela's words to sink in.

"That's a real basic explanation," Angela apologized.

"So, then, Marvin and I are working together," Mary K proposed.

Angela nodded. "Yes, absolutely."

"And Marvin and I will never meet?" she asked curiously.

"Well, mmm," Angela frowned. "Not necessarily. Sometimes twinned souls meet, sometimes they don't. Sometimes they incarnate together, as siblings, lovers, parents and children."

"Parents and children?" Mary K queried. "So, they don't have to be the same age? Like identical or fraternal twins. Born together."

"Nah," Angela shook her head. "That isn't a requirement. It doesn't make much difference on the soul level. You and Marvin might meet, depending on what kind of plan you've mapped out for yourselves."

"How do I find out what the plan is?"

"If I knew that, then I really would have figured this whole thing out!" Angela exclaimed with a laugh. "I don't have an answer for you. Different people have different ideas about that, and about whether there even is any kind of plan to begin with."

Mary K shook her head and smiled. "This is really, this is incredible stuff."

"I know," Angela replied. "Sometimes I just want to throw my hands in the air and walk away from the whole thing. But I hope I've offered this material in a way that's not only accessible to people in terms of understanding it, but also seeing how this is at work in their own lives. I'm not an evangelist or anything," Angela waved the idea away with her hand. "I'm not trying to convince anyone of anything. I just figured there were probably people in the world seeing and experiencing what I've noticed. By putting this material out there, in this book, it might help those people know they're not alone."

Mary K smiled gently.

"I don't think I realized that's why I did that until just now."

"I noticed there's no picture with your bio on the back cover," Mary K observed.

"Mmm."

"Was that a choice? Author photos are fairly standard these days."

Angela pulled one knee to her chest and sighed. "I know it's the regular thing to do, and that authors like to be recognized for their work. I wasn't quite comfortable with that. I'm still getting settled with this material. The reality of it. Not including my photo may be a small way of continuing to distance myself from it. But then also, I'm not really into public recognition. I've pretty much always shied away from that."

"I think your book will do quite well, Angela," Mary K offered genuinely.

Angela laughed. "I don't know about that. Actually, I don't really care. It was something I had to do, and now it's done. But with your article about the magazine," Angela gestured toward Mary K, "I think there will be more interest in MOMENTUM. If we do really well, hey, maybe I'll quit my job at America Online." Angela watched as Mary K transcribed her words into her notebook. "Wait! No, don't put that in the article."

"Don't worry," she smiled. "I wasn't writing that."

"I really appreciate your taking the time to come talk with us, for asking us to do this article," Angela told her. "You're our first big interview."

"The first of many, I'm sure."

"I hope not," Angela laughed. "I don't mean I haven't enjoyed my time with you," Angela stammered. "I just mean, I don't generally like being the center of too much attention. Like I was saying a minute ago, I like being acknowledged for my work, that kind of attention. But I told you about the band I was in, when I was a student. I really struggled with that decision, but as much as I love music I'm glad I chose school instead. It got to the point where those guys couldn't even go buy groceries without being recognized, sometimes even mobbed. I don't think I could live like that."

* * * *

"It sounds like the interview went well, then," Cheryl called out from the living room later that evening.

"Yeah, it wasn't too bad," Angela shouted back from her friend's kitchen. She grabbed two drinking glasses from a cabinet, frowning as soon as she heard the music from the other room. She fought the rhythm creeping into her system, her lungs becoming dead weights in her ribcage. She wrinkled her nose and walked slowly down the hallway.

"Umm, Cheryl?" Angela asked as she reached the living room, where her friend stood at the stereo cabinet. "What's that music, please?"

"The new Robin Michaels album," Cheryl smiled wryly. "Don't you have a copy?"

Angela swallowed hard as she put the two glasses down on the coffee table. "No, and I'm not going to get one, either."

"Oh, come on, Angie," Cheryl prodded as she swayed gently to the song's rhythm.

Robin's voice filled the room. Hearing his lyrics, his voice, Angela clutched her stomach and knelt down on the floor. "Oh, God."

Cheryl quickly bent down beside her. "Honey, are you okay?"

Angela covered her mouth with one hand. "I think I'm going to be sick."

Cheryl laughed. "Now, his music isn't that bad!"

"No," Angela complained, close to tears. She pointed toward the speakers. "I mean, I wrote that! Those are my words."

Cheryl reached for Angela's hands. "I thought you were doing better with this now."

Angela sniffed hard. "Yeah, I did, too."

"Look, this is just going to keep on until there is some resolution, right? So why don't you get in touch with him? Reach out to Robin."

"Oh, yeah, right!" Angela laughed. "What am I supposed to do? Just send an e-mail saying, 'Hello, Robin. This is your soul twin calling. Have a nice day'?!"

Cheryl smiled. "Why not? He already wrote you a letter, last year. Why not write back? You've got his address."

Angela climbed up off the floor and began to pace. Cheryl's eyes followed as she passed back and forth in front of her.

"No, he wrote a letter to the editors of the magazine, not to me," Angela protested. "That's entirely different. This whole thing is just nuts."

"Separate fact from emotion, Angie."

Angela stopped pacing and listened to the music, so familiar. "What's the name of this song?"

Cheryl smiled. "*Water Walking.*"

Angela placed her hands on her hips, looked down at her feet, and sighed.

"I guess I shouldn't loan you my copy of his biography then." Cheryl pointed to the coffee table, where Mary Katherine Baker's ROBIN MICHAELS: THUS FAR lay.

Angela shook her head and smiled sarcastically. "I've already got it. I can't read it."

"Why not?" Cheryl looked up at her from the floor.

"Every time I open it, just to some random page," her voice tightened, "all I see is my life and my words shouting back at me."

Chapter 53

July 1998

Virginia Beach, Virginia

Robin handed the cashier a $20 bill for the turkey wrap sandwiches and sodas he and Rose had ordered for lunch. "At least they're not overcharging their captive audience," he commented quietly as they walked away from the food court of the GTE Amphitheater.

Rose had invited her father to attend the Lilith Fair concert festival in Virginia Beach, an hour's drive from her modest Williamsburg apartment. After strolling through the historic district, visiting the small shops and craft houses, Rose had proudly introduced him to her colleagues at the Colonial Williamsburg Foundation, where she had been interning while pursuing her master's degree. She was anxious to convince him that she was in control of her life, and that she knew what she was doing.

Now, amid the curious blend of live music from several stages, Rose spread a large blanket on the lawn. Robin ran a wet wipe across his hands.

Sitting down, Robin bit ravenously into his sandwich, accidentally dumping half its contents down the front of his shirt. As he gazed, dumbfounded, on the chunky river of mayonnaise, lettuce, and tomatoes slowly making its way down his chest, his daughter burst into delighted peals of laughter.

"Oops," Rose teased. She tossed the paper napkins to him and reached into her knapsack for some spring water. Taking the plastic bottle from her hand, Robin's gaze lingered on her engagement ring. Rose sighed.

"Stop. We're not talking about this today." She bit into her own sandwich and looked away from him, scanning the festival grounds.

"Right." Robin poured some water into a wad of napkins and dabbed at the globs of food on his shirt, generally making the mess worse.

Rose filled the silence with a few more bites of her lunch. She put her sandwich down and pulled off her sandals, curling her bare feet beneath her broomstick skirt as she faced her father squarely.

"You've got to give Harris a chance," she said, her hands clasped in her lap.

Still cleaning himself up, Robin shot her an amused expression from beneath his greying eyebrows. "I thought we weren't going to talk about this."

Rose smiled and reached for her soda. "Okay, but I'm just going to tell you what you've already heard."

Robin put down the wet napkins and gave his daughter his full attention. He knew she had already made up her mind, and there was nothing he nor her mother could do to convince her otherwise. So stubborn. She had gotten that from him.

"I'm twenty-five years old," she began, looking down at the blanket as she placed her intended points in mental order. "I've completed my master's at William & Mary, and I'm ready to move on. It's a good time to make a change, especially geographically."

Robin resisted the urge to fidget.

"Harris has been in San Francisco for nearly a year. He's got a good job with that architectural firm. It's only a matter of time before he slides into something more senior, maybe even starting his own partnership."

He nodded, encouraging Rose to continue.

"We've been dating almost three years, living together here those last months before he moved. We know each other. There won't be any surprises."

"There are always surprises," Robin blurted out before he realized he had even opened his mouth. "I mean," he stammered in apology, "life is like that."

Rose sighed angrily and crossed her slender arms over her chest. "You think just because you and Mum couldn't make it work that I'm doomed to fail also."

"That's not true, Rose," he counseled, trying to placate her.

"You two married so young," she protested. "You were still babies. You didn't know who you were yet."

Robin studied the colour pattern of the blanket. Alice had made a similar argument to her parents, years ago. Self-knowledge was such tenuous wisdom, constantly shifting like sands with the tide.

"It's not my fault you get yourself into all these crazy relationships." Rose was shocked to hear the accusation on her own lips.

Robin looked up to face his daughter's anger. Their eyes met, for a moment, before Rose turned away in embarrassment.

It was true these last years had found him in a string of impossible involvements with all the wrong people. For all the wrong reasons. Following his split from a theatrical set designer, his recent dalliance with a twenty-year-old, Scandinavian model had provided the desired excitement and boost to his ego, though it had left him feeling emotionally and ethically bankrupt.

Robin sighed. "I don't know what to tell you, Rose. I can be a big, fat idiot sometimes."

The final strains of an artist's closing song and enthusiastic cheers filled the silence.

"This is my life," she said quietly. "And this is what I want."

He nodded, then looked up into his daughter's stern face. He could still see the child inside this young woman, staring back at him. He wanted to pave her path with daisies and jellybeans. He felt the fatherly advice welling up inside. He laughed privately, to think he might offer any reasonable answers, given the example of his own life. Robin took a deep breath, filling his lungs, and then released everything.

He leaned forward and touched Rose on the knee. "Harris is a wonderful fellow, Rose. No one is denying that. He's a good lad, a good person, with a good job and a great outlook."

She looked into her father's eyes, encouraged but not entirely trusting.

"Of course I'll worry. You're my baby girl." Robin could see her tears forming and felt his own eyes growing moist. "Your mother and I did a fairly poor job of laying out any kind of roadmap for you, so you're going to have to figure it out for yourself. I can't make your decisions, or your mistakes, for you. I wish I could take the pain of some of those experiences from you. But I can't. That's all meant for you, in your life. I just want for you to be happy, sweetheart."

"Oh, Daddy," Rose murmured as she wiped at her nose with the back of her hand.

"But San Francisco?" Robin leaned back and planted his hands on his knees. "It's so far away. It was one thing to have you here on the American East Coast. But now you're moving to California..."

Rose laughed her tears away. "You know you love it out there, Dad," she chided. "You can come visit, and I'll come home again. It's a wonderful area. Harris has found a place for us in Redwood City, so we can take the train in. And you love to fly. You spend half your life in the air as it is anyway. The Pacific isn't much further to travel."

"Alright," he said, chuckling. "But I'm still your father," he said, pointing a finger at Rose. "And I'm telling you right now... to finish eating your lunch. Or else."

She giggled appreciatively and leaned forward to kiss him quickly on the cheek. "Thanks, Dad."

There is nothing in this world, Robin thought to himself gratefully, like my child's smile.

* * * *

Cheryl had convinced Angela to run away with her for a long weekend at the beach. The Lilith Fair stop was an added bonus. Getting away from Reston was precisely what Angela needed.

The two friends had meandered arm in arm along the beach and the boardwalk, breathing the saltwater air and feeling the sand beneath their feet. Within a few hours of their arrival, Angela had managed to shake off the stress and anxieties of home, reclaiming the skip in her step and laughing easily.

Now walking the amphitheater grounds, Angela wandered through the food court alone, killing time while Cheryl enjoyed a twenty-five-dollar massage from a local vendor in a nearby tent. With each step, she concentrated on shooing away the thoughts that wanted to crowd in on her. She knew she was just procrastinating. Once she was home again, she would have to face her own music.

"Ron," she whispered to herself as she rounded a corner and began another lap. It was simultaneous thrill and dread she felt, thinking of him. He expected an answer when she returned. She honestly didn't know what to tell him.

They were comfortable together. They got along well. They had become trusted companions. She loved him; this much she knew. But was she in love with him? Had she ever been?

Angela stopped and leaned back against a light pole. She shoved her hands deep into the pockets of her blue jeans and kicked at the dirt with the heel of her shoe, digging a small hole.

"It makes all the sense in the world," she repeated Ron's own words, his less than romantic marriage proposal nearly a week earlier. She would be thirty soon. Time to settle down, right? If she wanted a family of her own, she'd better start making plans.

She felt the cool metal of the light pole on her bare elbows. She should be excited about this. She criticized herself for her looming ambivalence and tried to work her way around it, but it simply would not let go.

"I want to do this," she said aloud, looking up at the late afternoon sky. It was the right thing to do, the next logical step. Marry Ron. Have his children. Build a life around this partnership. But. whenever she tried to imagine a bright and happy future together, all she felt was a sinking dread in her gut. She looked down at her dusty shoes and gave her entire weight to the lamppost. "I can't do this."

Angela cleared her throat and sniffed back the tears she felt coming on. There was no decision to be made. She had learned not to go against her intuition, and it was clear what it was telling her. No deliberation. The best she could do would be to forget about this business for awhile, and enjoy this evening with her friend.

Her shoulders relaxed, finally free of this weight. She smiled peacefully as she sighed. This wouldn't be easy, but it was the best path. For everyone.

Angela bought a pink lemonade, a favorite from childhood. She sipped the tart sweetness and started back toward the massage tent, wondering if they offered additional body work. She laughed, imagining herself receiving an aura cleansing. "One of these days," she said to herself quietly, "I might actually believe in all of that."

She turned another corner and looked up. A familiar face caught her eye. She was unable to move, frozen in her tracks. Robin.

Angela blinked. Hard. He was still there. It was definitely him, standing a few yards away with a young woman. "Oh, my God," she muttered under her breath, her body filling with molten lava, pouring in from her feet upwards. Robin and his companion turned. They were headed in her direction.

She panicked. No, not now, not now! Angela managed to put one foot in front of the other, moving out of Robin's path. Though he had not yet caught sight of her, within a few seconds he would be right on top of her. There would be no way to avoid a meeting. She moved quickly.

Angela glanced furtively at him as he approached. He had his hand on the girl's back, guiding her as she walked in front of him. Angela could feel the building onslaught of energy. Something wasn't right. This was not an intended meeting. She was smart to get out of the way. She turned away from him, a bolt of lightning striking her solar plexus as he passed.

She braced herself against the internal electrical storm, though it evaporated quickly, retreating with each step he took. A shiver ran up her spine as she shook off his energy. She continued on her own path, silently kicking herself for being such a coward.

* * * *

"Dad, are you alright?" Rose had a supportive hand on her father's shoulder. They had turned a corner, heading toward the food court for a couple of sodas, and Robin had suddenly faltered in his steps, reaching for a lamppost to steady himself.

"What's wrong?" Rose asked in alarm. "Are you sick?"

"No, no," Robin tried to reassure her as he regained his breath. At first he feared he was having a heart attack, feeling slammed by a locomotive. But the pain had quickly subsided, leaving nothing but this feeling he could only describe as electrical shock.

"I'm alright," he panted, looking into his daughter's face with a confident smile.

"Shall I get someone? Do you want to sit down?"

Robin looked at the base of the lamppost. Someone had been digging in the dirt, with a stick or something, he thought to himself. His fingers tingled against the cool metal. He pulled his hand away, and the sensation stopped.

He touched the pole again and felt the buzzing. Odd. Stepping away from the lamppost, he shook his hands and adjusted his neck.

"I'm alright, sweetheart. Must be jet lag," he lied. They continued toward the food stands, Rose keeping close pace with her father. He looked back over his shoulder to regard that lamppost once more, then shook his head, still feeling slightly dizzy and definitely in shock.

Chapter 54

December 1998
Reston, Virginia

Ron had already begun packing. He shoved shirts and socks into a large duffel bag and reached for anything in sight he felt he should take with him. Despite the passionate flood of emotions visibly rushing through him, Angela felt nothing, standing in the bedroom doorway and watching. Numb.

"Ron."

He ignored her. He opened their shared closet and started pulling out his clothing.

"Ron, let's talk about this." Angela entered the room and sat down next to his bag on the bed.

Refusing eye contact, Ron rolled his belts and ties before placing them in the bag. "What is there to talk about? I think we've pretty much exhausted our resources there."

He stepped into the bathroom and gathered his shaving supplies. She looked down into his duffel. She was tempted to put his things back in the bureau, but she didn't move.

"I just don't understand why it has to be like this," she said, exasperated.

Hands heavily laden with shaving cream cans, cologne, and toothpaste, Ron stepped back into the bedroom. "You're kidding me."

"No, I..." Angela shrugged.

Ron crossed to the bed and dumped his load into the duffel bag. Standing over her, Ron looked down on the top of her head. "How much longer did you think I was going to wait, Angie?"

She looked up, meeting his gaze. Angela swallowed hard. Here come the emotions, she thought. "I don't know. But I'm being as honest as I can. I didn't want to be unfair."

Angela bowed her head and rested her face in her hands. Ron was leaving her. She searched inside for that magic light switch, to change her feelings about all of this. Was Ron really the wrong partner, or was it just stubbornness, even fear, that stood in the way?

Ron crouched down and placed his hands on her knees. "Angie."

She cleared her throat and pushed her hair back behind her ears. It was just a matter of time before the tears came.

"I'm really fighting here, Angie," Ron admitted. "I need to stay true to myself and the things I want, just like you. And it's not easy for me not to get angry about this."

"So you're not angry?"

"I didn't say that." Ron almost laughed. "I'm just tired. I want what I want. I'm thirty-seven years old, and I want to get married. I want to start a family. It's time for me to do that."

Angela pulled up her feet and sat cross-legged on the bed.

"I kept waiting for you to feel sure of me, to let go of this… independence, you keep saying you need."

"What's wrong with that?" Angela demanded. "What's wrong with wanting my own life?"

Ron stood again and took several steps away. "Nothing. There's nothing wrong with that, Angela."

"Okay, so then what's wrong with the way things are, for us?"

He stopped in front of the bedroom bookcase, surveying the volumes they had acquired together. He touched one of his books on chaos theory, considering pulling it off the shelf and packing it into his bag.

"I just saw this, living together, as a step along the way to someplace else." He turned to face her. "I didn't think this was going to be it. I thought we were moving forward, not stagnating. But if it hasn't happened in four years, then I guess it's just not going to happen."

Angela thought on his words, each one a cold stone in her stomach. She looked at the soft leather of his shoes. After too many moments of her silence, Ron returned to the shelves and began retrieving his books. Angela felt the wet warmth of a few stray tears spilling down onto her cheeks. She brushed them away quickly.

"One of these days, Angela, you're going to let your defenses down, or whatever it is that's got you stymied," he said with his back to her. "I don't know if it's perfectionism, or fear, or what. Maybe you simply don't…" Ron carried his books to the bed and dumped them on top of his bag. "I don't know. I realized I just got to a point where I would have taken even 'Maybe' over 'Not yet.' At least that would have been some progress. And that's a problem. I don't want to live my life compromising myself like that."

Ron reached for her hands and pulled her up off the bed. "I love you, Angela. But what is enough for you just isn't enough for me."

* * * *

She felt she were in a movie, caught up in the momentum of what was going on around her, but unable to take any action to influence the outcome.

Watching Ron pack and listening to his occasional advice on how she might change her outlook was an experiment in quiet torture. Angela retreated to the den and sat down with Rusty, disturbing their dog's winter nap. She wanted to lose herself in some vacuous television program, but quickly felt this was callous and inappropriate. She grabbed her coat.

Ron had decided to move out. He was packing up his things and would return for his share of the furniture the following weekend. The friendly relationship that had been her steady anchor for nearly four years had at last dashed itself against the rocks.

Inside a confusing vortex, Angela spun in a whirlwind of rational arguments and emotions. She wandered the dark streets of her urban neighborhood, pulling her coat close against the biting cold. She walked around and around, circling the block, returning to their duplex, each time comforted to see the lights still on. Ron was still there, but she was too shaken to go inside. Not just yet. And she would take another lap.

Now, she was ready. She must have been walking for an hour. She unlocked the street-level entry door and started up the steps to their second-floor apartment.

She stopped half-way up. Ron stood at the top of the stairs, ready to carry his last load to the car. They looked at each other, neither saying a word.

"Can I help with any of that?" Angela asked, breaking the silence. She climbed the rest of the stairs toward him.

"No, I've got it. This is the last of it." Ron started down the steps, passing her on the staircase without a glance.

Angela sat down on the top step, watching Ron open the door at the bottom of the stairs. He struggled with the doorknob, trying not to drop the boxes and bags he was carrying. He made it safely outside, and the door closed shut behind him.

She leaned forward, resting her forehead on her knees. She heard the familiar click of Rusty's toenails on the hardwood floor and felt him lean against her as he lay down. Still wrapped in her winter coat, Angela was uncomfortably warm, but she needed this protective layer. She closed her eyes and prayed for unconsciousness.

There was a hand on her shoulder. Looking up, she found Ron standing on the steps in front of her, smiling sadly. She must have dozed off. "You didn't think I was just going to leave like that, did you?"

Angela sniffed and returned his smile. "No."

Ron leaned forward and kissed her lightly on the mouth. She looked into his eyes, completely open to him. He pulled her heavy coat down over her shoulders, then took her hand and led her down the hallway.

* * * *

Ron sat on the edge of the bed and slipped on his shoes. Angela lay under the blankets, watching.

"Where will you go?"

He stood up and fastened his belt. "I'll go to Andy's, at least for a couple of days."

"I guess you've really thought this through." There was no anger in her voice, just quiet resignation.

Ron sat back down on the bed and leaned across to touch her chin. "There wasn't exactly a plan."

"Yeah." She looked into his face, so strong and familiar. Without a doubt, Ron was one of the best friends she would ever have, and this moment possibly one of the bigger regrets of her life. "I'm really sorry, Ron."

He gave her his sweetest smile of understanding, the smile that always melted her heart. "It's okay. It's going to be okay." He gave her hands a quick squeeze and winked. "I'm glad we got to say goodbye like this."

She kissed the end of his nose. When she pulled away to look at him, she felt an emotional nausea rushing in, threatening to flood the entire room. Her eyes filled with tears as her smile contorted across her face. "You'd better get going, I think."

"Yeah." Ron's voice was rough. It was time.

He got up from the bed, lifted his coat from the floor, and walked out into the hallway. She heard him say a quick goodbye to Rusty. Angela's breath came in quiet fits as she listened to his retreating footsteps echoing against the walls.

She heard the downstairs door close behind him. Angela pulled the covers back and swung her feet down to the floor. "Right," she said firmly. She pulled on her favorite pajamas and dug her ridiculously large slippers out from underneath the bed.

Angela padded down the hallway to the den and stood in front of the television, mindlessly flipping through the channels. She glanced out the window, looking down into the street below. Her breath stalled in her throat when she caught sight of Ron, standing alone on the sidewalk, gazing up solemnly toward the apartment they had shared. She never knew if he actually saw her observing him.

Weighing his keys in his hand, Ron turned and got into his car. Angela moved closer to the window, touching the cold glass with her fingertips as she watched him drive away. Her breath fogged the clear panes in quiet waves. Her cheeks were wet, and she didn't care.

"This, too, shall pass," she whispered.

Angela heard a strange buzzing, growing louder. It was in her skin, in her bones. Her entire field of vision went white.

She was standing, somewhere... No walls, no floor, no ceiling. Nothing but white. Bright white. She squinted against the intensity of the light before she realized she didn't have to. She looked down. She was still wearing her plaid pajamas and her fuzzy bunny slippers. This had to be a dream.

"Do you remember the map, Angela?" asked a familiar voice behind her.

Angela turned to find the smiling figure of Michael. She was vaguely aware of others, somewhere in the distance, but she couldn't make them out clearly.

"A map?"

"The map that Isis showed you?"

A table materialized in front of her, on it lying a great tome, opened to that same page she had seen years before. The swimming ocean colors, the vibrant blues, greens, and purples, swirled to life before her eyes.

"Yes." Her voice echoed across space. Or was it only inside her own skull?

Michael rested his hands on her shoulders as they looked down on the liquid soul map.

"There is always a plan, Angela," he whispered. "Everything is happening precisely as it should. There's no way you can get it wrong."

Angela spun on her heel to face him. She was nearly shaking with anger, frightened by its intensity. She wanted to scream. She wanted to slam her fists into his chest. She clenched her fingers as her jaw tightened.

"Tell me what to do!" she demanded. "Give me something I can use, something I can understand! Don't show me some messy watercolor and expect me to complacently accept—" She turned with the intention of knocking over the table and sending the massive book sprawling to the ground, but the space behind her was now empty. Instead, in the hazy distance, she could make out the vague form... of Robin.

Angela faced Michael again, nearly panting in frustration. His smile expressed such immense patience and love. She didn't know if she would laugh or cry.

The phone was ringing. Angela shook herself back into her body. Spontaneous soul journeys were not her preferred method of enlightenment. She held a hand to her forehead, allowing her eyes to adjust to the comparative darkness of the apartment. "Oh, man," she muttered as she shuffled across the floor to the phone, nearly tripping over the rug in her slippers. She would deal with this phone call and then go straight to bed, and she might stay there for several days.

She picked up the receiver and held it against her head. "Hello," she snapped.

"Angela? Angela Harris?" came the man's voice from the other end of the line.

Angela planted her fist against her waist in impatience. "Yes. Who is this?"

* * * *

"So we've got to focus on empowering individuals," Angela concluded, nearly jumping up in her seat in restless enthusiasm. "As opposed to just throwing information at them. Which is essentially what happens all the time, all around us. We're drowning in information. What's the term? Data smog."

Jeff Pleasant, an experienced entrepreneur in his own right, sat across the table from her at the small Mexican restaurant, jotting down a few notes as she spoke. It had been nearly two weeks since he had called her at home that evening, proposing they meet to discuss a potential partnership, as they had several times before. He liked Angela, admiring her creativity and conviction, and he was hopeful they at last had stumbled upon a means of combining her unique genius with his marketing and business acumen.

"Interactive," he commented.

"Absolutely." Angela reached for her iced tea. She enjoyed these brainstorming lunches with Jeff. But she rarely took any of this seriously. Previous meetings had yielded no results, and she no longer held any expectation around these conferences. Plus, reeling from her still fresh split from Ron, Angela felt raw, open. Her defenses were inactive. She was floating. She wasn't holding anything back.

"Listen," Angela directed as she drummed her fingers on the lunch table. "It's no mistake that new age titles and multimedia fantasy games have taken off the way they have. People have reached a point where basic needs are long past being met. That's ancient history. In this society, anyway."

Jeff sat back in his chair and smiled. She was almost preaching, with an excited energy that was easily contagious. More than youthful exuberance, the fifty-two-year-old thought to himself. Jeff put his pen down and simply listened, absorbing her passion.

"The economy is in such a state that we don't know what to do with ourselves. People today enjoy a level of financial success they've never had before, and it just keeps seeming to ramp up. More, more, more."

"And that's where the problem is," Jeff commented.

"Exactly!" she agreed. "We've become slaves to our own lifestyles. The television tells us we need this, that, and the other thing, in all different shades of the rainbow, if we're going to really be happy, if we're going to truly seize all that life has to offer. We need a huge, flat-screened television in every room of the house, with these gaming systems and DVD players hooked up to them. Surround sound in the bathroom, the basement, and the garage. A brand new convection oven that can cook three eighteen-pound turkeys at once. We need the latest thirty-passenger SUV that can go zero to a hundred and seventy in nine milliseconds. We need instant access to everything: T-1 lines in the house, video screens in the car, cell phones that glow in the dark, digital pagers that tie your shoes and valet-park your car."

Jeff laughed, enjoying the facetious fervor of her argument. Angela took a breath, settling herself in her seat. She looked directly into Jeff's eyes, pinning him down.

"Obviously, this isn't enough. It's not working. You will never, ever be able to get enough of what you don't really want."

"And you know what people want," he challenged.

Angela smiled. "I know what I want. And I can't imagine I'm alone in this."

* * * *

"Do you think we're trying to do too much?" Angela asked over coffee the following Saturday afternoon.

"It's aggressive, it's ambitious," Jeff responded, a pen clenched between his teeth as he read over a draft of their business plan. "But, you know, we're working out a schedule, we're tackling these points by degrees."

Angela frowned. She looked out the window of Jeff's study onto the back lawn, gauging the lengthening shadows of early winter.

"Hey, I've got another one," she said, looking back at him. Jeff pulled his pen out of his mouth and waited.

"Something that takes a bunch of those professional indicators," she began, stretching the fingers of one hand, then the other. "You know, the tools used by college and career counselors. Personality tests. That tell you what you're good at doing, what jobs and professions are best suited to you."

"Okay."

"Put them together on a CD-ROM," Angela gazed into a distant corner as she put words around her vision. "You have to license these. But structure an interface in such a way that the user doesn't have to take each test individually. Create one questionnaire, to answer all at once, or in stages, a couple of questions at a time."

"And this global questionnaire feeds the different measurement tools," Jeff offered.

"Exactly. The program builds an individual data file that lives on the hard drive, stores the information there to build the person's profile." Angela tapped her foot against the leg of the chair, unconsciously providing a steady rhythm for her thoughts. "You could have multiple users, each with his or her own data file."

Angela grew quiet for a moment. Jeff scribbled some notes on his legal pad. The only sound was Angela's fidgeting.

"So you end up with this comprehensive picture of who you are as an individual, though it's not intended as self-definition," she proposed.

"What do you mean?" Jeff looked up.

Angela shifted, curling up in the chair. "Well, the intention is not to ask a few questions and then spit out a profile that says, 'This is who you are, this and nothing else.' That's dangerous. Instead, it's a resource for gaining insight into preferences and talents you may have only peripherally been aware of before."

She reached for the mug on the table beside her and drank down the rest of the lukewarm coffee. "It could be used in schools," she suggested as she put down the empty mug. "Help students make choices about academic and career paths, maybe help figure out some of the things they want to do with their lives."

"Some of the things?" he asked wryly.

"Yeah," Angela smiled. "Can you imagine doing only one thing in your life, and nothing else? How boring is that? I'd probably shoot myself."

Jeff laughed. "And career counselors could use this, too, to help clients. Outplacement services. Or people just wanting to make a change, or discover a new interest. They could get this CD-ROM and use it at home."

"Yes." Angela took a breath and relaxed her body. She had a tendency to become restless as she gave herself over to such brainstorming. "But that's just an idea."

Jeff smiled at this last comment as he jotted down a few more notes. "Just another one. Did you just think this up, sitting here right now?"

"Mmm," Angela thought. "Yeah, I guess so. Sorry."

"Don't apologize!" Jeff chastised. "The best thing to do right now is give voice to all of these different ideas, throw them on the wall and see which ones stick. The only bad ideas…"

"… are the ones you keep to yourself, right?" Angela smirked.

"Right." Jeff pulled the proposal draft back into his lap and continued his review. He shook his head and smiled. "This world culture CD-ROM series…"

"I know, I know," Angela defended. "It's huge. Maybe impossibly so. I wouldn't want to be the one to have to put that together. That's a project that never ends. Like a big encyclopedia. Once you get the thing out there, you have to keep updating it every year, or more often than that. Hundreds of countries, hundreds of discs…"

Angela frowned. Jeff poured another cup of coffee. Suddenly, her face brightened.

"But think of the educational benefits, being a child in one place and exploring an entirely different corner of the world, without having to leave your desk," she continued. "Or finding out more about your own country. You get the language, the culture, the history, music, customs, religion, holidays…" Angela sighed.

Jeff looked up with raised eyebrows.

"It's gigantic, the undertaking. Maybe it can't ever happen." She started shaking her knee as she thought. "But I like the idea. People want to make better sense out of the world. This might be one way of doing that. Or, maybe start some kind of global, cultural exchange. Like the American Field Service. Take kids from underprivileged backgrounds and expose them to different cultures and ideas by taking them into communities in other parts of the world. Let the kids from different countries talk to each other. Offer them experiences that will let them think more independently, more inclusively…"

"Angela…" Jeff chided.

"Yeah, okay." Angela backed down. "I'll try to stay on topic."

Jeff returned to his reading, and Angela stared out the window again.

"Stay on track," said the voice inside. "Don't forget Spirit. This is your main focus."

"Mmm. Right," Angela responded aloud, gazing deeply into the middle distance, seeing nothing.

"What?" Jeff looked up from his work.

She was startled by his voice. "Hmm? Oh, nothing." Angela looked away again, tapping her fingers against her forehead.

"We should just call this company Angela's Brain," Jeff joked. "You're a think tank all by yourself."

Chapter 55

April 1999

Winchester, Hampshire

Robin turned over in his bed, dancing the fine line between consciousness and sleep, where he had his funkiest, most productive dreams.

He was swimming. The water was warm and clear green. His lungs filled with the emerald water as he moved beneath the surface, breathing in the green as his entire body filled with light. The warmth of the crystal liquid caressed every millimetre of his bare skin.

Coming to the surface, Robin could see the shore, just a few metres away. There was a woman standing at the water's edge, waiting for him. That same woman, her brilliant green eyes reflecting the light in his own.

Catching sight of him, she smiled. She knelt down and dipped her fingers in the deep green sea, running her hand back and forth as she absorbed the warmth into her body, sending gentle ripples out to Robin. He felt her energy reach him, entering his chest and radiating outward from his heart. She lifted her gaze to again meet his in a welcoming expression of intimate recognition. She extended her arms out to him.

Who was this woman?

Robin wanted with his entire being to go to her.

"GO TO NEW YORK."

Robin's eyes opened wide as he lay in bed, shaken awake by the reverberation of the voice through his body.

"Oh," he said awkwardly to the darkness. He stretched his hands under the covers and yawned. He squinted at the clock on his nightstand. It was just past 3 a.m.

"Mmm," he growled deep in his throat, turning onto his back and closing his eyes, ready to return to his dream. He tried to picture the woman once more...

"GO TO NEW YORK CITY," came the intuitive voice again, echoing against the walls of his skull and forcing alertness onto his sleepy brain.

"New York," Robin repeated as he sat up in bed. He switched on the bedside lamp, accidentally knocking the book he had been reading to the floor. He squinted down at the title—Angela Harris' ANGEL OF UNDERSTANDING—then leaned back against the headboard. He yawned again, long and deep, stretching his arms out to his sides.

He looked up at the ceiling. "Alright...?" he questioned the empty space. There was no response.

* * * *

It was nearly 10 a.m. when Robin finally wandered into the main building of New Haven.

After sitting up for an hour or so, waiting for more information or to at least go back to sleep, he had resigned himself to consciousness and got up out of bed.

Following a long, hot shower to stimulate circulation and wash away the blissful memories of his emerald ocean, Robin went downstairs, made some coffee, and sat down in front of the computer to catch up on e-mail. An increasing number of fans across the globe were figuring out his screen name. Soon, he would have to change his online identity, again.

Green, he thought to himself. I could just be Green.

He had then awakened several hours later, having dozed off at his computer desk.

"Good morning, Mr. Michaels," Betsy greeted him cheerfully as he pushed through the heavy glass doors of New Haven.

"Mmm. Yes. Morning," Robin responded, his head cloudy with broken sleep. He had walked from home, taking advantage of some clear weather. His shoes and the cuffs of his trousers were damp with dew from the grass.

"Your messages are on your desk, Robin," she commented while stapling papers together at the reception desk.

"Messages," Robin mumbled as he walked through the sunlit foyer, headed toward his office.

"Several came in from the States last night," she explained, not looking up.

Passing the reception desk, Robin stopped suddenly and turned back to face her. He was frowning, trying to figure out what he was missing. She looked at him and smiled.

"Kevin's on vacation this week, remember?" Betsy prompted. "I'm covering reception while he's gone. So if you can't find me in my office, I'm up here." She smiled at his vague confusion and returned to stapling.

"Mmm," he commented, pivoting around again and passing into the hallway.

Betsy had already unlocked his office door and turned on the lights, anticipating his arrival. When he saw the uncertain stack of demo CDs, no doubt deposited by his multimedia group in hopes of his feedback, he felt the skin around his mouth tighten. Robin stepped behind his desk to survey the day ahead.

"Oof," he released as he sat down.

Pushing the collection of discs aside, Robin reached for a more modest pile of paper messages and facsimile transmissions.

Nathan Pratt was proposing another film score collaboration, some movie about gladiators. Or Viking explorers. He hadn't decided yet, Nathan's hand-written fax explained. Rose had phoned to let him know she and Harris had returned from their honeymoon—"Yes, we're still married," she had dictated to the late night operator. Someone at Amnesty International had faxed the agenda for the upcoming New York conference, though he had long ago declined due to workloads at New Haven and Segue. Gareth and Priscilla's daughter, Joy, would graduate from Columbia University in the States next month; would he attend the commencement with them? Annie Lennox was inviting him to make a vocal appearance on a new album. Some woman he had never heard of had gotten his fax number and was requesting that he make an appearance to sing at her birthday party in Oregon; she had also faxed a photo of herself in a bathing suit. Habitat for Humanity wanted to know if they could count on his generous financial and promotional support again this year. XCel, a new American boy band, wanted to sample one of his older releases, claiming he should give them a break because they were a growing presence, and because their pop tunes would renew interest in his own material.

"Oh, boy," he muttered. Some days, he would trade anything he had for a few, blissful moments of absolute anonymity. No one pulling at him, wanting something from him. No one giving a damn who or what he was.

"Mmm," he commented, reading the next message. Mary Katherine Baker had called to request an interview, at his convenience, when he was next in New York. He felt the excited tug in his solar plexus. Holding this message up against the Amnesty itinerary and the commencement invitation, Robin smiled. "Ah, yes."

"New York, New York," he sang to himself as he lifted the telephone handset. "Kevin," he spoke into the receiver.

"Betsy," came the patient reply.

"Oh," he uttered in surprised embarrassment. "Ah, I need to make air travel arrangements."

Chapter 56

19 May 1999
Marriott Marquis, New York City
11:03 p.m.

Angela sat on the queen-sized bed in the hotel room and switched on the television. She and Jeff had just spent two hours over a late dinner going over last-minute details of their proposal and outlining strategies for any anticipated opposition from the Westone executives.

"We've got a killer plan, Angela," Jeff had commented in the elevator after dinner, mistaking her fatigue for anxiety.

"Sure," she had replied sleepily. "Everything happens precisely as it needs to."

She lay back on the stiff blankets and listened to the drone of late night television. She studied the white stucco ceiling and wondered how many others had stayed in this room before her.

"So here we are," she said aloud. "New York City." She had been feeling out of sorts all week, unable to focus. She felt guilty for her lack of attention, knowing Jeff was counting on her—her vision and her enthusiasm—to punch through and grab the hearts of the Westone ventures group. But her own heart wasn't in it. She believed in the proposal they had worked so hard to put together, but she felt something else at work beneath the surface.

"What am I doing here?" she asked the ceiling.

Angela held a standard issue pillow against her chest, wrapping her arms around its sterile softness. She closed her eyes and sighed, knowing she could easily drift off to sleep.

"The vibrational harmonies are in alignment," Angela heard the voice inside tell her quietly.

She opened her eyes and frowned. "What the hell is that supposed to mean?"

"Your soul has moved into phase with itself," came the patient reply.

"Mmm." Angela sat up and reached for the remote control. She had no idea what her intuition was talking about. She had developed the habit of simply accepting without question, generally ignoring the message until it began to make sense.

She turned off the television and got up on her feet. She unzipped her overnight bag and rooted around for her toothbrush.

"There is no such thing as coincidence," her intuition reminded her.

"Whatever." Angela dismissed the message with a wave of her hand as she carried her toothbrush and toothpaste into the bathroom.

Chapter 57

20 May 1999
New York City
1:32 a.m.

Angela stood on the hotel roof, looking out over the city so late at night. Through the din of never-ending traffic below, she felt the throbbing heartbeat of the metropolis. She wondered how she had gotten up here. Dressed in loose, white clothes, she glanced down at her bare feet. Why wasn't she cold? And where was that light coming from?

"Oh," she whispered, realizing that she was glowing.

* * * *

Robin teetered on the edge of the rooftop, catching himself just before he lost his balance. He stepped far back, clutching his chest as he recovered. "Close." What the hell was he doing up here, anyway?

A bright light from the centre of the roof attracted his attention. He walked toward it, moving through a cloud. He could make out a translucent table surrounded by four luminous chairs. Feeling soft cotton against his skin, he looked down at his clothing and wondered if he might be dreaming of a rooftop ashram.

* * * *

As Angela sat down, the quartz crystal molded to her shape. Spectres of color danced within the light itself in this sacred space. The sounds of the city had disappeared. Feeling a gentle buzzing beneath her feet, she gazed up into the stars and lost herself in the crisp beauty of the Milky Way. "I must be dreaming."

"You both are." The commanding voice brought her back into focus. Across the table, Angela found the blissful faces of Isis and Michael. She began to speak, but saw Michael nod to the chair next to hers. There sat Robin, just as bewildered as she was.

"The council has convened," Isis announced gently. In the middle of the table glowed a large stone, illuminated by an ethereal flame, deep blue-green, burning within.

Isis and Michael gazed upon their human avatars. Angela felt an intense wave of love wash over, permeating every cell of her body, eliminating all doubt. An electric charge of spiritual breath ran the length of Robin's spine, rushing out through his fingers and toes, releasing self-recrimination and insecurity.

"You have done well, both of you," Isis encompassed the two with her eyes. "Do I need to ask if you're ready?"

Robin smiled, truly grounded and confident. "No. I mean, yes. Ready."

Angela studied the side of his face. Gone was the anxious torment that had plagued her before. "Yes. It's time."

Michael clasped his hands in front of him on the heavy table. "Do you have any idea how close you've come so many times?"

Robin and Angela turned to each other, adrift in a mutual ocean of green as their eyes met.

"Part of the purpose behind soul twinning," he continued, "is energetic teamwork. When one twin is down, the other provides an essence lift. You have given each other necessary adjustments. You have come together time and again, to pull each other out of ruts, to spark new elements of consciousness, to help each other along this path of awakening. Neither of you would be where you are today without the other. You can take equal credit for all you have accomplished individually," Michael concluded.

"… And for all you will accomplish together," Isis expanded.

"There is to be a meeting," Angela confirmed, her voice no more than a whisper.

Her twin glanced at her familiar profile. "A conscious meeting." Robin smiled as his energy blended with Angela's radiating warmth.

Isis nodded. "There remains much work to be done. This is merely the resolution of your separateness, while you walked individual paths. The inward struggle with your same spiritual truth is over."

She reached forward and touched the stone. Its inner flame pulsed, the brilliant glow embracing the crystal table and the four sitting around it.

Michael laughed. "Do you know how close you are right now?"

Robin visually gauged the distance between their chairs.

"Not in this space," Michael chuckled. "There is no true separation here. You have no idea how close you are to each other physically, at this precise moment."

Isis smiled gently and nodded. "Soon."

The flame swelled again inside the stone, spilling upward into the open sky. Angela and Robin were engulfed by this radiant emerald, consumed by its light.

"Sleep," Isis suggested as the dazzling luminescence faded to darkness.

Chapter 58

20 May 1999
Marriott Marquis, New York City
7:12 a.m.

Angela sat in the hotel restaurant, waiting for her partner. She nervously shook one knee under the table and took small sips of cranberry juice. She checked her watch again, then looked up to find Jeff taking his place across the table from her.

"You have this thing about being early, don't you?" he asked as he yawned.

"Sometimes." Feeling a strange fluttering inside, she was more restless than usual.

"Okay, let's see here." Jeff perused the breakfast menu, then looked toward the buffet. He glanced at Angela's glass of juice. "You don't have to wait, if you're hungry."

She wrinkled her nose, her knees vibrating under the table. "I'm afraid I don't have much of an appetite." The juice in her glass trembled with the rhythm of her knees.

Smirking, Jeff looked quickly underneath the table. "You're not nervous, are you?"

Angela sighed. "I don't know what's going on with me this morning. I was totally fine last night. Actually, I wasn't even sure this was what I wanted to do anymore," she admitted.

"Angela…"

"Don't worry. I'm committed to this meeting," she reassured him. "I was just feeling like… this is done. It's out of my hands. Time to move on to the next big thing."

"What's the next big thing?" he asked.

Angela smiled. "I don't have any idea."

"This is a big day," Jeff offered. "It's alright to be anxious. Perfectly natural."

"Yeah," she commented quietly, looking away. "Big things happening today."

"Well, I'm going to get some breakfast," Jeff rose from the table. "Are you sure you don't want anything?"

"Yeah. Listen, Jeff," Angela caught his arm. "I'm just going to walk for awhile. Get this out of my system. I'll meet you at Westone, okay?"

Jeff checked his watch. "The meeting isn't for another two hours."

She nodded. "I just want to get out of here, move around. I'll be there."

"Yeah, okay."

Angela reached down to retrieve her canvas attaché from beside her chair. Within two minutes, she was at the reception desk, handing over her card key.

* * * *

For once, Robin had not overslept, up before the alarm had the opportunity to wake him. He couldn't sleep with this odd buzzing sensation meandering up and down his spine.

After nearly stumbling out of the shower, he had switched on the television. The sounds of CNN filled his hotel room as he stood in his bathrobe at the window, looking down on Broadway. It was a quiet meditation, watching this living city from so far above. He sighed and pressed his fingers against the glass.

"Time to get it together, old boy," he commented quietly, not having any idea what he meant to say.

The television news anchor announced the time. Robin turned away from the window and dressed quickly. He tossed his belongings into his case, slipped on his shoes, tucked the morning paper under his arm, and was out the door within minutes.

* * * *

"Room 2523 checking out," Angela told the clerk politely.

"Ah, yes, Ms. Harris," the young woman responded as she entered a few keystrokes into her computer terminal. "The bell captain has stowed your luggage until your return flight. Will you be leaving this account on your American Express?"

"Yes."

The printer behind the desk started up, and the clerk retrieved Angela's statement. "Here you are, Ms. Harris. I hope you enjoyed your stay with us."

"Yes, thank you," Angela replied, slipping the receipt into her bag as she hurried toward the exit. She needed to walk. A lot. If she got lost, she'd flag a taxi.

* * * *

"Room 2525," Robin announced to the young woman behind the counter. "Are there any messages?"

The young woman smiled and checked the message box. "Everyone's on the twenty-fifth floor!" she laughed.

"Oh?"

"Your next-door-neighbor was here a split-second ahead of you," she explained.

"Mmm," he commented. "Popular section of the building."

"Have you had breakfast this morning, Mr. Michaels?" the clerk asked as she handed him a slip of paper.

"No, not yet." He glanced at the note: "9:30, Robin. Mary K." He slipped the paper into his jacket pocket. "I'm headed that way just now. Cheers."

Robin stepped away from the desk and crossed the expansive lobby. He repositioned the newspaper under his arm and enjoyed a brief fantasy about what he would have for breakfast. He chuckled quietly as he made his way across the dark carpet. It's funny what becomes important as you grow older, he thought to himself. Within this persistent restlessness, he was certain good coffee and hot food were precisely what he needed to ground himself.

Chapter 59

20 May 1999
New York City
3:17 p.m.

Mary K walked Robin through the hallway toward the central bank of elevators. He was cheerful despite the fatigue in his face and his gait.

"So give us about two months for publication of this article," she advised. "We're currently slated for the August issue, but sometimes stuff comes up."

"If extraterrestrials land on the Eiffel Tower," Robin joked.

"Precisely."

They rounded the corner into the main corridor.

"I think we got some nice photos today," Mary K continued. "You'll be seeing your handsome mug on our glossy pages in no time."

Robin looked at her sideways. "You'll doctor those up nicely, won't you?"

Mary K laughed and patted her old friend on the back. "Sure, we'll make you look like you belong on the cover of GQ!" She cleared her throat. "Thank you, Robin. Thanks again for doing this. I know how busy you are."

Robin shrugged and smiled as they reached the lift. "No worries. It's no trouble. Something told me it was time to come back to New York. I've had a good trip."

"What time is your flight out?"

"Mmm. Not until about 10, I'm afraid." Robin yawned and quickly covered his mouth, laughing. "That will give me some time to return to the hotel for a quick lie down."

Mary K nodded as she checked her watch and frowned. Robin smiled.

"I know you've got another meeting. I can see myself out, thanks."

"Just an editorial review," she replied. "I'm not missing much."

"Go," Robin ordered affectionately. "I've taken up enough of your day."

Mary K smiled warmly and hugged him. Robin chuckled as she patted his back.

"Have a safe flight home," she said.

Robin nodded and smiled. He watched Mary K continue down the hallway toward the conference rooms, then turned and studied his reflection in the polished brass of the elevator doors.

* * * *

Henry Peters walked his two new partners toward the elevator. Standing between Jeff and Angela, he rested his fatherly hands on their shoulders.

"I'm glad we're doing this," he told them bluntly. "Should you have any trouble with the arrangements you're making, you just give me a call. There will probably be delays and roadblocks. But you know this, Jeff. This is par for the course." Henry smiled. "Things have a habit of working themselves out."

"Thanks again for taking the time to meet with us, Mr. Peters," Angela interjected.

Henry stopped and looked at her sternly. "Angela..."

She nodded and smiled. "Henry."

"Much better." Henry stepped back to address them both. "You've done well to partner together. Too many ventures fail because there simply wasn't the diversity in thinking and experience. I'm not saying this undertaking is a guaranteed success," he cautioned. "But I wouldn't get behind it if I didn't think it was a good idea."

"A solid plan also helps, generally," Jeff joked.

Henry laughed. "Of course."

"Angela!"

Angela turned, surprised to find Mary Katherine Baker approaching. "Wow. Hi!" she called out.

"I didn't know you would be here today! Hello, Henry," she acknowledged her colleague, then turned back to Angela. "What brings you to our offices?"

"We had a meeting with Henry and his staff." Angela gestured to her partner. "This is Jeff Pleasant."

Jeff extended his hand to shake Mary K's. "Hello."

"It looks like we're partnering with Westone to build a production and retreat facility," Angela continued.

"Cool!" Mary K exclaimed.

"I'm going to go ahead down," Jeff said to Angela.

She nodded in reply. "I'll meet you in the lobby."

"Angela, it was good to meet you, finally," Henry shook her hand. "I look forward to seeing you again next month."

"Yes, thank you," she responded as Henry continued down the hallway with Jeff.

"So you'll be back next month," Mary K commented. "You'll have to give a call this time, let me know you're coming. I'd love to sit down and talk with you again."

Angela raised her eyebrows in good humor. "Another article?"

Mary K laughed. "Perhaps. When do you head out?"

"On our way now, actually." Angela glanced at her watch. "Our flight is at 6."

"That's too bad," Mary K frowned. "But I was busy myself today. Pretty long interview. Oh!"

She took Angela's arm and began walking her toward the elevator. "I'm supposed to be in a meeting," Mary K admitted. "But there's someone I'd like you to meet."

* * * *

"Have a good flight back." Henry shook Jeff's hand in front of the elevator. "Expect a call toward the end of next week. I'll have more details then about our situation here. But this process shouldn't take long."

"Good," Jeff replied confidently. "We'll be in touch."

Henry left Jeff waiting for the elevator, standing next to another man. Robin caught Jeff studying his image in the reflective doors. They turned to each other and smiled politely, then looked away again.

The bell rang and the doors slid open. Robin and Jeff stepped into the empty carriage. Jeff pushed the "L" button. "Going to the lobby?"

"Please," Robin replied.

The heavy brass doors began to slide shut.

"Robin! Wait!" It was unmistakably Mary K's voice. Robin reached forward, unsuccessfully trying to catch the doors before they closed. He could feel the lift engage.

"Oh, well. Next time," he said.

Jeff tapped hard on the "Door Open" button and held it, certain it wouldn't do any good.

* * * *

Angela's heart was in her throat. It was him! He was here! A wave of anxious relief washed over her as she and Mary K reached the elevator just as the doors closed.

"Damn," Mary K cursed in a low voice. "I had Robin Michaels here with me today, and I know he would have liked to meet you."

Angela laughed nervously. "Why?"

Mary K pressed the "Down" button. "We'll get the next one, maybe catch him in the lobby." She turned to her and smiled. "He was the one who told me about your magazine in the first place."

Angela was dumbfounded. She stared at Mary K, blinking.

Mary K laughed. "Yes. He really liked your book, too, though I only just recently got a copy to him."

She expected panic. She anticipated her knees going weak, convinced light-headed dizziness would overtake her. But looking inside, Angela found she was perfectly calm.

"Oh, that's interesting," Angela heard herself say, managing a smile as she glanced again at the journalist.

Mary K peered deeply into Angela's green gaze. Angela looked back at her curiously.

"Oh, my God," Mary K stammered. "Your eyes..."

"What?" Angela asked.

Mary K apologized with a smile. "I swear they're the same. I never noticed that before." Shaking her head, she laughed at herself. "Nevermind."

The elevator doors slid open.

"Hey!" Mary K exclaimed as Robin saw her and smiled. "We didn't lose you after all. There's someone you should meet."

Robin stepped off the lift and turned to the young woman standing with his friend.

Angela and Robin took a deep, simultaneous breath. Letting go, the complementary rhythm of spiraling energy rose within the twins' separate bodies. Their eyes met.

And their Soul danced.

Acknowledgements (2001)

I would like to briefly acknowledge a number of individuals who have been instrumental in bringing RHYTHM to print:

Michele Anderson, for research assistance and for dragging me back to Africa so soon. Martin Brandt, whose subtle presence many miles away has been a reminder of what is really important. Robin Jones, for cheerleading and companionship, at home and abroad. Sean McAllister, for helping me keep things in perspective. Ames Hardymon Schnier, for laughing with me all these years.

My manuscript readers—Raymond Baker, Joe Breskin, Catherine Formusa, and Mike Rosenberg—for your honest insights and feedback. I cannot thank Cathe enough for her incredible wisdom and her enthusiasm for everything. She has been an angel of encouragement.

Everyone on the Web Integrations Technologies team, for playing and creating with me awhile. Lea Marshall and Al Marschall, whose pre-production expertise and friendly interest helped bring this manuscript to print.

My four parents—Joe, Lissa, Stan, and Suzanne—for life and love, and tremendous support in both. I also appreciate their affectionate acceptance of my quirky answers to standard questions.

I offer my express gratitude to the musicians of the world who share their souls with the rest of us through rhythm. From your albums, I have crafted this story's soundtrack, constantly in the background as I wrote. This list represents only a fraction of the artists on this journey with me:

Afro Celt Sound System, Natacha Atlas, Baka Beyond, Bayete, Deep Forest, Manu Dibango, Echoes of Incas, Emerson Lake & Palmer, Peter Gabriel, Mickey Hart, Nusrat Fateh Ali Khan, Daniel Lanois, Morcheeba, Monsoon, Nomad, Ayub Ogada, The Police, Hossam Ramzy, Sainkho, and The Who.

About the Author

Jennifer Willis is an author, essayist, and journalist in Portland, Oregon. In her non-fiction work, she specializes in topics related to sustainability, spirituality/religion, history, and health. Her articles have appeared in *The Oregonian, The Christian Science Monitor, Salon.com, The Portland Tribune, The Writer, Ancestry Magazine, Aish.com, Skirt!, InterfaithFamily.com, Vegetarian Times, Spirituality & Health,* and other print and online publications at home and across the globe.

In fiction, she focuses on urban fantasy and playful mayhem. Visit her online at Jennifer-Willis.com.

Author photograph by Rachel Hadiashar.

Printed in Germany
by Amazon Distribution
GmbH, Leipzig